THE GHOSTS OF SAIGON

Also by John Maddox Roberts

A Typical American Town

THE GHOSTS OF SAIGON

John Maddox Roberts

A Thomas Dunne Book

St. Martin's Press New York

A THOMAS DUNNE BOOK.
An imprint of St. Martin's Press

Graham Greene's THE QUIET AMERICAN published by
William Heinemann Ltd, extract reprinted by
permission of David Higham Associates.

ISBN 0-312-14345-1

First published in Great Britain by Headline Book Publishing

First U.S. Edition: July 1996

10   9   8   7   6   5   4   3   2   1

For the United States Army, 1967–1970

Bread and Salt

THE GHOSTS OF SAIGON

Book One

GHOSTS

Prologue

For the second time I flew into the city. The last time had been twenty-six years earlier. That time I had been in a Boeing 707 operated by Flying Tiger Airlines, the company founded by Claire Chennault that shared its name with the swashbuckling outfit of American flyers he had organized for the Chinese in their war with Japan. I had been with a planeload of scared young men, little more than boys, and like every one of them I was absolutely alone as we dropped out of the monsoon clouds and strained our eyes, peering through the thick little windows. It had been night that time, and we'd been able to see little more than some dim points of light as we approached from the sea, nothing like the glaring light-show a major American city would make. Then our tires had squealed on the runway of Tan Son Nhut airport.

This time it was daylight. I flew in a JAL jumbo jet with the most courteous flight attendants in the world. The plane was full of middle-aged men and their wives, all of them draped with cameras, most of the men wearing baseball caps bearing the insignia of military units from another time. I was with a woman I didn't know, didn't trust, and didn't much like.

The huge, multiple tires made no discernible squeal this time. The big aircraft slowed and taxied past the terminal. The building didn't look much different from last time. It might have been improved, but nobody was going to mistake it for a major world airport. We passed a big sign: WELCOME TO HO CHI MINH CITY.

Ho Chi Minh City, my ass. It would always be Saigon to me. It all began with a letter.

Chapter One

The letter was in my post office box that morning, solid and substantial in comparison with the flimsy junk surrounding it. I took the mass of paper over to a table and spent all of ten seconds sorting, then I threw everything except the letter into a trash can.

The envelope was made of thick, creamy paper, obviously expensive. Printed in the upper left corner in burgundy ink was 'Queen Productions', with a Hollywood address. Next to it was the company logo: a stylized crown. If you looked close enough, you could see that the crown was made of movie film. It all reeked of wealth and success, as was intended. Pretty good for a guy who used to bum cigarette money off me.

Carson Investigation Agency's Knoxville office was located in a newly renovated building on Union Street. I'd opened the office six months before and was at that time the only agent there, although I'd chosen spacious quarters with plenty of room for three or four more, if business should prove brisk enough. The main office was in Cleveland. Randall Carson, my boss, gave me the Knoxville office because an investigation I'd run had caused my name to stink in certain Columbus political circles, and he thought it best to send me out of state for a while. After a short spell of adjustment I decided I liked Knoxville. It was a big enough city to be interesting, but small enough to get around in easily. And it was a long, long way from LA. The laid-back mini-metropolis was just what I needed.

I'd always read the mail with my morning coffee – a meaningless ritual that helped fill the absence of a domestic life. I put on the Mr Coffee and looked at the letter lying on my desk while the machine groaned like an animal giving birth, yielding its dark brown stream. A delicious scent filled the office. I'd found a shop out on Kingston Pike that sold many varieties of imported coffee. This morning's was Ethiopian Yrgacheffe. When you've sworn off booze, you get finicky about things like coffee.

As I waited for the pot to fill I thought about Mitch Queen.

We'd been close once, serving together overseas in the Army. Back stateside we'd both lived in Los Angeles – Queen trying to break into the movie business in almost any capacity, me in the LAPD. For the first couple of years we got together frequently. In the usual fashion of such relationships we'd drifted apart as we found we had less and less in common. I'd last seen him years before, at my wife's funeral. I wondered why he was re-establishing contact now. At one time I would have wondered how he had located me, but in this day of the desktop computer there's no trick to it at all.

When the coffee was done I poured myself a large mug, added sugar and milk from a carton in the little office refrigerator, and sat back in my swivel chair to open the letter. The heavy paper made hard going for the letter opener, but it parted without producing fuzz or dust. Top quality all the way. The letter was on a single sheet of the same paper, embossed with Mitch's company logo. Also enclosed was a printed brochure.

Gabe, M'man!

I can't believe how many years it's been since we got together. I've just learned that the old outfit's having a reunion in Chattanooga next week and I'm going to attend. Since you're not far from there these days, maybe you'd like to go too. We can sit around and talk about old times over a few brews. I'm sending you one of their brochures for all the pertinent details.

Gabe, this isn't entirely a social occasion. I'm involved in a truly major – and I mean major – production, the biggest of my career. The screenplay's dynamite, the director's a multiple Oscar winner, I have commitments from bankable stars and heavy-money investors lined up with their checkbooks out. Now something weird has come up to deep-six the whole project and, believe it or not, it involves you and me and the old days.

I don't want to get into details just now, but if you'll meet me in Chattanooga next week I'll fill you in and if you want to take it on I'll hire your services at a very generous rate. You know I don't do things in a small way.

I really need you on this one, Gabe, please come through
for me. Remember the Racetrack.

Best wishes,
Gunslinger

What the hell? I read it over again. It was the damnedest
letter I'd ever received. It started out casual, just hey, old
buddy, let's get together. Then it went hyperbolic and boastful,
which was nothing out of character for Mitch Queen. Then it
turned pleading and almost desperate, which was not like him
at all. The last sentence needled me. Did he think I'd forget?
I'd have felt a lot more like hearing his problem if he hadn't
thought it necessary to throw that old debt in my face.

I looked over the brochure. It was from the 18th MP
Battalion Society. It proclaimed that the unit was having a
reunion for everyone who had served with it in Vietnam, and
listed the organizers, the guest of honor, a schedule of events,
all the usual stuff. Appended were details concerning the
convention hotel, nearby hotels, their locations and rates and
so forth.

I was amazed to learn that there was such a society, and
that it held reunions. My war wasn't like World War Two. I
knew that vets of gung-ho units from that war, like the
Marines and paratroopers, had held get-togethers damn near
every year for half a century. They felt they'd done something
to be proud of, and nothing that big had ever happened to
them in the years since.

Vietnam was different. We just wanted to go home, put on
civilian clothes and forget about the whole thing. I'd never
been interested in or had any use for old-soldier nostalgia
trips. I didn't have many good memories of the time, except
that that was where I met Rose.

But looking at the brochure I felt an odd, compelling
sensation that told me I should do this. In recent years I had
found myself remembering my Army days with a certain
fondness. I had even begun viewing the Vietnam year through
a golden haze of nostalgia. I would never fool myself into
believing that it had been a wonderful experience, but more
than a quarter of a century had passed. To hell with the
ugliness and terror of the actual events – when you reach my
age, *anything* that happened when you were twenty years old
starts to look good.

So I picked up the phone and called the Cleveland office.
'Carson Investigations. May I help you?'
'Delilah, this is Treloar in Knoxville. The boss man in?'
'Oh, hi, Gabe. Let me see, he was on the other line . . . no, he's free now. I'll connect you.'

A couple of seconds later Randall Carson's tobacco-wrecked voice came over the line. 'What you got, Gabe?'
'Something really strange just arrived in the mail. Listen to this.' So I read him the letter.
'And this Queen guy served with you in Nam?'
'Yeah, and we saw each other for a while after we ETSed. He went into the movie industry. I've seen his name on film credits over the years. Lately he's produced some big movies, but I hardly ever go to see films any more.'
'Just a minute. Queen? I think I met him at parties at yours and Rose's place. Tall guy, real blond? Talks a mile a minute?'
'That's him.'
'He struck me as a hustler.' Nothing wrong with his cop's memory for physical characteristics or character.
'He's in movie production. You've dealt with those people before. It's hustler paradise.'
'So what's your feeling on this?'
'I'm curious. Queen seems scared and I'd like to know why.'
'He the kind of man who doesn't scare easy?'
I had to think about that for a minute. 'He was as cool in action as anyone I ever saw, but I'm not sure it was really courage so much as . . . well, like I said, you've dealt with movie people. You know how sometimes their grasp of reality is a little tenuous?'
'Most of the ones I met were none too tightly wrapped, yeah.'
'I think that's the way it was with Queen. It was like he thought it was all a movie. Like even if he got hit the director would just yell "cut" and he'd get back up. I'm wondering what it'd take to get through that kind of attitude.'
'Did you guys see all that much action? Korea was my war; I remember how bad the MPs on the roads could get shot up. But I thought you big-city guys had it dicked.'
'You remember when I first joined the Department, you and all the older guys would tell me and all the newbies how bad it was going to be in Watts and South Central?'
'Sure. And they were bad, weren't they?'

'After Cholon, they were no big deal.'

'Okay, Gabe, catch the choo-choo and see your old buddy, see what's on his mind. One more thing I know about movie people: they deal in money that's mythical to the rest of us, but mostly they talk. See which way Queen's coming from. If he's really got the kind of funding he says, he won't mind parting with a big chunk of change to protect the rest. If you think his problem's something you can deal with, go with it. But get the money up front first – fifty per cent, non-returnable. Don't let him pull any personal shit on you. You're not a free agent and you can tell him this is straight from your boss. No dough, no action from Carson Investigations.'

'Got you.'

'What racetrack is he talking about anyway? Santa Anita? Hollywood Park? He give you a good tip once or something?'

'No. It was a place in Saigon.'

After we hung up I called the Read House in Chattanooga. It was the main convention hotel and the switchboard put me through to the front desk.

'Read House. How may I help you?' It was a male voice.

'My name is Gabe Treloar and I'm calling from Knoxville. I'll be coming in next week for the eighteenth MP reunion and I'd like to book a room.'

'Oh, we've been booked up for some time, but just let me check in case there's been a cancellation.' He was off the line for a minute, then, 'Treloar, you said?'

'That's right. Gabriel Treloar.'

'A room has already been booked for you, Mr Treloar. By a Mr Queen.'

So the self-confident bastard had been sure that I would take him up on it. I glanced at the clock on my wall. Still only a little after 7.00 a.m. in California. I was tempted not to call, just keep him guessing. Childish game-playing wasn't my style, though, whatever he was into.

I spent the rest of the morning catching up on paperwork, of which there is a great deal more in private investigation than there is action, adventure, gunplay, tense stalking and high-speed car chases. A detective's principal tool is the telephone, although the computer is catching up fast. A little past noon, as my belly started to demand lunch, I picked up the phone and called the number on the letterhead.

'Crown Productions.' The voice was female and very

trained. She was probably another aspiring actress who took a secretarial job in a production company for the contacts. If she was smart, she'd stick with it and forget about working in front of the cameras.

'I'm Gabe Treloar and I'm calling from Knoxville for Mitchell Queen. I have a letter from him here and he wants me to contact him right away.'

'Oh, yes, he left word that you might be calling, Mr Treloar. Mr Queen is away just now and he won't be back in the office for a day or two.'

'When he calls or gets back, tell him I'll meet him in Chattanooga.'

Chapter Two

The drive from Knoxville to Chattanooga took about two hours, all of it on Interstate highway through the rolling hill country of Tennessee. The hillsides were green again, although there was a lot of timber felled by the recent freakish winter with its unprecedented snow and ice storms. Now the summer was heating up, and it promised to be as severe as the winter had been. It was a far cry from nearly seasonless southern California. I liked it.

Traveling south on I-75, the land levels out for a while before you reach the Tennessee River Valley, then you climb a bit and the highway curves around the shoulder of a mountain and Chattanooga appears unexpectedly, spread out along the curving river, with the abrupt peak of Lookout Mountain rising dramatically from the south bank.

It's a quaint southern town now, slowly acquiring a Sunbelt sprawl, known to the rest of the country mainly because of a corny old song. Seeing the sleepy, seedily gracious old town it's hard to believe that it was once the focus of terrible carnage. But signs everywhere point to scenes of that long-ago bloodshed: Chickamauga, Stones River, Lookout Mountain itself.

The Read House turned out to be an agreeable surprise: a turn-of-the-century hostelry, all red brick outside and warm, dark wood inside, with potted plants and a mezzanine and a lobby ceiling adorned with near-baroque wood carving. It was a place from an earlier time. While the clerk behind the front desk saw to my registration, I studied a row of drawings on the wall opposite. They depicted a succession of earlier hotels that had stood on the spot prior to the present structure. One had been converted into a hospital for Confederate soldiers during the Civil War.

'Here you are, Mr Treloar,' the clerk said. She was a pretty young woman with a little too much make-up and a little too much hair. 'You're here for the eighteenth MP Society reunion?' she asked perkily.

'That's right.' I looked around the lobby. Men wearing nametags were meandering around aimlessly. A hardware dealer's convention must be sharing the hotel, I thought. 'Where's it going on? The mezzanine?'

'Registration's on the mezzanine. You can take the elevator or the stairs around the corner.'

I signed my name in the hotel register. 'What's the other convention here?' I asked her, jerking my head toward the men in the lobby.

She looked a little puzzled. 'There's just the one reunion here this weekend. Those people are here for it. I hope you enjoy your stay, Mr Treloar.'

I picked up my bag and went to the elevator in a semi-daze. These balding, paunchy middle-aged men were my contemporaries. Somehow – in some deep, irrational recess of my brain – I had been expecting to see the young men I had served with back in a decade now remembered more for its music than for anything else. Oh, sure, I knew that they'd look different – out of uniform, maybe a few lines on the face, a little gray at the temples – but somehow, otherwise, those same young men. I wasn't expecting *this*.

The elevator was as old-fashioned as the rest of the place, with an ornate bronze dial over the doors, its arrow tracing the path of the car as it descended. When the doors slid open a group of men and a few women got out and another group got on with me. I wasn't wearing a name tag, so nobody was squinting to see if I was someone they knew.

A man stood next to me in the elevator: bald, jowly, pot-bellied, a pair of heavy glasses balanced on his nose. I tried to reconstruct him in my mind as he might have looked twenty-five years before. A cop can get pretty good at that sort of work. He caught me studying him and smiled tentatively, sticking out a hand.

'Freddy Clark. Delta Company, '70 to '71.'

I took his hand. 'Gabe Treloar. Alpha Company, '68.'

He shook his head. 'Tet. Bummer.'

Then the doors opened on my floor and I got off. 'See you later,' Freddy said before I left the elevator and walked to my room.

It was a pleasant, single-bed arrangement with a view of the river and Lookout Mountain. I wondered if, on foggy nights, the ghosts of Rebels and Yankees still met to do battle on the slopes.

12

I wasn't ready to go down and register for the reunion. It wasn't what I had come for anyway, and seeing those men downstairs and in the elevator had given me an unexpected jolt.

I lay down on the bed and folded my arms under my head, wondering why. I looked up at the ceiling and let my mind range back, not trying to direct it – that's usually a good way to find answers to the things that eat at you, those itches just below the skin. This time it took me back to an earlier period, before the Army and the war. I was a high school kid in LA, newly arrived on the wide-open West Coast from the insular Midwest. My father had gone down to Long Beach for a reunion with his old World War Two outfit. The vets were doing it all over the country that year, celebrating the twentieth anniversary of the end of the war.

He had come home seeming falsely elated, then he sank into a deep depression, drinking heavily for three days straight, something I had never seen him do. With the usual self-involvement of that age, I was too wrapped up in my own problems to take much notice at first, but in time this got through even to me and I asked my mother what was eating at him.

She just looked sad and shrugged and said, 'He just found out that he's going to die someday.'

I had no idea then what she meant. Now I knew this was what Dad had seen down there in Long Beach: those splendid, vigorous, enthusiastic young infantrymen who had stormed on to Omaha Beach with him were now tired men in their forties, disappointed with their lives, marriages and jobs, grasping desperately at the camaraderie that they'd once felt when they shared a common purpose and life had been uncomplicated.

Dad had been at a low point of his life then, for reasons I had only recently discovered. Surely I wasn't going to let this commonplace, near-farcical *memento mori* throw me into a depression.

I got up and went into the bathroom. In the big mirror I studied myself. No, that twenty-year-old GI was gone for ever. But, I assured myself, I wasn't doing too badly for my age. In fact, I was in my best shape in years. I could chin myself twenty times and do a hundred pushups, and I still didn't need glasses. I had most of my hair, although a hat was definitely in order if I was going to spend much time in strong sunlight.

Teeth still okay, belly firm – although that was getting more difficult to maintain.

With horror, I realized that I was turning into one of those youth-obsessed jerks I thought I'd escaped when I left California. I decided I would have to eat unwisely for a while, maybe regain a little perspective.

I called the desk and tried to connect with Queen's room, but was told that he hadn't checked in yet. It was still too early for dinner and I didn't yet feel like hobnobbing with my fellow vets, so I left the hotel and took a walking tour of downtown Chattanooga.

I found that the old center of town was gentrifying after a long slide into inner-city decay. Like so many American cities, it had lost business to the fringe malls and population to the 'burbs, growing shabbier by the year, becoming the haunt of the displaced and the desperate. There were still a few blocks like that, but most of it seemed to be in an advanced state of recovery. I decided I'd have to come down here again soon, maybe see if the town was a good prospect for a branch office. I went as far as a lavish new fresh-water aquarium near the river and turned back.

I spotted Mitchell Queen as I came into the lobby. He was crossing from the desk to the elevators and he spotted me at the same time, breaking into a broad grin, dropping his suitcase and sticking out a hand.

'Gabe! I knew you wouldn't let me down.'

'Good to see you, Mitch.' I grabbed his hand and we shook. We didn't belong to the hug-and-kiss generation, although we hadn't missed it by much. We looked each other over. I couldn't tell if he approved of what he saw, but Mitch Queen had changed amazingly little. He was my height, with deeply tanned skin, and his short, crisp, wavy hair and clipped mustache looked exactly the same. His face was so unlined that I suspected plastic surgery, but I couldn't see any scars. He looked a good fifteen years younger than he should have – a real asset in Hollywood, where even the writers routinely lie about their age.

'You had dinner yet, Gabe?'

'I was waiting for you.'

'Good! They served dinner on the plane but I avoided it. Give me twenty minutes to get established in my room and meet me in the restaurant?'

14

'Sounds good,' I told him.

'Christ, it's great to see you, Gabe! It's been way too long.'

'It sure has,' I agreed, knowing we could have gotten together any time in the last fifteen or more years if there had been any real reason to. I wondered what the reason was. Why now? I guessed that I'd learn soon enough.

Mitch went to his room and I took the stairs up to the mezzanine to register with the reunion. The smiling guy behind the table gave me a badge sealed in plastic that gave my name in big letters, my company and in-country dates, all printed over the unit crest: an upright sword flanked by a pair of axes. I pinned the badge on and picked up a schedule of events.

Another desk held fliers put out by organizations offering veterans' tours. I studied these in some wonderment. They had tours to all parts of the country, promising old soldiers access to places where once they sweated and bled. The old names swam up out of the past: Cam Ranh Bay, Hue, Da Nang, Ah Shau Valley, Chu Lai, Pleiku, Khe Sanh, Ban Me Thuot, the Mekong Delta, the Central Highlands and, of course, Saigon. You could even visit the place few ever got to see except through a bombsight: Hanoi. They offered family rates.

Vietnam nostalgia. The mind reeled.

When Queen showed up I was sitting at a table in the restaurant with a glass of iced tea in front of me. He was only about ten minutes late, which wasn't bad for him.

'Sorry to keep you waiting.' He sat down and a waitress came over. 'I had to make a couple of calls.'

'May I bring you anything from the bar?'

'Sure, honey. Let's see, this is the South, isn't it? How about a mint julep? How about you, Gabe?'

'I'll stay with this,' I told him, tapping my glass.

'That's new, isn't it?'

'It's been a while.'

'Not a bad idea, I guess. Sometimes I tell myself I'm gonna quit but a few years ago I swore off cigarettes and then it was coke I gave up and I can only handle so much virtue. So, you've stayed with police work all this time, huh? First MPs, then the LAPD, now private work. I guess it must suit you.' All this in a single breath. He wasn't quite the motormouth he'd been, was a little more laid back now, but he still didn't pause much for wind.

15

'Old habits die hard,' I agreed. 'So you've hit the big time. Congratulations, Mitch. I don't follow the movies much, but even I run across your name from time to time.'

'Yeah, the industry's been good to me. Even Ahhhnuld returns my calls these days.' His rendition of the world's most famous Austrian accent cracked me up. Mitch had always had a dead-on ear for accents, dialects, peculiarities of speech and so forth. He was always John Wayne when making arrests. 'Not much of a menu, is it?'

I'd been studying mine. 'Looks fine to me. Come on, Mitch, we're supposed to be here celebrating our days of eating Army chow off a stamped steel tray. You're not into that nouvelle stuff, are you?'

'Nah, that was last year. This year it's meat and potatoes – you know, white trash food. Which is pretty much what we have here. But it's only in the places frequented by people in the industry that anybody eats the stuff. Outside, you look for what you like.'

'Yours is a complex business,' I told him.

'You have to keep up with these things. If you're not right on top of the fashion, people think you're not a phoney, and then they won't do business with you. Besides, we're not here to relive the great old days of wasting our young lives in the asshole of the world, Gabe.'

'Just why *are* we here, Mitch?'

'Can't give you the whole story just yet. There's somebody else you have to meet, be arriving in the next hour or two.'

'Why all the mystery?'

'No mystery, just easier not having to repeat a lot. I can tell you some of it while we eat.'

The waitress arrived with his julep and took our orders. Then Queen went on: 'Like you said, I've come up in the industry, produced some hits – I won't say blockbusters, but some features with impressive profit margins. Lots of hotdogs after me to read their screenplays, lots of people ready to listen when I tell them I've got an opportunity for them to make some money. Well, last year Jared Rhine came to me with a screenplay.'

I could tell this was supposed to be significant. 'I know I've heard or read the name someplace.'

At least he didn't act like I was feeble-minded. 'Rhine's written a string of hits the last few years, all of them top grossers: *Highrise, Adrenalin Rush* – you've heard of 'em?'

'The names. I don't go to movies much any more, and I don't have a VCR.'

'God, you're culturally deprived. Anyway, they're actioners – lots of violence, kinky sex, wild plot twists. He's hot, but he's known as a bad boy to deal with – throws tantrums if someone wants to change anything, threatens violence, that kind of stuff. A man with an attitude problem.'

'That for real or just a pose?'

'In my business it's hard to tell. I knew a guy, wrote good stuff, got walked all over because he was a nebbish, just sat at home and pounded his typewriter and got shafted year after year. One day he shows up at a meet, he's grown a big beard and he's wearing mirror shades, a sheepskin vest, gold studs in his nose, cowboy boots with silver-plated toes and heels. Somebody suggests changing a couple of words in the second scene, he hauls out a forty-four magnum and blows a big furrow in the top of a teak desk. Gets top dollar now. Nobody wants to cross him because he's such a bad dude. People are standing in line to get a look at his newest screenplay. It's make-believe city, Gabe.'

'That the story on this guy Rhine, too?'

'Who can tell? He's a recluse, lives in Santa Barbara, hardly ever comes out of his place in the hills. People seek him out, not the other way around.'

'Did you seek him out?'

'Not exactly. One day a letter arrives at my office, says Rhine wants to show me his new screenplay, says it's real special. That's all, but that's enough. I run up there. He's got a little canyon all to himself, only one way in and it's got a steel gate across it topped by razor wire; secure as the LBJ. It's got an intercom, and I push the button and identify myself and the gate unlocks by remote control, although I have to drag it open myself, then shut it after me when I drive through.'

'The guy paranoid or just cautious?'

'His precautions are reasonable but sort of low-rent, you know what I mean? A man who gets what he does for his work, you'd expect him to have an automatic gate. Anyway, I drive up this narrow little canyon and at the end of it there's this tiny house, just a cabin, really, and on the slope behind it there's a satellite uplink dish. I park and the man himself comes out. He's barefoot and wearing the bottom half of those martial arts type pajamas and nothing else, but what the hell, it takes all kinds, you know?' Queen was falling back into his old frenetic speech pattern. I figured he must have worked hard to gear himself back.

At this point our dinner arrived and we applied ourselves to it. At least eating made Queen slow down, and he delivered the rest between forkfuls of lobster salad. I knew better than to order seafood so far inland; I'd opted for the broiled ribeye with herbed butter. It looked like the most life-threatening item on the menu. I planned to order the pecan pie with ice cream, too, just to cast defiance in the teeth of mortality. Live dangerously is my motto.

'So we go inside and it's a cross between a hermit's cabin and a Zen temple. No furniture whatever, just those straw *tatami* things the Japs use. I mean no sit-down furniture. In one corner there's this beautiful computer set-up, state-of-the-art stuff. I mean – my God, isn't that an overused phrase? State-of-the-art? I'll try not to use it any more – for seventy-five years people hacked out terrific scripts on a typewriter, now nobody can write a grocery list unless they have a machine they could send rockets to the moon with.

'So Rhine sits on the floor and he's got this little tea pot and two little cups of tea and I sit down with him, my creaky old knees giving me hell the whole time, and I drink this goddamn tea, and finally, when he's achieved *wa* or whatever it is, he hands me this screenplay. The title grabs me right away. It's called *Tu Do Street.'*

'It takes me back,' I admitted. Tu Do Street was one of Saigon's sleaziest thoroughfares, a strip of bars and whorehouses that sucked the pockets of soldiers inside out before they went back to earn some more the hard way, maybe with a case of exotic VD to liven up the next ambush.

'I open it and I sit there and for the next couple of hours I don't even look up from it. Rhine keeps refilling my tea cup and I keep knocking it back until I feel like I have to piss like a racehorse, but I don't want to get up.'

'Pretty good, huh?'

He put down his fork and gazed at me with level eyes. 'Gabe, this story is not just dynamite. It's a fucking nuke.'

'There've been a bunch of Vietnam movies lately,' I said. 'I haven't seen any of them, but I know most of them lost money.'

'This isn't just about the war, Gabe, it's about now. And it's about one of the hot-button issues of the day: the POW–MIA question.'

I put down my own fork. 'Mitch, if my grasp of recent history hasn't slipped too badly, the POW–MIA scam played out three or four years ago. The Vietnamese want to rejoin the real world so bad they'd *create* prisoners to give back to us if they thought it'd help.'

He waved his silver knife like a baton. 'This one takes an all-new slant. It's nothing like that Rambo garbage. This isn't some wet dream commando fantasy, Gabe.'

I shrugged. 'It's your business, I won't presume to advise you. But you have some sort of trouble?'

'Not at first. To continue: I read this screenplay and it's saliva city. I want it bad and Rhine tells me what he wants for it and when I recover consciousness I go out to hustle.

'Now, a big part of my business is giving people a hint of what I have without actually letting anyone know what it is. Orson Welles was the first one to use this secret thing – now it's a goddam minor art form. If you do it right, nobody knows exactly what the hell you've been doing until the film premières. The rest is all leaks to the press, just like the government.' Speaking of the arcana of his trade, I could see that for all his flip cynicism he loved the business.

'A big part of a producer's job is to line up investors, but they're a skittish lot and they're just like the guys who invest in the stock market – which is to say they're superstitious. They believe deeply in magic.'

'Wait a second. I think you just lost me there.'

'There's no other explanation for it, Gabe. You think the big money people listen to economists? Shit, most of them consult psychics. They go in awe of signs and portents. Most of all, it's words and names of power. The right words, the right names – they have genuine mystical power that charms the money out of these people's bank accounts.'

'I think I understand what you're getting at,' I said. 'Like that time during the Carter administration when one of his cabinet people used the word "depression" in a speech and the next day the stock market lost about a hundred points?'

'Exactly!' He jabbed the air with his fork, dropping a small sliver of lobster on the table cloth. 'Remember what he did? He said that the next time he was tempted to say depression he'd substitute "banana". After that, he'd talk about "the great banana of the Thirties". Well, these people I work with are exactly that way. They wants words and names of power.

'Rhine's a magic name, but no writer is genuinely bankable. A few directors are bankable, and about a dozen stars. You have a low-budget film, you can cast anyone you want, anyone you can afford. You go above twenty million, you gotta have one or more of those magic names. There's a strict hierarchy of money. Your budget's forty million, there's maybe six stars that bankable.'

'What's your budget for this one?'

'A hundred million.'

I dropped my fork. 'Who'd you line up to direct this thing? God?'

'Pretty close. You know who Jed Goldfarb is, don't you? I mean, you haven't been living on Mars or someplace like that?'

'I know who he is.'

'Generally acknowledged to be the most successful director of his generation when it comes to record-breaking money-makers. But he keeps trying to make prestige message movies and those lose money. I showed him *Tu Do Street*, presenting it as an action spectacle that is also socially profound as well as being political TNT, and he signed on.'

'Did you get your bankable stars?'

'To begin with, I got Lawrence McKay. He's not quite in the magic circle yet, but he will be after this.'

'So the female lead is the bankable one?' I was already talking like an insider.

'I got Selene Gibson.' He gave me a smug, winner's smile.

'Selene Gibson. Damn. She's been a goddess for decades. But the movie business isn't really politically correct when it comes to box office – if that term is still in use. Isn't she a little past her peak drawing power?'

Now the smile was wider. 'Stars like magic too, Gabe.'

'Maybe I'm being obtuse, but what the hell are you talking about?'

He leaned across the table and actually looked around, as if somebody might be eavesdropping. 'The screenplay's just part of it. Film technology has grown so sophisticated it really looks like magic, Gabe. You saw the wild stuff they did in *Terminator Two*?'

'Uh-huh. I actually saw that one. It was amazing.'

'Well, I have a team lined up for the production with a process that makes that look like something Chaplin might've used. See, *Tu Do Street* takes place over three decades. It starts in the present, flashes back and forth and traces the lives of five people – three men, two women – as they intersect, from the early Sixties to the present. Selene's role is an ingenue type who's married to the US ambassador to Vietnam early in the Kennedy administration. She becomes a flaming anti-war radical in the war years and so forth until, in the present-day sequence, she's the ambassador herself.'

He took a deep breath. 'And the magic part is, she's going to play her character *the whole time*! No doubling, no hokey make-up, none of that. It's all gonna be done with the computers. When Selene plays a twenty-year-old newlywed, she'll look *exactly like the twenty-year-old Selene Gibson*, thirty years ago!'

'I'm impressed,' I admitted. 'The process is that good?'

'These guys gave me a demonstration and I don't mind telling you I about croaked on the spot. You'll never be able to believe your own eyes again. They can take an old geezer and give him the fountain of youth treatment, and there is *no way you can tell* it's a trick. They can make 'em look like anything else, for that matter. The art of make-up is about to become a thing of the past, Gabe. I signed the computer firm to an exclusive contract for this picture, to maintain absolute secrecy until it premières, signed in blood on the lives of our children. I've only clued in the stars and their agents and the investors. They'll keep quiet because it's their money and reps riding on it, too.

'You see what this means, don't you, Gabe? It's gonna revolutionize the way movies are made. More accurately, how they're cast. Jesus, Gabe, Liz Taylor'd work for free if you could make her look just like she did in *A Place in the Sun*! But this process is only gonna be new once – and it'll be for my project!'

I was actually getting to enjoy this. His kidlike enthusiasm was highly communicable, which probably was what made him a successful producer. Then I remembered that he had a problem.

'So what went wrong?'

His face sobered. 'I told you the people with the money believe in magic. They believe in curses, too. Let me call and see if our third party's here yet. We can go on up and talk over why you're here. You finished?'

'No,' I told him. 'I'm having dessert.'

He shook his head as he walked off toward the house phones. I guessed that pecan pie and ice cream was beyond the pale for a Hollywood type, even one hiding out in a foreign city.

The decadently Middle American meal made a comforting weight in my stomach as we rode up in the elevator. Our fellow vets were getting pretty talkative as booze and schmaltz lubricated their tongues and soothed the raw spots in the collective memory. Their wives mostly looked bored or disgusted. I could see them offering up silent thanks that this didn't happen very often. We got off on the seventh floor and walked down the carpeted hall.

'Come on in,' a female voice called when Mitch knocked.

We went in and there was a woman sitting at the little table next to the room's single window. The curtains were open, rippling slightly in the breeze and hum of the air conditioner. The lights of downtown shone beyond. She had a folder open on the table beside her and a briefcase closed at her feet. She got up and stuck out a hand as we came in.

'Connie, this is my old buddy, Gabe Treloar. Gabe, this is Connie Armijo.'

She was about five-three with a compact, almost chunky build, but she moved with an athlete's ease. Her hair made a short, curly cap around her head of the rare color called Castilian red – a sort of chestnut with an almost subliminal reddish tint. Her skin was pale with the faintest tinge of olive, giving her almost black eyes a dramatic contrast. Her face was closed, impassive, despite the full-lipped generosity of her wide mouth. She wore a severe business suit but she had slipped her shoes off and didn't bother to put them back on. Her handshake was extremely firm.

I made her for a cop immediately and she would have done the same but I was sure she already knew about me.

'Gabe, Connie's with the McInery Detective Agency.'

'I've come across the name,' I said. 'All women, isn't it?'

'We are an all-female agency and we represent an all-female clientele,' she said in a warm, slightly husky voice. 'Many women feel that they don't always receive the best representation from male attorneys. My boss, Darlene McInery, decided a lot of women might feel the same way about detectives and so she founded the agency. She was right. We never lack clients.' It was plainly her usual spiel, but there was a slight challenging edge to it.

'No argument from me,' I said. She looked a bit puzzled, as if she'd expected some snide, macho comeback.

'Let's make ourselves comfortable,' Queen said, taking a chair. 'Gabe, Connie's been retained by Selene Gibson for reasons about to be made clear.'

I sat by the table. Connie Armijo took the room's single easy chair, crossed her nyloned feet at the ankles and said, 'Miss Gibson retained the services of the agency when she received a threatening letter shortly after she agreed to appear in Mr Queen's film.'

'Miss, not Ms?' Queen said, quirking an eyebrow.

'She prefers to be called Miss Gibson,' she deadpanned, 'and we respect the wishes of our clients.'

'What is the nature of this letter?' I asked.

She handed me a single, typed sheet. 'This one's a copy. Miss Gibson has the original.'

It didn't take long to read.

To all persons involved in the production of the proposed film *Tu Do Street*:
The cast, crew and financiers of the above named project are hereby warned that they are not wanted in the People's Republic of Vietnam. Any attempt to film the picture in the People's Republic will be met with violence. The director and stars will not leave the country alive. There will be no second warning.

'Brief and to the point,' I commented. 'You're planning to shoot it in Vietnam?'

'It's like you said earlier: like half the world, they're desperate for hard currency. They got tired of being a pariah nation and they want international recognition. I floated the idea over there as soon as the restrictions came off and they jumped at it. It's a real coup, Gabe. We don't film in the Philippines or Thailand or Mexico. Every scene will be shot right on the spot where it all happened. The country's been in a twenty-year coma so hardly anything's been changed.'

'Even allowing for your usual hype it sounds good, but not worth the risk,' I said. 'Why not just shoot somewhere else? It sounds like you've got some old hardcore VC or NVA here, and we both know how fanatical they could be. You say your script's great and this new process is what everybody'll want to see anyway. Shooting it in Vietnam's just icing on the cake; you can dispense with it.'

Queen shook his head. 'I got the same letter. So far it's just Selene and me that's got them, but mine was a little more personalized. That letter I sent you said that it involved you and me and the old days?'

'I was wondering about that.'

'Well, here's why.' He reached into an inside pocket and took out another single, folded sheet of paper and passed it over to me. The letter was identical to the one Connie had, but there was a further line appended at the bottom:

P.S. Don't try to shoot it anywhere else either, or you're a dead man.

Martin Starr

I had to read the name three times before I was sure I had it right. It was a name I had never expected to see again, certainly not in a hotel in Chattanooga.

'Okay,' Connie said. 'So who is this guy Starr?'

'Let's tell her about Martin Starr, Gabe.'

Chapter Three

The plane had landed in the dark and we stood in four lines on the steel treading while our duffel bags were unloaded. Then we rooted through the piles of bags to find our own and got back in line. The sky was beginning to pale by the time this task was accomplished and I stood there woozily, wrung out by the long flight and half-stunned by the muggy heat. We'd left the States on a cool day in early January in the Pacific Northwest, and here it was a steambath. The tropical fatigues we'd been issued at Fort Lewis were new and not yet comfortable, and I wondered if anything could be comfortable here.

A bird landed on a telephone wire near the metal strip. It looked sort of like a sparrow, but something indefinable about its tail feathers made it alien. I was twenty years old and scared.

The sun was up and it was getting truly hot when four big olive-drab buses pulled up in front of us. I noted curiously that they were Toyotas. I'd never seen a Japanese-made bus before. The drivers called for us to climb aboard and we picked up our duffels. On the seats inside, holding our bags awkwardly in our laps, we noted that steel grates had been welded over the windows.

Somebody rapped one of the grates with his knuckles. 'That's to keep grenades out,' he said in an awed voice. 'This shit's for real.'

Even in the early morning the road was jammed with traffic: bicycles, rickety trucks, sideless vans jammed with people, jeeps full of Vietnamese soldiers, ox-drawn wagons. Only closed Asian faces were to be seen anywhere. We stared wide-eyed every time some skinny kid on a bicycle strayed too close. Back in the States we'd heard endless stories about how the VC sent seven-year-old kids to chuck grenades into groups of American soldiers.

The buses dumped us in a compound of long barracks like

25

tin-roofed shacks, with sandbags piled to waist height all the way around them. Above the sandbags the board sides were turned outward like louvers, backed by screens. In the middle was a big, unwalled shed covering rows of benches. A sergeant with a clipboard came out looking bored.

'Get under cover,' he said. 'You want to get sunstroke, you got a whole year to do it. Best not get it here and make paperwork for me. Get in there, siddown and have your papers ready.'

Like everybody else I was carrying a big manila folder with all my records, and I sat on one of the benches clutching it, studying the big map at one end of the shed, almost nodding off to sleep even though it was morning. It had just turned dark when we boarded the flight in Washington and the flight had lasted twenty-four hours, with a short stopover in Tokyo. Since we were flying west it had been night the whole time; the longest night of my life.

Somebody came along and collected our papers and we were assigned to bare bunks in the long huts and told to assemble in the big shed whenever the whistle blew. We learned where the chow hall, the shower hooches and the latrines were, and we were shown where to take cover in case of a rocket or mortar attack – long half-sections of corrugated steel culvert dug halfway into the ground and roofed with the inevitable sandbags.

We were as undifferentiated as newly-hatched baby mantises in our spanking new OD fatigues without insignia, waiting to be assigned somewhere. We pulled work details and fell in four or five times a day for the stomach-tensing wait to hear our names called. Men were called out singly and in groups of three or four for destinations most of us had never heard of: Bien Hoa, Can Tho, Da Lat; and some we had: Hue, Cam Ranh Bay, Da Nang.

By the morning of the fourth day there weren't many of my original planeload left. They'd been replaced by new arrivals and I was feeling like an old hand, showing the new guys where to put their gear and what they could expect, which was pretty simple. You waited around all day and at night you could lie on your bunk and watch lizards catch bugs on the screens. In between, you cleaned up the barracks, hauled trash to the dump and filled sandbags.

The first formation of the fourth day was roll call. The

second was an assignment formation, and my name was the second one called.

'Treloar, Gabriel, RA15809460, sound off!'

'Here, Sergeant!'

'Gitcher shit together and haul ass to the Admin hooch. You drew Saigon, you lucky prick!'

I ran back to the barracks and grabbed my duffel bag and carried it the twenty steps to the shack where all the paperwork was kept. I was grinning and the others gave me sad, sour looks. After all the places with the savage-sounding names, Saigon didn't sound bad. It was a big city, not some jungle or rice paddy. We'd seen a little of it from the buses that hauled us from Tan Son Nhut. It even had a cathedral.

Inside a tall young buck sergeant in MP uniform was collecting my papers from the man behind the desk. He was wearing decidedly un-regulation sunglasses with lenses that were nearly black, and he turned to study me through them.

'This my newby?' The name-tag above his right breast pocket said 'Queen'.

'This's your man,' said the clerk. 'Fresh outta Fort Leavenworth an' ready to make the streets of Cholon safe for truth, justice and the American way.'

The sergeant tapped me on the chest with the big envelope. 'Come along, m'man, we bound for the wicked city.'

I shouldered my bag and followed him out to a jeep where another MP sat in the rear with an M-16 propped between his knees. Queen got behind the wheel and punched the ignition button. I tossed my bag in back and climbed into the passenger seat. The wind blasted our faces as the jeep pulled away because the windshield had been folded down.

'Don't let your hat blow off, man,' Queen said. 'The windshield stays down 'cause explosives can blow the glass back in your face.'

'What's that thing?' I asked, pointing at a tall, vertical steel bar welded to the center of the front bumper. It was deeply notched every few inches of its five-foot height and the upper foot was canted sharply outward.

'Wire cutter,' he answered. 'The gooks like to stretch wire across the road about neck height. They imaginative little buggers, for sure. Don't worry – for now, we on the main highway. Don't gotta watch for that shit 'less we go out to the base camps. Y'see, m'man, you won't be humpin' a ruck through the boonies where you goin'. It's Saigon. Civilization, y'understand?'

'Hey, man,' said the other MP, 'you bring any albums?'

''Fraid not.'

'Shit.' He lit up a cigarette with a Zippo. 'We wore our *Sergeant Pepper* out. Only people ever think to bring albums over's the soul brothers, an' all they listen to is Aretha and Ray Charles.'

The drive to Saigon wasn't a long one. I saw a jarring mixture of architectural styles: at first mainly ramshackle slums that reminded me of pictures of South America, giving way to a few pagoda-like structures that looked generically Asian, then some more modern, tall, uniformly ugly concrete buildings, and a great many colonial places from the era of French occupation. These had a certain charm, the sort of European seediness I associated with some Graham Greene stories I'd read. Somehow, though, the place lacked the exoticism I'd expected.

But the streets were packed and everywhere you saw new construction going on. Shops displayed huge piles of fruit and vegetables in baskets on the sidewalks, and hawkers sold everything imaginable, much of it American-made. Everyone seemed unbelievably *busy*. If the Vietnamese were beaten down by years of war as I'd heard, the Saigonese sure didn't know about it.

We pulled up in a small compound lined with MP jeeps like the one we rode in. Some of them sported M-60 machine-guns on swivel mounts.

'Let's get you in-processed,' Queen said, piling out of the jeep. The other man was already walking away. Queen shepherded me through the dreary routine in record time, cajoling and browbeating a series of clerks to facilitate the process, talking non-stop and refusing to accept a negative.

First we went to the company orderly room. The clerk looked at Queen like he knew what to expect.

'This is m'man Treloar. I want him in my squad, to replace my former man Higgins, the lucky fuck that ETSed on me.'

'You want to partner with a newby?' The clerk had sardonic eyebrows and a thin little mustache.

'That's right. Get'm fresh and unspoiled, break 'em in properly. That way he won't have any bad habits to lose, y'understand?'

'You got him.'

Queen led me to a long squad bay where a big floor fan stirred the muggy air. I stashed my duffel bag in the only vacant locker. A middle-aged Vietnamese woman swept the floor listlessly with a short-handled room.

Next it was the finance office, where I dropped off my pay records. Then to all the others, ending up at the clinic where I left my medical records and got my blood typed.

'I don't get it,' I said to the medic. 'Every new post they send you to in the Army, they stab your finger. My blood type's been right here on my dog tags since my first day of basic. Are they worried it's going to change between one post and another?'

The medic shrugged. 'It's the rules.'

'Just one of the many mysteries of the Green Machine,' Queen said. 'C'mon, let's get you properly accoutered and armed and you'll be ready to face life in the Capital Military Zone, which is where we are, by the way.'

So we went to supply and I drew bedding and field gear and signed for all of it, then to the arms hooch for my weapons: an M-16, insubstantial and toylike after the massive old M-14s we had been trained with in the States, a .45 automatic pistol and a 12-gauge shotgun. I signed and was given a weapon card for each one, but they would stay in the arms room until I went on duty.

Outside Queen looked at his watch, a heavy, stainless-steel Zodiac. 'Hour'n a half. A new record for in-processing. Time for chow.'

Outside the chow hall the sergeant with head count duty had a bowl on the little desk in front of him. It was filled with fat, orange pills. He told me to take one of them as I signed my name.

'Wednesday's malaria pill day,' Queen told me. 'But don't take it all at once or you'll get the runs. Break it in three pieces, take 'em a few hours apart.'

Inside it was like any chow hall in the States except that all the KPs were Vietnamese. We slid the stamped steel trays along the stainless steel tubing and standard Army chow splatted into the depressions. The four-man tables had the usual cheap plastic table cloths. Floor fans at the ends of the long room stirred the grease-smelling air.

Queen sat across from me and split his malaria pill into three pieces with a GI table knife. He swallowed one piece and put the other two into a breast pocket. I did the same and washed down the bitter fragment with lime Kool-Aid. I poked at the food without much interest. I'd already learned that the climate left me with little appetite.

'Treloar. What kind of name is that?' Queen asked.

'It's Cornish.'

He took off his near-opaque shades and for the first time I saw that his eyes were blue. 'Cornish? That's a little-ass chicken.'

'Cornwall's a county to the west of England,' I told him. 'Used to be an independent country. It's part of England now. Names that start with "Tre" are usually Cornish.'

'My, my. Where you from before the Army got you?'

'Ohio originally. My family moved to Los Angeles about five years ago. That's where I signed up.'

'LA?' He grew animated. 'That's where I'm going immediately upon separation. I'm gonna use my GI Bill for business school, then get in the movie industry.'

'You want to be a movie star?'

'Naw, that's bullshit stuff. I'm going into the production end. I want to make movies, not prance around in front of the camera like a fairy. Production's where the money is. That's where you're in control. All those stars and directors whose names're up there in great big letters at the start of a movie? They ain't shit. The money men hire and fire 'em. They just grunts. The name on the check's all that counts.'

'Never thought of it that way,' I admitted, which was my way of saying that I hadn't thought of it at all. Clearly, Queen had thought of it a lot. The fact was, movies were about the last thing on my mind. 'What's it like here?' I asked, changing the subject.

'Depends. Mostly it's just police work. We ride patrol. We bust people. Lot of the time we get to travel around with ARVN MPs. They're pretty useless, but at least they can talk the language. But that's not much help in Cholon. That's the Chinese ghetto.'

'Who do we bust?'

'Mostly drunk GIs. We round up AWOLs, who're always to be found in the bars and whorehouses of colorful Tu Do Street, the Disneyland of Southeast Asia. Dope's getting to be a real problem, but we usually let the ARVNs bust the Saigon cowboys who sell it. Then there's the deserters.'

'Deserters? Jesus, where does anyone desert *to* around here?'

'A good question, and one that had me puzzled for a long time after I arrived. Fact is, the deserters just disappear underground in Saigon. There's some in the other big towns, and a few that've actually joined the VC and the NVA, but most of 'em stay right in Saigon, usually shacked up with some woman. They come out at night and deal dope, mug drunk soldiers, pull stickups and generally behave the way they would if they were back home.'

I was astounded. I had never dreamed of such a thing. 'How many of them are there?'

'For understandable reasons they don't fill out census forms. Best estimates go five hundred to a couple thousand.'

'Holy shit! I never heard of any of this in the States.'

'Oh, by no means. Bad for morale. No, these boys're all just AWOL or missing in action. Wouldn't do to admit that the capitol supports a battalion-sized population of deserters. The gooks call 'em "ghosts". You'll learn all about 'em soon. Nothing new about it. Ask Sergeant Major Poszesny sometime. He MP'd in England during World War Two, says the island was full of deserters from every Allied country. It was a deserter's paradise, because all the cities were blacked out. I guess there was a lot of basement trials and executions when the lights came back on. Maybe I'll back a movie about it sometime.

'The good part about duty here is there isn't much enemy action except the occasional grenade chucker. Best of all, you never have to shine your own boots or pull KP or clean the barracks. The gooks do all that. You just pull straight duty and your off-duty time's your own.'

That sounded better. 'What's there to do in our off-duty time?'

'Same as the guys we bust. Go get drunk on Tu Do Street.'

That afternoon I drew my .45 and my M-16 and rode my first patrol in the streets of Saigon. Queen drove and pointed out the sights and the reference points. We were paired with a team of three stony-faced Vietnamese MPs who rode in a jeep behind us. After a while Queen let me take the wheel to get the feel of the chaotic traffic. For a while I felt like there was a sniper on every rooftop and I had a big target painted between my shoulder blades, but I got over that quickly.

The days that followed established the routine, and soon

Saigon seemed no more alien than a typical Mexican border-town like Tijuana. I toiled over my Vietnamese phrase book, something few of the other guys bothered with. The streets were full of American soldiers, and they regarded us with about the same favor they showed the VC. I'd expected that, at least. A policeman's lot etc.

Mostly it was boredom, just like stateside service. We had movies in the barracks. The TV had an American channel that showed elderly US series in black and white, and a state-owned channel that carried mostly incomprehensible Vietnamese opera. Armed Forces Radio was better. Everyone agreed that the Beatles' new songs like 'Magical Mystery Tour' and 'Hello, Goodbye' were all right, but were nowhere near as good as 'Sergeant Pepper'. That month the theme from *Valley of the Dolls* was at the top of the charts and we were soon heartily sick of it.

Not everything was boring. There were some prize bummers to be had as well. We didn't have to be exactly gentle with the men we rousted, but I felt a little sick the first few times I saw ARVN MPs making a bust. They figured a man came along easier if he was unconscious. It was something you got used to, eventually. I learned that the back alleys of Saigon were like those of other big cities, and before long I'd seen my share of bodies – GI and Vietnamese, military and civilian. Where you have hookers and pimps and dope and mean, armed men, you get bodies.

The Americans, I discovered, were listed as killed in action. Nobody ever received a telegram saying, 'We regret to inform you that your son bled to death from razor cuts to the genitals administered by a Tu Do Street pimp whose whore he stiffed for a 200-piastre blowjob.' We found hookers murdered, too. Grunts could come out of the bush with a nasty edge on them, and pimps got vicious if a girl tried to leave. But there were always plenty more girls. Saigon was full of farm girls who had fled from the countryside to escape the war, no husbands, no jobs, no prospects.

Even settled into routine, it was an uneasy place to be. Every Vietnamese civilian was a potential enemy, but at least we respected the VC and the Northerners as tough, dedicated fighters. We had no such respect for our South Vietnamese allies. We considered them incompetent and useless as soldiers, and they probably regarded us the same way. We all knew that the governments we supported were corrupt to an extent that left the mind stunned with disbelief.

The GIs weren't much easier with each other. The first day I noticed how blacks and whites usually sat at separate tables in the mess hall and at the PX. Nothing official, of course, and not even a matter of social pressure. It was just an unspoken acknowledgement that we had little in common except the Army, didn't much trust or like each other. We worked well together on duty and there was little or no friction in the barracks, but an invisible wall was there and attempts to breach it from either side were seen as presumptuous at best. But that had been the same in the States. What was different was the alien country we were in and the war that was shredding it.

At the end of my first month in country, Queen and I got orders to drive out to Long Binh and pick up a prisoner.

I was sitting on my bunk, pulling on my boots, when Queen came into the barracks. 'Gitcher shit together, m'man, we're going to the LBJ to pick up a client.'

I'd heard about the LBJ – the Long Binh Jail, the Army's infamous in-country military prison. Rumor had it that it existed to prove that you couldn't escape Vietnam by murdering an officer.

'Sounds good to me.' I finished lacing and got up. I hadn't yet left the Saigon area and was curious to see the countryside. 'What do we need to take?'

'Go to the arms room and check out your twelve-gauge. That's SOP when escorting a prisoner. We'll be technically in the field, so bring along your flak jacket and steel pot. Might as well leave those spit-shines in your locker, too. You got issued jungle boots, didn't you?' He'd dropped his affected speech mannerisms and was all business.

'Uh-huh.' I sat back down and started unlacing. 'Who's riding with us?' I knew that MPs usually rode in threes when they left Saigon: a driver, a shotgun and a machine-gunner in back.

'We got some spook major riding with us,' Queen said. 'He's taking charge of the prisoner.'

I got the jungle boots out of my locker. They were mostly canvas, much lighter and cooler than the spit-shined leather boots. 'Spook? CIA? Is this routine?'

'Don't know, don't ask. Man, there's more weird shit goes

down in this country than you can shake your dick at. We once escorted a bunch of tribesmen out of Laos, little fuckers with their teeth filed to points, cannibals or some such. Don't know why they were here, don't know where they went. There's no bottom to the weirdness here, man.'

I took the flak jacket from the top of my wall locker where it had lain folded since it was issued to me. I slipped its massive weight on to my shoulders and tried to ignore the stink of old sweat and mildew.

I went to the arms room and then reported to the orderly room. The first sergeant, whose name was Washington, sat behind his desk. On the wall behind him was a big map of the country, covered with clear acetate and marked up with grease pencil. Queen came in right behind me.

'What's the sitrep, Top?' he asked.

Washington's brown face twisted into more wrinkles than it usually showed. 'Sitrep. Where'd you get that shit?'

'Heard it at a press briefing.'

Washington swiveled in his creaky old chair and pointed at the map. 'Things pretty quiet with the big holiday comin' up. Been some action in Deuce Corps area. Nha Trang and Ban Me Thuot got hit last night; Kontum, Da Nang, we heard Pleiku and maybe Qui Non was hit too.'

'Just harassment?' Queen asked. 'Rockets and mortars? They always throwing stuff into Da Nang and Pleiku.'

The first sergeant shrugged. 'Don't know. Got unofficial word Ban Me Thuot and Kontum got hit by big ground forces, but who knows what they been smokin'? A coupla gook kids and a water buffalo look like a division when you on smokin' status.' He swiveled back around. 'Capital Milzone's quiet, though. No action between here and Long Binh 'cept the traffic.'

The door to the CO's office opened and a major came out with the CO trailing behind him. The major's immaculate jungle fatigues were bare of everything except his rank, an MACV patch on one shoulder, and a name-tag that said Gresham. He had the kind of blank gray eyes I associated with LA cops who'd been in uniform too long, and he carried one of the clipboards that were Vietnam's version of swagger canes. He wore a .38 revolver holstered on his belt, instead of the usual .45 automatic.

'Sergeant Queen,' the CO said.

'Sir!'

'You are to hand-carry this officer to the LBJ and take charge of a prisoner held there. You will deliver the prisoner and Major Gresham to the American Embassy.' The CO wasn't quite insubordinate, but he didn't leave much doubt that he didn't like having to run errands for spooks.

'Rat own, Captain,' Queen said. It was that year's approved pronunciation of 'right on'.

'You do know how to say "yes, sir", don't you, Queen?' Washington demanded.

'Yes, sir,' Queen said contritely. He was doing a perfect imitation of Eddie Haskell on *Leave it to Beaver* but I didn't think the CO and the first shirt caught it.

'Bring your jeep around front and wait for me there, Sergeant,' Gresham said.

We went out to the motor pool and checked out our jeep. Queen took the log book and keys from the motor sergeant and signed the vehicle out for Long Binh.

'Why are we taking a prisoner to the embassy?' I asked Queen. 'The Seven-Sixteenth MPs are in charge of the embassy area.'

'You might's well ask why a prisoner's going to the embassy in the first place. There's some doors man was never meant to open.'

We went to our jeep and climbed in. I got in back with my shotgun because the major would be taking the passenger seat. I didn't much like going out without a machine-gun, but the trip from Saigon to Long Binh was regarded as a drive from the city to the suburbs, not a safari into the heart of darkness. Queen logged in the time and odometer reading and unlocked the steering wheel. The keys weren't for the ignition, which operated by a button on the dash, they were for the various padlocks on the vehicle, one of which fastened a chain from the steering column to the wheel.

We were waiting in front of the HQ building when Gresham came out and climbed in without a word. We pulled away with that deep-throated rattling chug that only jeeps have and headed out toward Highway 1.

At the edge of the city Queen pulled over to the side of the road. 'Injun territory for the next few miles, chillun. Lock an' load.' He took his M-16 from its mount beside him and jerked back the charging handle. I pumped a round into the shotgun's chamber and set the safety. Then we both charged our .45s and set their thumb safeties and reholstered them and fastened the flaps on our holsters.

'Feel safer now?' Gresham said, apparently bored by the warlike melodramatics.

'Eminently, sir, eminently,' Queen said as he pulled back on to the highway. 'Imagine our embarrassment should the VC make a social call. We'd be unable to receive them properly 'cause we gotta use one hand to drive or hold on to the vehicle. That's the sort of *faux pas* that gives Americans a bad name in these parts.'

The major looked pained. 'How long have you been here, Sergeant?'

'Just shy of five months, sir.'

'I've been here most of the last three years, and I have yet to see three men in a jeep come back alive from an ambush, no matter how they were armed.'

This depressing thought quieted Queen for a while and I concentrated on our surroundings. The outskirts of Saigon consisted of an enormous slum where people who had fled the countryside for the relative security of the city huddled in conditions of squalor that were simply beyond the comprehension of most Americans. I'd already seen the village that lived on top of the American garbage dump; they were among the better off. One thing Americans produce is a *lot* of garbage. Most of the shacks in the Saigon shanty town were made of sheet metal produced by rolling out aluminum cans with their absurdly cheerful colors. One shack would be made of red Coke cans, another of blue-and-white Schlitz cans, another of gold Miller cans. Innumerable old people and women and kids were everywhere. The younger men were away or keeping out of sight.

Past the shanty towns the highway ran through a string of villages separated by stretches of farmland. For a while it paralleled the Saigon River, and we saw people living in boats and little restaurants on rafts, decorated with strings of streamers and colored lights that would probably make them look almost attractive after dark. Gunboats churned the muddy water of the river, rocking the sampans and making a minuscule surf on the banks.

The road was a good one, laid out by the French and maintained by American contractors. It was jammed with the chaotic traffic I'd come to expect in Vietnam; vehicles of every conceivable sort jammed with more people than I would ever have believed possible. Animals too – both pulling vehicles and riding in them, or just walking along with or without human company. US and ARVN military vehicles bulled through everything as if they were the only things on the road, and I was reminded that we had taken more casualties from traffic accidents than from enemy action so far that month.

A few miles out of Saigon the land was rolling and hilly, full of cultivated fields and no sign of the jungles and rice paddies you always saw on the news in the States. I was amazed to see corn growing. We passed somnolent villages and innumerable roadside stands selling food and dubious-looking pop in scavanged bottles.

Once, a startling spectacle loomed by the road. It looked like nothing so much as a little, white clapboard-sided school-house, and mounted on a pole jutting above its roof was a huge gold swastika. I pointed at the apparition. 'What the hell's that?'

'Buddhist temple,' Gresham said. 'There are a lot of Buddhist sects in Southeast Asia and that's one of them.' He raised a hand to keep his hat from blowing off and I noticed that he wore a number of the brass and braided hair wrist bangles made by the mountain tribes. Having delivered this information he seemed to lose interest.

About an hour from Saigon we turned off Highway 1 toward the main gate of Long Binh. It was a little past noon, 30 January 1968.

A cluster of vendors squatted in front of the gatehouse, and when we pulled in they tried to sell us sunglasses, beer, monkeys, parrots and a number of things I couldn't name.

While Gresham presented our credentials I gazed out along the perimeter of the camp. At hundred-yard intervals big, earthen bunkers hulked out of the ground, their armament trained out over barbed-wire aprons and concertinas of the shiny, new razor wire that was terrifying to us but that VC sappers seemed to be able to waltz through without a scratch. Behind the bunker line stood skeletal, hundred-foot towers, their sandbagged tops mounted with huge searchlights.

The MP on the gate waved us through. I'd been expecting a fortified huddle of buildings, but Long Binh turned out to be mostly open country with widely scattered company and battalion areas separated by stretches of sandy, grassy ground. We passed marshalling yards of every conceivable sort of *matériel*: spools of rope like a giant's sewing box, long black bladders of aviation fuel that looked like fifty-foot waterbeds, motor pool after motor pool of jeeps, trucks, bulldozers, end loaders, cranes, anything that moved on wheels or tracks. There were airstrips for fixed-wing craft and pads for helicopters with sandbagged revetments around their perimeters. We passed a sprawling hospital where choppers with big red crosses on their sides came in like wounded prehistoric flying reptiles with blood dripping from their fuselages. The *whop-whop* of the choppers was unending, and everywhere I looked I saw them landing, taking off or cruising overhead: big, twin-rotor Chinooks and the ubiquitous Hueys, and little, buzzing, hornet-like recon choppers I hadn't seen before.

Queen pulled up at a vast yard surrounded by a high fence. It was full of the corrugated-metal Conex containers that had become the standard way of moving things by cargo ship and rail. They were stacked eight or ten high in squares the size of city blocks separated by regular streets. The squares stretched out as far as I could see.

'I want you to look at that,' Queen said. 'This is the Beer Yard. Those Conexes contain nothing but beer and pop: Coke, Pepsi, Seven-Up, you name it. I think this says something about American culture.'

'We're not sightseeing, Sergeant,' Gresham told him. 'Drive on.'

Eventually we reached the LBJ. It was yet another sprawl of buildings, only this time the razor-wire-topped fence had guarded towers at the corners. It looked like any ugly prison any place in the world. Gresham talked us through the gate and we drove him to the Administration building.

'This is going to take a while,' he said. He looked at his stainless-steel watch. 'It's thirteen hundred now. Go find yourselves something to eat and report back here at fifteen hundred.' With that he turned around and went up the steps.

'Fuckin' spook,' Queen said as I climbed into the front seat.

'There's a crate of C-Rations in back,' I told him. 'Think we can find some shade in this place?'

'Fuck a bunch of C-Rats,' Queen said, putting the jeep into gear. 'Let's go to the Loon Foon.'

A couple of miles from the LBJ we found a rambling, barnlike building that housed the base's Chinese restaurant. It looked like a favorite stop for grunts just in from the bush. A squad of filthy, unshaven men climbed down from the back of a deuce-and-a-half looking like visitors from another planet decked out in beads and strings of dried ears and sunglasses with heart-shaped lenses. The black guys wore bushy afros with little boonie hats perched on top of them. One tired-looking grunt stayed behind to watch their weapons and he carefully set his rucksack at his feet. Something wiggled under the flap of one of its side pockets and an ocelot or something poked its head out and stared at me with feral green eyes.

'Weird shit,' Queen muttered as we went in. The interior was a single, cavernous room where hundreds of GIs and a few ARVNs sat at tables while twenty or so Chinese waitresses hustled trays of steaming food, adroitly avoiding the almost mechanical assgrabs of the customers. We found seats and ordered fried wontons and barbecued pork and deep-fried shrimp.

'How big is this place?' I asked Queen. 'We haven't even seen the bunker line since we passed the gate.'

He leaned back in the cheap wooden chair. 'Biggest American installation in the world, so I've heard. Long Binh's a logistical base, that explains all the marshalling yards and the incredible heaps of shit everywhere. It's Eleventh Cav's headquarters, but they're out in the field most of the time. A little way up the highway is Bien Hoa, which is a tactical base. All around here's little fire bases serviced by all these choppers you see.'

'So we're in firm control of this area?' I asked hopefully.

He nodded. 'We are in the daytime. Come nightfall, it reverts to the original proprietors.'

Our lunch arrived and I tried out my technique with the chopsticks. A smiling waitress helped me out, repositioning my fingers and all the while keeping up a chatter of what were probably blistering insults in Chinese. By the end of the meal I was actually managing to pick up more than I was dropping.

After we left the Loon Foon another jeep was pulling up beside ours. A captain got out and went inside and his driver dismounted and stretched. The driver was wearing a pair of boots, shorts made from fatigue pants cut off at crotch level and a flak jacket, nothing else on his body but tan and dogtags. On his head he wore an NVA flag as a pirate-style bandanna, and mirrored aviator shades. In one hand he held a pump shotgun shortened to a pistol grip with about a foot of barrel cut off even with the tubular magazine. He looked profoundly unimpressed by our MP insignia.

'Man,' Queen said as he started up, 'there are some fuckers come out of the bush you do not want to mess with unless you have a lot of backup.'

We still had an hour so we drove around the base and there seemed to be no end to it. Most of it was of the familiar wood, screen and sandbag construction with tin roofs, but there were some big headquarters buildings of concrete, looking as permanent as the Pentagon.

'What do they do in those places?' I asked Queen.

'I wonder myself,' he said. 'Write each other memos and circulate 'em, I guess.'

Over everything hung a thin, foul-smelling pall of greasy smoke. I asked Queen about this and wished I hadn't.

'It's from the latrines. See, the shitters here are a tad shy of the American standard. They're mostly four-holers with half an oil drum under each hole – about an inch of diesel fuel in the bottom of each drum. Once a day the gooks drag out the drums, dump 'em into a trench behind the latrine, and set fire to 'em.'

'Christ,' I said.

'Yeah, but think what a nostalgia trip it's gonna be for these guys. Many years hence, whenever they catch the aroma of burning shit, it'll carry them back to the good old days at Long Binh, Republic of South Vietnam.'

We arrived at the LBJ right on time and we waited. After a while Queen went inside to check and came back out shaking his head.

'Some kind of paperwork screwup. Can't do anything till all the paperwork's done in triplicate.' He patted his pockets. 'You got any cigarettes?' I shook one out for him, already used to the ritual. Queen was providing for his retirement with the money he saved by not buying his own cigarettes.

The wait stretched on and on, all afternoon. But if soldiers know nothing else they know how to wait, since they do so much of it. We filled the time the way soldiers always do, smoking and talking. As the day dwindled, Queen glanced nervously at the sun.

'Be dark pretty soon,' he said. 'We gotta be on our way.'

'When do we have to be back?'

'It's not that. We can't be out on the highway after dark unless we're with a blacked-out convoy. Where's that goddam spook and his jailbird?'

Almost an hour later Gresham reappeared, accompanied by a pair of tall stockade guards carrying shotguns at port arms. Between them was our prisoner and he didn't look fearsome enough to provoke all the attention and security. He was a small man in his mid twenties with dark hair and fine, almost delicate features. The manacles and leg irons he wore seemed almost comical draping his slender limbs.

Gresham looked quietly furious. 'Sergeant, cuff him and let's get the hell out of here.' His clipboard now held a fat manila envelope bearing a large 'Classified' stamp.

'My very sentiments,' Queen said, taking a pair of cuffs from his belt while one of the guards unfastened the man's elaborate bondage gear. He clipped the prisoner's wrists behind him efficiently and we got him into the back next to me.

'Don't waste any time getting to the gate,' Gresham said, glaring at the red western sky as if he could draw the sun back above the horizon by force of will.

'Red sky at night,' said the man next to me, 'Charlie's delight.'

'Shut up, Starr,' Gresham said tonelessly.

The prisoner turned and gave me a shy, almost girlish smile. 'My host doesn't want me to communicate. That seems un-American, don't you agree?' He wore fatigues that were too large for him and on the back of the blouse had been painted a large, white capital P.

'You think you're our comrade in arms, jailbird?' Queen said. 'Disabuse yourself of that notion.'

'Oh, dear,' the man sighed. 'Am I to be the victim of police brutality?'

'That would be a violation of the UCMJ,' Queen said, referring to the Uniform Code of Military Justice. 'On the other hand, shooting you while trying to escape would be perfectly in order. Now I'm a peaceable sort myself, but my comrade seated next to you, PFC Treloar, is an infamous psychopath. He'll put nine big double-aught holes through your pretty white P.'

'Both of you can it,' Gresham intoned.

We drove on in relative silence, discounting the rumble of the jeep and the whopping of the helicopters, which had grown so monotonous that I no longer really heard it.

'Shit!' Gresham said as the gate came in sight. A half dozen vehicles were already there, stopped by the movable barricade. A couple of officers were talking to the MP officer in charge of the gate, but he seemed bored and unmoved. His expression didn't change when Gresham hopped from our jeep and tried to bully his way through.

'Lieutenant, I have to be in Saigon tonight! This is State Department business.'

The young looey studied the ID Gresham held in front of his face, then shook his head. 'Sorry, Major, no unconvoyed vehicles are to pass this gate after sundown. That's General Weyand's orders. There's a convoy leaving a little past midnight and you can hitch on with them. You'll still make Saigon tonight.'

Gresham fumed but it didn't do him any good.

'We can't have all these vehicles bunched up here at the gate,' the MP lieutenant announced. 'Take them out along the perimeter road and park them at regulation intervals. You'll be told when the convoy is ready to go through.'

Gresham got back in. 'Drive down three bunkers and park. I'll try their field phone.'

A broad dirt road ran around the perimeter. The bunker we pulled up to was identical to the others; about fifty feet long, maybe eight feet high, a bulldozed artificial hill covered with grass. A couple of men sat on top smoking, and a young buck sergeant stood by the entrance. They all wore a little circular patch, its device resembling the astrological Mars symbol turned inside out: a short, fat arrow pointing slantwise toward the center of a circle. It was the insignia of the First Logistical Command, known to one and all as 'the leaning shithouse'.

The buck sergeant came up and saluted. 'Making you wait? Happens every night.'

'I need to use your field phone,' Gresham said.

'Sorry, Major, the CO doesn't allow any non-perimeter traffic over our lines.'

'Think I give a shit?' Gresham got out of the jeep and disappeared inside the bunker.

'Who's that asshole?' the sergeant asked.

'Lady Bird's nephew,' Queen told him. 'Big pull in Washington. You got a cigarette, Sarge?'

He shook one out. 'Smoke 'em quick. We go under light discipline in ten minutes.' It was almost dark by this time.

'What outfit are you guys?' I asked.

'2077th Transportation. We're in charge of ten of these bunkers.'

'Ever get any action?' I asked.

He snorted. 'You think a base this big gets attacked? We catch a few mortars and rockets once in a while, but they get fired by remote from up in the hills. There's never anybody there when the choppers go looking for 'em. Doesn't mean there's never any shooting. Newbies think they got gooks in the wire every time a monkey farts. Last month one of 'em bagged a water buffalo. You wouldn't believe the paperwork.'

'Do you ever have the feeling,' our prisoner said, 'that you've stepped out of reality into a sort of alternate universe where the rules of comic opera apply?'

Queen turned around and gazed at him. 'As I live and breathe, we've an educated man among us. What's your name, yardbird?'

'Martin Starr. With two Rs.' He smiled his shy smile again, revealing small, perfect teeth. His eyes were long-lashed and he even had dimples. I wondered how a man like this fared in the environment of an Army stockade.

'And what brings you to the attention of our Langley ranger?' Queen asked.

'Oh, a misunderstanding. It'll all be cleared as soon as I get to present my case.'

'You're perfectly innocent, of course,' I said.

He gestured eloquently with his shoulders. 'Is anyone truly innocent? I'm sure I have my share of original sin. Obviously, my bad karma outweighs the good just now. But the wheel turns. My sad case is far from the worst blunder of American policy in Southeast Asia.'

'By God, I'm glad if we gotta be stuck it's with an interesting conversationalist. Last man I came out here to pick up did nothing but yell black power slogans for two solid hours.'

'The soul brothers have their own views concerning our government,' Starr observed.

'This fucker was white. I wonder how fares the spook?'

'Douse the butts,' the buck sergeant called. The guys on top of the bunker stubbed out their cigarettes and we did the same. In the distance, bright orange lights blossomed in the air and drifted dreamily; big 4.2-inch mortar illumination rounds. Searchlights swept from some of the perimeter towers and low-cruising helicopters shone their own lights on the ground, all of it in silence except for the faint whopping of the distant choppers. It was an eerie sight. Vietnam was two different worlds and I'd heard the saying: 'The night belongs to Charlie'.

'Decent light show,' Queen commented. 'I hope someone calls in a target for the choppers. They fire those miniguns; the tracers come out so fast it makes a solid beam of light. Get a bunch of them firing, they look just like those Martian ships from *War of the Worlds*.'

'It's all so goddam alien,' I said. 'What the hell are we accomplishing here?'

'Do you know what you'll find if you go out there?' Starr said, gesturing toward the outer dark with his chin. 'Within a mile of here you'll find massive old concrete pillboxes left behind by the French in the early fifties. And just a few yards from them you'll see old, caved-in bunkers that the Japanese dug here in World War Two. Dig beneath those and you'll find the bones of Chinese and Cambodians. We're just the latest in a long line of interlopers here. A few years ago we weren't here. In a few more years, we'll be gone. We're just ghosts to these people.'

'That's some deep stuff,' Queen said. 'Ah, here comes the good major.'

Gresham didn't look happy. 'You two keep an eye on this man. If you want to go into the bunker for a smoke, take him with you. I don't want either of you going to sleep, either.'

Queen whipped around and gave him a flat stare. 'Piss on that noise, Major. Me and my partner *never* sleep on duty!'

For an instant, Gresham almost looked as if he knew he'd said too much. 'Just see that you don't.' He turned and strode up the rear face of the bunker, then sat crosslegged on top of it, staring out over the flare-glimmering landscape.

'Too bad you're not in the field,' the young buck sergeant said quietly. 'Officers like that, they're the reason God created frag grenades.'

'Spooks come and spooks go,' Queen grumbled. 'Not much difference between a spook and a ghost, eh, Starr?'

'Enlightenment comes to him who meditates,' Starr affirmed.

'Looks like he's meditating up there,' I said, nodding toward Gresham. 'Think he'll find enlightenment?'

'Meditating upon his sins, one hopes,' Starr said. 'It can't hurt.'

After a while we went down into the bunker to smoke. It was surprisingly cool inside. A black soldier with a pockmarked face sat behind an M-60. Two other soldiers lay on a bench dug into the sandbagged dirt of the back wall. Their rifles were lined up on the parapet next to the machine-gun. Below the parapet the firing devices of a half-dozen claymore mines dangled on their electrical cords. The firing slot was about four feet wide and ten inches high.

We ducked below the slot to light up, then straightened. I leaned on the parapet and looked out. The world out there looked even more ominous thus viewed. The claustrophobic interior of the bunker provided little sense of security.

'Seen anything to shoot at?' Queen asked the gunner.

'Sometimes I wish I would. Might help keep me awake.' In the far distance we heard an M-60 cut loose. 'Some nervous shit seein' things. He'll regret it. You shoot one of these things you got to clean it. Takes about six hours to do it right.' He leaned down and lit a cigarette, keeping his eyes tightly shut as he did to preserve his night vision. He straightened, blowing smoke. ' 'Least it's early yet. Somebody shoots like that around four in the morning, everyone else jerks awake and starts shooting, too. Pretty soon the whole bunker line's firing away at nothing. There's about twenty miles of perimeter around Long Binh, bunkers ever' hundred yards. Makes a hell of a racket.'

'Gooks won't bother us for the next few days,' said one of the reclining men. 'They's a truce on for the new year or some such shit.'

'Ain' no truce in this fucked-up place,' said the third man. He lay with his head propped on his helmet, staring up at nothing.

A couple of hours later the convoy arrived and we attached ourselves to its tail end with the other orphans. The officer in charge told everyone that he was assuming no responsibility for us and we accompanied him at our own risk. Then we got moving.

The night had clouded over and it was unbelievably black. It was nerve-wracking to drive along in the dark, even at the glacial pace of the convoy. The truck in front of us was just a slightly blacker shape in the gloom. The only illumination was provided by the ridiculous little cat's eyes – dim, rectangular lights no more than an inch wide mounted on the bumpers of the vehicles.

'They taught you convoy procedure at AIT didn't they?' Queen asked me.

'Uh-huh.' I hoped he wouldn't tell me to drive. Just riding made me nervous enough. The road had no centerline or side lines. It was like riding on ink.

'Remember how to maintain interval?'

'Watch the cat's eyes,' I said. 'Make sure that the vehicle in front of you always shows two. If you see three, you're too close. If you see just one, you're too far back.'

'Rat own. I'll make an MP of you yet.'

The convoy trundled on, a line of lost souls trying to find the other side of the Styx. In contrast to the road, the villages we passed were brightly illuminated. The Vietnamese liked colored lights, and the villages looked like a succession of carnivals in the distance. The American installations were islands of brightness as well. Only the perimeters were blacked out, the interiors lit up by floodlights on tall poles. In this war the enemy had no aircraft and the greatest security lay in being able to see at night, unless you were out in ambush country.

From time to time the convoy slowed and a vehicle or two would pull away on to a side road leading to one of the US installations. We were down to a dozen trucks and a jeep or two when we finally saw the lights of Saigon ahead of us.

'Home again, home again, jiggity-jig,' Queen said as the dismal shanty town closed around us. 'What time's it getting to be, bro?'

I looked at my PX Seiko but the luminescence had long since faded from its dial, so I flipped on the anglehead flashlight that hung on the front of my flak jacket. The red night-time filter leached color from the watch and my arm alike. I flipped it off. 'Just coming up on 0200,' I reported.

'Twenty minutes to the embassy,' Queen said, 'an' twenty-five more to the barracks and some well-earned sack time. We'll be cuttin' Zs by 0300. I'll let you check the jeep into the motor pool, Treloar. I know you won't mind . . .'

He was cut off when the lead truck, impossibly, stood up on its rear wheels, balanced on top of an enormous, orange fireball. The tremendous detonation that accompanied the spectacle was something that I felt in my eyeballs and viscera and bone marrow rather than anything I could hear with my ears. Explosions are something movies never convey well.

M-60s mounted on top of the other trucks began hammering, and troops opened up with their M-16s. They were answered by the slower chatter of AK-47s. The streams of red tracers from the American guns met the greenish arcs from the AKs, crossing and recrossing like a kids' pissing contest. The flat bang and orange flash of a grenade silenced the fire from the rear of an American truck and I looked wildly around for someone to shoot at.

'What the fuck!' Queen yelled. 'They ain't supposed to do this here! This is *Saigon*, for Christ's sake!'

'Get us out of here!' Gresham shouted.

But Queen was already slamming the jeep into low gear and flooring the accelerator. The little vehicle jumped forward and slewed around the truck ahead of us, then past another that was on fire with bodies hanging off it. The smoke that blew on to us was fouler than any at Long Binh. Queen took a corner on two wheels and two men with rifles jumped out from behind a tin shanty to block our way. Queen jerked the wheel to the right and caught one of them with a fender. The small man flew back against the flimsy shack and the thin metal crumpled inward like tinfoil. I thumbed off my safety and fired at the other and he disappeared back between two buildings.

Then we were driving down nameless alleys where people huddled in terror inside the false security of their pathetic hovels. After the chaotic firefight, the relative quiet was stunning. I was breathing heavily, thinking that I had just killed my first man. Or maybe not. He might have just ducked as I blazed away at nothing. How could I know?

'Head for the Y Bridge,' Gresham shouted, naming one of Saigon's more distinctive landmarks, connecting Cholon with the administrative part of the capital.

'Fuck that,' Queen told him. 'Charlie's open for business tonight and he's got that bridge sighted in for sure!'

'Screw where we're going,' I said. 'Where the hell *are* we?' We were all talking at the tops of our voices, both from excitement and because the detonations and the gunfire had set our ears ringing.

Abruptly, Queen stopped the jeep and shut off the engine.

'What are you doing, Sergeant?' Gresham snapped. 'Get us—'

Queen held up a finger. 'Shh. Listen.' He'd regained his cool and it seemed to steady the rest of us. The sound of gunfire came from every direction and we could see the glow of huge fires beginning in several parts of the city above the low roofs of the shacks. Besides the rattle of small-arms fire and the flat bang of grenades, we heard the blast of mines like the one that had destroyed the truck, along with the massive *whumps* of mortar rounds and Chinese-made rockets.

'Major,' Queen said, 'this ain't a few sappers out for a night of mischief. This is a fucking offensive. It takes a division to deliver the kind of fire we're hearing. Out here on the fringes they're just disrupting traffic and stalling reinforcements and counterstrikes. You know goddamned well what they're concentrating on: the Tan Son Nhut airbase, MACV headquarters, the radio station, the presidential palace and the United fucking States embassy! You sure you want to go there?'

'Remember what you said about three men in a jeep?' I reminded him.

'Now, I *know* Cholon,' Queen said, 'and that's where our buddies are, and I know they'll have a secure perimeter established around MP headquarters.'

Gresham sat silent for a minute. 'All right. Head for Cholon. Drive slow.' Queen started the jeep, put it in gear and we crept on. Gresham slammed a fist against his knee. 'Damn! They can't be attacking! This is Tet!'

We entered an area of shabby but permanent buildings. Starr turned and smiled at me as we passed beneath a streetlight, his fine, almost pencilled brows arching, his perfect teeth gleaming.

'It's the Lunar new year,' he said. 'Fun, mystery and magic.'

There was something hallucinatory about it, and I was to learn that this was true of the whole war. Probably, it's true of any war. Only years afterward do things seem to make sense in retrospect, filtered through books and films and commentators. We drove through streets that might have been the night-time streets of almost any city. The streetlights were on, as were a few neon signs. Not even a flicker. We'd patrolled streets like these since my arrival, but on this night combat teams dashed from corner to corner. Some of them spotted us and then Queen would make a fast turn while AK bullets pinged from the pavement. I fired a couple of times but the range was too great for the shotgun. Over the rooftops we saw the graceful rainbows of heavy machine-gun tracers and parachute flares like a gaudy fireworks display.

Once, a team of sappers crossed an intersection not twenty yards in front of us. They were men and women both, wearing city clothing, not the black pajamas and straw hats of the countryside. They held small arms and carried heavy satchels on their backs, almost certainly explosive charges. They glanced at us warily as they crossed the street, but took no other action. They were grimly determined upon their mission, and we formed no part of it. We gaped after them, too surprised and relieved to take any action ourselves. We drove on.

I was beginning to think we were going to make it home without a fight when a pair of teams chanced to cross in front of us and behind at the same time. Queen grabbed up his M-16 and fired one-handed while Gresham stood up and popped away with his silly little revolver. I worked the pump on my shotgun and something hit the calf of my leg and clunked to the floor of the jeep. I looked down and saw the grenade rolling there and thought: well, shit.

Starr scooped up the grenade with both hands, cuffed behind him as they were, squatting weirdly to do it. He stood, dropped it, and back-heeled it out of the jeep, laughing like a kid playing a new game. The thing exploded and I felt something punch the back of my flak jacket but I was too busy firing to pay it any heed. The VC or whatever they were seemed to be everyplace.

Queen tried to drive us out but something hit one of our front tires and the jeep lurched sharply to the left. I fell and something leapt over me and I dragged myself up to see Martin Starr running for an alley.

'Halt!' I yelled inanely. I lined up the shotgun and the big, white P on his back was poised perfectly over the bead.

'Shoot him!' Gresham yelled. 'Kill the sonofabitch!' He was fumbling rounds into the cylinder of his .38.

My finger tightened on the trigger and I thought: I'm in a

war zone in a foreign country in the middle of a firefight and I'm about to shoot a fellow American. Screw that. Then Starr was in the alley and out of sight.

'You stupid bastard!' Gresham howled. 'You let him get away!'

'Sorry, Major,' I said. 'We need every round for Charlie tonight.' I looked around. The vicinity had become quiet. There were a couple of bodies in the street. 'Where'd they go?' I said.

Queen shrugged. 'Must've had pressing business elsewhere.'

I couldn't believe there were just two bodies on the street. I could have sworn at least a dozen were killed in the first few seconds, and I was amazed that none of us had been hurt. Then I realized that the VC probably thought they had killed all of us. It's a rare soldier who can keep track of what really happens in a firefight.

Queen gave the steering wheel a radical right-hand twist to compensate for our flat tire and we limped on. Gresham glared and muttered the whole way, as if his little problem was the biggest event of the night. I knew we were in for some trouble, but mortal fear drives off all lesser considerations.

'There's our boys!' Queen whooped. Just down the street was a roadblock. Behind it we saw the shiny MP helmets, so different from the camouflage-covered field helmets of the grunts.

'That you, Queen?' shouted a gangly Spec 4 named Andrea. 'We figured you'n Gabe done got your asses waxed.' They dragged parts of their makeshift barricade aside and we drove through. Queen braked and we jumped out. Suddenly I felt wobbly.

'What the fuck's been goin' on?' Queen asked. 'We crashed this party without an invitation.'

'Goddam if I know,' Andrea said, dragging a razor-wire coil back into place. ' 'Bout 0130 the CQ caught a flash report somebody was attacking the US Embassy. But that's Seven-Sixteenth territory so he just put us on alert. 'Bout twenty minutes later the shit commenced to fly and it ain't let up.'

'I reckon Uncle Ho done come calling,' said Sanders, a black private from Georgia. He held an M-79 grenade launcher, a stubby weapon like a single-barrelled shotgun. It looked like a toy in his massive paw. His eyes narrowed and I followed his gaze to a flicker of movement on the corner of a roof half a block up the street. The launcher made its peculiar little cough and two seconds later the grenade turned the wooden parapet to splinters. Something that looked like a scarecrow flew back from the brief yellow flash.

'Sniper?' Queen asked.

Sanders shrugged. 'Maybe. Dogmeat now.'

'Where is your CO?' Gresham demanded.

'Comin' yonder,' Sanders said, jerking his chin toward a jeep that was approaching from down the street.

The jeep pulled up and the CO got out. He was a captain named Crandall and he had the harried look of a man who had to be everywhere at once. The first sergeant was driving the jeep. A machine-gunner and a radioman crouched in the back. Crandall stuck out a hand and the radioman gave him the handset of the big Prick-25 field radio, bolted into its mount on the back of the jeep. Its long, flat antenna whipped back and forth mindlessly.

'I need reinforcements here!' Crandall yelled into the mouthpiece. 'Cholon's crawling with VC! I've got a secure perimeter here but Charlie's got units spotted all over the place. Center of activity seems to be the Can Tho racetrack. I think that's where they've set up their command post. We need infantry to clean out these nests in the tenements and armor to take back to the racetrack.' He listened for a while, his face getting gloomier, then said: 'Out.' He gave the handset back to his RTO and walked over to us.

'Thought we'd lost you two,' Crandall said. The first sergeant got out of the jeep behind him.

Queen saluted. 'Sergeant Queen and PFC Treloar all present and accounted for, sir. Sorry to report a flat tire.'

'These two,' Gresham said, furious, 'these two let my prisoner escape!'

Crandall looked at him like he was an apparition conjured up by magic. 'Say again?'

'The man hopped out in the middle of a firefight and made like a jackrabbit down an alley,' Queen said. 'Can't fault him for balls, though his good sense may leave something to be desired.'

'You uncuff him when the shooting started?' First Sergeant Washington asked.

'Didn't have time,' I said. 'He took off with his hands cuffed behind him.' I decided not to say anything about Starr's feat with the grenade. They'd put it down to battle hysteria. I was beginning to doubt it myself.

'This man,' Gresham said, so angry there was a quaver in his voice, pointing a finger at my face, 'had his weapon leveled at my prisoner and wouldn't shoot! Refused even after I gave him a direct order! I want him court-martialled!'

Washington took a cigar from his breast pocket and stuck it in his mouth. 'I can't believe I'm hearing this shit.'

'Major,' Crandall said, 'if you think I give a rat's ass about your prisoner you're even crazier than you sound! I'm outnumbered in the middle of an enemy offensive and I've been short two men and a jeep because they had to nursemaid you out to the LBJ and back. If your prisoner is out there alone and wearing cuffs, he's going to be dead by morning or else he'll turn himself in to the first soldiers he sees, so you can take your sorry spook ass to Langley right now, Major. I have a war to fight!'

'Captain,' Gresham said with what he probably thought was withering scorn, 'this is insubordination and goddam near mutiny. It all goes in my report.'

'Major,' Washington said, 'you can go to our headquarters and borrow a typewriter to make out your report.' He gestured in the direction of HQ with his cigar. 'Then you take it to General Westmoreland. He's the one you CIA fuckheads told there wasn't gonna be no fighting over Tet. Truce or some such, you said.'

We all ducked as mortar rounds started landing close. Gresham whirled and started walking back down the street, stiff-spined. I thought: Where the hell does he think he's going?

'We've got more ammo coming up,' Crandall said, climbing into his jeep. 'It's gonna be a long night. Call for help if you need it, but no false alarms. We're spread thin enough as it is.'

'Rat own, Cap'n,' Queen said, saluting as if he were in charge.

The mortars let up and Andrea took me by the shoulder, turning me half around and looking at my back. 'Treloar, 'less you shit your pants, I think you better go see the medic.'

'Huh?' I reached back and felt the rear of my trousers. They were soaked with something sticky and my hand came away covered with blood. 'I felt something hit my flak jacket when that grenade blew,' I said. 'I never felt anything hit me.' No wonder I'd felt woozy when I got out of the jeep.

Queen grinned and took me by the arm. 'Coupla you guys get the spare tire on this jeep, okay? I got to take m'man Treloar to the medic, collect his aspirin and his Purple Heart.'

'Some fuckers do anything to get out of a little fight,' Sanders grumbled.

'Come along, young trooper,' Queen said. I suddenly felt very tired as we went toward the aid station. Nothing hurt yet but I felt wrung out. Queen shook his head, chuckling.

'What're you laughing about?' I demanded.

'That guy, Martin Starr.'

'What about him?'

'Wasn't he one crazy son of a bitch?'

Chapter Four

'That's it?' Connie Armijo said. 'You saw him disappear into the slums of Saigon on the first night of the Tet Offensive of '68, still wearing cuffs, and you never saw him again?' She had the cop's habit of making sure the facts were straight and everything in the right order.

'Not exactly,' Queen told her, 'but it was certainly the incident that left the most lasting impression. First impressions are important, don't you agree?'

'First impressions, last impressions, it's all the same.' She fixed him with her black, Hispanic eyes. 'My first impression of you was you're a professional bullshit artist. That's still my impression.'

'We saw him again,' I said. 'At least, I think I saw him one more time. Mostly we heard about him. After Tet his body wasn't found and he didn't turn himself in. But in the following months ghost activity got more intense, more organized. Word had it there was a man behind it, an American deserter who'd become king of the roost in the Saigon underground. The name Martin Starr kept coming up.'

'How could he have survived in conditions like that?' she asked. 'How did he get out of his cuffs?'

'Our acquaintance was brief,' Queen told her, 'but the man just wasn't a normal human being.'

'Crap,' she said succinctly. 'You picked him up at a prison, even if it was a military stockade. He must've had contacts in the Saigon underground. He knew exactly where he was going when he jumped out of your jeep. It's the only thing that makes sense. What was he in for, anyway? Why was he being moved, and why to the embassy?'

'It was spook business,' I said. 'We were curious, sure. We tried to find out, but it was all in paper files in those days, no computers you could play with. Neither of us even had a secret clearance, much less the kind of top-level clearance you needed to get at spook files. And we had other things on our minds. For the first couple of months we assumed he was dead anyway.'

'You said ghost activity increased. What sort of things happened?'

'Random robberies and muggings turned into complex, well-planned hijackings, for one thing,' Queen began. 'Shakedowns of the local merchants got real organized. Black marketeers had another payoff to make, besides the ones they were already making to the VC and the Saigon government.'

'You have to understand,' I interjected, 'we were operating in a milieu so corrupt, with so many different criminal elements, that it took a while for us to understand that a new element was at work.'

'And American criminals could operate there?' She shook her head. 'That's a little hard to picture.'

'The ghosts operated mainly out of Cholon,' I explained. 'Cholon was Saigon's Chinese ghetto, almost like a foreign town set down in the capital. That gave them a further layer of protection from the Saigon government and gangs. Plus, they had some advantages the others lacked. For one, they could impersonate regular GIs to pull jobs.'

'And they had contacts within the American military establishments,' Queen said. 'Remember, this was the Vietnam war and most of the men were draftees and unhappy about being there. Dope was getting to be a big problem. The deserters and their buddies still with the units co-operated to buy it and smuggle it to the US. All the movies and books are about the grunts and the pilots, so most people think that's all we had in Vietnam. But it was like any other modern war. There were about a dozen support personnel for every poor bastard out there busting bush. The support people had a lot of time on their hands and they sat on top of a lot of goods and those goods were valuable on the black market. The ghosts did a lot of business with them. Their contacts in the administration offices could usually tip them in time whenever we tried to crack down on them. Their major difficulty was they couldn't rotate back home. They just stayed there, year after year.'

'So you think a lot of those MIAs people are always agitating about in Congress were really these ghosts?'

'I'm afraid so,' I told her. 'The Army didn't like to admit that there was any such thing as in-country desertion. Mostly they were carried as missing in action. A few of them got so sick of it they'd turn themselves in and there'd be a quiet court-martial.'

'That was another thing that changed after Starr waltzed away from us,' Mitch said. 'Renegade ghosts started dying shortly after they arrived at the LBJ. Pretty soon, no more were turning themselves in.'

She nodded. 'Real organized crime stuff. I never knew so much of it went on over there. Did they fight much with the other gangs?'

'We heard rumors,' I said. 'They must've co-operated on some things – had to, really. But they were like any other ethnic minority setting up gang activity in a new place. They succeeded by being tougher, meaner and more violent than any of the others. And they were the best-armed gangsters in history, at least until the gangs here took up military hardware in the eighties. Most of them deserted with their personal weapons and any sort of American arms could be had on the Saigon black market.'

'We found vaults that'd been blown with anti-tank rifles,' Queen told her.

'So what happened to them after the war?' she asked.

'I'd always assumed that they were rounded up and executed when the Hanoi government took over in '75,' I said.

'That's what I thought,' Mitch said. He held up the letter. 'Until this came along.'

'Mitch,' I said, 'what you have here is a very serious-sounding death threat. Have you considered your legal position? If this turns out to be for real and you don't tell the people involved and someone is hurt as a result, you're responsible.' I saw Connie nodding emphatically at that.

'You think I haven't thought of that? The question is, is it for real? That's where you come in, Gabe. I have to know whether this is a credible threat. Remember what I said about investors? I just don't want them rabbiting over nothing. Even if Martin Starr really sent this, how do we know that he can carry it out? He was a bad dude twenty-five years ago, but so what? By now he could be an old derelict cadging drinks in a bar someplace. He may've got wind of the project and this is some sort of revenge for things that happened to him a long time ago.'

I looked at Connie Armijo. 'What's your agency's position on this?'

'Darlene told Miss Gibson, emphatically, that she should have nothing to do with this project. The threat sounds serious and it doesn't read like the work of someone with a pickled brain.' She gave Queen a look that said what she thought of his hopeful theory. 'I have to tell you that everything you have said reinforces my own opinion that it isn't worth the risk to her. My God, the woman's worth millions. It isn't like she needs the work. But Mr Queen seems to have hooked her with his computer gimmick. She's desperate to be on screen looking the way she did thirty years ago.' Her voice was perfectly calm, but a very faint Hispanic accent had crept into it, a sure sign that she felt deeply about this. Or maybe that she just didn't like Queen.

'Vanity impels people to extreme behavior,' Queen said. I saw Connie's generous lips tighten. He was digging at something.

'Let's keep this professional,' she said. 'The fact is that, whatever our recommendations, Miss Gibson has retained us to watch over her interests in this matter, to be sure that the investigation is properly conducted and ascertain whether a threat to her welfare indeed exists.'

'In other words, you're not about to trust an investigator hired by me.'

'Why should she?' I said. 'Face it, Mitch, with as much as you have riding on this your objectivity has to be in question.'

He clapped a hand over his heart. '*Et tu*, Gabe? All right, Connie, are you satisfied with my man here?'

She nodded. 'No problems so far. Being your old friend was no great recommendation, but I see now that he knows both the suspect and the milieu. And, of course, he has plenty of investigative experience.' Of course she knew all about my LAPD service record. Well, it had been a good one until near the end. She took out a gold pen and wrote something on a pad. She was left-handed and I noticed the engagement and wedding rings, worn so long that they were sunk into the flesh of her finger.

'Great!' Queen said, clapping his palms together. 'Now we can get to work on this.'

'Just a minute,' I said. 'I haven't agreed to take this on.'

'What's the problem?' Queen said, honestly puzzled.

'For one thing, I'm not Philip Marlowe. I work for an agency, Mitch. I'll have to consult with my boss, and he's going to have to be satisfied with the situation and the case. He's also going to have to be satisfied with the money.'

He waved a hand airily. 'Oh, sure. Whatever it takes.' I guessed that a man who could raise a hundred million dollars for a movie project wouldn't worry about what a private investigations agency might cost him.

'I imagine you two want to talk your business arrangements in private,' Connie said. 'I have some phone calls to make myself.'

We took the hint and stood up. With promises to get together over breakfast in the morning, Mitch and I left.

Mitch was shaking his head as we walked toward the elevators. 'I've had stars pull prima donna stunts before, but siccing an all-female detective agency on me is a new twist.'

'Selene's the bankable one, you said so yourself. You'll just have to put up with what she wants.'

'You think I don't know that? Thing is, pretty soon they'll *all* be doing this!'

We sat for a while in my room talking price, then Mitch left and I made a call to my boss. It was late, but he was a widower like me and put in late hours at the office. I outlined the situation for him and for a while I heard nothing from his end except raspy breathing.

'This is stranger than anything that's come across my desk in a *long* time,' he said finally. 'I mean, even for film people this is way out there.'

'He didn't argue about the fifty per cent up front non-refundable,' I reminded him.

'Yeah, and the money's good, but, I don't know . . . What's the chance this is some sort of wild publicity stunt?'

'I've thought of it, but I can't believe that's it. For one thing, I think they usually wait until a movie is near release time before they pull publicity gimmicks. This can only hurt the production.'

'Do you want to take this thing on? I don't care how good the money is – if you think it's too fishy, don't do it.'

'I have to admit that I'm intrigued, since it involves me, even though it was a long time ago. I've often wondered what happened to those deserters.'

'Are you saying you want to take the case?'

I made up my mind. 'Yes, I am.'

'Then you got it. I can send Mayhew down to cover the Knoxville office if you need to be away for a while. What sort of time frame do you estimate we're looking at?'

'I have no idea just yet. It's going to call for some travel. This one I can't handle over the phone.'

'Where are you going?'

'LA first,' I said reluctantly. 'Bad memories there. I'm going to have to talk to people I'd sooner not look in the eye—'

'Screw that,' Randall interrupted. 'Jesus, you think you're the only guy ever fell into a bottle?'

'I got Murray killed,' I said leadenly.

'He was a cop, and walking into bullets is what cops do sometimes. You were a damn fine cop for sixteen – seventeen years, and people will remember that. You got over this a while back, remember? You talk to whoever you need to. Now, what's your plan?'

'LA is where the movie people are. I need to talk to Selena Gibson. I'm not taking Queen's or Armijo's word for her take on this, I want a face-to-face interview. There's also this guy Jared Rhine. I want to talk to him.'

'He sounds like a hard man to approach.'

'When people know their money is on the line, they co-operate.'

'Very true.'

'Also, I still have some contacts in the West Coast Vietnamese community. I want to see what I can turn up there.'

'Do you still keep up with those people?'

'Not much since Rose died. After that we didn't have much left in common. It would've been different if we'd had children. But they're pretty punctilious about things like Christmas cards and wedding invitations, social obligations like that. I have their addresses and phone numbers. Rose and I sponsored her brother and his family when they had to run after Saigon fell. We located them in a refugee village in Hong Kong. I'll start with him. He may have kept in contact with his friends from the old days.'

'Okay, play it as you think best. But Gabe?'

'Yeah?'

'Don't go all Hollywood on me.'

The next morning I found Connie in the hotel's grill. It featured a massive breakfast buffet with grits and gravy prominently featured to remind you that you were in the south. I loaded up a plate and joined her. On the table in front of her there was a huge bowl of granola-type cereal and a plate piled with fruit. She eyed my mess of eggs, bacon, sausage and waffles with wary horror, as if it all might leap off the plate and attack her arteries.

'Some commit suicide fast,' she said, 'some prefer to do it slow. I guess that's as good a way as any.'

I dropped the napkin in my lap. 'Yesterday it suddenly came to me: I'm going to die no matter what I do, so what the hell?'

She downed a crunchy mouthful. 'You experience this sort of epiphany often?'

'Every month or two.'

We were sitting by a window, and the morning light allowed for a better reading than I'd been able to manage the night before. Connie was in her upper thirties somewhere, maybe forty. About five-four, she had to go at least 145 pounds, but she wasn't overweight. It was all arranged on a compact, big-boned frame. Her face was unlined except for a couple of deep, c-shaped marks that framed her mouth like parentheses. They were visible even when she wasn't smiling. In fact, I had yet to see her smile.

The waitress filled my coffee cup and I sipped it. 'You don't like Mitch, do you?'

'Gee, you really must be a detective after all!'

'It's how I make my living. Perceiving those little subtleties of attitude and body language is what made me a success.'

At last she smiled, revealing big, exceedingly white teeth. 'Okay, we've used up the day's ration of sarcasm. I'm sorry. I know he's your friend and you go back together a long way, but no, I don't like him. I don't like anyone who lets money substitute morals. And using his gee-whiz computer gimmick to hook Selena was a nasty piece of business.'

'Selena Gibson's a big girl,' I said. 'Surely she can make her own decisions.'

She looked pensive. 'If she wants to look thirty years younger on the screen I guess that's all right by me. Maybe it'll even extend her career. But I don't think she understands what a dangerous situation she could be walking into.'

'She was cautious enough to hire you,' I pointed out. 'Does she have bodyguards?'

'Two from the agency. Jeanette and Holly. They're good. Holly was with the Detroit police for ten years. Jeanette paid her way through college working the women's wrestling circuit.'

'They're probably good enough to handle the usual deranged fans. We're looking at something different here.'

She shrugged. 'I won't argue with that. But at least she's got some sort of protection.' Connie gave me the same once-over she'd given me the night before. 'So you were with the LAPD?'

'That's right. You?'

'Houston Police Department. I've been with Darlene for four years.'

I didn't ask her why she'd left the Houston PD, and figured she would extend me the same courtesy. We weren't investigating each other, after all. Queen joined us a few minutes later. He wasn't a breakfast eater, and limited himself to orange juice.

'Seen any of our old buddies yet, Gabe?'

'Not one so far.'

'How would you know?' Connie asked. 'It's been a quarter of a century. Forget the faces. You have to squint at name tags and see if you recognize names.'

That made me wince. 'Jesus, thanks for the observation. When you start calculating your life in sizable fractions of a century you know you're getting along in years.'

'I don't think I'm really up to schmoozing with these guys anyway,' Mitch said. 'It seemed like fun when I first read about it, but now that I think back, there's maybe a half-dozen of those guys I remember clearly. I already checked the membership list, and I didn't see any familiar names. I mean, it wasn't like World War Two, where units were raised here in the States and trained together and shipped overseas together and fought and came back and got demobilized together. Those guys lived in each other's pockets for four years or longer. Nam wasn't what you'd call a camaraderie-building experience. You checked in, put in your year and went home. It's the events you remember more than the people.'

I looked over the schedule of events. 'Actually, I'm beginning to find the whole thing depressing. That aquarium up the street looks more enticing than this.'

'I thought you guys all liked to go to the Vietnam Wall in Washington and cry and leave little mementos,' Connie said.

'No such thing,' Mitch told her. 'Hell, half the guys you see bawling at the Wall never went to Nam. There's a whole little subculture of Vietnam vet wannabes; guys that served but never went overseas, guys who never served. Hell, shrinks get people suffering from post-Vietnam stress disorder that weren't even born when we pulled out. The Nam war gave weird people something new to be weird about.'

'I'm going out to California,' I told him. 'I need to speak with Selena Gibson, and I'm going to talk with my brother-in-law. He may still be in contact with family members in Saigon. They didn't all get out.'

Connie glanced sharply at me, surprised.

'Old Duke,' Mitch said. 'I'd almost forgotten him. How's he doing these days? He must own half of Orange County by now. Look, I can put you up at my place, save your boss a little money. I've got a guest house by the pool, has its own garage, beats the hell out of a hotel. Connie's been staying there part time since Selena hired her. You like it, don't you, Connie?'

She shrugged. 'It's a nice place. The pool's a good one.'

'See? Is that praise or what?'

I wasn't too keen on the idea, but we had standing instructions to save the agency expenses wherever possible. Carson was a tight man with an expense account. 'Okay. Thanks, Mitch.'

'Mr Queen,' Connie said, 'why didn't you just invite Mr Treloar out to LA? Why did you drag us all to Chattanooga?'

'Like I said, it sounded like fun at the time.'

She stood. 'If you'll excuse me, I need to make some travel arrangements.' She walked off, back and shoulders stiff, hips swiveling.

Queen grinned after her. 'She likes to swim,' he said. 'Wait'll you see her by my pool. You're in for a treat.'

'What's that mean?'

He shook his head. 'I won't ruin the surprise.'

After breakfast I sat figuring out logistics over a last cup of coffee, the caffeine buzzing in my bloodstream. I decided I'd drive back to Knoxville, put my car and apartment in mothballs and catch the first flight out for LA. I half-listened to a couple at the next table.

'I don't know why you men make such a big deal over this,' she said wearily.

'It was Vietnam, for Christ's sake!' he said, pleading for understanding. 'It was where we left our youth!'

She was unsympathetic. 'You'd've just left it somewhere else. You wouldn't still have it.'

When I got back to my room the message light was blinking

on my phone. The operator told me Ms Armijo wanted me to call her. I punched in her room number.

'Yes?'

'Gabe here.'

'Oh, good. Would you come up to my room for a few minutes? I want to discuss a few things with you.'

When she opened the door her suitcase was on the bed, fully packed. 'I'm flying out this afternoon,' she said, closing the door behind me. 'I wanted to clear up a few things with you, in private.'

I walked over to her window and looked across the river to Lookout Mountain. 'That's fine with me.'

'All right, what's with this reunion crap? I could tell he wasn't interested from the first.'

'It's reinforcement,' I told her.

'Come again?'

'Mitch overdoes things. Always has. He's calling in a marker, reminding me of an old debt. He figured being surrounded by the old outfit might put me in a more receptive mood, increase the obligation.' I took out the letter he had sent me and handed it to her. 'Here, read this.'

She read it and handed it back. 'Okay, he's scared. I knew that. I could smell it on him. What's this about a racetrack?'

So I told her about the racetrack.

Chapter Five

Everyone remembers the Tet Offensive of 1968. Only those of us who were there, and maybe a few historians, remember that they came back again in May.

I'd met Rose by then. She was working as a secretary at Battalion HQ, and I was pulling every string I had to get assigned there so I could see more of her. Like so many of the upper-class Saigonese she was a French-educated Catholic, trilingual – and the most beautiful woman I'd ever seen. This was saying something, because Saigon has more beautiful women than any other city in the world.

I was an old Saigon hand by that time. I'd picked up a Spec 4 rating and I could sling the in-country jargon with the best of them. The Beatles' 'Lady Madonna' was fading from the charts and the Mamas and the Papas were coming on really big.

I was driving our jeep, Mitch riding beside me, chattering on about nothing much. He was getting short, only about two months left before heading home, and he got more frenetic as the great day drew nearer. We were on a street packed with Saigon cowboys on Hondas with their girls sitting sidesaddle behind them, farm trucks loaded with produce, people delivering vast loads on bicycles, saffron-robed Buddhist monks walking in groups, their shaven heads gleaming in the sunlight. Along the sides of the street ancient temples abutted Toyota dealerships. At little sidewalk tables people sat eating lunches of an international nature. I'd found that a typical Saigon lunch might consist of a bowl of rice, a stubby ear of corn on the cob and a sandwich made of a split French loaf piled with vegetables and shrimp, laced with pungent *nuoc mam*. Life went on, although sizable sections of Cholon had burned down during Tet.

'Turn here,' Mitch said, and I wheeled left into a narrow street that wasn't much more than an alley. People had to step back against the walls to make way for us and they didn't look happy about it. We came to a wider cul-de-sac and Mitch told me to pull up at an open-fronted barber shop. Above its open shutters was a long red sign with Chinese writing in gold paint. Inside, two barbers eyed us boredly. In one chair an elderly Chinese man was getting a scalp massage. The other chair was empty.

'Now I know you don't need a haircut,' I said.

'By no means,' Mitch said, getting out of the jeep. 'You wait here, make sure nobody takes our vee-hicle.'

'Shit, Queen! You dealing greenbacks again? You're gonna get caught and you'll be in the LBJ until General Vo Nguyen Giap ETS's out of North Vietnam!'

'I'm merely another example of the drive and initiative that made America a great nation. I'm gonna need boocoo P to supplement my GI Bill when I get home. Abide here the nonce, m'man. I'll be back shortly.' He went inside and disappeared through a rear door.

I muttered curses as I dismounted the jeep and fired up a cigarette. I'd learned about Queen's currency dealing early in my stay. American personnel weren't supposed to possess US money and we were warned of dire consequences should we try to smuggle any in. We were paid in MPC – military pay certificates; scrip redeemable at the PX and other approved businesses. For spending in town, we could convert them at the bank into Vietnamese piastres, referred to as P, which were supported at an outrageously inflated rate by America, though at the banks we got only the official rate.

On the black market, greenback dollars brought in at least five times the number of P set by the US. You could sell your greenbacks and convert the P at the bank, which had to redeem them at the official rate. This turned you a tidy 500 per cent profit, assuming you didn't get caught.

The risk annoyed me, but I was way beyond being morally outraged. The atmosphere of corruption was so thick that Queen's little money racket seemed no more reprehensible than a boyish prank. Guys going out of country on R & R picked up US dollars in places like Hong Kong, Bangkok, Tokyo and Sydney, and gave them to Queen to exchange with his contacts. Queen assumed all the risk and took a twenty per cent cut. It was a good deal all around.

I stood there smoking in the miserable heat when a little kid maybe three years old waddled over and squatted near my boots, grinning up at me. I'd acquired a pair of aviator shades and I took them off to smile back at him. Immediately, I got that bullseye feeling between my shoulder blades. Slowly I turned and scanned the windows and rooftops behind me. No snipers.

I turned back and wondered what the hell kind of place was this, where you couldn't smile at a kid without thinking he was setting you up for a bullet in the back? A few minutes later Queen came out and climbed into the jeep.

'*Dee-dee mao*, brother,' he said. 'Let's cut us a chogi out of this place.'

'You make out okay?' I asked, putting the jeep in gear.

'Numbah one. Pretty soon I'm gonna be the John D. Rockerfeller of Southeast Asia.'

'Bit shot, huh?' I was getting annoyed, mainly over my scare with the kid. 'So you get what? Maybe five hundred bucks against fifteen to twenty in the stockade?'

He grinned through his black shades. 'Shit, m'man, in this place we're all under suspended death sentence and making thirteen cents an hour. Might as well get the five hundred to sweeten the situation.'

We went back to the barracks. That night we were sitting in the enlisted men's canteen having a beer when the VC let us know they were back in town.

Captain Crandall called a hasty formation and addressed us through his bullhorn: 'Okay, gentlemen, it's not like this hasn't. happened before. You all have your posts assigned. You newbies who missed Tet, stick close to the vets and watch what they do. First platoon stays at HQ as our flying force.'

First platoon. That was us.

'It's going to be different this time,' Crandall said. 'The ARVN will be handling most of the fighting. We just secure our areas and render assistance when asked for.'

'Yeah,' Andrea muttered behind me, 'I believe that shit.' Our confidence in our allies was not great.

So we sat in our jeeps in front of HQ, hugging our weapons and watching the fireworks and listening to the noise of battle while somebody's Japanese tape recorder blasted out 'Eight Miles High'.

Around midnight a group of ARVN MP vehicles pulled up and a young Vietnamese captain got out of the lead jeep.

'Them VC can hang it up now, boys,' Queen said in his

Walter Brennan voice. 'Duke Wayne's done arrived.' The captain's name was Duc Nguyen, which, pronounced in Vietnamese, sounds a little like 'Duke Wayne'. Queen thought it was funny as hell. Duc was also Rose's brother. He'd wangled her the job at Battalion in the usual Saigon fashion.

A few minutes later, First Sergeant Washington appeared in the HQ doorway. 'First platoon, stand by.'

'Well, shit!' said hulking Sanders, throwing down the butt of his cigarette and stomping on it. 'Them ARVN done got they ass in a crack agin an' we gotta get it out for 'em!'

Crandall appeared, accompanied by Duc Nguyen. 'The VC have set up a command post in the racetrack again. You are to accompany Captain Nguyen and assist his unit in prying them out of there.'

Our platoon sergeant was a lanky Texan named Overstreet. 'Why not just shell the fuckers out of there, Captain?'

'There's a complication this time. They have at least three round-eye prisoners.'

That straightened us up. 'MPs?' Overstreet asked. There was a hierarchy of round-eyes in Vietnam as far as we were concerned: first came MPs, then the rest of the Army, and after that came the other services. If these poor fools were Coast Guard they wouldn't get much sympathy from us.

'These are civilians,' Crandall said. 'Two PA&E employees and at least one other, status unknown.'

There was a collective splutter of indignation. We had gradations of contempt, too. At the very bottom – even below the Saigon government – were the round-eye civilians, especially the Americans. They had no business being there, we thought, and they were making big bucks out of our danger and suffering. PA&E was Pacific Architects and Engineers which, along with Vinell Corporation, were the biggest civilian contractors in South Asia. As near as we could tell, they recruited solely on a basis of loudmouthed, boorish loutishness, and they did more to ruin US–Vietnamese relations than any number of village massacres.

Overstreet was dumbfounded. 'You mean we're supposed to put our asses on the line for *them*?' He packed a whole load of contempt into one short word.

'No,' Crandall said coldly. 'You're expected to obey orders.'

Overstreet held his gaze for a few seconds, then whirled to face us. 'Mount up!' he bawled.

We got into our jeeps and fired up the engines. A minute later we roared out after the ARVN contingent, Duc Nguyen in the lead. I was driving, Queen sat next to me, and behind us a newby manned our M-60. He was hearing his first shots fired in anger and was as tense as a bowstring.

'Here's your chance to shine, m'man,' Queen said, grinning. 'The way you been pantin' after the fair Miss Rose, you should welcome an opportunity to impress her brother.' In the streetlights his eyes had a funny look, one I hadn't seen before.

'What're you so cheerful about?' I asked. 'I never knew you to harbor a secret admiration for PA&E.'

'Shit, no! They lower than the correspondents at the Continental Hotel bar. But you know how there's a Chinese word that means "danger" if you read it one way and "opportunity" if you read it another? That's exactly our situation this very night. When we get to the racetrack, we stick close to the Duke and seize the first chance to go in and rescue our distressed compatriots.'

'You two assholes crazy or something?' cried the newby, scanning the rooftops as if they were packed with snipers.

'Young trooper, you don't have to go in with us,' Queen reassured him. 'You can supply what the grunts call suppressive fire and make sure our esteemed ARVN allies don't steal the tires off our jeep.'

Then the racetrack heaved into view. The old colonial powers had brought Western-style horse racing to Asia, and now there were racetracks in all the major cities. The Saigon Racetrack was in Cholon, probably because nobody in the world loves to gamble like the Chinese do.

It was a big, typewriter-shaped building of reinforced concrete, not much different from the stands at Santa Anita, Hollywood Park, Saratoga or, for all I know, Ascot. We approached from the side opposite the track itself, which consisted mainly of a rubble-strewn parking lot. There was heavy fire coming from various parts of the building, but most of it was directed away from us. It looked as if an assault force was assembling on the opposite side. Even as we watched, a couple of Sheridan tanks pulled up on the opposite side and cut loose, firing into the bleachers.

We halted in a line at the edge of the parking lot and dismounted, crouching behind our jeeps, rifles pointed toward the hulking building.

'Come on,' Queen said. 'Let's go join the council of war.'

We duck-walked along behind the line of jeeps to where Overstreet and Duc Nguyen crouched, conferring.

'Well, that's it,' Overstreet was saying with obvious relief. 'Let the armor take care of those fuckers.'

'My orders are to rescue those civilians if at all possible, Sergeant,' Duc said. His English was near-perfect, a rarity even among upper-class Vietnamese, who all spoke perfect French but rarely English.

'My ass!' Overstreet protested. 'We got nothin' but rifles, shotguns, forty-fives and a few thirty caliber machine-guns. Them armored boys got fifty calibers, cannons and flame throwers. Let them settle it. We go in there, they as likely to kill us as Charlie.'

'Now, Sarge,' Queen said, waddling up to him, 'you are fully aware that Captain Nguyen is in charge of this operation. I would deem it an honor if you will allow me to lead the assault.'

Overstreet looked at him as if he'd just stepped from a flying saucer. 'What you been smokin', Queen? Lemme see your eyes.'

Queen ignored him and looked straight at Nguyen. 'What'll it be, Captain? You and I both want those civilians, don't we? Me'n my man Treloar'll back you.'

The ARVN captain hesitated for a moment, evaluating, then he nodded curtly. 'Very good. You go in with me.'

'What angle you workin', Queen?' Overstreet demanded. 'You go in there, you're dead for sure.'

'Don't get your balls in an uproar,' Queen said, grinning. 'There's plenty more where me'n Gabe come from.'

Overstreet nodded, resigned. 'That's God's own truth. Okay, go on, you dumb fuck. Don't get killed and make paperwork for me.'

So we worked out an assault plan. The machine-gunners were to spray the hell out of the building's upper works and, under their cover, Nguyen's ARVN MPs would charge across the parking lot with Queen, Duc and me in the lead. Once we were in, the rest of First platoon would follow, except for the guys on the machine-guns, who would keep up their suppressive fire and cover us in case of a retreat.

'How'd you find out about the round-eyes?' Queen asked Duc in a low voice, as we crouched in the shelter of a jeep while

70

Overstreet gave the gunners their instructions.

'We have a man in this cell. He contacted us a while ago.'

Queen's eyebrows went up. 'You infiltrated the VC? Far fuckin' out!'

'The Tet offensive nearly wiped them out,' Duc explained. 'They are desperate and recruiting many newbies. Easy to plant our agents with them now.'

That explained why the Second Battle of Saigon – soon to be termed 'Mini-Tet' – lacked the scope of the earlier offensive. They were throwing against us kids without five months of training. Much later we figured out that it was a coldly calculated ploy by the Hanoi government to wipe out the remnants of the old Viet Cong infrastructure. They had no intention of including the southerners in their government when they reunited the country.

I had no such comforting thoughts at the time, though. I just had the usual dry-mouthed, wet-palmed, loose-bowelled feeling of sick anticipation common to most men about to go into action. This was not police work as I had anticipated it. I knew perfectly well that a teenage kid with an antique French rifle and one cartridge could kill you just as dead as a whole NVA division.

'We go now,' Duc said, standing. Like most Vietnamese he was a small man, but his erect bearing made him seem taller. Still, he looked like a ten-year-old standing between us. The MPs recruited for size. Like all Vietnamese of the officer class, he was immaculately presented, his uniform so neat and starchy you'd never guess he had spent the last few hours fighting all over the Cholon.

We went into a half-crouch, as if we were about to begin a hundred-yard dash, which in fact we were. Overstreet shouted 'Go!' and the machine-guns began to rake the building. We started our run.

We should have spread out, or run across one at a time, or at least zigzagged like broken-field runners – but we did none of those things. Our best chance lay in the hope that no one would dream that we would do such an idiotic thing. Besides, we figured they'd be distracted by all the heavy fire coming from the other side of the building. I thought I heard bullets pinging off the tarmac all around us, but it was probably my imagination.

We'd almost reached a big doorway that led beneath the

stands when a couple of Vietnamese in civilian clothes cradling SKS carbines appeared and gaped at us. They didn't get their weapons lined up before being hosed down by just about everyone in our little force.

Then we were inside and Duc was barking orders to his men. Under the stands was a warren of passages and small rooms and the ARVN MPs began clearing them, first rolling grenades in then charging through after each blast.

'You're gonna kill those civilians this way!' I yelled, my ears ringing so loud I could hardly hear myself.

'They aren't in this part,' Duc said. 'Come with me.' He shouted something to his men and opened a steel door, then went down a flight of stairs with Queen and me close behind him. Oddly, Queen shut the door behind us.

It was deathly quiet after all the racket above. The stairway and the corridor beyond were dimly illuminated by low-watt bulbs burning in steel cages set at intervals along the ceiling. When we reached a door at the end of the corridor Duc held up a hand, halting us.

There were four bodies on the floor, pushed against the walls to leave the center of the passage open. They wore civilian clothes and they looked Chinese to me. We tracked through the blood that covered the floor; it was so sticky under our boots that I knew those men had been dead for hours.

Queen raised a foot and glanced at Duc. The captain nodded and Queen kicked. The door banged inward, a big, bloody footprint in its center. Two Vietnamese whirled around as we entered. One of them got off a shot with a Chinese-made pistol before we cut them down.

The three civilians were seated against a wall of the little room, their hands bound behind them, legs straight out, ankles tied. Their eyes were wide with shock, then, when they realized who we were, their relief was almost embarrassing to see. Two were men in their thirties, deeply tanned and with big beer guts. One of them was blond with a crew-cut, the other darker, with a Zapata mustache. The third man was a little older, slender and graying at the temples.

'Oh, Jesus!' the blond guy said. 'Jesus, are we glad to see you guys!' Big tears streaked his face.

'I'll just bet you are,' Queen said, shoving a fresh magazine into his rifle. Then he drew his bayonet, stooped and cut the cords binding their ankles. 'Now just who are you guys?' he asked as we helped them to their feet. They exuded a rancid stink of fear.

'Tom and me are with PA&E,' the guy with the mustache said. 'Hey, how about cutting our hands loose? My God, I can't tell you how happy I am to see you!'

Queen ignored him and turned to the other man. 'And who're you?'

'James Quentin. I'm a pilot with TWA.' He was a little more self-possessed than the other two, but he was sweating.

'Two engineers and a pilot. My, my.' Queen looked from one face to the next, smiling. Duc wasn't smiling, and neither was I. 'And just how did you three happen to be here at the racetrack when the VC came to usurp the place?'

'Hey, what is this, Sarge?' Blondie tried to chuckle but it came out as a croak. They all winced as the building rocked and concrete dust filtered down from the ceiling and the lights flickered. 'What are they doing up there, shelling? Come on, Sarge, cut us loose and get us out of here!' His voice went shrill on the last words.

'Close the door, Gabe,' Queen said quietly.

'What is this shit, Queen?' I demanded. But I shut the door anyway.

'Yeah, what is this shit, Sergeant?' Zapata demanded. Then he shut up as Queen jammed the muzzle of his rifle into his nose, as if he were trying to force the flash suppressor up one nostril. It was hot from all the shooting and the man yelped.

'You boys picked the wrong time and the wrong place to meet with your chink buddies outside, didn't you?' He cocked an eye at me and grinned. 'Gabe, these boys was here dealin'. Question is, what was they dealin'?' He turned back to Zapata and barked: 'What was it, fuckhead? Money or dope?'

'You can't do this, Sarge!' Blondie said, but his eyes crept sideways to a small satchel and a big suitcase. The pilot looked disgusted. Duc picked up the bags and set them on a folding table and opened them up. The satchel held neatly bundled greenbacks: fifties and hundreds. The suitcase was stuffed with Vietnamese piastres.

'Money,' Queen said, nodding. 'Good, that simplifies things. Captain, what do you say you keep all the P and me and my buddy'll split up the greenbacks? I could never move that much P.'

Duc looked stern. 'I will take the P and one third of the American currency.'

Queen sighed. 'Well, I guess you rate a finder's fee. Okay, divvy it up. We gotta move.'

'You can't do this, Sergeant,' the pilot said.

Queen stared at him coldly. 'Be a shame if we was to fail in our mission of bringing you back alive.'

'If you have any complaints,' I said, 'you can take them to General Westmoreland. I hear he has a sympathetic ear.' I didn't like the deal, but no way did I feel any sympathy for these parasites.

'I knew my prayers were answered when the third man said he was a pilot,' Queen said, poking the TWA man in the belly with his muzzle. 'These're the fuckers that move most of the greenbacks into the country. You got that money counted, Captain?'

There were three even stacks on the table. Duc scooped one stack into his uniform and picked up the suitcase. 'It is time to go,' he announced.

'You three get out of here,' Queen ordered as he picked up one of the stacks. I opened the door.

'At least cut our hands loose,' Zapata pleaded.

'I like you just the way you are,' Queen said. 'This way you don't get foolish thoughts and pick up weapons. Now git. Be careful, now, it's slippery out there.'

They hustled out. Duc went out behind them, toting his suitcase.

'Grab your money and let's go, m'man.'

'I don't want it.'

He gaped. 'Don't want it? What's this, scruples or something? This is found money, Treloar. It ain't like we stole it. It was about to finance the People's Liberation Army. If we turned it in, it'd just end up in Army pockets, not a bit of it would ever find its way to the US Treasury. Fuck that.'

'You take it,' I said. 'Bad enough I risked my life for it, I don't need to go to Leavenworth by way of the LBJ.'

Queen shook his head as he stuffed the rest of the money into his shirt. 'I always reckoned you were a sweetheart, Gabe; now I know you're a friggin' saint.'

'Just scared,' I told him, 'just like any other sane human being.'

'Let's get out of this place, m'man. There's no more profit to be had here.'

Duc and the civilians were nowhere to be seen as we ran down the corridor and up the stairs. There was still desultory firing going on upstairs. The air in the warren was thick with powder and grenade fumes. I knew I was due for a racking headache from the explosive fumes. As we tried to find our way back outside I started to laugh.

'I just knew you'd see the humor of the situation,' Queen said.

'It's just that you've been telling me for months that you want to be a Hollywood money man. I never guessed—'At that moment three VC holdouts dropped out of some sort of ceiling trap. Even as I fumbled my rifle around I saw that these were no kids; they were hard-faced men with centuries of war behind their eyes.

My first shot went wide, then three AK bullets caught the edge of my flak jacket, spinning me around and down, my rifle flying from my hand. I looked up from the floor and saw the AK muzzle centered on my face. I had just enough time to realize that I was going to die before the VC seemed to disappear in the spray and smoke and continuous roar of gunfire. Queen loomed over me in a sudden, ringing silence.

'How bad you hurt?' he said, kneeling beside me, opening my flak jacket, concern showing on his face for the first time.

'Fuck if I know.' I was almost numb, my hands and feet tingling, ears buzzing. 'They dead?'

'We're alive, so you may assume their demise. Shit, m'man, you just bloodied up a little bit. Chewed up your side some, but I don't see anything vital spilling out. There's some nicks on your legs but that looks like what the medics like to call secondary missiles – bits of concrete and such kicked up by all those AK rounds. C'mon, let's get you on your feet and out of here.'

'They get you?' I asked.

'They wouldn't dare.'

He wrestled me up and I found that I could stand. Queen picked up my rifle and I looked around us. The three VC lay in a heap. The next morning the outfit would come in and police up the bodies and count shell casings. Nobody would figure out how Queen had come through it unhurt. This was where he earned his nickname of Gunslinger.

We hobbled toward the parking lot with my arm over his shoulders and his around my back.

'Now you're all set, Gabriel.'

'What you mean?' I said woozily. Wounded twice in less than five months. I didn't like this place at all.

'For starters, you pull some sack time in the hospital. You're gonna be Captain Crandall's fair-haired boy now, assuming those dumbfuck civilians got out alive. He won't fuss if you want to be reassigned. Master Sergeant O'Dell is head of Personnel at Battalion. In six months he's gonna top out twenty and retire. He's feathering his nest against the day. I'll slip him a little of this green and he'll station you in Miss Rose's lower right-hand desk drawer if you want. You got it made now.'

At that moment it all sounded good, even using that money. I'd been about to die meaninglessly in a stupid situation in a tremendously unpopular war, and that gave me a whole new outlook – at least temporarily.

And I knew I owed Queen for saving my life. The fact that he'd endangered it in the first place didn't mean much, because the whole war was such an absurdity. The episode in the Saigon Racetrack was just one more seriocomic skit in an endless soap opera. And he'd given me a real shot at Rose. Somehow, I had a feeling he'd be calling in the debt someday.

The parking lost was swarming with ARVN when we got out. The local firing had stopped, although it was still going on all over the city. Duc was nowhere to be seen. The civilians were standing among the American jeeps, their hands finally freed.

'Hey, Queen?'

'Huh?'

'Thanks.'

'Rat own.'

Chapter Six

Queen's house was, naturally, in Beverly Hills. It was a three-story white stucco pseudo-Spanish edifice with a red tile roof. It looked as if it dated from the twenties, and had probably once been the pride and joy of some long-forgotten silent star or some megaphoned director in beret, riding boots and jodhpurs.

I parked my rented car in the driveway and climbed the Spanish tile steps, squinting against the glare of the California sun on the white façade. I hadn't been away all that long, but the sun and the smells of the LA atmosphere and California vegetation already seemed alien. Mitch Queen had the door open before I got to the top. To my mild amazement, he was dressed in old jeans, a T-shirt and rubber zori sandals.

'Gabe! How was the flight? Hell, don't tell me. They're all the same, aren't they? Three hours of boredom in a flying building, followed by reclaiming baggage. C'mon in.' He had a way of supplying all the idle chitchat for both parties. The front door opened on to an atrium that rose the full three stories. Vast twin staircases led to the upper floors. The center held a three-tiered fountain.

'Nice place,' I commented.

'Yeah,' he said delightedly. 'Isn't it the most pretentious piece of garbage you've ever seen? This was built when people knew what this *nouveau riche* stuff was all about. The Trumps are amateurs by comparison. Of course, the current fad is to buy a perfectly good mansion like this, tear it down, and build another one on the site. It's supposed to demonstrate something.'

'Potlatch,' I said. 'Kwaikutl Indian ceremony to show off how important you are by how much wealth you can afford to destroy or give away.'

'I guess that's it. Well, there are depths of vulgarity to which even I won't descend. I'll spare you the tour since you're not here to give me money. Let's drive around to the pool house.'

We went back out and got in my car. Mitch directed me to a gravelled drive that led around the house, past the groundskeeper's shed and some disused stables, to a single-story structure with parking space in the rear. A white Toyota was already parked there.

'That's Connie's,' Mitch said. 'She came up this morning.'

He helped me get my bags out of the trunk and we carried them in. In welcome contrast to the mansion, the guest house was modern and of modest proportions. A spacious living-dining room, fronted with a plate-glass window facing the pool, was flanked by a pair of bedroom suites. Mitch conducted me to mine. There was no sign of Connie, so I presumed she was in the opposite suite. Its door was shut.

'Let's see . . .' Mitch glanced at his watch. 'It's two-thirty. I've got an appointment in an hour. Want to get together for dinner at seven?'

'Sounds good to me.'

'Then rest, freshen up, have a swim. If you didn't bring a suit there ought to be a few in the closet. I'll see you later. If you need anything, call the housekeeper on the intercom.' He pointed to a tabletop phone. 'Her name's Julia.'

When he left I unpacked, found a bathing suit and put it on. I was a little jet-lagged. It was three hours later where I'd been that morning. I was hungry, so I looked over the little kitchen and put together a sandwich out of some deli items from the fridge. Among ranks of bottled designer water I found some fruit juice.

On my way out to the pool I stopped by Connie's door. I was about to knock when I heard her talking on the phone. Her accent had grown heavy.

'You think you want to go out with that creep? He's too old for you and I think he's married and lying to you about it . . . Don't you talk to me like that!' There was a short pause, then she cut loose with a volley of paint-peeling Spanish.

I passed on by without knocking and carried my plate out to a poolside table. I ate slowly, savoring the rich, sybaritic ambience of big-money Southern California – a dream life most of us never have a chance to experience. Even second hand like this, I could understand the temptation. I wondered how much of it was for real, as far as Mitch was concerned. Did he really own this place, or was it all front?

When I finished eating I swam a few laps, revelling in the bracing coolness of the water, the chlorine sting in my nostrils that always took me back to my early teenage days on the coast. When I was winded I got out, dried off and resumed my chair. As I did this the glass door of the guest house slid open and Connie came out wearing a simple, two-piece bathing suit. Immediately I saw what Queen had been getting at.

I had never seen a woman bodybuilder before. No wonder, I thought, she carried so much weight so well. Her musculature was striking; bulky for a woman yet graceful. Except for her washboard abdominals she didn't have the razor-sharp muscular definition I'd seen in pictures of bodybuilding competitions. Instead she was smooth and sleek, like a racehorse. She lowered herself into a chair opposite me.

'I'm sorry. I was on the phone to my daughter. I'd've come out to say hello sooner.' She shook her head wearily. 'Teenagers.'

'You've spent a lot of time on the weights,' I observed. 'How'd you get into bodybuilding?'

'It started out as therapy, physical and mental. My husband was a cop in Houston, like me.' She gazed down at the rings on her left hand. 'We were in a car wreck one day. Wasn't in the line of duty. We were on our way to church Sunday morning. A drunk driver swerved across three lanes of traffic and hit us head-on. Mick was killed.' She said it tonelessly, as if it were an old, often-told tale. 'My legs and back were badly injured. When I was healed up enough, the orthopedist put me on a schedule of weight training to help restore the atrophied muscles. I found out that I liked it.'

She glanced back up at me. 'I mean I liked all of it: not just the way it made me look, but the exertion, the sweat, the fatigue, even the pain.' She added, hastily, 'Don't take that wrong. It's the only kind of pain I go for.' With one fingernail she traced one of the C-shaped lines that bracketed her generous mouth. 'These are what they call pain lines. They come from the awful faces we make when we crank out those last few reps.'

'You ever compete?'

'For a couple of years. I placed ninth in the Ms Olympia one year but that was enough. It's not really healthy. At that level of competition the women starve themselves and aerobicize their bodies half to death to get rid of their last traces of fat. They want to have the same kind of muscular definition that the male competitors have. The problem is, the female body is designed to carry a higher proportion of subcutaneous fat than the male. They drop below the minimum fat level and systems start shutting down because the body thinks it's dying. Their periods stop, they get dizzy spells, they're weak and have a hard time concentrating.

'At the Ms O, I walked off the stage after my posing routine and fainted. It's not uncommon. I decided the hell with this and stopped competing. I still do the workouts but I eat like a reasonable human being. I may not ripple like Queen's buddy Ahhnold but I feel great.'

'How long have you been doing this?'

'Mick died eight years ago. We were married twelve years.' She looked down at the rings again. 'I've never been able to bring myself to take these off, that's why they're so embedded. I went to a jeweller the other day to see about having them resized. He said he'd have to cut them off first. At least they help me to get rid of guys who hit on me in bars.'

'I know the feeling,' I said, holding up my hand to show her the ring I hadn't removed since Rose died.

'So your wife was Vietnamese?' She seemed a little uncomfortable, knowing we had even this much in common.

'Uh-huh. I'm going to call my in-laws this evening, when I feel up to it.'

After a while she got up and dove into the pool, raising almost no splash. She swam laps as tirelessly as a seal. I admired the energy and power with which she cut through the water. We had more in common than she knew. We go crazy in our own ways, dealing with grief and despair. I'd done it with a bottle, she had turned to barbells, driving out one pain with another. At least she had something to show for it.

The sun dropped low and I went in to shower off the chlorine. I wasn't looking forward to calling Duc. It wasn't that I thought he wouldn't help me out. I knew he had a powerful sense of obligation, and I had been his sister's husband and the sponsor for him and his family when they'd fled Vietnam. But I felt crass, as if I was calling in an old debt on account of what was, after all, a business matter. A little like the way Queen had roped me into this.

I had his number in my address book, but I checked the phone book first to make sure he hadn't moved. It had been that long. I found his name, among about a hundred other Duc Nguyens – the name being the Vietnamese equivalent of John Smith. He was still at the same address in Eagle Rock. I knew he also had a real estate office in West Hollywood, but I figured it was late enough to catch him at home. I dialed quickly and listened to the ringing at the other end. I'd about decided that no one was home when it was picked up.

'Hello . . . yes?' It was a young woman's voice, somewhat shaky.

'Hello, this is Gabe Treloar. I'm trying to reach Duc Nguyen.' There was something distraught in the woman's voice and it bothered me. 'We're relatives,' I added, lamely.

'What? I mean—' I realized that she had been crying hard for a long time. 'I mean, please excuse me. I'm sorry. Is this Uncle Gabe? This is Margaret Calvin. We tried to call you last night but got your answering machine.'

Margaret was Duc's oldest daughter, abut five when they'd immigrated. Last I'd heard she was teaching at a school in Glendale and married to an architect. And now she was upset to the edge of hysteria.

'Margaret? Yes, this is Gabe. I flew into LAX this morning on business and I'm staying with a friend in Beverly Hills. That's where I am now. Margaret, what's wrong? What's happened?'

'Uncle Gabe, Daddy's dead! He's been killed!' Her voice rose to a little-girl squeak on the last couple of words. I heard her sobbing on the other end until, amid a mutter of voices, someone else took the phone.

'Mr Treloar?' The voice was male, young but self-assured. 'I'm Greg Calvin, Marge's husband. I don't believe we've met.'

'No, no we haven't. I've been out of touch with the family the last few years. What's happened?'

'Yesterday at five o'clock my father-in-law was gunned down on the street. It was a drive-by and nobody has any idea about who or why.' He sounded bitter but matter-of-fact. You can't live in a major American city and be mystified about random violence.

My cop reactions clicked in. 'A drive-by? In Eagle Rock?'

'No, not here. He was leaving his office in West Hollywood. He didn't make it all the way to his car.'

'Was anybody else with him? Anyone else killed or hurt?'

'No, he was alone. Some people still in his office heard the shots and ran out. All they saw was the car hauling out of there.'

'Listen, I'm on my way. If the traffic's not too bad I should be there in about an hour.'

'Okay. You probably won't be able to park very close. It's not just the family. About half the Vietnamese community's coming by to pay their respects.'

I thanked him and hung up. For a while I sat there, trying to shift mental gears to meet this new development. Quite aside from the personal angle, everything was wrong about it. The time was wrong and the place was wrong. I was still sitting like that, my hand still on the phone, when Connie came in, toweling herself off. She stopped abruptly when she saw my face.

'What is it?' She didn't change expression when I told her, but her body stayed perfectly still, even though she was breathing heavily from all those laps. She had perfect focus of attention, an invaluable asset in a cop.

'I'm going up there,' I told her. 'Want to come along?'

'I'm with you. Give me a few minutes to change.'

I scribbled a note for Mitch and left it with his housekeeper. Ten minutes later we were heading out on Sunset toward the freeways in my rented car. Connie had dressed in a dark business suit, and her hair was still a little damp. Every few minutes she gave her head a little shake to help it along. In the meantime, we talked.

'I suppose coincidence is out?' she said.

'I can't rule it out completely,' I said. 'Recreational murder is more common than ever. But the timing makes it unlikely, what with death threats in the air about our time in Saigon. And Duc's office is in West Hollywood, just off Beverly Boulevard. That whole area's commercial.'

'And gang-type drive-bys are usually in residential slum areas.' She gave her head another little shake. The tight cap of curls was resuming its shape. Either she had a hellishly resilient perm or it just grew that way naturally. 'So this looks more like a deliberate hit. Still doesn't mean it's connected, though. Maybe he was mistaken for somebody else. Or maybe he was mixed up in something you don't know about. You said yourself he wasn't above improving his condition through extra-legal means.'

'That was Nam,' I insisted. 'Ripping off crooks was legitimate business there. He was strictly a straight arrow here.' The look she gave me said she didn't think much of sentiment as a tool of logic. 'Besides,' I pressed on, 'he's been here damn near twenty years. With that much time to get into some kind of trouble, it's asking a little too much to believe it'd come to a head right now.'

'Okay, I'll buy it for now. What're we looking for?'

'I don't know,' I admitted. 'But his family may know if anything offbeat has happened in recent weeks. It's worth a try.'

Traffic was heavy on the Glendale Freeway, the usual rush-hour jam complicated by a few minor crackups. With relief I took the exit into Eagle Rock. The little foothill community looked much as I remembered it: a typical, mainly postwar middle-class area, not quite as staid and respectable as Pasadena to the east. When I came to the Nguyens' block I saw right away that I wasn't going to park anywhere near the house. I found a spot in front of a video store on the nearest business street.

We trudged up the steep hill back to the house and I envied Connie the effortless way she took the slope. I'd been trying to keep in shape, but running along the flat Knoxville streets was a little different from this Alpine exertion. She was tactful enough not to note the discrepancy.

The house was a postwar frame bungalow: extremely modest for a man of Duc's means, but then his concept of the American dream was to put about twenty grandchildren through Harvard Medical School. There were a number of people standing in the tiny front yard. Most of them were Asian, all speaking in low voices. We went up the steps on to a crowded porch and into the living room. I could hear sobbing, some of it coming from other rooms. A sandy-haired man in his twenties spotted me and came through the crowd.

'Gabe Treloar? I'm Greg Calvin. I'm glad you could make it.' We shook hands.

'I'm sorry it had to be at such a time. This is my associate, Connie Armijo.'

He took her hand and scanned the throng. 'Marge is in here someplace. I think Duc belonged to every Vietnamese society in Southern California. Not to mention his business associations.'

'How is Anne?' Anne was Duc's wife. For some reason, Vietnamese Catholics often give girls Christian names, but not boys.

'Taking it hard. The doctor gave her some sedation this afternoon. She's sleeping now, I think. Why don't we step outside where it's cooler?'

We went out on to the porch and found a relatively uncrowded corner where we could lean against the railing.

'Have the police turned up anything yet?' Connie asked.

'Not a thing that I know of.'

'Who's handling the investigation?' I asked.

'A Deputy Lowry – let me see, he gave me one of his cards.' He rummaged in his pockets and came up with an LA County deputy's card; it informed me that Lowry was to be found at the West Hollywood Sheriff's station.

Greg shook his head while I studied it. 'It seems so ironic. Duc used to talk sometimes about the two of you in Saigon in the old days. Jesus, to live through all that and then get gunned down in LA!'

'He saw a lot more of it than I did. I was only there a year. He saw the whole war. Hell, he was born when they were fighting the Japanese, and he watched the war with the French while he was a kid. His time here was the closest thing to peacetime he ever experienced.'

'Uncle Gabe?'

I turned to see a lovely young woman with huge but extremely red eyes, her face a little swollen and blotched from weeping. I hadn't seen Margaret since she was about sixteen. Her hair was short now, but otherwise she had changed amazingly little. We exchanged a hug and kiss on the cheek and I introduced Connie.

'Margaret,' I said, feeling awkward, 'at a time like this I hate to talk like a cop instead of a relative, but do you know if your father experienced anything unusual in recent weeks? Any threatening letters? Did he act as if he felt endangered?'

She frowned, puzzled. 'I don't . . . why?'

Connie stepped in, a note I hadn't heard before in her voice: friendly, comforting and businesslike at the same time. 'I know it seems unbelievable, and it caught us by surprise too, but Gabe and I are working on a case that involves some things that happened in Saigon when he and your father served together there. There may be no connection to what happened yesterday, but we have to look into it.'

'You mean it may have been deliberate?' Greg said.

'It's a long shot,' I told him. 'Connie and I are with different firms. We've been hired by some people involved with making a movie in Vietnam. The producer is another man who was with us in Vietnam in '68. He's received death threats because of the project and wants the matter investigated. I wanted to speak with Duc because I thought he might still have contacts in Saigon – maybe they might know why somebody doesn't want a movie filmed there. Instead, I find Duc's been murdered.' It sounded brutally terse put that way, but grief-stricken people are easily distracted.

Connie gave me a disapproving glance. 'Do you think there might have been any connection, Mrs Calvin?'

Margaret blinked and swallowed a couple of times. 'My God! I certainly wasn't expecting anything like this.'

'It may be nothing, just a coincidence,' Connie said. 'But if there's a chance, we have to follow it.'

'How about it, Hon?' her husband said. 'Your Dad say anything to you?'

She frowned. 'Greg and I live in Glendale. I don't get over to visit as much as I'd like, especially during the school year. But Dad was never directly involved with the movie business. He never indicated there were any problems. But I haven't seen him much in the last six weeks or so. Most of my visits, my mother and I went out shopping or for lunch. Dad spent so much of his time at the office.'

'How do you mean, "directly"?' Connie prodded gently.

'Dad's business is real estate. Commercial properties, not houses.' She shrugged. 'This is LA. I guess he probably dealt with people in the film industry from time to time, but only in regard to property and buildings. He never would have invested in something like film production.'

Greg put an arm around her bowed shoulders. 'Duc used to lecture me about the foolishness of gambling with capital. As far as he was concerned, the movie business might as well have been craps or roulette.'

'What about your mother?' I asked. 'Did she indicate anything might have been wrong?'

'No, and she's not up to being questioned right now. The doctor has her under sedation.'

'I understand,' I said. 'Just tell her I was here and give her my love, and if she's feeling up to it in the next few days, I'd like to talk to her about any problems Duc might have had.'

'Of course. If there's any chance this awful thing can be—' Margaret started to choke, took a few deep breaths, then went on. 'I'll give you a call when I think Mother is up to it. Where can I reach you?'

We exchanged phone numbers and another hug, then she went off to see to the multitude who'd come to pay their respects. There were more arriving every minute. I'd had no idea Duc was such a wheel in the community. By no means were all of them Vietnamese or other Asians. The Southern California real estate business and its attendant business associations are pretty multicultural.

'When and where will the funeral be?' I asked Greg.

'There's a Father Padilla here someplace. He'll be able to give you the details.'

We shook hands and I thanked him, then scanned the crowd, looking for a clerical collar. I finally spotted it on a short man chatting gravely with a small group on the lawn.

'There's the padre,' I said to Connie. 'I need to talk to him. I guess I'll have to shop for a dark suit.'

I went down the steps and joined the little group. While I waited for a chance to talk to the priest, a black Lincoln limo pulled up on the street in front of the house. There were no parking spaces but the driver stopped and got out. He was a tall, very thin black man with short graying hair that was receding at the temples. His brow was deeply furrowed and a thin salt-and-pepper mustache lay between a small nose and a thin upper lip. He limped slightly as he walked around the front of the limo and opened the rear passenger door. He glanced idly around the crowd on the lawn, then his gaze sharpened on me for a fraction of a second. I felt the tiniest of memory-flutters somewhere in the back of my brain.

A leg emerged from the limo. It wore a pinstriped charcoal trouser leg and silk hosiery, and terminated in Italian footwear as expensive as any I'd seen. It rested on the pavement for a moment as the driver stooped and said something to the man inside. Then it rose, withdrew back inside, and the door closed. Without a glance in my direction, the driver resumed his place and drove smoothly away. Nobody seemed to have noticed the little scene.

Father Padilla looked amazingly young. He had dark hair and clear blue eyes, a cherubic face and a left earlobe that wasn't wearing a ring but clearly had been pierced. Apparently, the Roman Catholic clergy had changed a bit since my days at St Anne's back in Monticello, Ohio. I identified myself and we went through the ritual mutual condolences – his for my lost brother-in-law, mine for his lost parishioner. He told me that the Medical Examiner's office had released Duc's body and the service would be on the following Thursday at 2.00 p.m. I thanked him and turned to find Connie at my elbow.

I looked out to the west. The sun was already down. 'It's getting late. We might as well go on back,' I told her. She nodded and we made our way back down the steep sidewalk.

Back in my car as I pulled out into traffic, she turned to me and said, 'What was that business with the limo all about?'

'You don't miss much, do you?'

'Do I look blind? Or just retarded?'

'God, you're prickly!'

'That's right. And I'm used to being underestimated, and patronized, and condescended to. I don't like it. I don't guess it happens much to you.'

I thought about it. 'People underestimate me sometimes. They think just because I'm soft-spoken and slow and easygoing that I'm a nice guy.' I turned and glared at her. 'They don't understand what a vindictive, vengeful, dangerous psychopath I am.'

The corners of her mouth quirked in a reluctant little smile. The little Cs deepened. 'Okay, so what was it with the limo?'

'I wish I knew. The driver saw me, saw something he didn't like, and said something to the guy in back, who thought better of getting out to pay his respects.'

'The driver knew you? You know him?'

'That's what I've been thinking about. I think I must, but I can't call anything up. Maybe he's some guy I busted years ago. That's a lot of faces to sort through. I may have to give it a rest and let my subconscious work on it for a while.'

'Sometimes that works,' she said doubtfully. 'But who was inside? You get the license number?'

'Yeah.'

'So did I.'

Chapter Seven

Selene Gibson's house was in Malibu – one of her houses, anyway. There was also one in Aspen, not to mention the places in Gstaad and St Tropez. As Connie had mentioned, it wasn't as if Selene was hurting for money. Malibu isn't a long drive from Beverly Hills, but the last stretch is along the Pacific Coast Highway. In order to be properly exclusive, the Malibuvians have campaigned hard to keep their community inaccessible by freeway. Except for the snobbery, I can appreciate their attitude. But the highway has some bad memories for me.

'What's bugging you?' Connie asked as we drove along a section of sheer cliffs. I wasn't aware that I'd let my expression change, but she picked up on it.

'Bad place for me.' I pointed to a spot we were approaching where the drop was two hundred feet with jagged rocks at the bottom. 'My father drove his car over the edge there in '66. That stone wall wasn't there back then, just a flimsy guard rail. It didn't even slow him down.'

'Suicide?' She didn't put on a big show of sympathy. After more than a quarter century it couldn't be a raw wound.

'The police report said accident.'

'Yeah, sure. That means he didn't leave a note. I've been by this stretch a lot of times. Even with a flimsy guard rail, he'd've had to be accelerating straight for it to go over.'

'He was. But I only found out why last year. I'll tell you about it sometime.'

She didn't respond. It seemed she wasn't inviting any intimacies that day.

A few minutes later we were in the high-rent district. 'Turn here,' Connie said. The road was nondescript, not even a name or number. It wound over some low hills thick with fragrant eucalyptus, then we were in a breathtaking little cove where the surf pounded on a low sea-wall of rugged boulders. Above and just behind the sea-wall was a house made of stone, concrete and glass, all planes and angles like a million other postwar 'modernistic' houses, but this one fitted its surroundings so perfectly that you knew it was designed by one of the rare architects who actually knew what he was doing with that style.

We parked in a circular drive at the foot of a long stairway that curved up to a verandah. I guessed it was called a verandah, anyway; it was entirely too grand to be a porch. A woman opened the front door and stood there, leaning against the jamb with her arms crossed. Not until we were at the top of the steps did I realize how big she was – at least two inches taller than I, with a broad, mobile face. Her broken nose lent it a raffish air. This had to be Jeanette, the lady wrestler.

'Jeanette, Gabe Treloar. Gabe, Jeanette,' Connie said succinctly. 'Anything new?'

Jeanette nodded my way but didn't offer to shake hands. 'Pleased to meet you. Nothing unusual. I can't keep her away from the windows and this place is half glass. She won't draw the drapes.' Jeanette scanned the hillside behind the house like an infantryman. 'She says snipers are for heads of state. Movie star freaks like to do it up close. I tell her we're not dealing with obsessed fans here, but I'm not making much of an impression. Other'n that, she mostly does what I tell her.'

Jeanette stood aside and we walked in. The woman sitting on the sofa was reading a magazine, wearing a pair of big Gloria Steinem-type glasses. She stood, took off the glasses and set the magazine on the marble table in front of her. It was *Architectural Digest*. All the magazines on the table were *Architectural Digest*.

'Hello, Connie,' Selene Gibson said. 'And you must be Mr Treloar.' She held out a slender hand and I took it.

I have the usual American problems with royalty. No matter how many drunk or druggy actors I hauled into Division headquarters for booking, the real stars always seem to be a species apart, especially the classy ones. This one had class in spades. At fifty-plus, Selene Gibson still had the astounding, ethereal beauty that had made her a star when she was fourteen. The perfect bone structure of her face accounted for most of it. When beauty is of the flesh it goes early; when it's in the bone, it lasts for life. I saw signs of discreet plastic surgery, but it was minimal. The famous chestnut hair now came from a bottle, if it wasn't an incredibly expensive wig, but even without those embellishments she would still have retained most of her looks.

I tried to think of something to say that wasn't too inane, and settled on, 'It's an honor to make your acquaintance, Miss Gibson.' It was absurdly intimidating being in her presence. Maybe, I thought, there's something to this glamor stuff after all.

'And this is great fun for me, too – meeting real private detectives after dealing with so many fake ones in my movies. Please, sit down.' Not playing a role, she spoke with a pronounced Alabama accent. I'd only heard it in one of her movies, some Tennessee Williams thing back in the sixties. It was a shock, hearing the movie queen talk like the sharecropper's daughter her publicist claimed she'd been.

'If you'll forgive me, Miss Gibson, you shouldn't be enjoying yourself. You should be scared.'

'Why should I forgive you?' she asked.

I must have looked foolish, because she grinned, exposing the legendary imperfection that set off her beauty: a set of dazzlingly white but crooked teeth. She patted me on the shoulder. 'Just kidding. And call me Selene. Let's see, your name is Gabriel, right?'

'Gabe,' I said.

'Okay, let's make it Gabe and Selene. Look, on my very first film, I saw an actor fall from a horse and break his neck. Vic Morrow was a dear friend of mine, and he was killed in a helicopter crash filming *The Twilight Zone*. Believe it or not, the film business is not without its risks.'

'Those are accidents. We're talking death threats here,' I told her.

'So we can't let the insurance people hear about it or they'll go through the roof. Your line of work can put your life in danger too. How much do *you* get paid for it?'

I looked around at the fabulous house, one of four. She had a point.

'Frank Lloyd Wright, 1927,' she said. 'Doesn't look that old, does it? I won't tell you how much I paid for it. I *will* tell you that I waited twenty-five years for it to come on the market. Kept my eye on it the whole time.' It was oblique, but I felt she wasn't just babbling on.

'Your point being?'

'I *wanted* this house. And I *want* this role in *Tu Do Street*.'

'My God, did this character Jared Rhine type this thing or did he bring it down Mount Sinai carved on stone tablets?'

'You don't know the tons of garbage you have to wade through to find one decent screenplay. And it's ten times as hard to find one with a first-rate role for a woman. I got into this business as a child and this is the best I've ever seen.'

'Not to mention Mr Queen's magic process,' Connie commented.

Selene smiled again. 'Okay, it was a hook, I admit.'

'Mitch tells me it's going to revolutionize movie casting,' I said.

'Mitch Queen's full of shit,' Selena said.

'What do you mean?' I said, shocked.

'I mean like every other hustler in this business, he's hyping this process way out of proportion. Sure, it's going to make me look like I did when I was twenty, and I'll be first to admit that it won't be nearly as big a job for me as for most women. They'll fix up my face, and smooth out these.' She held up the backs of her hands. They were wrinkled, the only real signs of ageing she showed. 'And it'll work, because all I have to do is stand around and deliver my lines, same as the others who undergo the big reverse ageing process. There's a couple of minor action sequences and we'll have stunt doubles for them. It's a dandy process, and it'll work beautifully for this film. After that it'll be old stuff. It's really better suited for animation, the pure fantasy stuff, not live actors.'

'I don't get it,' I said.

'Then consider this: to impress me, they ran a clip from one of Sean Connery's recent films. Then they ran it again, only this time his face was the young Sean, more than thirty years ago. I was impressed, sure. But there's more to acting than your face. Sean's in his sixties now. So now they can make him look like he did in *Dr No*. Do you think they can make him *move* the way he did when he was not only a young actor but an athlete? It'll be grotesque; a bunch of elderly actors tottering around with twenty-year-old faces!'

'I hadn't thought of that,' I admitted.

'Jesus, you should've heard these kids at that lab!' She threw back her head and laughed full-throatedly. It might have been a thespian gesture but it looked great. 'One of them, I swear he couldn't have been twenty-five, told me: "This is going to change everything! We'll be able to take any actor, give him Bogart's face, or Cagney's, or anybody's. Any actress can be Jean Harlow!" I'm not kidding, he really talked like that.'

She shook her head. 'I mean, do these children think Bogie was just a *face*? I had a supporting role in a film he made just before he died. I learned more about acting just talking to him between takes than I could've learned from five years with Lee Strasberg. That man radiated talent! He was one of a kind, and this computer magic is no more than a sophisticated rubber mask.'

'Mitch has some pretty heavy hitters lined up,' I said. 'Have you worked with any of them before?'

She shook her head. 'Most of the people I worked with are retired or dead or irretrievably has-been. The current crop of wunderkinds came along in the eighties. Goldfarb's the biggest thing in the industry now, and I've only made three films since he started. Jared Rhine's some sort of hermit and he's only worked with a tight little group that came out of USC film school, and I don't know any of that bunch; all beer-drinking buddies from their student days. You see a lot of that since the old studios went under. I've met Lawrence McKay, but only socially. I've asked for Ed Nakajima as principal cinematographer, but Queen won't give me a straight answer. I think he wants another film school whiz kid, whoever Goldfarb's favorite may be. They'll let me pick my own costumer as a sop for my wounded pride.'

'You sound a little cynical,' I observed.

She smiled wanly. 'I love movies. But the business? After more than four decades it's a little hard to retain the starry-eyed enthusiasm. But I'm not yearning for the good old days. It was just as nasty and cutthroat in the fifties, and the studio contracts were *much* worse. No, I have no cause for complaint. I'll get screwed over from about six directions, but it'll be worth it to get this film done. Then maybe I'll retire.' She leaned back and loosed that great laugh again. 'God, I can't believe I'm still saying that! I've said the same thing for my last six films. Twenty years from now I'll be planning my comeback, like Norma Desmond with a dead writer in my swimming pool.'

'You get full marks for courage, Selene,' I said. 'I think you're being reckless, although you showed good judgement in retaining an agency to look after your security. May I see the letter you received?'

She got up. 'I'll go get it.' I noticed that she rose a little stiffly, and that as she walked from the room there was a slight, arthritic hesitation to her steps. She was right: even with her young face back, she was going to need a stunt double for anything the least bit strenuous.

While she was gone, Connie and Jeanette conferred about the security arrangements: the cook, the gardener, the chauffeur and so forth. I was all too familiar with this aspect of the work. Nobody escaped suspicion while the client was under threat, and with good reason. When you're investigating a kidnapping, extortion or blackmailing, you find a trusted employee involved more often than not. The rest of the time, it's usually a close family member.

After a few minutes Selene returned with an envelope. When she handed it to me I looked over it first. I hadn't seen the envelope in which Gabe's letter had been sent. This one was a plain white 4 ⅛" × 9 ½" envelope, exactly like millions of others that are sent through the mail every day. It had been addressed with a typewriter or a superior word processing printer. There was no return address – not an uncommon phenomenon where threatening letters are concerned. There was no stamp or postmark.

'How was it delivered?' I asked.

'I'd like to know that myself,' Selene said. 'When Mitch Queen was laying out his pitch he got his principal players together at San Ysidro Ranch – me, Jeff Goldfarb, Lawrence McKay, plus a half-dozen of the heavy investors he was lining up. He rented suites for everyone. Have you ever been there?'

'Afraid not.'

'It's a beautiful little resort hotel in the Montecito hills. We were all there four or five days. I stayed on for another week because I like the place and I have friends in the area I wanted to visit. One evening, four days after the meeting broke up, I came back to my suite after dinner at a friend's house. I found this on my pillow, right next to the chocolate.'

I glanced at Connie.

'I looked the place over. No security worth speaking of. The suites opened on to the outdoors, not on to hallways. Any kid with half a brain for locks could get in.'

'That didn't make me feel much better about it. He was telling me he could get close to me, and he proved his point.' Selene tried to act nonchalant and unconcerned, but her body language said otherwise. Her elbows were close to her body, her hands nested together in her lap. She might feel confident here in her Frank Lloyd Wright castle, but she hadn't felt that way at the resort hotel in alien hills.

'There was no personal note appended?' I asked her.

'Actually, I thought this was plenty personal. What do you mean?'

'Starr, or whoever it was, added a hand-written note to the bottom of Queen's copy of this letter,' Connie told her. 'You would have told us if you'd gotten one, wouldn't you?'

'Of course.' Her tone sharpened. 'What sort of note?'

Connie told her. 'It seems this man Starr and Queen – Gabe here too – go back a ways.'

'I want to hear about this,' Selene said, sounding more intrigued than alarmed. Now I was beginning to wonder about her grasp of reality. So far she'd seemed a bit more firmly rooted than most in her business, maybe because she dated from the studio days before cocaine became the second currency of the film business. Or maybe that was just my illusion as an outsider.

'Gabe, why don't you give her the story?' Connie said. 'I've heard it. I want to go over the security here.' She got up. 'Jeanette, give me a tour of the grounds.'

The two women got up and went outside.

'Why don't we go out on the deck?' Selene said. 'It's a nice day and I'm tired of being cooped up. If I want to go out, Jeanette insists on going out with me and she's not much of a conversationalist. I've learned all about the Women's Wrestling Federation. Sly Stallone's mother was her manager for a while.'

'You meet all kinds in this business,' I told her as I got up.

'Can I fix you a drink? My housekeeper's off today, but I can actually do a few things myself. I used to be a pretty competent bartender. My first two husbands were boozers and they were particular.'

'If you have any iced tea I'll take some.' I saw no reason to tell her I'd quit drinking. Few things are more boring than a reformed drunk talking about it, and she'd done nothing to deserve it.

'I can manage that.' She went round a broad counter that defined the kitchen area.

The deck ran along the width of the house and extended fifty feet on cantilevered supports, hanging out over the sea-wall. The tide was still in, and the surf was raising a fine spray against the huge sandstone boulders. A waist-high stone wall ran around the deck's periphery. Atop the wall, a gimballed support held what looked like a set of oversized binoculars. Out of curiosity I raised its lens covers and peered through the eyepieces. I lined up a yacht that was almost on the horizon and was amazed by the power and clarity of the image. I could see individual figures moving around on the deck. Superimposed on the field was some sort of gauge – intersecting vertical and horizontal lines marked off with arcane symbols and numbers.

'That's a naval range finder,' Selene said. I abandoned the view and turned to see her setting a tray on a little table near the wall. 'A friend of mine who's a retired Navy man gave me those. He got them off his old cruiser when it was sent to the scrap yard.'

I joined her at the table. She had a crystal goblet of white wine in front of her. My tall tea glass had a sprig of fresh mint in it. I wondered where that had come from at short notice.

'So – let's hear the story.'

I told her, not rushing it, as interested in getting a feel of her and of this place as I was in informing her. She listened without comment, her face intent but utterly without change of expression. I wondered what she was hearing: was it a recitation of personal experience, or a film treatment?

'That is one of the craziest stories I've ever come across,' she said when I was done. 'Really, you just can't beat that for drama. I mean – mysterious spooks, a surprise attack, hair's-breadth escapes, combat . . . It's great stuff. But this *is* real, isn't it?'

'I'm beginning to wonder myself. I know it happened; I still have the scars to prove it. But it was a long time ago in an alien place, and sometimes I think it must've happened to someone else. Starr showing up after all this time just adds to the sense of unreality.'

'Do your war wounds still bother you?' For some reason she sounded interested.

'They never got all the shrapnel out. When you're young you heal quick, and they didn't bother me for more than twenty years, but the last couple of years they've started to remind me they're there; sudden twinges of pain when I least expect it.'

She nodded intently. 'It's a myth, isn't it? I mean, that you really heal. You never fully recover from injuries. I broke my leg skiing when I was twenty-two or -three. I was assured that it was completely healed, but sometimes now I'll wake up around three in the morning with terrible pain in that leg. It happened again just a month or two ago.'

She stared off toward the horizon. The yacht was no longer in sight. 'Back around 1920 Lillian Gish made *Way Down East* with D. W. Griffith. There was a famous scene at the end where she's drifting down a river, unconscious, on a hunk of ice. The hero has to save her before she goes over a waterfall. Her hair and one of her hands are trailing in the water. The scene only lasts a few minutes on film, but it took days to shoot and Griffith was a bear for realism. He shot it on a real river where the winter's ice was breaking up. Lillian had to lie on a real slab of ice for days, with her hand in water that was barely above freezing. She got pneumonia, and more than seventy years later that hand still pained her.'

She took a sip of wine and returned to the present. 'I guess I'm wandering. I don't know why. Maybe it's just a jolt to find out this business goes back that far.'

'If it does,' I said.

'What do you mean?'

'I'm not yet entirely persuaded that this isn't some sort of super-elaborate publicity gimmick. It's unlikely, but I have to look into all the possibilities.'

'It'd be the dumbest stunt I ever ran across, and I've experienced some lulus. And,' she pointed out, 'Mitch Queen would have to be behind it. You and he are probably the only ones alive who remember this Martin Starr character. Not that I'd put it past him, it's just that I don't think the project needs to be pre-sold.'

'I take it you don't like Mitch.'

She looked genuinely surprised. 'Did I say that? I didn't mean to give that impression. Sure, he's a hustler, but that's his work and he's good at it. You have to look at everything he says from every angle, but that's not a bad idea on general principles. There are some truly reptilian lowlifes in the movie business and compared to them he's Mother Theresa. No, personally I like him fine. I never heard that he's ever shafted or ripped off anyone, and if you don't hear rumors like that about someone it's a pretty good sign that they're safe to deal with. Besides, he's good company. You never have to worry about those awkward silences at parties if you invite Mitch.'

I decided that this was what constitutes a sterling character reference in her business. 'Connie dislikes him, and I think it's affecting the way she's handling this case.'

'Would you have said that to a client if she was with your agency?' Selene could be plenty incisive when she wanted to.

'No. But I'd say it to my boss, and ask that one of us be taken off the case – preferably her. But she's probably going to say the same thing about me, since Mitch is an old friend. I just think you should know all the factors here.'

'I appreciate that.'

'A lot of Mitch's job seems to involve lining up investors. What sort of people has he got behind this project?'

'I don't know who all of them are. That can be for a number of reasons: Queen probably likes to keep some of his money sources to himself, and there are sound business reasons for that, these being shark-infested waters; and some investors demand anonymity, usually because of taxes or business associates who don't like what amounts to gambling, or they just don't want to be pestered by a lot of other hustlers with projects to finance.'

'What about the ones you saw at the San Ysidro Ranch?'

'Let's see . . . there were three suits from Paramount. They've picked up financing on his projects before, but never anything this steep. Bert Schuster was there. His mother was one of the biggest stars of the forties. He tried acting for a while when he was younger – not much talent, decided there was more future in the production end. He likes to risk money on quirky, original projects from time to time. Those were the ones I know had some previous connection to the industry.'

'What about the others?'

'There was a man from New York named Morris, a financier who'd made a bundle in foreign currency speculation, looking for places to spread his new money around. I read him as a guy who thinks he's smart when he's just been lucky. That sort is the natural prey of a man like Queen. The other one was a mysterioso named Armitage. He put out the impression he was some sort of banker, but if he is, it's probably one of those offshore firms that specializes in cleaning up dirty money – very smooth and confidence-inspiring – but he never said much about himself.'

'Has Mitch really lined up a hundred million to finance

this project, or is that just more hype?'

'I don't see how he can get it done for much less. Oh, I know what you're thinking: these days the publicity flacks are always yakking up the bucks, as if a string of zeroes amounted to a decent film. It used to be that sums like that meant disastrous cost overruns, but now movies are actually budgeted at a hundred mil. But what does it mean? If they pay twenty million for a bankable star and forty mil for publicity, then maybe forty million gets up on the screen, if it's spent wisely. Usually it isn't, and they can't understand why the audience is disappointed after all the build-up.'

'But you don't think this is that sort of project?'

'Queen's lined up some awfully good talent, and unless there's been some under-the-table dealmaking, nobody's getting paid those obscene sums that've become so common. He seems really intent on putting the whole budget into the project. I can't say there won't be a little larceny involved along the way, but I don't think it'll be anything that would adversely affect the finished product. After all, the size of everyone's *next* paycheck will go ballistic if this film plays the way we hope.'

'I see your point.' There didn't seem to be any motive for anyone to want to sabotage the project. This was not conclusively significant, though. I still didn't know much about this business or the people involved. And any business where people threw such gigantic sums of money around so casually was as foreign to me as the space program.

Connie returned with Jeanette. For a moment they both scanned the horizon, as if they expected a submarine to surface out there and open up on us with its deck gun. Some people carry this security stuff too far.

'The setup isn't too bad,' Connie reported. 'But it's still too open for my liking. I'd really recommend you move to a hotel for the duration.'

'Not a chance, dear. Hotels are for location shooting and trips away from home. I've bought houses in my favorite places because I've lived so much of my life in hotels. Forget it.' Polite but firm.

'You've retained us to look after your safety,' Connie told Selene, Jeanette nodding away over her shoulder. 'You're making it difficult for us to do our job.'

'Actually, I retained your firm to determine whether I'm in

real danger or not. It hasn't been established yet.'

'It's our practice to assume the danger is real until proven otherwise,' Connie said, beginning to steam a little, that faint Hispanic accent tingeing her vowels and consonants. 'Proof of danger could come in a pretty unequivocal form: a bullet through the head, for instance. Then it'd be too late to start taking the warnings seriously, wouldn't it?'

'Lay on more guards if you have to,' Selene said. 'I can afford it. But I'm staying here.'

'It's your choice.' Connie's mouth formed a tight line – not an easy feat with those generous lips. She glanced my way. 'Gabe, was there anything else you wanted to see or discuss?'

I got up. 'I don't believe so. Miss Gibson, it's been a pleasure.' I took her gracefully proffered hand. 'It's unfortunate that we had to meet under such circumstances.' I saw Connie wince. I felt like an utter jerk, falling back on hackneyed phrases, reduced to inarticulacy in the presence of big-time Hollywood glamor.

She smiled sympathetically. 'But then, we probably never would have met if it weren't for something like this. There's serendipity to be found even in death threats. I'm glad to know you're on the case, Gabe.' Class all the way.

We got out of there before I made an even worse impression.

Both of us were silent during the drive from Malibu. I had a lot to think about. I wasn't sure about Connie. She kept glancing at me sidelong, as if she was waiting for me to say something, probably something stupid.

'Okay,' she said at last, 'what do you think?'

'I think I'm starving. How about you?'

'Yeah, I guess I could stand to eat.'

'There's a great little Chinese place not far from here. At least, it used to be there.' You never knew in California. Whole blocks simply vanished sometimes.

'Sounds good.'

It was still there: a mom-and-pop operation sandwiched between a dry cleaner's and an electronic game emporium. Murray, my LAPD partner of many years, had turned me on to dim sum and Chinese noodles two decades before they became chic in America. The place was mainly takeout but there were a half-dozen tiny tables. We took one of them and ordered. The waitress left us a pot of aromatic tea and we sipped cups of the scalding brew.

'So what do you think of the big movie star?' Connie asked.

'I think she has the usual problem people in her business have: difficulty in perceiving the real world as real. She's rich and famous and used to getting her way. Aside from that, I like her. Not that we're required to like our clients.'

'Same here. She's a terrific lady and a royal pain in the ass to guard. Her life has been threatened but to her nothing can be as important as her big comeback role. Her life's on the line and she sees it as a threat to the *production*, for God's sake!'

'Movie people can be narrow-focused. So can the rest of us.'

'What's on your mind?'

'I don't think well when I'm hungry,' I told her. At least she refrained from firing back the obvious rejoinder. A few minutes later the waitress returned with our orders: for me, a mixed platter of spring rolls, steamed pork buns and shallow-fried dumplings; for Connie, a huge bowl of noodles with fish and vegetables floating on top. We didn't talk while we ate. I noticed with approval that Connie knew how to eat noodles Oriental style – slurping them in without regard for decorum. When all the solid fare was gone she picked up the bowl with both hands and drank the last of the stock.

She set the bowl down just as I was blotting up ginger sauce with the last pot sticker. 'Okay, Treloar. What are we missing?'

'I think we've been distracted by the pure weirdness of this thing. We've had Hollywood glitz coupled with the war and spooks and maybe a master criminal right out of Dick Tracy with a grudge going back more than a quarter of a century.'

'It does sound pretty far out when you put it that way,' she acknowledged.

'But one thing keeps coming up that's a lot simpler and a lot more basic, and it's the sort of thing that customarily motivates people to things like fraud and theft and murder. It's just sort of been buried under all the luridness.' I poured myself another cup of the green tea.

'What's that?'

'A hundred million dollars. I think we should ignore the extravagant personalities for a while and concentrate on the money.'

She looked at me for a few seconds, her large brown eyes unblinking. 'Treloar, that's the first really intelligent thing I've heard you say.'

Well, it wasn't much, but it was a start.

Chapter Eight

It's an old investigator's principle and I don't know why it took me so long to recognize it. Once, Murray and I had been assigned to assist some feds who were investigating massive corruption among government contractors in southern California. An old fed with a banker's face and cop's eyes had laid it out for us succinctly: 'Ignore the personalities and ignore the talk. Just follow the money. Find out where it comes from, where it ends up, and the route it took to get there. That will tell you who did what and why they did it.'

This is a very fundamental concept, and it holds true whether you're investigating street pushers, major corporations, organized crime or national governments. In fact, the larger and more complex the organization, the less often any other factor applies at all. At big-business and government level, crimes of passion are rare, but crimes of greed occur in overwhelming profusion. I've been told that, above a certain level, big business, big crime and big government become almost indistinguishable. This could be an exercise in cynicism, but you never know.

That, together with a number of other things, was on my mind as I drove to the West Hollywood Sheriff's Station. Connie wasn't with me this time. So far, there was no definite connection between Duc's killing and our mutual investigation. Connie was off on errands of her own. Maybe, in her way, she was being tactful. This was my first foray into local police territory since I'd left it so ingloriously a few years before.

I was familiar with the building, although I'd never worked in West Hollywood, which is county territory. The second I stepped over the threshold I was hit with a mixture of nostalgia and dread. It was all so familiar: the sounds, the smells, the atmosphere that was an almost military combination of bustle and lethargy. Even the faces seemed familiar, although I didn't see anyone I remembered. But there's a look to police officers and, to a lesser extent, the department's other employees share it. Often as not, the

103

people they haul in off the street share a look too, but it's a different look.

But between me and all this familiarity there was a wall. I didn't belong here any more. I no longer deserved to be here. I felt that everyone was sizing me up, evaluating me, that they could all tell I'd been a cop and were wondering what I'd done to screw up so badly, if they didn't know already.

It was ridiculous, of course. LA has a police force, taking city and county together, that is bigger than a lot of towns. You can have a long and varied career with it and never encounter ninety per cent of your co-workers. And these people had plenty on their minds. It was absurd to think that the long-past woes of Gabe Treloar could weigh heavily on their thoughts. The feeling was no less real for that.

I asked the desk sergeant where Deputy Lowry was to be found and he directed me to Homicide. I could have located it by myself, but he obviously didn't want any dumbass civilians wandering around lost in his headquarters and making trouble for him.

Vernon Lowry seemed unbelievably young for the seniority of his job, a good index of my own advancing years. I'd been a detective at about the same age I judged him to be, back when I was a young hotdog earning commendations and making rank fast. He got up from his desk and shook hands when I entered his cubicle; a taut-bodied man with buzz-cut blond hair and eyes that flickered from my scalp to my shoes and back in the traditional cop's once-over. I handed him my card and he gave me one of his. He waved me to a chair that was so close to his that our knees nearly touched.

'How can I help you, Mr Treloar?'

'Margaret Calvin's husband told me that you're handling the Duc Nguyen murder. Margaret is Duc's daughter. She's my niece.'

His pale eyebrows rose fractionally. 'I know who she is. She's your niece?'

'Duc was my late wife's brother.'

'Then this isn't a business matter?' He held up my card. At least he didn't show the contempt cops often feel for private investigators.

'Well, actually it is. At least, it may be.'

Lowry sat back and frowned. 'I want to hear this. What do you say to some coffee?'

The coffee was pretty good. He doodled on a pad while I gave him a radically abbreviated version of my current employment and its possibly tangential connection to Duc's murder.

'It sounds like you and Mr Nguyen go back a ways,' he said when I'd finished. At least he pronounced the name right; most people say Nooyen.

'As I've said, we drifted apart. But this job I'm working on, and his being gunned down at just this time . . . I don't like it. I don't like the coincidence.'

'That's reasonable. You sure you can't tell me any more about this film project?'

'My client's adamant about maintaining a lid on the production, which is understandable when you consider how much money is involved. And the connection is pretty tenuous, anyway.'

'It's that all right. But if, later on, I decide otherwise, you may be looking at a subpoena.'

'No problem,' I told him. 'I'm not about to stick my neck out for a bunch of la-la-land investors, no matter how much money they stand to lose.'

'Okay. What did you want to know?'

'What do you know so far about the shooting?'

He took a folder from his desk and flipped it open. There were only a few sheets of paper in it. 'On Friday at 5.07 p.m., 911 received a call about a shooting on Charleston Avenue near Western and Beverly. The first unit arrived at the scene at 5.19. Found dead at the scene was Duc Nguyen, identified by associates as a local businessman whose real estate office was only a few yards from the murder site. Witnesses reported hearing shots, then the sound of a car speeding away.' He glanced up at me. 'You want to read the transcripts of the witnesses' statements?'

'I'd rather talk to them myself. Did anybody actually see anything?'

'Do they ever?' Lowry shrugged. 'One kid here, name of Thomas Kim, says he saw a dark, late-model car tearing around the corner, but he was too rattled to see any more than that. Otherwise, the victim's associates said that he left the office, just like he did every work day, and he didn't make it to his car. They heard shots, they looked outside and saw him on the sidewalk and someone called 911.'

It was about standard. Most people aren't too observant at the best of times. Put them in a situation that's completely outside their experience and they rarely have anything useful to report. At such times, impressions are so subjective that witnesses of the same event will give outrageously differing accounts. But cops have to take down their statements anyway. You never know. The dark, late-model car could turn out to be a gray delivery van. The kid might have been looking in the wrong direction. The shooter's car may have been behind him, or already gone.

'Have you ever had a drive-by shooting in that area?'

'Not so far, but the gangs are always coming up with new ways to make our work interesting. Nobody'd heard of freeway shooting until some bozo gave it a try. Next thing you know, it's all the rage. Commercial-district drive-bys may be the latest fad. Maybe we'll be seeing lots of them from now on.' He didn't sound especially bitter, just hard to surprise. You get that way after a while.

'What did the scene look like?'

He finished his coffee. 'Want to go take a look at it?'

I finished mine. 'Let's go.'

It wasn't far from the station to Duc's office. We took my car and killed the time on the way with small talk. Lowry didn't probe much about my LAPD past. I knew he'd check the files as soon as he got back to headquarters.

Charleston was a street like a lot of others in the vast sprawl of LA. It was more prosperous than most, though certainly not in the same class as Rodeo Drive. But then, what is? On a sunny LA afternoon it didn't seem like the sort of place where sudden violence could erupt. Everything was bright and well maintained; there were no collapsible grates across the windows, no gang graffiti sprayed on the walls. It was the sort of street where people with funds to invest or disposable income to spend could expect to go about their business with perfect peace of mind. It just goes to show you.

Duc's business was in the middle of the block, flanked by a branch bank and a fairly tony boutique. Across the street were a computer outlet, a Thai restaurant, and a three-screen theater with its parking lot. The street was lined with cars, so I parked in the theater lot and we walked across the street.

The murder site was still fenced off with yellow crime scene tape. It was about a dozen paces from the door of the real estate office. Some passing pedestrians stopped and gaped at the chalk outline of the body, but mostly they just walked by with eyes averted.

We stepped across the barrier and I squatted by the chalk outline, trying to associate it with the man I had known. But I couldn't tag it to an individual. Instead, it was a terribly evocative abstraction, like those ghost shadows left on the walls and sidewalks of Hiroshima, where the bodies of human beings had shielded the brick and concrete from the furnace blast in the instant before they were vaporized.

It looked as if Duc had fallen on his back. The legs were drawn together with the knees slightly bent. His arms were close to his body. He had probably lived for a few seconds after falling, maybe even been conscious. Instant unconsciousness followed immediately by death would have resulted in an untidy sprawl. There was a broad, dark stain on the sidewalk.

I stood back up, feeling a slight protest in my right knee. 'How was it done?'

'His car was parked there,' Lowry said, pointing to a spot two paces away where a white Toyota now resided. 'The shooter's car stopped there.' He pointed to the street, a spot midway between the white Toyota and the car in front of it. 'We know that much from the angle of the fire and the peel marks the shooter's car made hauling ass.'

'What did the coroner's report say was the cause of death?'

'He was struck six times near the center of the chest by medium-caliber bullets, right through the pump and lungs. Death was near-instantaneous.'

'The weapon?'

'It was full-automatic fire, so it was probably a sub-machine gun of some description – Uzi, Mac 10, one of those. We recovered six shell casings from the street. They were European military, from a Portuguese arsenal with headstamps from the mid-seventies. All the slugs passed on through and hit the wall over there. We recovered three, all regular military hardball. The rest must've ricocheted all over, maybe landed in someone's back seat and they drove away with the evidence.'

I went over to the wall. The marks were there, just below chest height for me: six shallow gouges in the brick, forming an irregular group I could cover with my palm. The copper sheathing of the slugs had left faint smears and there were some brownish blood specks. If this had been the movies, there would have been huge, gory splotches all over the wall. A few years back, the special effects guys got a little carried away and started showing blood and flesh and bone flying every which way even when the weapon was a small-caliber pistol. These days, when it's a sub-machine gun, they really get extravagant.

Reality is a little different. Sub-machine guns fire pistol ammunition, most of them the 9mm cartridge that was developed near the turn of the century for the old German Luger pistol. Its power is marginal, and copper-sheathed military bullets don't expand at all. They just punch on through. They don't pick bodies up and throw them around and most of the bleeding is internal, although considerable blood may drain out under the body, depending on how it falls. Exotic ammunition is another movie conceit. Only an idiot would use hollow-point slugs in a weapon that depends on consistent ammo to work at all. Modern military ammunition is relentlessly reliable, even if it lacks cinematic panache.

'How do you see it, Treloar?'

'A professional job,' I told him. 'Six rounds fired, six hits in a vital area. Everybody has those little sub-machine guns these days, but hardly anybody knows how to use one.'

'That was my thought. A gang-banger would've sprayed the whole neighborhood, maybe bagged a couple of innocent bystanders.'

'The shooter got out of the car. A pro wouldn't've tried to do it from the front seat. Too chancy that way. So there were probably two: the shooter and a driver.'

'Right again.'

'So much for how,' I said. 'That leaves why.'

'There's always mistaken identity,' he said.

'A possibility. But somebody went to a lot of trouble to pull a professional hit. That's an amateur mistake. Still, it's not impossible. Do you know if there were other Vietnamese in the area?'

'In your brother-in-law's business over there, sure. But how many people can spot the differences between Asians? That restaurant across the street's owned by Thais; the kid who thinks he saw the car is Korean. LA's got Cambodes, Lao, Hmong – and that's just naming the exotics. Plus there's the garden-variety Chinese and Japanese, who've been here forever. That spreads out the likelihood of a mistake.'

'It does,' I admitted.

'Your brother-in-law have any undesirable business associates?'

'Like I said, we've been out of contact for a long time. That's something I plan to look into.'

'Good idea. I'll be doing the same. This isn't the sort of thing I'm used to seeing on my beat. Other places, sure. But not West Hollywood, for God's sake. It's . . . what's the word I'm looking for?'

'An anomaly?'

'That's it. This is an anomaly. I don't like anomalies on my turf. Hell, I don't like *any* of the evil shit that happens around here. But as long as I know what's going on I can deal with it. I don't need any anomalies.'

We stepped back over the yellow tape and went into Duc's offices. The lettering on the front window read: GOLDEN STATE PROPERTIES. I remembered helping him pick it out years ago. He wanted something that sounded grandiose and substantial, but local at the same time. It was a bonus that gold is a lucky color in Asia.

There were three desks in the front office. Behind the first desk sat a middle-aged Asian woman, her graying hair pulled back in an old-fashioned bun. A younger man and woman sat at the other two desks. The man looked Vietnamese, the woman was Caucasian. They had the drawn look of people who had suffered a shock followed by anxiety.

The graying woman rose to greet us. 'Good afternoon, Deputy Lowry. We weren't expecting you today. Have you learned anything?' She spoke without an accent, unless you count Californian as an accent.

'Afraid not, but we're working on it. This is Mr Treloar. He's a private investigator and he was Mr Nguyen's brother-in-law. I was just showing him the site and acquainting him with how things happened.'

The woman extended a fine-boned hand. 'I'm Sarah Cho, Mr Nguyen's personal secretary. I'm afraid I never met his sister. I came to work for him just after she passed away.'

'Mr Treloar's firm is investigating a matter here in LA and there's a possibility it might be connected with Mr Nguyen's murder. The likelihood isn't great but we have to pursue every lead.' Lowry knew how to reassure the citizens all right. 'I hope you'll be as co-operative with him as you've been with me.'

'Certainly,' she said. 'What is it you are investigating?'

'It involves a film production,' I told her. 'The details are confidential, but I'd like to know if Duc had any dealings with the film community recently.'

She looked thoughtful. 'Let me see . . . certainly nothing to do with the big studios. In recent years they've been getting rid of property in Los Angeles, not buying it. Occasionally we dealt with businesses on the fringes of the motion picture industry – lens companies, title companies and so forth. They're mostly independent and they need commercial property just like other businesses. I can check, but I'm pretty certain that there haven't been any of those within the last year.'

That didn't sound promising. 'Did he have dealings with the Vietnamese? I don't mean with the immigrant community. Had he recently done business with people currently residing in Vietnam?'

'Not that I am aware of. Naturally, he had innumerable business contacts with the Vietnamese community here.'

I'd been paying attention to the other two. The Caucasian woman was doing her best to eavesdrop. The Vietnamese man was equally intent on his own work, ostentatiously paying us no attention at all.

'Were any of his relations with the Vietnamese, local or otherwise, in any way difficult or hostile?' I asked. The Vietnamese guy was working even harder at his own business, not minding ours at all.

'I couldn't say that. Sometimes voices would be raised, but they usually conversed in Vietnamese and I don't understand that language. I don't believe I heard any real arguments, though. Everyone was always smiling when they came out of Mr Nguyen's office. Why are you concerned about the Vietnamese?'

'Oh, just a hunch I'm playing.' Civilians always like it when you use words like 'hunch' and 'clue'. It makes them feel like they're taking part in a real detective movie. 'On Friday, when he left the office, did he act troubled in any way?'

'Well, he was preoccupied, but he was often that way. He didn't seem afraid or apprehensive, if that's what you mean.'

I took out one of my cards and scribbled my guest house number on it. 'I'm staying here in LA and I can be reached at this number. Please call me if you think of anything that might be helpful. Don't be embarrassed if it seems obvious or trivial. You never know what might be important.'

She took it. 'Certainly. I'm sorry I could help so little as it is. It was just all so unexpected. I've been assuming that it was one of those meaningless, random things that are always happening – someone having to kill somebody to join a gang, that sort of thing. So much of life has become grotesque in recent years.'

'It may be just that,' I told her. 'But we have to pursue any leads we have.'

'Please accept my condolences, Mr Treloar. We all thought so highly of Mr Nguyen.' She was undoubtedly much closer to him than I was, but I accepted gracefully. She didn't look like she was about to burst into tears, but maybe she just had a lot of self-control.

Back out on the sidewalk Lowry grinned at me. 'Playing a hunch, huh? Do you pack a roscoe down these mean streets?'

'It works,' I said. 'Admit it: you say the same stupid things to the civilians.'

'Yeah, we all do,' he admitted. 'I talk about my "informants" and "contacts". I'm always searching for "clues". Why break their hearts and tell them that most of the time we catch the assholes because they're incredibly stupid or their friends rat them out, or both?'

'No reason. The world needs make-believe. The people I'm dealing with now live in it twenty-four hours a day.'

'Is there anyone else you want to see here?'

'Just the kid who saw the car.'

'May have seen the car,' he corrected. 'He works across the street. Let's go see him.'

It turned out to be the computer store. The place was full of all that mysterious stuff I've never learned to use, which is a major sin in my business. Computers scare me because I grew up during the decades when only governments, banks and major businesses had computers, and we knew that they were up to no good. It was all *1984* stuff: computers were going to be used to keep tabs on people and control and oppress them. Okay, I was wrong, but the fear is still there. My generation never guessed that teenagers would use the damn things to spy on the government and big business, not the other way around. Come to think of it, that's just about as scary.

Thomas Kim was behind the counter. He wore the youth uniform of the day: backward baseball cap, Metallica T-shirt, baggy shorts, oversized sneakers without socks or laces. He looked about sixteen years old. He probably sold a half-million bucks' worth of computers and gear every month. Lowry introduced us and the kid accepted my card.

'What can I do for you, Mr Treloar?' His accent was pure LA. If he'd come off a boat it was before he learned to talk.

'Come outside with us and describe for me what you saw when Duc Nguyen was killed.'

'Well, to start with, I was right here when I heard the shots.' He came out from behind the counter. 'Then I heard a car door slam and the car burning rubber. I ran for the door...' he pushed it open, '... and I see this dark car hauling ass around the corner, over there.' He pointed to the corner of the theater parking lot.

'Could you see how many people were in the car?' I asked.

He shook his head. 'Uh-uh. It had smoked glass. Couldn't see a thing. And it was going so fast I couldn't get a look at the license plate, except that the colors were California.'

'What did you do then?' I prodded.

'Well, I looked across the street and I saw Mr Nguyen lying there. Actually, I didn't know his name at the time, I just knew that he was one of the people I'd seen around here most days. I knew he worked in that office. Anyway, I yelled back inside for Penny or Antonio to call 911 and I ran across the street. I saw right away there was nothing I could do. You can't give CPR to someone who's had most of the CP part blown away.' He was trying to act nonchalant but his face twitched a little. 'I mean, maybe I should've tried mouth-to-mouth, but there was all this blood and stuff coming out...'

'Wouldn't have done any good,' I told him. 'You knew it was gunfire when you heard it?'

'Sure. I've heard automatic weapons fire before, just never so close.' His cockiness came back as his thoughts veered away from the blood and gore part.

'It was brave of you to run out like that,' I said.

He shrugged, pleased none the less. 'I would've stayed put except I heard the car hauling. I didn't think they'd hang around.'

'What was the tempo of the shots?' I asked him.

He frowned. 'What do you mean, tempo?'

'I mean, was it sort of slow – *boom-boom-boom-boom* – so you could count the shots? Or was it faster?'

'Real fast, like cloth ripping. I heard later there were six shots, but it could've been three or ten just as easy.'

'You've been a big help, Thomas,' I told him. 'If you think of anything else, just call me at that number I gave you.'

'Sure. Look, you need any equipment, I can give you a good rate. In your business, you really need a good system. It'll take care of ninety per cent of your work for you. You'd be amazed.' He had my number all right.

'I'll keep you in mind.'

He went back inside.

'Time for me to get back to the office,' Lowry said.

'Nothing to keep me here,' I said. 'Let's go.'

As I got behind the wheel of my car I was hit by a sudden, shocking pain in my lower back. It wasn't the worst pain I'd ever felt, but it was so unexpected that I gasped as if I'd just inadvertently set my hand on a hotplate.

'What is it?' Lowry asked, concern on his face.

For a moment I couldn't think what it might be. I'd have thought someone had shot me, except that I'd never felt anything the times I'd been shot. Then I realized what it had to be: the shrapnel still in my back from the first night of Tet. Some of it had been too close to my spine to dig out and it didn't seem dangerous at the time. The docs had warned me that it would give me trouble eventually. Just the day before I'd mentioned it to Selene Gibson. I'd felt twinges before, but nothing like this.

'Nothing,' I told him. 'Just an old friend come calling.'

'You sure? You went white as a toilet bowl. You want to run by a hospital? Cedars-Sinai's just down the road.'

'I know where it is. No, this is just an old back problem. It's nothing.'

But it wasn't nothing. As I drove I thought of what Selene Gibson had said: that you never really recover from injuries. It was true. All the old hits, all the old cuts and wounds, they never really go away. They're always waiting to come out of nowhere and get you again.

When I got back to Queen's I found him out by the pool. He grinned and waved me to one of the chairs by the little poolside table. 'You learn anything from the LAPD?' I sat and gave him the outlines and he shook his head. 'Hard to believe, something like that happening to old Duke.'

When I'd told Queen about the murder he'd been shocked and intrigued, but it was like another unreal event on the fringes of his unreal world. 'It is that,' I said. 'But I'm not ruling out a connection between the killing and the threats.'

'I don't see how there could be.' He took a sip of something colorless in a frosted glass. 'He wasn't involved with the production.'

'He was in Saigon back when you and I and Martin Starr were there.'

Queen snorted over the lime slice that decorated the rim of his glass. 'Have you looked in an LA phone book lately? It's full of people who were in Saigon and its environs back then. Hell, it's no wonder the Vietnamese government's desperate for foreign business. There's probably nobody left there. Everyone came to California. You're making the mistake all us old 'Nam vets tend to make.'

'What mistake's that?'

'We act like that war didn't involve anyone but us. What's that word that means seeing the world like you're the only thing that's real? Sloppy-something?'

'Solipsism.'

'Right, solipsism. We were a bunch of self-centered kids back then, and we just saw the draft and the Army and the war and that whole goddamn country like they were all created just to make things inconvenient for us. We saw pictures in the magazines, all those long-haired hippie guys and bare-boobed hippie chicks romping and doping and humping, and there we were missing out on it, like that was the worst thing happening. But it was all just solipsism, see? We didn't count for diddly squat in the great scheme of things, Gabe. We were just a blip in the long, long span of Vietnamese history, just one more pack of foreign dickheads who came along to make trouble for them. Hell, no sooner were we gone than they went and invaded Cambodia. This conflict stuff is the breath of life to them.'

He leaned forward and tapped a finger against his temple. 'It's only here, in our own minds, that we were important, or that war counted for anything. Solipsism.'

'You've become a philosopher in your old age, Mitch,' I said.

He sat back again. 'Actually, I picked up some of that from

Jared Rhine's screenplay for *Tu Do Street*, but it got me thinking. Do you realize that people voted in the last election who weren't born when the US pulled out of Vietnam? And *that* was damn near five years after you and I were there. You think any of it means anything to these Gen-Xers? They don't know Tet '68 from Gettysburg. Hell, I've got a teenage nephew who asked me what I did in World War Two! I told the silly little prick that I wasn't born then and he says, "I mean, y'know, that war back then." Y'see, Gabe, they think there was a generic war sometime before CDs were invented: Vietnam, Korea, World Wars One and Two, it's all the same.'

'They lack our wisdom,' I agreed.

'Damn right. Rhine really gets into this stuff. Y'see, we were the last generation to have a sense of being a part of history, of being at the culmination of a long series of events, trying to influence the course of future events. Now it's all digitals.'

'Digitals?'

'Right, digitals. Look at these watches.' He held up his gold Rolex. 'Mine's classier than that piece of PX shit you wear, but they've both got dials, right? Dials with hands. Right now the hands are on 3.22, but you can see the whole face of the dial, that just a little while ago the hands were on 3.15, and before that they were at noon. You can also see that there's a future, that those hands are going someplace – past, present and future all in one little circular frame of reference.'

He leaned forward again and spoke intently. 'Digitals don't have that, Gabe! They just give you the present moment, with no reference to past or future. Jesus, is it any wonder those brainless little schmucks don't have any attention span? It's not MTV! It's the goddamn digitals!'

'This is some profound stuff, Mitch.'

He sat back again. 'Damn right. That's what Rhine's screenplay is about. It's about our fleeting moment in what may have been the world's last stretch of real history. And it's not just Western history, Gabe. Western history is linear. Asian history is cyclical. Rhine deals with both.'

'Sounds ambitious,' I allowed.

'It is. It's Vietnam as the culmination of two thousand years of Western domination and colonialism and missionary chauvinism. It's the deathsong of WASP culture. Is that a story or what?'

'It must be, but what the hell are you talking about?'

'Take a drive around LA, Gabe. Hell, you've lived here since high school, maybe you don't even see it anymore. Think of yourself as someone from that Mid-Western whitebread hometown of yours, somebody who's never left the comforting womb of middle-class, white, Protestant heartland America. Plunk him down in LA, give him a long street-level tour, not failing to linger in the Black-Hispano-Asian ghettos that make up such a substantial part of the community. What does your mayonnaise-gobbling Lutheran Anglo see?'

I thought about it. I wasn't entirely unfamiliar with what he was getting at. 'About what he'd see in New York or Miami, with a slightly different ethnic mix. He'd see pandemonium, sort of Hell's suburbs.'

He smiled like a teacher who's gotten his point across to a difficult student. 'He'd be seeing the future, Gabe, though he might not know it. He's been living in a museum all his life, thinking it's the real world. There's fifty different cultures stewing together in this city alone, and mostly they don't see the world or history the way we were taught, and they don't always hold the same values we were brought up with. It's a new America in the making and it won't be the one Norman Rockwell painted and Frank Capra made movies about.'

'Hell,' I told him, 'that America didn't exist even *then*! That's all myth and propaganda.'

'You think I don't know that? Myth is what the film industry is all about. But it's how we define ourselves. This crowd who took over Congress think it was real and they want to go *back* to it, for God's sake! You've seen it, Gabe. Nativism's been a big part of American life for almost two hundred years. In the last century they got all hysterical because they thought they were getting inundated by other types of *Europeans*! They thought the Irish and Italians were going to make them all worship the Pope and eat flounder on Friday or something. But now the people are really different and the numbers are much, much greater.'

'Thus bringing about the end of history as we know it?'

'Yeah, pretty much. At least, that's Rhine's take on the situation. Okay, it's pretty far out, not what you typically think of as cinematic, but there's a lot more to it.'

'I imagine there has to be. Mitch, I want to see this script. I want to see what's in it that has Starr or whoever it is in such an uproar.'

He drew in a little, his body language going defensive. 'I don't know, Gabe. My contract's downright brutal about who gets to see the property. Besides, the threats have nothing to do with the screenplay itself.'

'Do you know that?'

'Of course I know that! There's only three complete copies of the screenplay and they've been under security you wouldn't believe. The Declaration of Independence gets treated with negligence compared to *Tu Do Street*!'

Now it was my turn to snort. 'Even you don't believe that.'

'Well, no. But I don't see how the screenplay has anything to do with it. Either the whole thing's a hoax or somebody just doesn't want us making a movie in Vietnam, period.'

'Can I read it?' I pressed.

'I'll have to ask. Maybe Rhine'll bend a little.'

'Tell him he'd better, or you're just wasting your money hiring detectives.'

One of the major pains of the business is the client who doesn't want to give the investigator everything he needs to work. They're amazingly numerous, maybe even the majority. They tend to think they know better than the investigator – who is a mere hireling – how to handle the investigation. Sometimes I wonder why they bother to hire us. In the Army they called it 'need to know'. Don't tell this moron anything more than he absolutely needs to know.

There is a conclusion to be drawn concerning such clients: one and all, they have something to hide.

Chapter Nine

That evening Connie arrived looking cheerful, so I told her about the end of history as we know it.

'When you and Queen were in Vietnam,' she said, 'were you ever exposed to that Agent Orange stuff?'

'They never needed to defoliate Saigon. Anyway, I think he got most of this from Jared Rhine. The guy must be a real case.' We were sitting at the little table by the picture window overlooking the pool. The remains of a pastrami sandwich sat forlornly on a plate in front of me. 'I guess he has a point, though. Any modern American big city has to look pretty shocking to Joe Whitebread from Middle America.'

'Sure, but so what? That's just the country boy in the big, wicked city. Been that way since the Bible. Did you know that the Hebrew word for "whore" translates as "foreign woman"?'

'I guess they never taught us that at St Anne's.' This was turning out to be an educational day.

'I think this Rhine character has a case of American White Male angst. He probably got passed over for a job in favor of some Asian woman and he's been sulking about it ever since.' She reached into the handbag on the floor beside her and took out a rubber ball, which she began to squeeze rhythmically. For a moment I flashed on Captain Queeg's steel marbles, but I figured she just had to keep her grip strong so she could pump maximum iron.

'No,' she continued, 'it's really the other way around. Native cultures are in retreat everywhere. People worry that Mexican immigration's going to turn the US into a Catholic country? My father and uncle are Baptist ministers. All over Latin America evangelical missionaries are converting people in droves!'

'Sure, but—'

'Forget about it!' she said, riding right over me, squeezing the ball so hard and so fast that I expected to see it squish out between her fingers. 'You think Asia's any different? They may not be interested in Western religion but they sure like Western material culture. And if they want that sort of economy, it looks like only Western political institutions are suited to it. And if that's true in Asia, it's ten times as true here. Sure, some first-generation immigrants cling to old-country ways. They always have. In the twenties there was a whole Yiddish theater system in America. There were dozens of Yiddish newspapers. Not any more. That generation's gone. Same'll happen to the latest wave. Go out there and talk to some seventeen-year-old girl whose parents came here from Laos in the seventies and now she's working at McDonald's. You'll get an earful of pure Valley Girl talk.'

'Am I the only one who hasn't been thinking about this?' I said, a little nettled. After all, I was the one with all the Vietnamese in-laws.

'I guess you must be,' she said, settling a little, switching the ball to the other hand. 'Look, I know you heartland white guys get worried that you may not be on top much longer . . .'

'Me? It's this Rhine character and—'

'. . . but you've got nothing to worry about. Well, not much anyway. Western culture is still the most powerful engine in history, and the US is its locomotive. Remember a few years back when all those people were dancing on top of the Berlin Wall?'

'Sure.'

'Didn't you notice that it looked like an ad for Levis? There wasn't one butt in fifty up there that wasn't covered by some sort of blue jeans! I mean, you want to see a symbol of the triumph of the West, what more do you need?'

'You have a point.'

She nodded with the certitude of a drunk. 'Damn right. You know what's gonna happen when Queen gets his movie made? *If* he does, I mean?'

'Tell me.'

'It'll be shown here, where it'll make money or bomb – I don't know. But whichever happens, it'll go on to show in theaters all over Europe and Asia and Africa and the Middle East and what used to be the Soviet Union and South America, then it'll run on their television and the videotape'll be sold in Bangkok and Kinshasa and Buenos Aires. In fact, it'll be seen everywhere that the laws don't forbid American movies. And it'll be seen even in *those* places by anyone with a satellite dish, and they'll copy it and pass it around. When did you last see an Indian film? Or one from China or Egypt?'

'It's been a while,' I admitted.

'Uh-huh,' she said triumphantly. 'For most Americans, it's more like never. But Cairo and Bombay and Hong Kong and Taiwan turn out a hundred times more movies than Hollywood. The only ones that ever make it here are the kung-fu movies. Does that tell you anything about the direction culture flows in this world?'

'You feel pretty strongly about this,' I said.

'Yep.' She tossed the ball back to the other hand and continued squeezing the hell out of it. 'You know, when the Goths invaded the Roman Empire, they weren't trying to destroy it. They wanted *in* on it and they were pissed off that the Romans wanted to keep them out and weren't willing to share. For hundreds of years everything that was attractive and desirable and alluring in their world was Roman and they wanted to be Romans themselves. The Romans wouldn't let them in but they came anyway. I learned that in a Western Civ class.'

She dropped the ball back in her purse, thoroughly throttled. 'So you see, you have nothing to worry about.'

'Me? This isn't about me!'

'Yes it is,' she insisted, giving me the evil eye.

'Anyway, those barbarians did end up destroying Rome,' I pointed out.

'Yeah, well, the Romans fucked up, didn't they?'

'So much for the world situation. What've you been able to find out?'

'Okay, small stuff first – and on the subject of kung-fu movies, guess where our boy Rhine got his start?'

'Tell me. You're the detective.'

'I checked with someone who owes me a favor and works for the Screenwriter's Guild. It turns out he scripted about fifty chop-socky epics in Hong Kong and Singapore back in the seventies. Our big-time screenplay honcho used to churn out grade-Z hack work for the Shaw brothers and even lesser lights.'

'I guess even Hollywood hot dogs have to start somewhere. Jack Nicholson started out in Roger Corman horror cheapies. Why should a writer be any different?'

'You might consider it before giving too much weight to his historical philosophy.'

'I'll keep it in mind. Anything else about him?'

'Just that he showed up here in the early eighties with his portfolio of martial-arts movies and got work as a script doctor – working the kinks out of other people's screenplays, got something of a reputation for turning losers into winners. By the mid-eighties he was selling his own work and turned out to be a wizard at the newly popular action-suspense-thriller genre. He's difficult and a hermit-style recluse, at least that's his pose.'

'Okay, but I'm more interested in the money people. Did you find anything on them?'

'The Paramount guys and the movie star's kid are straight industry money people and there was no point in looking into them beyond establishing that,' she said, all business now. 'Queen's is just one of several projects they're involved with at present.

'Morris, the money speculator Selene reads as mediocre but lucky, seems to stack up as just that. A couple of years ago he turned a small bundle into a big one by buying up European currencies with dollars when the dollar soared for a few days because those bozos in Moscow tried to topple Yeltsin. He resold them when things settled down and went back to more cautious speculation. When NAFTA went through he invested in Mexican pesos, then dumped them just before the bottom dropped out.'

'That doesn't sound dumb to me,' I said.

'Our financial investigator says he's the kind of guy who thinks he has great natural instincts and is privy to inside information. He gets top expert advice and then ignores it to follow his own hunches. He's been right a couple of times so now he thinks he knows more than the experts. You know, like Hitler: he ignored his generals' advice and invaded the Sudetenland and Czechoslovakia and France and he got away with it. It convinced him that he was a great natural military genius. He didn't guess right again, but he never lost faith in his instincts.'

'Damn, aren't we historically-minded today? Okay, so much for Morris for the present. But I want to keep an eye on him anyway. How about the other one – Armitage?'

'He's a cutie. Calls himself an investment banker, has firms in the Cayman Islands, Bermuda, Grenada, places like that. Always seems to have big money to invest, gives very little to the tax man, and – get this – was never indicted or even investigated, as far as we can learn.'

'Never *investigated*?'

'So it seems. Think he's connected? One of those guys with a mysterious flag on his file?'

'Maybe. But then Treasury can keep pretty tight wraps on an ongoing investigation. They can take years, and nobody's going to hand out progress reports to just anybody who asks. But this looks promising. Let's stay on him. I want to know about this guy.'

That evening I got a phone call I'd been half expecting. Connie was doing some stretching exercises on the floor next to the phone and picked it up on the second ring. 'For you,' she said, holding it out.

I took it, automatically glancing at my watch: 10.15.

'Mr Treloar, this is Ngia Van Minh.' The voice was heavily accented. 'You saw me earlier today at Golden State Properties. I worked for Mr Nguyen.'

'Yes, I remember you.'

'I overheard your conversation with Mrs Cho. She was telling you the truth, but there are things she doesn't know because she doesn't understand Vietnamese. These things have been bothering me.' His enunciation was clear, but I could hear the distress in his voice. It's something I could pick up on from my years of marriage to Rose. Most people, unused to the cadences of Vietnamese speech, would have missed it.

'Then maybe you should tell me about it.'

'I think so, but not over the telephone.'

'Where do you want to meet?' It's an old game. They all watch too much television. They feel so much better if you let them pick the place. I hoped it wouldn't be an underground parking garage or the Griffith Park Observatory. Not only too much TV, but they all see the same movies.

'There is a school playground at the corner of Charleston and Lamar Street, about two blocks from our office. Do you know it?'

'I'm not real familiar with the area, but it should be simple enough to find.'

'Will you meet me there in one hour?'

'Sure. There'll be someone with me, a colleague who's working on the same case.'

He paused for a moment. 'Well . . . all right. One hour, then.'

He hung up and so did I. 'Do you feel up for a little

excursion?' I told Connie about the call.

'Sure.' She got up off the floor. 'Let me change clothes and get some shoes on.' She was in a leotard and tights, looking as solid as a box of rocks, although not nearly as angular.

'You told me you thought he looked hinky,' she said when she got into the car on the passenger side.

'Nothing wrong with my instincts,' I said with a little satisfaction. 'But I was thinking I'd have to look him up privately and lean on him. This is going to be easier than I thought.' That's the sort of statement you should never make.

'I wonder why he didn't want to meet at his home,' she mused. 'They usually feel more confident that way, more in control.'

'Doesn't want his family involved, is my guess. Not much sense in speculating.'

'A school playground in the middle of the night. Maybe we can sit in the swings. I haven't done that in years.'

Traffic was light all the way. It usually is at that time of night. Finding the playground was no problem. Some kids were just wrapping up a late game of basketball as we arrived. Otherwise the whole block was all but deserted. Aside from the basketball court there were the usual teeter-totters, a jungle gym and some swings. The swings were in deep shadow next to the school building, not a good place to meet someone, so we passed them up, instead stationing ourselves next to a merry-go-round made of steel plate and pipes, nearer the sidewalk and a streetlamp.

'You notice how they like to pick places with good visibility?' Connie said. 'Like maybe somebody's going to be hiding somewhere nearby? I guess this is as close as he could get to a public park.'

'Park benches are hard to find in this part of town,' I agreed.

We'd been there about ten minutes when a slightly built man approached us along the sidewalk, hands in pockets, hunched a little, looking uneasy.

'Mr Treloar?'

'That's right.' I took his hand, feeling the tension. 'This is Connie Armijo. She's a detective, too.'

'Yes . . . well, hello. I am sorry to bring you out to a place like this at such an hour, but . . .'

'That's perfectly all right,' Connie told him. 'We're anxious to hear what you have to say. We want to find out who killed Mr Nguyen.'

'Yes, Duc Nguyen was a good man, a very good man. I do not want these people to get away with this. It is not right. We are not in Vietnam any more.'

At last we seemed to be getting somewhere. I started to speak but Connie broke in again. 'Why don't we sit down here and you can tell us about it.' She sat on the steel merry-go-round and Ngia Minh sat next to her. She seemed determined that she was better than me at setting people at ease and getting them to open up. Well, maybe she was right. I sat on his other side.

'I would have invited you to my home, but I am afraid to involve my family.'

Connie arched her eyebrows at me. 'You think they might be in some danger?'

'You saw what happened to Duc Nguyen.'

'What did Mrs Cho miss?' I asked him.

'Duc Nguyen does . . . did a lot of business with the Vietnamese community. Most of it was just ordinary dealing in commercial property. But lately men approach him he does not want to deal with. Some of them are . . . were, I mean, officials of the old government and military men. They act like the war is still going on and they can do as they please because they are the men with the power.'

'You mean they've become gang leaders here?' I asked him.

'Well, yes, I suppose that is how you would say it. They are bad men.'

'And Mr Nguyen wanted nothing to do with them?' Connie prodded gently.

'Of course not. But . . .' His hands did a little butterfly movement as he tried to find the right words. '. . . but the situation is very complicated. Duc Nguyen was a man of substance and position in the community; once an army officer and of an excellent family. He was a man much respected. But this is not Vietnam and in this place our position is not so firm. He did not wish to cause ugly discord within the community.'

'So he dealt with them,' I said.

'Only to let them have the properties they wanted,' he said hastily. 'Mostly these were warehousing and trucking facilities, a few retailing properties. He would have nothing to do with their activities.'

125

'So what gave them a reason to kill him?' Connie asked. 'There must be more.'

'I don't know everything, of course. But about a month ago, some of these men I speak of came to the office. With them were two other men, also Vietnamese, but these men were not immigrants. They were in from Saigon.'

'Are you certain?' Connie asked.

'I could tell from the way they were talking. I brought them some tea from the place across the street, and I saw one of the men take a pack of cigarettes from his pocket.' He pantomimed the act. 'When he did, he took out a passport and wallet with the pack. It was a Vietnamese passport.'

'Okay,' I said, 'what did they talk about?'

'It was not so much talk as argument. These men wanted Duc Nguyen to be partners with them in some sort of business. You understand, I could not hear everything, just sometimes when they raised their voices. They spoke Vietnamese, so Mrs Cho couldn't understand them. At around noon she left to have lunch and it was then that the arguing was worst. For a while they were shouting at one another.'

'Where was the other woman I saw at the office?' I asked him.

'That is Jerri Batchelor. She was out that day, taking clients to tour some property. She wasn't there at all when those men were in the office.'

'Did you get any idea what kind of business was involved?' Connie asked.

'I think it had to be smuggling. You know, people like this do not speak plainly, even among themselves. They used words . . . language that hid their real meaning.'

'I know what you mean,' I assured him. 'What words did they use?'

'They spoke about "salt" and "flowers", and I think by this they meant drugs. Other things I don't know: "tigers", "snakes", "ghosts". I have no idea what they meant, but Duc Nguyen did not like any of it.'

Connie and I locked eyes at that last strange word. 'Ghosts?' she said.

'Yes. They used the word several times, and it sounded like they meant people. I think maybe illegal immigrants.' He thought for a moment. 'But maybe it is the name of a gang back in Vietnam. They talked of "the Ghost". They used a form of the word . . . what is it when you speak of the biggest?'

'Superlative?' Connie said.

'That is it. They used the superlative form, like "the big ghost".'

'Do you have names for these men?' I asked.

He glanced around again. He wasn't exactly trembling and wringing his hands, but he was the next thing to terrified. 'One of them was Ngo Pham. He owns a fruit market, but everyone knows he is a broker for illegal immigrants from Southeast Asia, not just Vietnam. Another was Tran Van Loan. He is a car dealer. Once again, it's a cover for something else, but I don't know what. The other local men I do not know, just faces I had seen once or twice before. The two just in from Vietnam were not introduced to me. I only got this from when they raised their voices, which was much of the time. They were very angry with Duc Nguyen. I heard what Mrs Cho said to you earlier. But this time, when the men left, they were not smiling.'

'How did Duc act after they left?' Connie asked him.

'Just like always. He was not an easy man to scare. He saw much war in the old days.'

'Did he say anything to you about this conference?' I asked.

'Just that this was something that did not work out and I should forget about it. He said we would not be seeing those people again.'

'Did any of them ever come around again?' Connie said.

'Not that I saw. They did not come into the office while I was there.'

'Why didn't you tell this to the police?' Connie asked him.

'What do I have?' he said bitterly. 'Some pieces of overheard conversation? The police must know who those men are, the local ones. They should have been arrested long ago. But the police have nothing on them or they have the authorities paid off. It is not easy to prove something against someone here. The police would do nothing. But those men would find out that I had accused them. They would make me pay. Then they would make my family pay.'

I knew what he was saying. He came from a place where the authorities were always the enemy. It didn't matter who the government might be, and the police were just their enforcers. If you were smart you kept your mouth shut.

'But you wanted to tell us,' Connie said.

'I had to tell someone.' He looked at me. 'You were related to Duc Nguyen. You were the husband of his sister. I thought you had a right to know this, and maybe you would know what to do with it.'

'Do you think I can keep you out of it?' I asked him.

He got up. 'I hope you will. I want to live a long time and have grandchildren. I . . .' His head jerked around as a black car burned around the corner of the block, tires squealing. The passenger window was down and something poked out of it.

'Down!' Connie and I both yelled at once, each of us jerking Minh by an arm. It's a wonder we didn't disjoint him like a chicken. We rolled under the merry-go-round just as the shots started; the ripping stutter of a sub-machine gun, not the slow chug of an assault rifle. The spang of the little copper-jacketed bullets off the sturdy steel flooring of the merry-go-round was deafening but reassuring. With a creak, the plaything began to rotate lazily. Connie had a massive revolver out and she began to return fire. The muzzle blast damn near deafened me and I felt bits of unburned powder sting my cheek.

The car hadn't quite stopped. Abruptly it accelerated and vanished around the next corner. We crawled out and brushed ourselves off shakily.

'Why didn't you shoot?' Ngia Minh demanded indignantly.

'No gun,' I told him. People have funny ideas about how carry permits work.

'Mr Minh,' Connie said, efficiently emptying her cylinder into her purse and snapping in fresh rounds from a charger. 'I think you'd better get your family together and take them on a vacation. Maybe you have relatives in Texas or Florida or someplace you can visit.'

He had gone dead white. 'I hope you find who killed Duc Nguyen,' he said, 'but I am through with this. Goodbye.' He walked off at a fast clip.

'Shouldn't we report this?' Connie said, nodding toward the merry-go-round. Long, shiny gouges decorated its surface.

'This is just vandalism of city property. You can report it if you want, but you'll probably get arrested for discharging a firearm within the city limits. I think I'm going for a little drive.'

'I'm with you. To hell with it.'

We made a short run back to the car and got in.

'Think you hit anyone?' I asked.

'Probably wounded their car. I wasn't really trying to pick out a target. I just didn't want them to hang around.'

'Sound policy.'

She was breathing fast and her eyes were wide. I probably looked much the same.

'Ever been shot at before?'

'I've had dirtbags pop off a round or two at me when I was chasing them. Nothing this serious.'

I shook my head but my left ear kept ringing loudly. 'That cannon of yours is rough on the hearing.'

'Poor baby. If that bastard's aim had been a few inches lower he would've minced us. I'm not ready for a toe-tag yet. I always heard that people tend to shoot high under stress. I was just keeping his stress level elevated.'

'I wasn't complaining.'

I didn't head back to Queen's. Instead I drove up to Mulholland and stopped at one of those view points where you get the postcard vision of the lights of the city as a fairyland – not what it's really like at all. I shut off the engine.

We'd both stopped shaking and were anxious to prove to each other how unshaken we were.

'How'd they locate us?' she said.

'Maybe they tailed Minh, maybe there's a bug on our phone. I'm wondering why they bungled an easy hit like that when they pulled such a professional job on Duc.'

'Different team maybe, amateurs. The team that got Duc may've left town as soon as they pulled the job. Pros would've done that.' She slammed the dashboard with the heel of her fist. 'Damn! All we've got is that your ex-brother-in-law got himself mixed up with Vietnamese gangsters. This isn't what I'm supposed to be working on!'

'They were talking about ghosts,' I pointed out.

'They were talking gangster slang. It probably doesn't mean what it did twenty-five years ago. Maybe he was right. These days ghosts may be illegal immigrants.'

'They talked bout a "big Ghost", superlative. Maybe that's what Martin Starr is these days.'

She didn't say anything for a while, and I didn't prod her. She opened her door and got out. The car sagged a bit when she sat on the front fender with her feet on the bumper. I got out and joined her. For a while we sat there watching the lights and hearing the faint noises of the city below, seeing the police choppers shooting their unearthly beams into darkened neighborhoods, the strobing lights of emergency vehicles flashing from all quarters.

'You said you saw Martin Starr one more time,' she said at last. 'Or you thought you did. Tell me about it.'

So I told her.

Chapter Ten

Republic of South Vietnam, November 1968

When I came off duty I marked off another day on my short-timer's calendar. I'd bought the calendar in the PX when I'd passed my sixth month in country. Short-timer's calendars were objects of superstitious reverence and ritual among GIs. I'd sneered at the other guys' elaborate daily placations of the gods of fate and fortune back when I'd had the bulk of a long, long year ahead of me. Now, with my year almost up, I was as abjectly ritual-bound as the worst of them. I wouldn't turn in my ripped-up flak jacket because it had probably saved my life twice and might do it again. I always wore Queen's black sunglasses because he'd rotated home without a scratch and had solemnly presented them to me when he left for Tan Son Nhut to catch his freedom bird.

'Won't be needin' 'em m'man,' he'd said almost four months before. 'The sun's more benevolent where I'm goin'. Look me up when you get home.' I even wore the damn things at night.

When I'd bought the calendar I'd superstitiously crossed off all the days since my arrival, then had marked off each subsequent day when I came off duty, usually in the early morning hours. Some guys only marked off a day after sunrise the next day, arguing that this improved your chances of making it home alive. They wouldn't have known the word hubris if they'd heard it, but they knew that the gods didn't like presumption or a smartass attitude.

I counted the Xs – more than three hundred of them. Some cautioned against counting your marked-off days. They said it was like counting your money during a poker game, sure to bring on a losing streak. I did it anyway, feeling that certain severely limited defiances of fate helped the process along; that an utterly slavish subjugation to placatory ritual was unsuitable, especially for an American.

I was getting antsy, too – jumping at every loud noise, snapping at people and generally being a pain in the ass. It wasn't just being short that did it. Suddenly I had a lot to live for. Rose and I were to be married on an auspicious day just after Christmas and a few days later we would be in the States, the World, the Land of the Big PX. I'd pulled strings with Personnel and my future was arranged: fifteen months of soft duty at Fort Ord and then I could separate three months early to get into the LAPD Academy. If I could just live that long.

Our platoon sergeant came into the bay. He was an E7 from Dallas named McKay. 'Ever'body get some sack time while you got the chance. Headquarters company's bein' pulled off regular duty for the day. We got a special mission tomorrow night. There'll be a special formation at 2100, but that don't mean you don't make the other ones. I wanna see my squad leaders in my hooch right now.'

I shut my locker and followed McKay to the tiny room at the far end of the bay that he shared with the sergeant of the Second Platoon. By now I was a buck sergeant squad leader. Promotion was fast in Vietnam. I led the first squad of First Platoon, Head and Head, which meant Headquarters, headquarters company. Head and Head supplied the personnel for Battalion headquarters, was attached to Battalion HQ, and had an extra platoon to accommodate all the extra cooks and clerks and whatnot. Otherwise, we pulled regular MP duty. For us, a special mission usually meant escorting some visiting VIP. At least it was a break in the routine.

The little room was jammed when the three other squad leaders and I wedged ourselves in with the platoon sergeant.

'Who's coming to call?' I asked. 'Our new commander in chief?' Richard Nixon had been elected a few days before. Speculation was rife whether he'd prove as big a disaster for the war as Johnson had been. There were few optimists.

'Ain't VIP duty this time,' McKay told us. Everyone was smoking and the atmosphere in the confined space grew dense. McKay stared at me through the haze. 'Your future brother-in-law's been huddlin' with Colonel Tapia all day.'

Uh-oh. He had his larcenous moments, but Duc Nguyen was a notoriously efficient and conscientious police officer. A powwow like that meant a serious operation in the works.

'Charlie comin' back?' someone asked. 'I thought we kilt 'em all last time.'

'Don't nobody open their mouth when you walk from this

room,' McKay cautioned, 'but it looks like we're goin' ghost huntin'.'

My stomach knotted. 'Aw, shit, McKay, you've gotta get me out of this!' I said. 'I'm so short I can sit on a dime and swing my legs and I'm getting married in less than a month! I can't afford to lock asses with a bunch of doped-up deserters now! I don't want my fiancee to be a widow. C'mon, get me off. I'll pull all your extra duty till I DEROS.' This was one of those military acronyms: Date of Estimated Return from Overseas. Acronyms seemed to outnumber conventional words.

'Nevah happen,' McKay said, shaking his head. 'I don't give a fuck if you DEROS the day after tomorrow an' marry Lucy Baines Johnson at Tan Son Nhut while waitin' to catch your plane. Long as you're with this platoon you take the same chances as everyone else.'

I looked around and didn't see any sympathetic looks. Heartless bastards. 'Well, shit,' I commented.

I wished he hadn't told us ahead of time. At least I'd have been able to get some sleep. All I could think of was that I was sure to get waxed this time. I briefly considered turning ghost myself. Only Rose would never go with me. She had a serene faith that everything was going to be okay and we were going to get married and go to the States and achieve the American Dream. Of course, she'd lived her whole life in this war-ravaged cesspit and had a more philosophical attitude than I could manage.

Morale fell into three phases in Vietnam. When you first arrived, you were scared to death, certain you would be killed in your first action. Then you entered a resigned period, knowing that you were there for a long time and that worrying didn't help anything. Then, when you were short, the fear came back with irrational force. Every bullet and grenade frag had your name on it. This was true even for rear-area time servers like me. It was much worse for the grunts in the bush, but nobody in The Nam ever admitted that someone else was having a worse time of it.

A few months earlier I'd have welcomed a ghost hunt. Lately, ghosts had replaced VC and American civilians as the people we hated the most. We imagined them all living high, with their dope and their stolen money and their shackjobs. Just then, though, I couldn't work up much indignation. I was leaving and they were staying and that seemed like punishment enough, as far as I was concerned.

I fumbled my way nervously through the next day, trying to find a way out of the night's mission. Sick call came and went without me being able to dream up any believable symptoms. I racked my brain for debts to call in, but I'd already used up all my credit lining up the sweet deal I was so concerned about losing. The Army didn't dare forbid GIs to marry Vietnamese women, for fear of offending our esteemed allies. But they certainly didn't encourage it. The posting to Fort Ord hadn't been easy to come by, either. It wasn't Hawaii, but anything in California had to be better than the swampy, isolated Southern posts that made up about three quarters of all stateside Army property.

I couldn't even take my worries to Rose. Duc had talked me up to her after the racetrack, and I didn't want her to see me acting like some trembling newby. So when my PX Seiko said 9.00, which in military parlance is 2100, I was in formation with the rest of my platoon and the other three operational platoons. Fifth platoon, which had all those cooks and clerks, was excused the formation.

After the customary wait, the brass showed up. Colonel Tapia, the Battalion commander, was there, along with his XO, Major Moore. HQ Company's CO, Captain Schultz, arrived along with Duc Nguyen. Sergeant Major Posezny, the top Battalion NCO, walked alongside the company First Sergeant, all of it in that formal hierarchical order that was a mystery to lower-grade enlisted men. The first shirt called us to attention. Then they all stepped back, leaving the Battalion CO standing in front.

'At ease. Gentlemen,' Tapia said, 'we're going out tonight to scour out a large nest of deserters and it's about damn time. They're having a get-together in a warehouse by the river. Most of you know the district. Captain Nguyen's men will be guiding us but they won't be going in. This is our mess to clean up and it's an American job.' He looked us over, hard-eyed. 'This is a different sort of mission. It's not soldiers we'll be dealing with; not even VC we can at least respect as fighting men. These are deserters. They're traitors and criminals. I don't want to lose any men because someone was slow on the trigger. So don't take any chances. There won't be any board of enquiry held over tonight's action. Take all measures necessary to defend yourselves and I'll back you one hundred per cent. We move out at 2300.'

'Ten-hut!' Posezny shouted. We popped to and the higher brass marched off, leaving Captain Schultz and the First Sergeant, a stringy old-timer named Woodruff.

'At ease,' Woodruff said. 'When you fall back in, I want ever'body in full combat gear: steel pots, flak jackets, jungle boots, the whole nine yards. Tape all your loose gear and slings so you don't make no sound. Weapons and ammo to include bayonets and grenades. These fuckers gonna blow the lights the minute we come calling, so supply has flashlights for every man. Squad leaders and assistant squad leaders are to draw illumination grenades as well. We wanna see these pricks so we can shoot 'em. Any questions?'

'Top,' McKay said, 'them warehouses down by the river's nothin' but wood an' tin. Illumination grenades gonna set 'em on fahr.'

Woodruff's eyes went wide. 'Oh, excuse me, Sergeant McKay. You in the insurance business now; you worryin' about shit like that? Let the fuckers burn!' Everybody laughed and McKay looked sheepish.

'If there are no more dumbass questions,' Woodruff said, 'then get your shit together. Ten-hut! Dis-miss!'

McKay and the other platoon sergeants about-faced. 'Fall out!'

We changed clothes and gear and went to the arms room. Standing in line waiting to get our weapons, everyone was chattering nervously. By now I was senior to most of them. They thought of me as a hardened vet. My assistant, a Spec 4 named Russel, wore a look of wonderment that came from more than the prospect of a fight.

'Did I hear right?' he said. 'Did we just get orders to kill these assholes on sight?'

'No, you didn't,' I told him and the rest. 'Best you remember that, too. Fuck what the bird colonel said. He's not the Defense Department. Sure, the Army wants to keep this ugly crap under the carpet, but if there's a sober reporter over at the Continental tonight, it could get out. Then there'll be court-martials up the ass if we pull any summary executions. And Tapia can testify with wide-eyed innocence that no indeed he never said *kill* those bastards, he just said be extra-special careful. If you listened closely you'll notice that that's all he did.'

'Well, shit,' someone said. 'An' here I thought we just got a 007 license to kill.'

'That's what he wanted you to think,' I told him. 'But I've been in the Army long enough to listen to what's said to me.' I came to the half-door of the arms room and collected my .45 and my shotgun and the incongruous bayonet that fastened to the lug below its muzzle. 'On the other hand,' I added, 'if one of them actually points a weapon at you, better wax his ass quick. I've been in the LBJ, and I'd sure as hell kill you to stay out of that place.'

At the reinforced ammo bunker we picked up rifle and pistol rounds and shotgun shells and frag grenades and, for me and my assistant, illumination grenades. We charged up our weapons and hung the rest of the warlike paraphernalia variously about our harnesses. Sticks of greasepaint were passed around and we darkened our faces and hands, just like we were going out in the bush. Well, Saigon was as bad as any jungle.

At supply we collected big, five-cell flashlights made of heavy aluminum, and I showed the newbies how to tape them to the M-16s so they'd shine where the weapons were pointed. Those of us with shotguns were issued regular GI flashlights with angled heads. Taped down tight to the harness they'd shine where the wearer was facing. Of course they'd draw fire too, but you can't have everything.

When we fell in I saw that the jeeps had been mounted with searchlights. Woodruff called us to attention and Captain Schultz laid out the operation for us.

'At 2300 all will be mounted in the jeeps and the deuce-and-a-halfs. Captain Nguyen will lead us to within a couple of blocks of the warehouse, where we'll dismount and proceed on foot. The Second, Third and Fourth Platoons will throw a cordon around the warehouse and establish a perimeter. First Platoon will go in and flush them out. When they go in, the jeeps will come up with searchlights and we'll bag the bastards as they try to escape. The river patrol will be bringing up boats to catch any who try to escape by water. And you heard the Colonel: nobody's going to miss these bastards, so let's save the Army the cost of a few court-martials, okay? Any questions?' There were none.

We stood around for a while, waiting for things to get underway. Some talked, but most were occupied with their thoughts, and I was willing to bet that the more thoughtful were wondering why, in the middle of a war, they were going into battle against other Americans. I, personally, had stopped marveling at the craziness. I just wanted to get home. It occurred to me that this pack of ghosts was standing between me and Rose and our freedom bird. Despite what I'd said to my squad, I knew that I wasn't going to brook much resistance from anyone. I had too much to lose.

Just short of midnight we got orders to mount up. Searchlight crews had been assigned to the jeeps and I rode in the back of one of the trucks with my squad. The covered-wagon tarps had been stripped from the vehicles and few people even bothered to glance at the little convoy as it rolled slowly through the dark streets. Not that there were many people to watch anyway. I stood at the front of the cargo box, leaning over the top of the cab, wishing I could smoke, wondering if I'd catch another round this time, maybe one through something vital.

We were far from the bright lights of Tu Do Street. Ramshackle tenements sprawled along the river, reeking of garbage and smoke. There was no sound but the rumble of the vehicles, and nothing moved except darkened helicopters far away, and way off in the distance I could see orange balls drifting dreamily – four-deuce illumination rounds hanging from their parachutes. Some fire base out there was under attack.

With a hiss and a squeal the convoy stopped. 'Unass the truck,' McKay said quietly. We dismounted cautiously, awkward in all the unaccustomed battle gear. Everyone was sweating heavily, from tension and from the way the heat built up under the heavy flak jackets.

'Lock and load,' I said. The mechanical clatter of the weapons being charged seemed intolerably loud in the still night, but there was no help for it. There was a multiple click of safeties being set, then silence again. I stuck another shell up the magazine of my shotgun and waited.

Duc appeared. 'First Platoon, come with me.' He wore plain fatigues, no flak jacket, and a black head scarf instead of a helmet or cap. He didn't carry a rifle but he had a .45 in his hand, the hammer back and the safety on.

We followed Duc into an alley and behind us we heard the other platoons moving out to take up their positions, guided by

Duc's team. I wondered whether there was any possibility we could take them by surprise. Surely somebody would have tipped them. With luck, there'd be nobody there. Ghosts wouldn't try to shoot it out with a whole company of MPs. But they might booby-trap their hideout. The thought of what a single claymore mine could do to us made my stomach lurch with fear. A man is very alone with his thoughts in such a situation.

We came out of the alley, passed between a couple of boat sheds and stood on the muddy bank of the river. The air was rank with the fecund river smell. I looked out across the water, trying to spot the river patrol. I saw the lights of some good-sized vessels and the surface sparkling with reflected glitter from lights on the other side, but if the boats were there they were blacked out, waiting for the signal to come in.

We walked along the bank, our boots making no sound in the mud. I retained enough professional interest to feel proud of my men. Even the newbies were carrying it off like vets. Then Duc held up a hand and we halted.

We stood beneath the pilings of a small wharf. It extended maybe twenty yards into the river, adding its creosote smell to all the rest. Its other end was attached to a hulking wooden warehouse that looked like it had been old when the French arrived. Very slowly, Duc climbed the slippery bank, keeping in the shadows of the wharf, his pistol held close against his hip. McKay followed him, then me and the rest, maintaining a few yards of interval between us to keep from tangling each other up and minimizing the casualties should hostile fire erupt unexpectedly. The quiet and the tension magnified even the tiniest sounds we made – the unavoidable rustlings of cloth and the shufflings of bootsoles on soft dirt.

We stopped again. We were at the top of the slope. There was a narrow alley between the warehouse and a similar building next to it. I came up even with Duc and McKay, straining my eyes into the dark alley to see why we had stopped. Then I caught a tiny orange glow from the alley midway along the warehouse's wall. Somebody was smoking a cigarette. They had posted a lookout. For the first time, I thought we might really catch them by surprise.

Duc began to step into the alley, cautiously and soundlessly as a cat. We did our best to emulate him. I was sure the lookout would see or hear us. He wasn't asleep after all. Then

I began to make out the dim figure in the light of the cigarette tip and I saw that he was facing the other way, toward the landward end of the alley. Of course. Nobody expected trouble to come from the river side.

Duc was less than a yard away when the lookout sensed something and whirled. His eyes almost crossed when he saw the muzzle of Duc's pistol trained an inch from his face, just above the bridge of his nose. There was a tiny click as Duc slipped the thumb safety. It was a Vietnamese kid, maybe thirteen or fourteen years old. The cigarette dropped from his fingers and I thought he was going to faint. Duc took a step forward and the kid took a step back.

'It is all yours,' Duc whispered as he marched the boy backward toward the mouth of the alley.

'This's it,' McKay said tightly. We were standing in front of a doorway that opened onto the alley. There was no door, just a heavy blackout curtain. There were no windows on this side of the building, no light leaking through the boards. All was black.

If there was a claymore inside, we were all dead. A claymore is a slab of plastic explosive the size of a hardcover book, bowed into a slight curve. The convex face is embedded with hundreds of steel balls and when the thing is set off the balls shred anyone standing within seventy-five feet. It is detonated remotely by an observer, or it can be hooked to a tripwire or another booby-trap device. It would be like standing inside a shotgun barrel when somebody pulled the trigger.

I didn't think the kid would have been there if they were setting up a claymore ambush, but this was a place where crazy things happened all the time.

'Let's go,' McKay whispered. Cautiously, he pushed the curtain aside with the muzzle of his M-16. Still no light. We crept through Indian-style, stepping high, coming down on the sides of our bootsoles and rolling the rest of the foot down. It looks absurd but it's quiet.

When everyone was inside we paused. It was dark but we could hear heavy, stertorous breathing. 'What the fuck?' somebody whispered.

'Shh!' McKay tiptoed to the source of the noise. The room seemed to be full of bales of something or other wrapped in burlap. Cautiously, I turned on my flashlight, just for a moment. A man lay on top of some of the bales, unconscious.

Next to his limp hand was a syringe, a bent spoon and a battered Zippo. I doused the flash.

'Come on,' McKay said. Using only brief flashes, we found a stairway that led down into some sort of cellar. From the top of the stair we could hear heavily muffled raucous voices.

'Jackpot,' McKay said, and I could hear the smile in his voice. 'Okay, dudes. It's party time.'

There were three more blackout curtains on the stair, and as we passed through each one the noise grew louder. We pushed the last curtain aside and light spilled through. It wasn't bright, but after the gloom we'd come through it was startling. For a few seconds we paused, letting our eyes adjust and scanning the scene.

The doorway opened on to a landing maybe six feet deep and a dozen feet wide. The landing stood about ten feet above a pitlike floor with stairs leading down to it from each side. The main room was at least forty feet long with heavy vertical timbers supporting the floor above. Smaller rooms opened off the main one. The main room was illuminated by drop lights using low-wattage bulbs, but brighter lights came from the side rooms where hissing Coleman lanterns burned. That was good, because the Colemans would be harder to extinguish than the electric lights.

There were forty or fifty men in sight, mostly grouped around tables. Tables and floor were littered with beer and liquor bottles. The marijuana smoke was so dense you could get high from a sniff. Most of the men were round-eyes but there were a few Asians. There were women too – all Asian, naturally. Dope packets littered the tables and men were shooting up as casually as if they were lighting up cigarettes. There were card games going on and deals were being cut. Stacks of currency changed hands, goods were being sold and traded, lots of vociferous, Asian-style bargaining filling the air. The men were dressed in uniform and pieces of uniform and civvies, Filipino and Hawaiian shirts seeming to be favored. Nobody was looking our way.

Against a far wall I saw a tall, graying man standing with his back to me, leaning over a table and yelling at somebody on the other side. Something about the little scene caught my eye, but just then McKay bulled through. I followed out on to the landing and the rest poured through behind us, taking both sets of stairs down into the pit.

'Hands up, assholes!' McKay bellowed. 'You're busted!'

For a moment things froze, the ghosts and their associates unable for a while to comprehend what had descended upon them. Then a stratosphere-cruising junkie loosed a shrill giggle and all hell broke loose good and proper. Women screamed, men shouted, people began to bolt. I figured that they'd have plenty of escape routes, and that was all right with me. Let the guys outside bag them. I was no glory hound.

We were screaming too; the usual 'Hands up!' and 'Freeze!' and 'Drop it, motherfucker!', plus a lot of incoherent yelling and waving of weapons to keep them confused and scared.

Then the lights went out and the first shot was fired. It was a pistol, so it wasn't one of us. The pit went dim but the glare from the Colemans came in from all sides, the light jerking crazily as people ran back and forth before the doors setting the lanterns swinging. Muzzle flashes added their unearthly strobe effect and our flashlights came on, making us look like robots from outer space, the beams caught by the heavy smoke.

I was still standing atop the landing, pressed against the waist-high railing. In the fantastic light I saw the graying man jump aside, the flash of something that might have been a weapon coming from his right hand. I lined up the shotgun, then froze as I saw the man sitting at the other side of the table. It was Martin Starr, his eyes straight on mine, smiling the way he had during the Tet fight. Then his hand came up with a big revolver and I fired over the heads of the frantic crowd below, seeing wood splinters fly from the table. Then a tall black man, wearing jeans and a Filipino shirt, grabbed Starr's shoulder and jerked him through a door and into one of the side rooms.

The Colemans were going out one by one. I heard a bullet hit a flak jacket with the sound of a boxing glove smacking into a heavy bag. The man beside me cursed and went down. I pulled the pin from an illumination grenade and tossed it into the center of the floor. It popped and fizzed in midair, then the blinding magnesium glare increased the chaos. McKay tossed one, and then another, into the corners of the room. Bullets were cracking around in all directions. I heard men and women scream as they were hit.

I saw a crazed drug freak jump on to an MP's back and try to cut his throat with a knife, but the high collar of his flak

141

jacket saved him long enough for a buddy to blow the loon off him with a twelve-gauge. Two MPs went down when fire came from a side room. Instantly, their squadmates hosed the room with automatic fire. There was a flat bang and whoosh as Coleman fuel exploded and flames burst from the room amid screams. Men and maybe some women ran out with their clothes on fire. The illumination grenades were igniting fires in other spots.

'Pick up the wounded and haul ass!' McKay shouted. Those of us still on the landing rushed into the pit to pick up our buddies. There weren't many of the ghosts and their friends left in the pit. Those that were mostly lay on the floor, writhing and screaming, some of them on fire. The luckier ones were already dead. Blood and bottles and shell casings made the floor treacherous. I saw that our wounded were all being evacuated and headed for one of the side doors.

'Haul ass!' McKay yelled again. 'It's crispy critters time in this place! Let the boys outside have the rest of 'em. Gitcher ass outside now! *Didi mau! Didi mau!*' Then he caught sight of me. 'Treloar! Where the fuck you goin'?'

I didn't turn around. 'Gotta talk to a man over here. Be with you in a minute.'

'Get back here, you dumb fuck!'

But I wasn't paying any attention. After those ferocious moments of insane brutality, I was filled with a sudden, inexplicable serenity. I felt like nothing could touch me; like Queen under the racetrack. I felt wonderfully alive and good, as if I were in exactly the right place at exactly the right time, doing exactly what I had to do. I guess it was a state of grace.

Heat from the flames bit through the greasepaint and tightened the skin of my face. The fire was using up the oxygen fast and making it hard to breathe. I passed through the doorway and found a litter of bodies. I saw an old Chinese man, his pockets stuffed with greenbacks and a bullet through his heart. A few feet past him was a beautiful young woman in a green silk *ao dai*, dead from something that didn't leave any visible wound. A crew-cut young blond guy sat at a card table with a butcher knife stuck through his chest. Somebody had taken advantage of the confusion to settle a personal score. Another door led to a passageway and at its end I saw two tall men supporting a smaller one between them. One of them sensed me and pushed the other two through as he whirled, a .45 coming up in his fist.

I fired and he spun around, a massive, bloody wound in his thigh. He still got a round off but it smacked into a beam over my head. I ran up to him, jacking another round into the chamber. He was a thin black guy and he dropped the gun, spreading pale spidery fingers before him as if they could stop buckshot.

'I give up! I surrender, man!' My face must have been unearthly, because now he looked really scared. I had the big muzzle straight on his face and my finger was tight on the trigger. 'Hey, I said I surrender! *Chieu hoi*, motherfucker, *chieu hoi!*'

I stepped over him, intent on Starr. He screamed as a big flame licked into the passageway. I paused, then turned around and grabbed his collar and started dragging him along the passageway. I heard guns firing from somewhere and then we were at a low doorway that let out on to a truck loading dock. The scene outside was a milling zoo almost as wild as the mêlée in the pit.

Searchlights swept everywhere, like some movie premiere in hell. People were running to escape, shooting and being shot, clubbed, cuffed, held huddling at gunpoint. Flames were jetting from the old warehouse and the dock was getting hot under my feet. From the other side I heard the slow chug of heavy machine-guns cutting loose. That would be the boats on the river. Maybe they were firing at people in the water, or someone was trying to escape by boat.

A knot of MPs rushed over to me, clubbing their way through the terrified mob with their gun butts. The shooting had tapered off, but not the yelling, crying and wailing. The MPs were the remnants of my platoon.

'Come away from there, dipshit!' McKay called. I drew up to him and he pointed at the man I was dragging. 'You stayed down there for that?'

I looked. The guy was going into shock, but he had enough sense to keep his hands clamped around his skinny, ruined thigh. You can bleed to death quick from a severed femoral artery. A medic came over and began tying a tourniquet around the shattered leg.

'Oh,' I said woozily. 'Almost forgot about him. No, I was

chasing Martin Starr. Saw him down there. Think I wounded him.'

Somebody stuck a cigarette between my lips and lit it. 'Shit!' one of the newbies said. 'There ain't no Martin Starr. Fucker's just a legend.'

I was beginning to wonder myself. The light had been uncertain, I'd been keyed up, the distance had been extreme. Was it Starr? I hated to think I'd let him get away twice.

'Yeah,' I said, 'maybe he is.'

We trudged through the herded prisoners, the ones still alive and unwounded now on their knees with their hands on top of their heads. A clutch of officers stood around a jeep and they didn't look happy.

'All of my men are out now,' McKay reported.

The company CO nodded curtly, then turned back to Colonel Tapia. 'Goddamn! I have a dozen wounded and some of them may not make it! We should've thrown a cordon around the place and torched it! Shot 'em as they ran out.'

'I agree,' Tapia said. 'Sending a platoon in was unnecessary.' He sighed. 'Too late to change our tactics now. I never could've got permission for an operation like that anyway.'

'Colonel,' his XO said, 'what the hell are we gonna do with all these civilians?'

'Give them to Captain Nguyen. He can kill them or let them go for all I care. I just want the Americans.'

'Fire trucks on their way,' a radioman reported.

'The goddamn reporters won't be far behind. Let's get these people in the trucks and get them out of here. Captain,' Tapia turned to Schultz, 'while this is a secret operation, you and your men will receive commendations for tonight's work. Congratulations on a job well done.' Tapia walked off with his flunkies and Schultz turned to us.

'He won't be writing the next-of-kin letters. You did a good job, men. Mount up and let's get the hell out of here.'

Much later I heard that the operation had been turned into a raid on Saigon's VC headquarters. There were so many commendations and decorations handed around you'd have thought that we took North Vietnam single-handed. I never learned what had happened to the ghosts we captured alive. Or the civilians, either, for that matter. Starr was never caught.

Not that I cared. By that time I was married and Rose and

I were departing for the States. My year was up and I was leaving Vietnam and Martin Starr behind for good.

Or so I thought.

Chapter Eleven

Duc's funeral was held in a parish church the size of a small cathedral. It was packed with mourners, most of them Vietnamese, with a sprinkling of others. I looked them over, wondering if Tran Van Loan and Ngo Pham and the other gang leaders were there. It wasn't unlikely. It wasn't even necessarily hypocritical, given the traditions of their culture. Even if they were Buddhist or Confucian or Cao Dai, like the bulk of the population, they might pay their respects. In South Asia spirits and ancestors often rate higher than the living.

I was in the pews reserved for the family, of which a respectable number were present. Duc and Rose had been alone among their siblings to survive the war. Rose and I had never had children, but Duc and Anne had done their duty by the ancestors. Their two sons and four daughters were there, along with a small crowd of grandchildren. There were also miscellaneous uncles and aunts and cousins who had managed to escape Vietnam after the collapse of the Saigon government. Once established here, Duc, using his old contacts, had scoured Hong Kong and Taiwan and Singapore and other places to locate them and bring them to the States.

I was touched that they all regarded me as a full member of the family, even though they hadn't seen much of me in recent years. As the sponsor who had been responsible for bringing Duc and Anne and their kids to the States in the first place, I was regarded as something of a patron, due a special respect.

The service provided the expected comfort for the bereaved. Father Padilla spoke eloquently of the tragedy of a life cut short by senseless violence. The smell of flowers was heavy in the air. As always, there seemed to me something unfinished in the service, something left undone. It's because I was raised in a Catholic parochial school in the pre-Vatican II days. Somehow, a Catholic service never seems right to me without the old Latin liturgy.

Afterward the motorcade wound its way to the beautifully

situated cemetery in the San Rafael Hills, where Duc was buried next to his sister. He was the second of his family to be buried in American soil, and certainly not the last.

After the brief graveside ceremony I went to stand by Rose's grave for a while. Silently, I told her about the many strange turns my life had taken in recent years, although I was sure she knew already. I knew perfectly well that Rose wasn't down there beneath the headstone. A grave isn't a resting place for the dead. It's a shrine where the living can come from time to time to get back in touch. I've always liked the way Asians go to cemeteries to give the ancestors periodic reports on how the family is doing, and the way Mexicans hold festivals in graveyards on the Day of the Dead so the living and the dead can celebrate together.

I was standing there, all but oblivious to my surroundings, when I felt the lightest of touches on my arm. I looked down and saw that it was Anne, Duc's widow. She was a tiny woman, wearing a black dress and hat. In Vietnam she would have worn white, but she and the others had adopted the local mourning custom.

'I am sorry to disturb you, Gabriel, but I must go now. Later on, after the others have left, we must talk.'

I took both her hands in mine. 'Certainly. But I don't want to burden you at a time like this. Maybe later on . . .'

'No,' she said firmly. 'This evening, after the callers have left.'

'I'll be there,' I told her.

She nodded, then she bowed her head toward Rose's grave and said a few words. She spoke Vietnamese in a voice so low that I could barely hear her, and all I caught was the word for 'sister'.

In the evening I went back to the house in Eagle Rock. There were still some callers there, so I visited for a while with Duc's children and their wives and husbands. I'd become an exotic figure to them, somehow: the drunk ex-cop who'd sobered up and become a private eye. They all watched too much television, too.

After a while Margaret came to me. 'Mother wants to talk with you.'

I followed her to a small deck that jutted from the back of the house, overlooking a little arroyo full of tangled growth.

This was one of those neighborhoods where the raccoons and coyotes come down from the hills to raid the garbage cans. Most people don't realize that the Los Angeles complex is on the edge of a wilderness. The deck was framed on two sides by a wooden trellis overgrown with morning glory and trumpet vine. Pots of begonia blazed along the steps leading down to the garage. The sun was almost down. In the far distance I could just make out the skyline of the downtown area through the haze.

Anne sat at a little table with a cup of tea before her. Another steamed on a fragile saucer and I took the only other chair. For a while neither of us said anything.

'This was our favorite place,' she said at last. 'In the evenings, after he came home from work, Duc and I would sit here and watch the sun go down. The air here is glorious in the evenings.'

'Anne, I'm sorry,' I said, my throat closing on the words. 'I thought I was taking you away from the war.'

She looked at me sharply. 'Gabriel, don't talk like a fool. For days I have been hearing condolences. Some were heartfelt, some were not. But no one suggested we made a mistake in coming here. If we had stayed at home Duc would probably have been executed by the Communists. The best we could have hoped for would have been a "re-education" camp. From what I have heard, those were just death camps. In Hong Kong or the Philippines or the rest of Asia? We would have been refugees, no better than beggars. I remember the refugee camps too well. We would have watched our children die of hunger and disease.'

She placed a tiny hand atop mine. 'We have had twenty wonderful years here. Duc created a successful business. Our children have enjoyed a first-rate education. In the old days they would have had to travel to France for that, and we never could have afforded it. No, what you and Rose did for us we can never repay.'

I didn't know how to reply to that, so I sipped at my tea to cover my confusion.

'But I did not ask you here to talk about that. I want to tell you that Duc's murder was not some random act. It was deliberate, and there are men who must not be allowed to go free and enjoy their profits after they have murdered my husband.'

This much I knew already, but you don't burden informants with your own knowledge and suspicions. That only taints what they have to tell you. You let them give you the story in their own words.

'Tell me about it, Anne.' I took another sip of tea. There was no rush.

She looked out across the arroyo, into the vast urban basin below, back across the years.

'When we came out of Hong Kong to live with you and Rose, there were only a handful of Vietnamese here. But the trickle of refugees turned into a flood as people here became established and worked to bring their families across. We helped each other and that was good. Other things were not so good. It was not just the best people who came here. Some were criminals and they did not change just because they had changed nations. And the young people – the ones who arrived as small children or were born here – some of them began to imitate the gangs they saw all around them; a great disgrace. But of course you saw much of this when you were a police officer.'

'I did,' I acknowledged. 'But it's what you see in any big immigrant community. It was the same with the Chinese in Cholon.'

She looked down at her hands. 'It is not just the lowest people. I am ashamed to admit it, but some of the very worst men are former officers of the Army of the Republic of Vietnam. They are violent, brutal men. In the war they grew accustomed to treating people like cattle, worse than cattle. They thought nothing of beating and killing villagers as if they were not even human beings.'

'I remember how it was.'

'When they came here, these men made much of being war heroes. They formed their own businesses and protective associations. They found that being "heroes" gave them an advantage in getting loans and favors from the government. Soon they began preying on the community – extortion, protection money – they have many ways of making it appear legitimate. They call it contributions to their fraternal societies and they have other covers, but it is just . . . What do you call it when criminals run and loot legitimate business for their own profit?'

'Racketeering?'

'That is it. At first some of them tried to get Duc to join them, but he would have nothing to do with them. You understand, he did belong to other veterans' and business-men's groups, but not with these thugs.'

She paused when Margaret came out from the kitchen with a fresh pot of tea. She refilled the cups and left without a word. Anne was silent for a while and I didn't prod her.

'Duc never spoke to the children of these matters. He wanted them to have a new life here, not to relive the past and its failures. But he told me about it, and about other things that troubled him. He would tell me these things out here in the evenings, as I am telling you about them now. He never went to the police, because he knew it would do no good. These bad men are subtle and the police have worse to deal with every day.'

It was pretty much what young Ngia Minh had said, though Anne would never offend me by admitting that she was as mistrustful of the American authorities as other immigrants from despotic regimes.

'A few months ago things grew much worse and Duc grew very worried. He said some new men were moving in from Asia: from Hong Kong and Taiwan, from Singapore and other places, and there were some Saigonese with them. They were making deals with the immigrant gangs. The Hanoi government has made peace with America and trade is beginning to start. These Saigonese want local people to deal with and they want property in the heart of the Vietnamese community, where they will be insulated from the authorities. Duc knew that these people would be involved in far worse things than extortion and . . . and racketeering.'

'That would be a pretty safe bet,' I said.

'Well . . .' She massaged one hand with the other, as if reluctant to go into the next part. 'Well, about two years ago, Duc sold some property to a man named Tran Van Loan. Two of the places were for ordinary use, just car lots. Tran Van Loan is a car dealer. Then Tran wanted a truck garage and Duc agreed to that. Then, a few months ago, Tran and another man, Ngo Pham, approached him about another place he had acquired, a big warehousing and shipping facility in San Pedro, next to the docks. I do not think I have to tell you what that meant.'

'Smuggling. Big-scale smuggling.'

'Exactly. For a while Duc put them off, tried to stall. But they became impatient, more demanding. They began to threaten. Then they brought two of the men from Saigon to pressure him.

'My husband looked at who these men were and the places they linked together, and he knew that half the drugs in Asia would be coming through that facility. And the illegal immigrants. You've seen how those people get shipped here?'

'I've seen the pictures on the news,' I answered.

She snorted delicately. 'I think those have been some of the luckier ones. It is no better than a slave trade. People mortgage their lives and the lives of their children for passage on a hell-ship and the life of a fugitive in this country.'

She paused again and I thought about the desperation of people who could even consider taking such a step. 'Did he sell it?'

'He was going to. He hated even to consider it, but the threat these men represented was very great. You see, as long as it was just the local Vietnamese gangsters, my husband told himself that he could protect himself and his family. He never stopped thinking of himself as a soldier, a warrior. I told him he was being foolish. They had guns and many men. He said that he had a gun too, and he was worth all their men put together.'

Tears spilled down her cheeks, but her mouth quirked up at the corners. 'What a man he was. And what a fool.'

'I'll agree with the first part. So why didn't he just sell them the property and be done with it? Nobody could fault him for it. He wouldn't be responsible for the uses they put the facilities to. That's a job for the Coast Guard and for Customs and Immigration and half a dozen other agencies.'

'This time was very different. They didn't just want him to sell them property. They wanted him to go into partnership. And he knew what the next step would be. They would want to be partners in his real estate business.' The tears had stopped and she levelled her eyes at me. 'You see, these people didn't want merely to deal with him. They wanted to *own* him, just as they want to own everybody they touch. He would become a part of them and he knew that he would be one of the first to die when the war began.'

'The war?'

152

'He knew there would be one. There would have to be. Criminals from Hong Kong and Singapore and Taiwan, maybe from Korea, Cambodia, Thailand, mainland China, even Burma? All of these people *co-operating*? He knew it could only be temporary, until each could consolidate a position here, taking advantage of the opening up of trade, the barriers coming down. Then they would begin to fight among themselves, forming alliances, breaking them, until one dominates or even controls everything. And you know who dies in such wars. It is never the big ones. It would be people like Duc Nguyen. And they do not spare the families, either.'

'So what did he do?'

'He refused to be in business with them. He showed the world a stone face, but he was truly frightened. He made enquiries about selling his business; he looked into places we could move to, away from the West Coast. Away from *any* coast. But they did not allow him that time. He should have pretended to co-operate, to buy himself time. But they made him angry with their arrogant demands, and he drove them from his office.'

She blinked back tears and stared off across the distance. 'They could not allow such defiance, such loss of face. They killed him.'

'Was there no one he could go to?'

'There might have been, if he had had time. Not here, not any more.'

That sent a cold jolt down my spine.

'But Duc still had friends back in Vietnam. One way and another, over the years, he kept in contact with them, the ones who survived the re-education camps. They have to stay low and show a humble face to the government, but they are not without power in Saigon. Duc thought there was a chance that he could cut off the head of this snake, and its tail here in California would die.'

'Do you think it would have worked?'

'I thought he was being unrealistic,' she gave me the level look again, 'but soldiers of lost wars are dreamers.'

I sighed. I could feel it coming down on me. 'Who are these men in Saigon?'

She nodded, knowing she had what she wanted. 'There is one who counts: Nguyen Chi Thanh. You remember the name?' In Vietnamese fashion, she'd used the family name first.

'He was chief of police for Cholon when I was there. I heard he became chief of all the police in Saigon just before the fall. Is he a relative?'

'Perhaps a thousand years ago. There are at least a million Nguyens in Vietnam. Nguyen Chi Thanh has a café called the Apple Orchard. It's somewhere near the city center. He is a leader of the . . . I suppose you would call it the underground; a group of men who have lived through the changes and have not given up hope.' For a moment that almost-smile appeared on her lips again. 'How strange it is. Over there, *they* are the criminals, more dangerous to the government than mere smugglers and gangsters.'

'Anne, did Duc ever mention "ghosts" to you? Or someone called something like "the big ghost"?'

'I remember that he said there is a gang in Saigon that call themselves "ghosts". I do not remember a "big ghost".'

'Did he say if these ghosts are Americans? Deserters from the war?'

She looked puzzled. 'No. Surely there cannot be any of those men left alive.'

'That's what I thought,' I told her.

Connie found me by the swimming pool. I had gone out for a half-hearted run but had been in such mental turmoil that I'd almost been run over twice. In belated self-preservation I'd gone back to the guest house and sat down to brood.

'The limo's a rental,' she said disgustedly. 'It's owned by Elite Wheels. The driver was a licensed chauffeur named Archie Dupre. Ring any bells?'

I thought about it, or tried to. 'Nope.'

She sat down. She was glowing slightly and looked more pumped than usual, obviously just back from a workout. 'Anyway, our man Archie checked out the limo on a company credit card belonging to Southeast Consolidated Investors. Sound vague enough for you?'

I shrugged.

She snapped her fingers just beneath my nose. 'Hey, Treloar! You there? Am I just talking to myself?'

I shook my head. 'Sorry. I'm just . . . Southeast Consolidated Investors, huh? Could be anything. Could be . . .' I trailed off.

Now she looked concerned. 'Look, Gabe, I know you spent

the day at a funeral, but you said yourself you hadn't seen that family in years.'

'It's not that. Not entirely, anyway. I don't want to talk about it.'

'Sure you do.' She stood up and grabbed my hand. 'Come on. We're gonna take a little drive.'

I stayed where I was. 'I'm not in the mood.'

'Crap. What've you got to do here? Sit around and sulk and think about going back to the bottle?'

'Shut up!'

'You think I don't know the signs? Come on, Treloar. I'm gonna make you feel lots better.'

I let her drag me up, not because I wanted to go with her, but because I lacked any will to resist. She tugged me along to her car and shoved me into the passenger seat.

'Where are we going?' I asked as we rolled down into the city.

'The one and only place for a guy in your condition. I mean, at this stage it's the bottle or suck on a gun barrel or this. You'll like this better, I promise.'

'Where was it you said you got your degree in psychology? Was it the Sorbonne or Heidelberg?'

'Houston PD. You already tried to drink yourself to death, didn't you?'

I could feel my whole body clenching like a fist. 'You've checked up on me. You know I did.'

She looked across at me without pity or sympathy, which was a good thing because I'd have punched her if she had, and then we'd probably both have ended up as traffic fatalities. 'As a matter of fact, I haven't. You're just easy to read. You ever try the other? I mean, if you did, you must've missed.'

'I used to think about it a lot. Tried it other ways, usually in a car, like my dad. I always chickened out. Anyway, I got over it. I'm not suicidal now, just pissed off.'

'That much I figured out.'

'My sister-in-law just laid a hell of an obligation on me.'

'How?'

'It's an Asian thing. You wouldn't understand.'

'Shit,' she muttered. 'Treloar, I wish you wouldn't try to tell me what I can and can't understand. Here we are.' We pulled up in front of a big, glass-fronted gym. The interior was brightly lit, the action inside looking like a movie running without sound.

'A gym? Is this your gym? What do you want me to do, lift weights?'

'Nah. Come on, I'll show you.' She slid out of the car and I did the same, mystified.

The woman behind the little counter at the door looked surprised. She had white-bleached hair standing in a ridge along her scalp like a cockatoo's crest, and a set of muscles that made Connie look anorexic. She wore glasses with '50s-style pointy frames and had a volume of Proust open on the table in front of her.

'Back already? You just left.'

'My friend here needs a workout. Charge it to my account.'

'You got it.'

'Come along, Gabe.'

I followed her through the long, iron-clanking room. It was past 11.00 p.m. and the place was full. There are gyms in LA that stay open twenty-four hours a day. The crowd was fairly representative: a few confirmed narcissists who were into competitive body building; some middle-aged crazies striving to regain their lost youth and suffering mightily. Most seemed to be like Connie – mildly obsessed sweat junkies.

At the rear of the gym was an area carpeted by thick mats. The back wall was lined with mirrors and a few professionals were in front of them, stripped to thong bikinis, male and female, practising their posing routines. It was difficult to believe that real people could look like that, but then they achieved it by renouncing every other human activity.

Some other people were on the mats doing stretching exercises, about to go out and wrestle with the iron or else winding down from their workouts.

In one corner were a couple of old boxer's standbys: a speed bag and a heavy bag. Connie walked up to the heavy bag and gave it a punch. It was a good punch, powered from her rear heel, her fist starting at her right hip, her hand twisting around at the last instant, her knuckles connecting at waist height. She could have cracked a man's ribs with a punch like that.

'Ever work out on a heavy bag?' she asked.

'A long time ago.' When I was a rookie patrolman I had tried my hand at boxing; went into a few matches representing my division as a light-heavy. I quickly found out I had no future in boxing. I had the size, the speed and the moves, but I lacked the savage killer instinct a champion boxer needs. Above all, I didn't like to get hit.

She hit the bag again. The smack echoed through the gym, but the bag barely moved. It was about four feet long and maybe sixteen inches thick.

'There's about two hundred pounds of leather scraps in this,' she said. 'It'll absorb a lot of punishment. Give some back, too.' She went to a rack and picked up a pair of gloves and tossed them to me. 'So punish it.'

I weighed the gloves in my hand. They weren't boxing gloves, more like fingerless work gloves of extra-thick leather. I drew them on and pulled the wrist-thongs tight. They were stiff with somebody else's sweat.

'Okay,' I said. 'I'll humor you.'

I stepped up to the bag and gave it a tentative punch. It barely moved on its suspension chain. I tried a few more easy punches with each hand, felt my wrists warming up, and began to hit harder. As my arms and shoulders began to pump up with blood I tried a little footwork to go along with the arm exercise. Pretty soon the moves started to come back to me and I threw in combinations, hitting harder as I got into it, the rhythmic smack of my gloved fists on the thick vinyl shocking me all the way to the shoulders and strangely satisfying.

I started to breathe hard and to sweat, my attention narrowed, magnifying the bag in my vision. I focused intently on the spot I was hitting, trying to drive my fists right through it. I felt my frustration and anger boiling up my spine and I struck even harder, seeing the bag actually bend in the middle with each blow. My waist started to ache from the way I was twisting my body from the hips, throwing extra power into my punches.

My breath whistled in my nostrils and my shoulders burned. All I could see was the impact point on the bag, surrounded by a vibrating circle of light. I was building up an oxygen debt that was charging me compound interest, but all I cared about was hitting the bag, working out a rage I had been unaware was in me, punishing the bag as if it had inflicted all my demons upon me. God, but it felt good.

Then I could hear only a loud ringing in my ears. The bag

was no longer in front of me, only a wilderness of dark spots and flashing lights. I didn't seem to have any body. Slowly, my vision cleared and the ringing resolved itself into muttering voices. I was sitting on the mat, utterly drained, too weak to move. The woman with the cockatoo hair drifted into my vision, prodding the heavy bag.

'I think he killed it,' she announced. A small circle of people stood around looking concerned.

'He's okay,' Connie said from somewhere outside my peripheral vision. 'Just had to work some things out.' They wandered off to their weights and machines. Then she was squatting by me, peeling off the soaked gloves. My hands were so swollen that she had to tug hard to get them off. When they came away my knuckles were smeared with blood.

'Like I said, the heavy bag punishes you right back.' She looked up. 'Megan, help me get him on his feet.'

The cockatoo woman stooped and grabbed me under an arm. 'Are you sure he'll be all right? He isn't on maybe like angel dust or something?'

'No, just a little tired, that's all,' Connie said, taking my other arm. They hoisted me easily, but I was shocked at how wobbly my legs were.

'I guess I'm a little out of shape,' I said, even my voice shaky. 'Ten minutes on the heavy bag never made me pass out before.'

The woman named Megan laughed a big, country-girl laugh. 'Connie, you sure he's not on something?' Then, to me: 'Buddy, you been pounding the shit outta that bag for forty-five straight minutes, gruntin' and snortin' like a bull in a pasture full of cows. I was about ready to call the cops but Connie said you'd drop pretty soon.'

'Help me get him out to my car,' Connie said. By the time we'd reached the front door I could have been walking on my own, but it had been a long time since I'd had my arms around two women at once, even if they were pretty strange specimens. I knew then that my mood was lightening. They maneuvered me into the passenger seat.

'He's gonna get your car all bloody and sweaty,' Megan said. 'You want some towels?'

'No, it's a company car. My boss can always buy a new one. Thanks, Megan.'

''Night, hon.' She swung back into the gym, the spread of

her back like the hood of an angry cobra.

I laughed weakly. 'You have unusual friends.'

She put the car in reverse and backed into the street. 'I never went in for the suburban kaffeeklatsch housewife type.'

I almost dozed off as we drove back to Queen's estate. When we arrived I managed to get out under my own steam, waving off Connie's attempts to help.

'I'm going to take a shower,' she announced. 'You go take a swim and try not to drown. Then we'll talk.'

Tired as I was the pool seemed awfully attractive. I stripped off and plunged in. The cool water was wonderfully rejuvenating, even if my lacerated hands stung like hell. I swam a few laps and then soaked for a while. I sort of hoped Connie would come out and join me but she didn't.

I climbed from the pool and towelled off, then went back into the guest house, showered the chlorine off and got dressed. By the time I returned to the living room Connie was sitting on a couch at a coffee table, dressed in a fleecy jumpsuit. She'd made a pitcher of something colorless and full of small ice cubes. She poured an oversized glass full and handed it to me.

'Here, you're probably dehydrated. This'll help.'

I took it and sipped. It was some sort of designer water with a little lime juice. I gulped down half the glass and sat opposite her.

'How're you feeling?' she asked.

'Sore. Hands hurt like hell.'

She nodded. 'That's nothing compared to how you're going to feel tomorrow. Want to tell me about it now?'

'I'll try. I don't know if it'll make much sense to you.'

'Try me.'

I told her about the funeral, and about my conversation with Anne that evening. 'You see, she wants revenge for what happened to her husband. And I'm the one to do it, because in a sense she holds me partly responsible for Duc's death.'

'Okay, you lost me there.'

I swirled the ice in my glass. 'I don't want to lay my whole history on you all at once. Maybe, if you want to hear it, I'll give you the details someday. Basically, what happened was this: I was a hotshot young cop getting commendations and making promotion fast. Then Rose died of ovarian cancer. I became a drunk cop. As a result I got Murray, my partner, killed. I was booted off the force. This took years, but those are the basic facts.'

'Got you so far.'

'The way Anne sees it, I failed my wife's family when I became a drunk and lost my position. I'd have had almost twenty-five years on the force. I'd probably be a lieutenant, maybe a captain by now. I might even be higher than that. I was good at the work and I kept earning college credits; I was qualified for the top positions.'

'Well, what about it?'

'Don't you see? Those bastards would never have dared to move on Duc if he'd had connections like that. As far as Anne's concerned, I left the family without protection.'

'But your wife would still have died years ago,' she said.

'That wouldn't make any difference as far as they're concerned. Not even if I'd remarried.'

'I thought Asians believed in fate and karma and kismet and all that stuff.'

'That's Hindus and Islamics. Not Buddhists and Confucianists and Daoists, and not Vietnamese Catholics, either.' I slumped in the chair, a numb lassitude seeping through me.

'Gabe, you lost your connection to these people years ago, whatever they may think. They have no real claim on you, certainly not to the point of demanding blood vengeance. This is America.'

'Maybe it's another symptom of the end of history as we know it. Whatever it is, I feel responsible whether it makes sense or not. My parents died years ago, I was an only child and the family back in Ohio was never more than nuclear. I guess the Nguyens are the closest thing to a family I have left. I can't help feeling that I let them down, and Anne knows which buttons to push.'

'She knows you suffer from an overdeveloped sense of responsibility. She and Rose must've had a lot of little heart-to-hearts concerning you.'

'Anyway, I'm still not satisfied that Duc's death and Queen's problem aren't tied together somehow. We've got Saigon racket guys and ghosts . . .'

'We don't know that. It's tempting, I admit, but that makes it all the more suspect as far as I'm concerned. That's not relevant here, though. What bothers me is this personal angle.

It's the kind of thing that can confuse your thinking; make you draw conclusions that aren't there.'

'You think I don't know that?'

Chapter Twelve

The next morning I felt as if I'd been run over by a truck, but that was only upon first awakening. Once I got up it was entirely different. Then I felt as if a whole freight train had rolled over me. I'm not ordinarily a masochist, but on some strange level it felt good. A few laps to work out the stiffness and a hot shower to further relax the muscles, and I felt almost ready to face the day. On the first try I dropped a glass of orange juice because my hand wouldn't close properly, but I learned to compensate.

'I've been all over the phone connection,' Connie reported as I drank the juice. 'I even climbed the pole. No sign of a bug, but that doesn't mean there wasn't one on it the day before yesterday.'

'Long as it's safe now,' I said, picking up the phone and awkwardly dialing Lowry's number. As I did this an errant thought came to me and while I waited for the call to go through I said, 'Has it ever occurred to you that dial telephones have been a thing of the past for years, but we still say we "dial" a number? Why is that?'

'God, that's such a profound question. I wouldn't know how to begin to address it.'

'We still lack a satisfactory verb. It just doesn't sound right to say you punched a number or poked a number. Maybe someday . . .'

'Lowry here.'

'This is Gabe Treloar. I'm wondering if you can check out someone for me. It's a licensed chauffeur named Archie Dupre, spelled D-U-P-R-E.' I gave him the license number Connie had supplied me.

'Is this relevant to the Duc Nguyen case?'

I described for him the little scene outside Duc's house. 'It may be nothing, maybe he's just some jerk I busted years ago, but it feels wrong. Will you see if he has a record?'

'Sure. I have a few other things to take care of first but I'll get back to you this afternoon.'

I thanked him and hung up. 'You know, we still say "hang

up" even though most of the time we actually set the handset down.'

'Yeah, and ships still sail even though they use every kind of power these days except wind. English is a funny language. Will you please keep your mind on business?'

'Sure. The leetle gray cells are always at work. What's your next move?'

'I'm going to check out Southeast Consolidated. I suspect it's going to be one of those corporate amoebas that squish out between your fingers when you try to grasp them, but I might as well try. What about you?'

'I'm going to pump Mitch. Getting straight answers out of him is a chore, but it's his hundred million and his professional future on the line.'

'I think I have the easier job,' she said. We agreed to get back together for lunch and she left in her company car. I set off in search of Mitchell Queen. I couldn't find him in the house and the housekeeper told me he was somewhere out on the lawn. I finally located him on his putting green, practising.

'You're up bright and early,' he said, tapping a ball into the cup. 'Jesus, Gabe, what happened to your hands?'

'I'm thinking of getting back into boxing. Mitch, tell me about your friend Armitage.'

He stooped and fished the ball out of the hole. 'Where'd you hear about him?'

'Selene Gibson told me.'

'Isn't Selene something?' He shook his head and placed the ball six feet from the hole. 'Kelly, Bacall, Bergman – they had nothing on Selene when it comes to pure class, even if she did start out in a shrimp-packing plant in Biloxi.'

'I thought it was a sharecropper's shack.'

'That was earlier. The story has it by the time she was thirteen she'd graduated from the dirt-floor shack to the shrimp factory in classic Southern Gothic violation of the child-labor laws that were in force even when she was a kid, and she was discovered by DeMille when he was down there location scouting for *Reap the Wild Wind*.'

He putted and sank the ball. 'No, hell, that was too far back even for Selene. Anyway, it was something like that.'

'Okay,' I said patiently, 'but what about Armitage?'

'What about him? He's a guy with money to invest.'

'What kind of money?'

'He's a banker. One of those offshore things.'

'You mean he launders money?'

He lined up another putt. 'That's what most of those banks do, I guess.' He caught my expression. 'Oh, come on, Gabe! Do you think anyone in this town or this business or, for God's sake, *any* business, really cares about where money comes from? Half the banks in Florida would collapse if they didn't process dope money. Same for arms and, these days, pirated software. It's the goods that're illegal. Once they're converted into money all that counts is that the taxes are paid up, and that's between Armitage and the government as far as I'm concerned. Who was that Roman emperor who wanted to raise dough by taxing the public urinals, and his son said that would be dishonorable, and the old man held a coin under the kid's nose and said that money has no smell? Was it Hadrian?'

I thought about long-ago Latin classes. '*Pecunia non olet.* I think it was Vespasian.'

'There you go. Armitage has money to invest and he wants a big chunk of *Tu Do Street*, and that's what I do: I line up people who have money with projects that appeal to them. I've sniffed his money and it smells fine.' He frowned at the ball, tapped it too hard and missed his putt. 'Shit. You weren't always so delicate about where money came from.' The racetrack again.

'That was a long time ago in a war.'

'Yeah, well, it always seems to go back to that, doesn't it? Sometimes it's like you and I never left the goddamned place. It's like the whole country hit the pause button in '75 and can't figure out what to do next. Every time some president wants a pissant war to get his ass out of a crack everybody yells about how it's going to be "another Vietnam". Those Republican politicians that want me to give them money think the country's still menaced by long-haired hippies in beads and sandals wearing peace symbols. Do you remember the last time you *saw* a peace symbol? Fucking lulus, every one of 'em. And people say *my* business is full of flakes.' He putted and missed again. 'Gabe, you're ruining my game here.'

'You really have a way with the non sequiturs, Mitch. I'm not talking about politics here. I'm not talking about Vietnam or the war or born-again conservatives with their brains stuck in the Eisenhower era. I'm talking about money, Mitch. I'm talking about a hundred million bucks. I can't believe that you can put a hundred million dollars and some larcenous human beings together without ending up with a criminal enterprise on your hands. I'm beginning to doubt that old Martin Starr is still around, but that hundred million and your buddy Armitage have me really intrigued.'

He'd been bent over, doing that comical little butt-wiggling, club-waving thing that golfers do prior to putting. Now he straightened. 'Have you had breakfast?'

'Just some orange juice.'

He turned around and started walking toward the house. 'You need more than that if you're going to put in a long day tracking down the bad guys. Especially if you're in training for the Golden Gloves, too. Come on, Gabe, m'man. I'll get Julia to lay on some breakfast for us and we'll talk about money.'

Julia had already laid out a minor buffet on the terrace, and there was already a place setting for me. I passed up the huevos rancheros and had fruit salad and coffee. My brief affair with suicidal cuisine was over. I was back in California.

'Okay, a few words about money.' Mitch went into his fork-as-conductor's-baton routine again. 'We talk about big sums of money, the picture people get in their heads is bundles of bills with bands around them, stacked in a suitcase like ransom money. The reality is a little different, at least it is in my business. In the first place, no one guy and no one company is going to put up all the financing for a big-budget movie; not with what they cost these days. I mean, the big ones have the money but they're not going to put it all into a single project. They spread it around among a number of projects to minimize the risk, should an overbudgeted production prove to be as popular as toxic waste at the box-office.'

'Makes sense,' I said, spearing a canteloupe ball.

'Damn right. Now, when my investors commit to a project, we form a production company for that particular film and they put a specified percentage of their money into an account where their accountants watch it like vultures. They want periodic statements detailing what every last dime went for, and they'll send people to the set or the location to check up on me and my team to be sure nobody's stiffing them, letting a brother-in-law double-bill the production, buying coke and putting it on the catering bill, that sort of thing.'

'Not a trustful bunch, huh?'

'Gabe, we're talking large money here. Large bucks and

trust do not go together. They're right to be suspicious, too, because that's exactly what people will do to you if you let them. I have to watch everyone, too. I run a tight ship, Gabe; I'm a very hands-on kinda producer. Sometimes it makes me unpopular on the production, but I make sure nobody picks my pocket and my investors are getting value for their money.'

'Unless the movie flops.'

He waved the fork philosophically. 'That's the risk factor, like in any business. You're always addressing a market and the market can change. But every other factor can be controlled. When some dufus of an auteur director runs a production way over budget, you can be sure that some producer is letting the business disappear up his nose or just lacks the balls to keep the silly jerk in line. You have to be able to crack the whip when it's needed. And you don't dick around with guys like Armitage or Bert Schuster, who's been in this business since he was a kid, or those money brokers from Paramount. They'll all dole out their end and keep an eye on the others to be sure they're doing the same. It's not impossible to pull a major ripoff in this business – it's been done before – but if you have the smarts to do it, you really ought to be stealing from a business that deals in truly big money, like investment banking or the government.'

'That helps to set my mind at ease, Mitch.' I was reserving my judgement, though. A man who knows intimately an arcane business seldom finds it difficult to flimflam someone who doesn't.

'These misconceptions about how the film business works are so common, Gabe,' he said, sounding put-upon. 'I mean, I wish these reporters and talk-show people would talk to producers for a change; we're the ones who know what's going on. They always want to talk to actors and directors and they don't know shit, and they're inarticulate to boot.'

'A problem from which you don't suffer,' I commented, sipping the sumptuous French coffee.

'Never. But do they ever ask me on those talk shows? No, they do not. I mean, one night a few years ago I saw Cimino on one of the late-night talk shows, and they were grilling him about *Heaven's Gate*, which was a real stinkeroo and a flop, but he could've handled the guff a lot better than he did. This host – I forget which one it was, but it was one of the nasty ones – asks Cimino how he managed to lose a hundred and twenty million or whatever it was, and the twit just looks down at his shoes like a kid getting scolded by the teacher and mumbles so you can't even hear him. That's what I'm talking about. Directors. They can communicate beautifully with pictures, but don't expect them to use language better than your average fourth-grader. I could've fielded all those questions better than the whole Director's Guild together.'

'How would you have answered them?' I asked, knowing how anxious he was to tell me.

'For starters, I'd've told him what I just told you: that the money doesn't come in the form of stacks of bills; mainly it's parcelled out in people's paychecks. A big film loses money, people act like somebody soaked the money in lighter fluid and set a match to it.

'Get this: that talk-show guy came up with an image for *Heaven's Gate* that about made me choke. Some economist or something did some calculations and said that the money wasted on that production would've supported eleven families for a hundred years! I mean, where do they find these people? How did he come up with that exquisite calculation? Is he talking about mom and pop and a baby, or a Chinese extended family with fifty people in one house? Does he really know what the median family income is going to be in the year 2095 or whatever? There are paid supposed experts who can't say what a gallon of gas is going to cost next year.'

'It does seem arbitrary,' I admitted.

'To say the least. You know what I would've said to that guy? I'd've said, look, when we get money to make a movie we don't go out into the desert and dig a hole and bury it, for Christ's sake! We *spend* it! We hire people. Those pictures don't appear up there on the screen by magic, you know. Besides a director and writers and actors, we pay camera people and costumers and electricians and lighting technicians and sound people and prop men and stunt men and key grips and boom operators and best boys and God knows what all. You know that endless list of people that rolls on forever after the end of a movie? We pay all those people. If we shoot on location we're paying hotels and caterers and local extras, and we're renting land and houses and spending money in local restaurants and bars and the local shopping mall. Plus, there's the advertising and distribution people. Hell, I even pay myself! That money isn't destroyed. Most of it's out circulating in the economy right now, where it's supposed to be.'

He paused for a breath. 'I don't know if *Heaven's Gate* would've supported eleven families for a hundred years, but I'm willing to bet that it supported eleven hundred families for a year! Gabe, do you know what happens when a movie flops?'

'What happens?'

'What happens is, some big-money investors take what is known in the Mexican movie industry as *el batho*. Now I ask you: do you really care? Does that talk-show host care? Are great big tears being shed over some guys who're just going to take it off this year's taxes?' He knocked back a glass of pineapple juice angrily. 'Anybody who ruins himself investing in a movie never deserved to have money in the first place. But a movie drops a bundle and people act like it's proof that Armageddon is at hand. Fucking jerks.'

'You've convinced me,' I assured him.

'Good, I'm glad to hear it. Now do you think you can get your mind off the dazzling piles of bills and back to locating Martin Starr for me?'

'I'm working on it.'

'Any progress?'

'I've been hearing some disturbing things about Vietnamese gangs. Not the juveniles, the big guys. Duc could've helped me there, but that wasn't to be. Every big West Coast city has a Little Saigon these days. The gangs from Asia are moving in, trying to take over. It struck me that that's a logical place for Starr to be, assuming that he hasn't mended his ways. During the war, when he was running the ghosts he co-operated with the local gangs. Maybe now he's a man who can move in both worlds.'

Queen leaned back in his chair and it creaked faintly. 'I don't know, Gabe. Starr operated in Cholon, and Cholon was mainly Chinese. From what I hear, most of the ethnic Chinese got booted out of Vietnam when the Hanoi government took over. Most of the boat people were Chinese.'

'You remember what it was like in those days. If you operated in Saigon, you co-operated with the Saigon gangs and you paid off the government officials. I'd say he had contacts in every camp. He may have kept up his contacts even if he had to flee the country. It's looking like all the Asian gangs are a little giddy over the new world order, Mitch. Their commitment to the free-market economy is second to none. They're co-operating in this move into the States.'

'Those bastards've always cut each other's throats at the slightest opportunity.'

'And they will again, but for the moment they're in town and cutting a lot of deals. It's looking like a deal that soured that got Duc killed. I haven't found the tie-in yet, but I can't help but feel that Duc's murder and your problem with Starr or someone else who remembers the old days are connected somehow.'

'Damn! I'm gonna have to get a research staff on this, hire a good writer and sit down for a brainstorming session. Asian gang movies could be the coming thing, Gabe. The dumbass Russians left us high and dry for intrigue when Marxism went belly-up. Could be the Yellow Peril is poised for a comeback. Maybe an update on the old Fu Manchu character. I wonder who owns the rights to him?'

'Now who's losing contact with the business at hand here? I know you live and breathe this stuff, but that's why you hired me: so you could keep on breathing.'

'Okay, old buddy. So what's your next move? I've got things in motion here and I can't stall. We'll be committed to principal photography pretty soon and there's no turning back then. I've got to know if I have anything real to worry about.'

'I may have to take a little trip. I'm not sure yet – I don't want to do it, but it may be necessary.'

'Whatever it takes.' He gestured expansively. 'Just don't let it take up too much time. That I don't have.'

It was nearly three o'clock when Connie came back. She kicked off her shoes and sat on the couch, laying her briefcase on the coffee table.

'Discover anything?' I asked. As I walked in from my bedroom I caught a glimpse of myself in the mirror over the little wet bar. I was getting a tan already. How quickly we revert.

''Bout what we expected.' She popped the latches, raised the cover and took out a folder. 'Southeast Consolidated Investors has been very busy the last few months. They seem to be moving out of garden-variety money laundering in the Caribbean and moving on to the mainland, investing in businesses and property, mainly along the Gulf coast.'

'Like where?' I asked, sitting down and flexing my sore fingers.

'Cities like Corpus Christi, Galveston, New Orleans, Gulfport-Biloxi, St Petersburg, that sort of place.'

'All towns with substantial Vietnamese communities.'

'Yep. I have an old friend with the Galveston PD. She tells me there's a lot of unrest in the Vietnamese community, has been for a while. Trouble was, all the friction between the immigrant fishermen and the entrenched native-born fishermen sort of kept things confused. They assumed that all the problems were race-oriented. They were exchanging shots out there on the shrimp boats, you know.'

'I heard about it.'

'But there was a gang there called the Golden Dragons. Real original, huh?'

I shrugged. 'They all saw the Fu Manchu movies, too.'

'Come again?'

'Never mind. What else did your friend tell you?'

'These Golden Dragons did the usual stuff: they shook down the local grocers and noodle shops, took a percentage from the shrimpers, ran gambling and narcotics, but kept their activities pretty much within the Vietnamese community. They feuded with the Chinese some, but they never messed with the Caucasian Gulf Coast mob. The New Orleans Mafia is powerful and very, very mean.'

'So I understand.'

'Anyway, some new guys started moving in a while back: very smooth, very well organized and backed by heavy money. They didn't even have a name or a special tattoo or any of that childish gang stuff. They simply announced they were taking over and started buying up waterfront property and transport facilities. The Golden Dragons tried to assert their prior claim and a few of them turned up floating in the bay or in alleys with their throats cut, no attempt to hide the stiffs. Since then, the surviving Dragons've joined the new guys.'

'What about the other gangs?'

'The Chinese have been oddly compliant, although my friend hasn't heard rumors of active co-operation between them. The white mob has yet to be heard from. But here's the kicker: there's a team of federal narcs in town trying to keep an eye on this bunch and not having much luck. My friend's acting as liaison between this team and her department, and she's been out drinking with them a few evenings after work. They told her the new gang's being financed by some money-laundering banks in Grenada and Grand Cayman.'

'Did they mention Southeastern Consolidated Investors by name?'

'No, but the properties they've acquired in Galveston are mostly adjacent to the ones the new guys have picked up. You already know my opinion of coincidence.'

'Good work, Armijo,' I said, meaning it.

'I have my moments.'

The phone rang and I picked it up. 'Gabe Treloar here.'

'This is Lowry. I ran a check on your guy Archie Dupre.'

'Just a second. My partner needs to hear this. She's going to pick up the other phone.' Connie got up and went into her bedroom. When he heard the click, Lowry went on.

'Okay, your man did hard time, but it doesn't look like you're the one who busted him.'

'How's that?'

'He was a federal prisoner. Did his time in Leavenworth. Released in '80 and kept his nose clean since. Hasn't been caught, anyway. He's lived in Culver City since last May; 445 West Briarwood, Apartment 79a.'

'What was he in for?' I asked.

'Get this, it's a new one on me. He was a private in Vietnam in '67 and he deserted! I think I've run into everything but that one. Anyway, Jimmy Carter decided to leave office in a blaze of compassion and he signed a lot of pardons that year. Archie was one of the lucky ones.'

Click. Another piece fit into the puzzle. Well, it fit in somewhere, anyway. It was another connection. 'You say he deserted in '67. Did you find out when he was busted?'

'No, just that by mid-'72 he was in Leavenworth. This any help?'

'More than you can guess. I owe you one, Lowry.'

'You sure do. Keep me informed.' He hung up and so did I.

When Connie came back in I was standing in front of the picture window, watching the play of sunlight on the water of the pool. It cast ripply silver waves on the ceiling of the guest house.

'So Archie was a ghost,' she said.

'So it appears. I wish I knew when he was picked up.'

'Want to go talk to him?'

'I doubt if we'd find him home. He made me, so he must figure I made him. Even if he's still there he won't tell us anything. It's the man inside the limo I want to talk to, anyway.'

'So what're you going to do?'

I'd known what it was going to be since I'd talked with Anne after the funeral, but I'd been putting off making the decision. No way out of it now.

'I've got to go talk to a man named Nguyen Chi Thanh. I'm going back to Vietnam. Want to come along?'

She blinked twice, slowly, started to speak, then stopped. Then she took a deep breath, seemed to come to a decision. 'I wouldn't miss it for anything in the world.'

Book Two

TOO LATE, MY BROTHERS

Chapter Thirteen

Inside, the airport was a dump. It looked as if nothing had been changed since the Americans left and time had taken its inexorable toll. Amid the crowd of new arrivals I looked around and tried to make the place call back memories, but I couldn't. I'd only been here twice. When I first arrived, I'd been bussed directly from the airstrip. The day I'd left I'd been too excited to notice my surroundings; waiting with hundreds of other GIs and Marines and airmen for the legendary aircraft – the Freedom Bird. For hours I'd held Rose's tiny hand while we inched forward amid muttering and loud talk and half-hysterical laughter.

Once, we'd been within minutes of boarding a plane when a couple of busloads of ARVN officers arrived on the strip and proceeded to bump the rest of us. They were headed for special training somewhere in the States. I'd burned with rage at the injustice and presumption of it all. I'd been sure, absolutely *certain*, that the next minutes would bring a heavy mortar attack and we'd be killed waiting to get on the next plane. I'd been equally enraged and embarrassed at the indignant shouts from all around me: 'Fuckin' gook assholes got our seats!', 'Get them dinks offa that plane!'

An MP sergeant on security had whipped around. 'Can it! Uncle Sam still own you mizble fuckheads an' don't forget it! We still got plenty room down the road in the LBJ, if you rather be there than here.'

My face had flamed but Rose just squeezed my hand. 'It's all right, Gabe. We be in the States soon.'

Before long another plane had pulled up and everybody's good mood was restored. We boarded that one. It was a TWA 707. Everyone had held their breath as it taxied out to the runway and accelerated, everyone unconsciously trying to make the plane lighter, to give it more power, willing it into the air. A huge cheer had erupted as the landing gear lost contact with the strip and we were airborne. But not me. I just kneaded Rose's hand until I was sure we were out of rocket range. Then I cheered and hugged Rose and wept.

'Hey, Treloar. Get a move on.' Connie nudged me in the side. The line waiting at customs had moved on ahead of me. Nope, I didn't remember a single thing about the terminal at Tan Son Nhut.

It had proven amazingly easy to arrange a flight to Vietnam. A phone call to a travel agency, some hurried immunizations, a little packing, and we were on our way. The new world situation still had me caught in a cultural time lag. There seemed something positively *unnatural* about easy travel to a country that still called itself Communist, not that that means much these days. That, plus the uneasy sensation that the war really hadn't ended. There'd been no surrender or ceremonies or rituals to proclaim that the state of war was ended and it was okay not to kill each other any more. There was a sense of something left unfinished that was as maddeningly persistent as a phantom itch in a severed limb.

I'd expected a lot of bureaucratic red tape and obstruction, but there was nothing of the sort. The US saw no reason to put obstacles in the way of travel, and the Vietnamese were desperately, almost pathetically eager for foreign visitors with hard currency to spend.

Since it was Queen's credit card, we'd flown first class, with the vets and their wives in tour groups and a bunch of Japanese businessmen who'd boarded in Tokyo. Economy was full of American Vietnamese who were going back to visit their families safely for the first time in many years. Things might have relaxed, but I wasn't betting that it was easy for the homeland Vietnamese to travel the other way. Besides, few of them could afford it.

Customs didn't take long. We were traveling with minimal luggage. It wasn't going to be a long stay and we weren't planning any excursions to the colorful, nostalgic battlefields. Da Nang and the Au Shau Valley could quietly revert to jungle as far as I was concerned.

We'd booked rooms at the Continental, so as soon as we'd cleared customs we caught a taxi toward the center of town, the part that had been the government center back when Saigon was the capital of a nation.

'Does it take you back?' Connie asked as we made our slow way through the dense traffic.

'Some.' Actually, it was a disturbing mixture of sameness and difference. The pedicabs were there, the beautiful women in *ao dai*, the throngs of pedestrians, the signs in their mixture of lettering systems. But something was jarringly different, and it took me a few minutes to realize that it was the near absence of military traffic. There were no truckloads of GIs and ARVNs, no jeeps of military police patrolling endlessly. The few uniforms in sight were those of what had been the North Vietnamese People's Liberation Army, now just the Vietnamese Army I suppose, looking strangely archaic in this closing decade of the century. And the Vietnamese military lacked their American counterparts' prodigal way with vehicles and gasoline. Motorbikes seemed to outnumber everything else.

Smell is the most powerfully evocative of the senses, and the smell of Saigon was exactly as I remembered it, compounded of cooking smells and perfumes and inefficient sewage disposal and incense from the temples, and perhaps not quite so much motor exhaust as a quarter-century ago. For millions of years of evolution our ancestors depended on smell far more than on sight or hearing. The primitive, animal part of our rear brain files every last odor and never forgets it. Smell something fifty years after the last time, and you remember exactly where you smelled it before.

The oppressive heat was unchanged. It was even more unpleasant now, because I was older. Connie didn't seem to mind. She was dressed in a sort of modified safari outfit and she looked cool and composed despite the heat after the long flight. Well, she had lived for years in Houston, which is not far from Saigon on the heat and humidity scale. She looked out the open window of the cab with interest, though not rubbernecking despite the exoticism of the surroundings. That seemed surprisingly cosmopolitan. Even LA isn't so bizarre that it leaves you jaded where the mysterious East is concerned.

'What do you find most changed?' she asked, as if reading my thoughts. But then, what else would I be thinking about?

'We can be pretty sure a kid on a bicycle won't ride up and toss a grenade through the window,' I said. And in that moment I realized that was exactly what I was nervously scanning the surroundings for. That old bullseye-between-the-shoulderblades feeling was back as if it had never left me.

The hotel had been growing seedy back when it was a headquarters for American and European journalists covering the war. Now it was seedier than ever, despite some new paint and half-hearted renovations. I'd booked rooms there in a fit of nostalgia because staying in a new, first-class tourist hotel seemed like a desecration when visiting Saigon. Besides, the travel agent had warned me that most of the new hotels were still under construction, despite the claims in their brochures.

The staff worked hard to maintain the old French colonial ambience, however, and the porter guided us down the threadbare carpets to our rooms as if he were leading us to staterooms on the *Normandie*. Our rooms were adjoining, and each had its own bathroom and a small balcony and an honest-to-God lazily-rotating ceiling fan – not the kind you can buy nowadays in your local home improvement store, but fans that had probably been there in the thirties.

Stiff and grimy from the long flight, I took a shower in the little stall, put on clean clothes and walked out on to my balcony. Connie was already on hers, sitting on a wrought-iron chair and sipping from a glass of what appeared to be Coca-Cola.

'How do you like your room?' I asked her.

'It's livable. I've spent enough time in Mexican hotels not to expect Hilton standards in third-world places. I wouldn't even want them. It always makes me feel like the big sahib lording it over the natives. This is fine.'

I nodded. 'I like it too.' We were on the second floor overlooking a bustling traffic square. 'You know, this is the Saigon I always wanted to see and never got to: the Graham Greene Saigon. If I still drank I'd be having a tall gin and tonic.'

She smiled, exposing big, white teeth to the sun. 'There you go. Let's find a tailor and get you a white suit. Maybe I can find a parasol.'

I shook my head. 'Parasols are before Greene's day. Maybe Conrad or one of those guys.'

'When do you want to look for Mr Thanh?'

'Mr Nguyen,' I corrected. 'Family names first here. Chi is his given name. We'll look for him later, when I'm alert. I've never been able to sleep on a plane.'

'I know what you mean. I'm jet-lagged. I know I won't be able to sleep, either. Besides, it's only late afternoon here, whatever our internal clocks say. Want to go for a walk?'

'Sounds good to me. I want to get a close look at this city.'

We went down to the lobby and fended off the many would-be guides and cabbies who wanted to take us to the bright lights. I was gradually losing my case of atavistic nerves, mentally kicking myself for the viscerally self-centered attitude. I even told Connie about it as we walked along a street that was exactly like it was when I'd been there before, except for the obnoxious beeping and squawking of video games coming from inside the many small businesses.

Connie favored me with one of her rare laughs. 'You've fallen into your pal Queen's solipsism, Gabe. Deep down inside, you expected this place to be exactly like it was when you left. Like time was supposed to stand still here while you were away, and resume when you got back, with VC still itching to waste you and the population with nothing on their mind but the war. But these people went right on with their lives. We left twenty years ago.' She stopped and looked up and down the street. 'We left and they stayed. Hell, half the people on this street weren't born when you went back home. The average age here's probably around nineteen.' She looked at me with sardonic, brown eyes. 'You're ancient history to them, old man.'

'God, you know how to make a guy feel good.'

We found a little café and had a wonderful noodle soup with shrimp and peanuts. Nobody in the world makes soup like the Vietnamese.

'I keep wondering about Cholon,' I said to her while we lingered over a pot of tea.

'We can catch a taxi and go there,' she suggested.

'I'm afraid to. What happened there after the South fell was what newspeople these days like to call "ethnic cleansing". I'm not ready for that big a downer.'

'This is some sentimental journey, huh?'

'We're not on vacation,' I reminded her. 'This is business. Let's go.'

We wandered aimlessly, trying to work up enough genuine fatigue to sleep soundly. Nobody paid us much attention except for the kids who wanted to be our guides or sell us stuff. They weren't especially persistent, because there were plenty of other marks around. We were far from the only Americans on the sidewalks. The vets were there in some force, most of them with half-stunned looks on their faces, searching for resolution. I hoped I didn't look like them.

Then we turned a corner and stared. Across the street was a huge sign over a bar entrance. It read: APOCALYPSE NOW.

'This I just have to see,' I said.

We crossed the street and went inside and stood there, stunned. The interior was huge and the decor was made up entirely of war memorabilia: belts of machine-gun ammo draping the walls like garlands, photos of GIs and battles, crates with the inevitable military stencilling, dummy grenades and rockets, painted unit crests, chopper crew helmets. In the center was an entire jeep with a big white star on its hood. From the sound system blasted the voices and instruments of Jim Morrison and The Doors singing 'The End'.

Everywhere there were Vietnamese girls dressed as period bar girls. Their customers were men dressed mostly in a motley of combat fatigues in a variety of camouflage patterns, most wearing shirts with the sleeves ripped off to show off their well-tanned, well-fed muscles. From all the loud conversation going on I could tell that not all of them were Americans. Apparently there were European war buffs as well. I didn't see one who looked old enough to have been there during the war.

At our entrance the guys nearest the door turned and looked us over disdainfully. I spotted a Rolex that never came from a PX and a pair of combat boots from L.L. Bean.

'Come on,' Connie said tiredly. 'Us old squares don't belong in a hip, with-it place like this.' We went back on to the street. Behind us I could hear 'Light My Fire' starting.

'God, that's depressing,' I said, but I was talking to her back. Connie had set off at a quick step, arms folded, hands gripping her upper arms near the shoulders as if she were cold. At the first corner she turned left without hesitation. At the next she turned right, as if she knew exactly where she was going. A niggling little suspicion formed at the back of my skull.

I only had to follow her for a few minutes. She stopped and stared across a wide, French-style boulevard at a towering, ugly building that looked like a ten- or twelve-storey parking garage. I hadn't been in this part of the city very much but I recognized the place. For a few days in '75 it had been the most famous building in the world. The one you saw on all the newsreels, anyway: the United States Embassy, location of the final scene in the US pullout from Vietnam.

I stepped up behind her and put my hands gently on

her shoulders. 'Tell me about it, Connie.'

For a long time she said nothing, but I felt subliminal trembling that vibrated her whole body. The sun was going down and the top of the tall building glowed.

'They came from that direction,' she said at last, still gripping herself, nodding jerkily down the boulevard. 'My God, there were at least a million of them. They packed the boulevard from side to side. They were jammed into the compound over there and they were trying to climb over the fence to get in. The Marine guards were beating them off the fence with rifle butts. You've seen those pictures of Saint Peter's Square at Easter when the Pope says Mass and talks to the crowd? That place is deserted compared to what it was like here on April twenty-ninth.'

She looked up at the roof of the Embassy. The famous roof. 'I was up there at first. I was a Navy nurse and they choppered me in from the USS *Mercy* with a bunch of other medical people. They started taking people off the roof right away, then they brought choppers down on the parking lot and by the Embassy fire station. I was up there patching up the wounded between choppers and I couldn't believe there were that many people in the world! They were packed in the boulevard and the side streets as far as I could see. Off in the distance you could see the fires and explosions at Tan Son Nhut, fires all over the city, rockets landing everywhere. A few minutes after I got there someone yelled and we all looked up and there was a big C-119 cruising overhead. It was on fire and it went down near the edge of the city. The explosion was huge but you couldn't even hear it over the other racket.'

She paused a moment, drawing a deep, shuddering breath. 'In the afternoon they sent me down to the main gate. They were letting people in a few at a time, the ones who had evacuation passes. Those things were beyond price that day and half the people in Saigon seemed to have them. You know what they had me doing? The hell with patching up the wounded, they had me sorting out the *dead* ones! People were coming in carrying old people and children and babies, and they wouldn't turn loose of them, even some that hadn't been breathing for hours.

'We tried to load the choppers to capacity and keep order, but it was like trying to stop the tide with a plastic bucket. People were terrified beyond all reason. When the choppers lifted they were clinging to the skids, sometimes kids ten or twelve years old. The choppers couldn't fly like that and the ones inside were trying to beat off the ones hanging on the skids. Sometimes they were a couple of hundred feet up before the last of them fell off.'

She twisted around and glared fiercely up at me. 'I was nineteen-God-damned-years-old, Gabe!'

She jerked back around and stared at the building. 'I stayed on the gate till almost dawn of the thirtieth. There were still people trying to get in, people who'd made the mistake of believing in us. A couple of Marines grabbed me under the arms and dragged me back into the Embassy and up the steps. I kept trying to pull away and tend to the wounded. The place was full of smoke from all the documents they were burning. Hell, they were burning millions of dollars in American currency up on the roof. Couldn't haul it out, didn't want to let the winners have it.

'The Marines threw me into a Huey and somebody strapped me in and we took off. It was still dark and off in the distance we could see big fires. I heard somebody say: "That's Bien Hoa." Then the pilot pointed to some really big fires, looked like a whole city burning. He had that macho pilot's drawl. "That's Long Binh," he said. "I was in the 91st Medevac there in '70. They're burnin' my hooch right now." ' She managed a little smile. 'You know how those helmets with the goggles made them look like bugs from another planet? Well, that was the first time I saw tears coming down from under the goggles.'

She hugged herself like she was really freezing now. 'You and your friend Queen and all those other vets, you act like you were the only ones who were ever here. You had a year of it and I had a day. But you guys had the good times. I got to see the shame.'

She turned and started walking tiredly back to the hotel. I put my arm across her shoulders and she didn't object.

'So there's my claim to fame, Gabe. I was on one of the very last choppers out of Saigon back in April '75.'

'Do you look for yourself in those TV retrospectives?'

'I never watch them. And I've never gone to a Vietnam movie and I never read Vietnam books. I don't like to listen to vets bullshitting about the war. I told Mick about it and that's it. Even my kids don't know I was here.'

184

'How many did we leave behind?'

'Hundreds, maybe thousands. Oh, and one more thing: those evacuation passes I mentioned?'

'What about them?'

'A lot of them were counterfeit. I saw a lot of people holding them that never worked for us – fat cats in expensive suits and women with suitcases full of jewelry. The legitimate refugees were very angry about it. And I kept hearing one name mentioned in connection with those forged papers: Martin Starr.'

Chapter Fourteen

We slept until late the next morning. In my usual jet-lag fashion, I'd woken three or four times during the night, disoriented. There was an all-night restaurant nearby, and once I woke to an aroma that was so much like one of Rose's favorite dishes that for an instant I reached for her on the bed beside me. It took me a long time to get back to sleep after that one.

Connie and I got together downstairs for breakfast: coffee and croissants. They even had marmalade.

'So what's on the agenda?' she asked. 'Are you feeling up to confronting our Mr Nguyen Chi Thanh?'

'The restaurant probably won't be open for a while,' I told her.

'I don't imagine it'd do any good to go to police headquarters, ask them about the ghosts?'

'Sure. They're doing all they can to encourage tourism and foreign investment, they're going to be real anxious to tell us all about their organized crime problems.'

'It was just a thought. So what's it to be, then?'

'We're tourists, aren't we? We'll do tourist stuff this morning: sightsee, hire a pedicab, maybe take a cruise on the river. Then we'll go find our man.'

'Great. Travel is so broadening. And we can revisit the sites of so many happy memories.'

'I'm sorry, Connie,' I told her. 'I know you miss your gym. If we learn all we need tonight, we can be out of here tomorrow.'

'Don't worry about the gym. I brought along some weights.'

It might have been true. That porter had been listing to the side with her suitcase.

We hired a pedicab in front of the hotel. Like most Americans I have an aversion to being trundled around by another human being's muscle power; it's too much like turning people into beasts of burden. But it was his rice bowl, and I wanted to be able to talk without shouting. Most of the city's motor vehicles were old and the Vietnamese still hadn't heard about mufflers.

187

The guy pedaling asked where we wanted to go and I told him to head for the outskirts, up the old main highway toward the Cambodian border. That seemed to surprise him, but he forged on, yelling at people to get out of his way.

'Where are we going?' Connie asked.

'The scene of the crime.'

The cabbie turned around and grinned at us, his gapped teeth clamped on an ancient, amber-colored cigarette holder in which a French Gauloise burned foully. 'You American vet, no?' Going by his face, he was around seventy years old, but the body that powered the pedicab was decades younger. I read him for around my own age. Life had dealt him most of the bad cards in the face.

'Eighteenth MPs,' I said. '1968.'

'Here in Saigon?'

'That's right.'

'You here for Tet?'

'I was. You?'

He threw back his head and laughed around his cigarette holder. 'I was captain in Fortieth People's Combat Team. Maybe we shoot at each other. I command mortar company, shell Tan Son Nhut.'

'Then we missed each other. I was in Cholon.'

'Plenty hard fighting there.' He broke off to harangue a farmer whose high-piled ox cart was blocking the narrow street. When the obstacle was past he went on. 'Lots you American vets here these day. Like old time again.'

'But you won the war,' Connie said.

He grinned again and shook his head. 'Not us. The North win the war.'

The clustered buildings grew further apart and dwindled out. There were no American-style suburbs. The transition from city to country was abrupt. 'Stop here,' I said.

Connie looked around, puzzlement wrinkling her brow. 'Where are we?'

I got out of the cab. 'Starr escaped somewhere around here,' I told her.

'Are you sure you're remembering right?'

'Pretty close.' I knew why she was mystified. The vast shanty town of bamboo and cardboard and tin-can sheet metal was gone. Once it had stretched as far as you could see in all directions, a mind-numbingly vast expanse of poverty and misery. It had all been cleared away. The ground was mostly cut up into small farms now. Arable land never goes to waste in Asia.

'What happened to the people from the country?' I asked our cabbie.

He shrugged. 'Most go back. Out to the villages.'

'But a generation grew up here,' Connie said. 'You can't just go out in the country and farm if you've never done it before. Didn't a lot of them starve?'

He stuck another Gauloise in his holder and lit it with an old Zippo. 'Some, maybe.' The thought didn't seem to upset him much.

'What did you mean when you said the North won the war?' Connie asked.

This time his grin was rueful. 'I was Viet Cong. We fight to make one Vietnam. Hanoi say we are brothers. We drive out the Saigon dogs and their Yankee allies, then rule the country together for good of all. First they get most of us killed on Tet. They plan, we fight, we die. When Ky and the last dogs run, we are in the streets, everyone cry *Giai Phong!* War is over and now the people will rule.'

He kicked idly at something in the dirt. It was a cartridge case, black with age probably .50 caliber. 'Soon, there is big victory parade, but we do not march. No Viet Cong in parade. We are to have no part in new government. We are just Southerners. I am colonel by end of war. Now I pedal taxi. My commanding officer flee to France, write long books for last twenty year.'

'Rough deal,' I said, not exactly overwhelmed with sympathy.

His grin stayed in place and he shrugged again. This guy grinned and shrugged a lot. 'Still alive. Not many my friends still alive. I live to see the northerners go beg to the Yankees. That make me feel good.'

We got back in the pedicab and he took us back into the city. 'Tu Do Street,' I said.

It was in the heart of the city. Long ago, in another life, it had been a long strip of sleazy bars and whorehouses side by side with expensive shops, classy nightclubs, press offices and all manner of headquarters for the innumerable spook operations conducted by the US, Europe, the Soviets, and – some of us speculated – Martians.

Compared to the old days, Tu Do was downright staid. There were still bars, but they looked like the kind of place where, if you got too drunk, they'd take you back to your hotel instead of dumping you in the alley out back with your wallet missing and maybe your throat cut. Mostly it was shops and professional offices and headquarters of businesses, many of them with American names on signs so new you could smell the paint.

'I think you were right, back at Queen's,' I told Connie. 'It can't be long before McDonald's opens up a Tu Do Street franchise. Can Wal-Mart be far behind?'

'Jeez, Gabe,' Connie said, pointing up the wide, tree-lined street, 'you never mentioned *that*!' At the end of the street you could see the twin spires of the cathedral.

'Saigon was always a city of contrasts,' I told her. 'If you could wangle a weekend pass, you could start out Friday evening at the riverfront dives at the south end of Tu Do,' I jerked my thumb back over my shoulder, 'drink your way north, and by Sunday morning you could get absolution along with your hangover at the cathedral.'

'Damn macho paradise,' she said. 'I don't know why you ever left.'

'Some didn't,' I reminded her.

It was with that thought in mind that I spoke to our cabbie for the last time when he took us back to our hotel. We paid him twice the regular rate. I suppose it was guilt money, but he pocketed it without comment.

'Have you been here in Saigon ever since the war ended?' I asked him.

'Most time, yes.'

'What happened to the American deserters who were left behind? Are any of them still around?'

For the first time he scowled – an expression made up of disgust and contempt. 'Dead,' he said. 'All dead long ago.'

We rested during the fiercest of the afternoon heat. There was a brief, heavy rainstorm and for a few minutes after that things were cooler, but it didn't last. Not until the sun was almost down did the heat become tolerable.

The Apple Orchard wasn't hard to find. It was only a few blocks from our hotel, a modest, white-fronted building recessed a few yards from the street, the recess forming a little courtyard where a few tables were set up beneath an awning, surrounded by potted rubber plants. They looked inviting in the evening breeze, but we went on inside.

A bar with a half-dozen stools, two of them occupied, lay along one wall. Tables covered with flower-print cloths and candles burning in the necks of old wine bottles were set around a floor tiled in blue and green. A double row of fans overhead stirred the muggy air. From unseen speakers came the reedy sounds of traditional Vietnamese opera. Couples or little groups sat at each table.

A waiter came up to us. 'No table free now. You wait?' He swept a hand toward the bar.

'We need to speak with the owner,' I told him. 'Mr Nguyen Chi Thanh.' He seemed unsure how to reply so I added: 'It's about Nguyen Duc.'

Now he smiled. 'I get! Joe send me, yes?'

'Just tell Mr Thanh.'

'You wait?' he said again.

'We wait,' I told him. He seated us at the bar and we ordered drinks. Connie had a white wine and I ordered a beer I didn't intend to drink because, somehow, it seemed unthinkable to order designer water or soft drinks in this city.

'Do you think he even understood what you were saying?' Connie asked.

'He got it. When I asked about Chi Thanh he was surprised. When I mentioned Duc he was shocked.'

'How do you . . . oh, yeah, I forgot.'

The bar had one other customer: a Caucasian with a lot of deep lines in a heavily tanned face, his white hair in a brush cut. He was dressed in an odd but practical combination: outside-the-pants Filipino shirt, khaki chino pants, huaraches on his sockless feet. He had an Aussie Black Swan lager in front of him.

'You folks just in from the States? I'm Pat Hacker.' He stuck out a broad hand that had performed hard work in past years. His grin was engagingly piratical. He had old Asia hand written all over him.

We introduced ourselves. 'Arrived yesterday,' I said. 'We're just now recovering. You?'

He rolled the condensation-beaded bottle between his palms. 'I've been here off and on for most of the last year. Doing consultant work mostly. Lots of new businesses locating here – import-export, computers, banks, hotels, you name it.

There's plenty of work for somebody who knows the place and the language.'

'So you've been here before?' I said.

'You got that right. I did three tours here in the Marine Corps. The place got to me. I took my discharge here after my last tour in '72. Haven't spent more than two-three months at a time in the States since.'

'Where've you been living all this time?' Connie asked. 'It couldn't've been here.'

'Lotta places: Port Moresby building docking facilities, newspaper stringer in Hong Kong, ran a trucking line for a while in Singapore, hotel security in Seoul. Asia gets into your blood. It's good to be back here, though, with nobody shooting at me. Vietnam's the most beautiful country in the world. I'm working with some investors now that want to start a four-star resort up near Cam Ranh Bay. You watch – in five years it'll outdraw anything in Acapulco or the Bahamas.'

'Is the business climate here all that good?' I asked him.

'Oh, hell yes. Up north they've pretty much given up on that Commie shit and here in the south it never took at all. The Hanoi gang's a bunch of puritanical ideologues but they never made a dent in the Saigonese. Look around you. This is a hustler's town and always has been. You a vet?'

'We both are,' I told him. 'But we're not here on a tour.'

'Business?'

'Matter of fact, we're handling what you might call advance security for a movie outfit that's going to be filming here later in the year.' Connie glanced at me sharply, but decided not to interfere. 'Have you heard about it?'

His attention sharpened. 'I've heard rumors about a half-dozen movie and TV projects coming up, couple from Japan, one or two from the States, a German nature documentary. Which one are you involved with?'

'They're keeping it sort of secret, but it's a movie involving the war years.'

He took out a card and handed it to me. 'If your employers need a good hand when they get ready to start shooting, I can handle it all: hiring, translating, transportation co-ordinating, liaison with the government, crew bossing, the works.'

I tucked the card into my pocket. 'You've done movie work before?'

'Sure. I worked on *The Year of Living Dangerously* when

they were shooting in Indonesia and the Philippines. Just ask Mel and Sigourney. We're old buddies.'

The title tickled a memory of an old magazine article. 'Wasn't there trouble on that production? Threats by political extremists?'

He snorted contemptuously. 'Yeah, some bunch of left-wingers threatened to kill the actors and shoot up the locations. It was all bullshit, but the producers chickened out and that's why we moved the whole thing to the Philippines.'

'Anything like that here?'

'What do you mean?'

'I mean, we're checking out some threats mailed to some people involved in the production. Don't try to film in the People's Republic or you'll be slaughtered, that sort of thing. Are there any groups here that'd be inclined to do what your guys in Indonesia did?'

He shook his head. 'Doesn't make sense. If you've got good, hard American dollars to spend, the government and businesses here will kiss your ass all the way to Hanoi and back. They may want proof they you're not going to make Uncle Ho look too bad, but other than that, they're all co-operation.' He contemplated his beer bottle for a moment. 'No, what I'd say you've got there is a shakedown artist looking to turn a buck. That's something you can definitely expect here. I'll bet pretty soon you'll be contacted and a price will be named. You want me to look into it? I'm good at this sort of stuff and my rates are reasonable.'

'Not just yet,' I said. 'You're probably right and it's nothing. We've got some nervous investors, that's all.'

'Is there any other kind?'

'If it's blackmailers,' Connie said, 'would it be a good idea to pay? How serious are they?'

'That's up to your investors, but I'd show your threats to your government liaison man. Their police are pretty good here. They'll probably find your guys and they'll take them out in the street and shoot them if that's what pleases you.' He glanced at his watch and swallowed the last of his beer. 'Gotta go meet some people,' he said, standing. 'You keep me in mind when you get ready to move operations here. If you don't know how business is conducted in this part of the world, you can waste a lot of time and money learning the ropes.'

I told him we wouldn't forget.

Soon a table was vacated and we were seated. I didn't see the waiter I had spoken to, and we went over the menu slowly. Our waitress had only rudimentary English.

'I noticed you didn't ask him about the ghosts,' Connie said when we'd ordered.

'Maybe the less we talk about them, the better. We don't know anything about that guy and he could be blowing smoke about what an expert he is. We're here to talk to Nguyen Chi Thanh.'

'Speaking of whom, where is he?'

Within minutes the first course arrived, and we didn't talk a lot as we worked our way through a first-rate dinner. My thoughts were occupied by this fantastic city with its – I struggled to find the right words – its *unsettling* attitude. It seemed all but oblivious of the war that still obsessed Americans. They could tolerate the apocalypse bar with its TV-parody war theme, and even our ex-VC cabbie seemed to regard his weird fate as the next thing to a joke. But it wasn't as if they'd forgotten. You saw too many cripples in the streets for that.

It wasn't just Vietnam. It was Saigon. Most of the country was generic rural Asia: peasants and rice paddies and tiny villages, water buffalo, quaint thatch and hardship, and old women in black pajamas and straw hats squatting and smoking beside the roads. Hanoi was the grim city of Marx and Ho. But Saigon was different. With its cosmopolitan mixture of Asian energy and European decadence, Saigon was a match for anything history could throw at it.

I suppose Connie was thinking similar things. This had to be as strange a trip for her as it was for me. I was about to ask her about it when our waiter reappeared.

'If you are finish, Mr Nguyen Chi Thanh see you in back.'

The chair legs scraped faintly as we pushed away from our table. The waitress was already clearing away the wreckage of dinner. We followed the young man through a doorway curtained with strung beads that clacked faintly and evocatively as we passed through.

The corridor beyond was dim, lit only by a single bulb of low wattage. My stomach tightened because, if this were a movie, we would be attacked here. But it wasn't a movie and the waiter opened a door through which brighter light streamed. We went inside and the door was closed behind us. Through the thick pall of cigarette smoke that hung in the air I saw a man sitting behind a table, the room's sole occupant.

'Please forgive me for not rising,' he said with only the faintest of accents. 'I fear I can no longer do so.'

I had seen Nguyen Chi Thanh a few times when he'd come to confer with my battalion CO, but I wouldn't have recognized the man who sat across the table. He had aged far more than the intervening years, and one side of his face sagged slightly, the eye on that side plainly blind. He raised a cigarette to his lips with fingers that had been broken and healed crookedly. His body was skeletal, dressed in a traditional robe instead of the more common western attire favored by most Vietnamese men. Apparently, the re-education camps were as rough as advertised.

'Please be seated.' He waved the twisted talons of the other hand and we took two of the chairs opposite his. The seat was slightly warm beneath me.

'Mr Nguyen,' I began, 'my name is Treloar. This is Consuelo Armijo. We don't wish to compromise you in any way, but there is information we need.'

'How might you compromise me?'

'I have been told that you have your finger on the pulse of the Saigon underground, that the government would consider you an enemy if . . .'

He smiled slightly and a tiny laugh wheezed and bubbled in his chest. 'Mr Treloar, you misapprehend somewhat. The government here is in great disarray. It is much the same situation as in China: a group of old men desperately trying to shed Marxism while retaining power. I assure you they have far more pressing problems to concern them than poor, ruined old Nguyen Chi Thanh. Now, you told my nephew that you wished to speak to me concerning Nguyen Duc?' Plainly, he wasn't going to waste any time on amenities. Well, to look at him, he didn't have a lot of time left to expend wastefully.

'To begin, my wife was Duc's sister.'

'I know who you are, Mr Treloar. You married Miss Rose when you were a young soldier here in 1968. Later, you sponsored her family for immigration when they escaped at the fall of Saigon. That was a very responsible, dutiful thing to do. We could wish that your government had been equally mindful of its obligations.'

'A few days ago, in Los Angeles, Duc was killed. He was gunned down in the street.'

His eyelids drooped fractionally. 'It saddens me that my old friend Nguyen Duc has died. He was a brave man and a fine soldier.'

Maybe it saddens you, I thought, but it sure as hell doesn't surprise you. 'I've learned from his widow that he was under heavy pressure from criminal gangs in California – Vietnamese gangs. Just before he was killed, he was visited by two men from Saigon. They were putting together a coalition of native and immigrant Vietnamese gangs, together with operators from all over Asia. I need the names of those two men.'

'You think these two killed Nguyen Duc?'

'Whoever pulled the trigger, they were responsible.'

'Mr Treloar, when governments decline, when empires crumble and nations are in turmoil, then the criminals and the parasites flourish. So it is in much of Asia, but you need only to look at Russia to see what I mean. The Communists were stupid, but they were strong. Now there is neither wise government nor strong police, and the vermin operate much as they please. You will be seeing far more of this in America.'

'The international situation doesn't concern me,' I told him. 'This is personal.'

Again the faint smile. 'This I respect. I will find the names for you.'

'Mr Nguyen,' Connie said, speaking for the first time, 'there is something else we need to know.' Her eyes were a little red from all the smoke but she soldiered on. 'During the war there was an underground population of American deserters. They were called "ghosts". Are any of them still here?'

'When the bulk of the American forces left Vietnam many deserters were left behind. They were a great nuisance, but our enemy was Hanoi and we had little attention to spare for them. After Saigon fell, I was . . . away for a number of years. When I returned, much had changed. The new government had no tolerance for dissenters and foreigners. Most of those who could not flee to other countries were apprehended and executed immediately, without trial. For police who were willing to take the appropriate measures, they were not difficult to locate. In Saigon, a non-Asian could not fail to be conspicuous and there was much inducement to turn informer.'

'You said "most",' Connie pointed out. 'There were some who remained?'

'Oh, there were a few who had achieved enough importance to be of a certain value to the Communists. Even Marxists of a hermit mentality need someone who can conduct unofficial business with the outside world. The Communist Chinese knew enough to leave Hong Kong alone when they could so easily have taken it. So it was with Hanoi. Some of these ghost leaders had valuable contacts in the outside world and their activities could be tolerated. There were only three or four of these, though. The rest were mere thugs and were killed. Why do you ask about them?'

'It's relevant to an investigation of ours that might be connected to Duc's murder,' I said. 'We've heard mention of a "Big Ghost", and of ghosts still operating here.'

Nguyen shook his head. 'Gangs like to take fearsome names. There is such a gang here in Saigon, but it is purely Vietnamese, I assure you. As to those surviving deserters, none of them are now resident in Saigon. I have heard of the one called "Big Ghost". He is seen here from time to time, but now he is a semi-legitimate businessman. There are some who remember him as the master of all the American deserters and so he has that name.'

Finally. I felt the tingle deep in my belly, the feeling that at last I was close to him. 'Would his name be Martin Starr?'

His mouth pursed and his eyebrows rose slightly. 'I remember that name from the old days. I never saw the man Starr, nor have I seen the Big Ghost. Whether they are one and the same I cannot say.'

'Could you find out?' I asked.

'I will make enquiries.'

'We're staying at the Continental,' I told him. 'But not for long.'

'This may take some time. And remember, he will certainly not be using his old name. Such men have many passports. I will get word to you back in America. I am not without resources.'

'One more thing,' Connie said. 'There is a film company coming here soon to make a movie about the war. They've been threatened, told to stay away. Would you know anything about that?'

For the first time he showed the slightest surprise. 'A film?

Hollywood coming here to make a movie? I cannot imagine anyone being concerned with it other than as a business opportunity.'

We rose. 'Thank you for your co-operation, Mr Nguyen. You have been of great assistance to us.'

He nodded. 'Good fortune to both of you. And, Mr Treloar?'

'Yes?'

'Be very careful. As Nguyen Duc learned, the war is not over. It never ends.'

Out in front of the café Connie took several deep breaths. 'Let's walk back to the hotel, Gabe. I need fresh air.'

'I was afraid you'd go all California on me and demand he put out his cigarette. I'm proud of you, Connie.'

'That was way too much smoke for one guy. There was a meeting in that room just before we went in. Five or six people, at least, and all of them smoking like freight trains.'

'I know. My chair was still warm. But maybe it was just his weekly poker game.'

'Yeah, sure. Poker games don't happen in this place. Conspiracy happens. He's not real mobile and he kept us waiting a long time. He must've called in all his buddies to talk over how to handle us. Did we really get anything tonight?'

'Maybe. We might just have a line on Martin Starr now.'

'What we got is a lot of this stuff.' She waved a hand at the night-time fog that made the neon signs hazy.

'Nobody's going to lay it all out for us,' I told her. 'Don't expect someone to drop us an anonymous letter that explains everything, ties up all the loose ends. We have to sort through a mountain of lies and evasions to pick out little nuggets of truth. Everyone's playing mind games, here and back home.'

'I hope that's not something you figured out just now.'

There were still a lot of people on the streets: people hitting the cafés, bars and gambling joints, tourists, a few police, and that massive bulk of people who always seem to be so *busy* in Asian cities, bustling around on nameless errands, carrying unidentifiable burdens, making things, selling things. We passed a flower shop still open that filled the street with fragrance, another that sold caged birds, still singing beneath the artificial lights, even at that late hour.

'By the way,' Connie said, 'it's Constanzia.'

'What?'

'My name. Constanzia, not Consuelo.'

'Oh. I was guessing. It just seemed inappropriate to use a diminutive.'

'I've always hated the name Consuelo. Only Spanish female name that ends in O. It just doesn't sound right. Of course, I've never been crazy about Constanzia, either. On the subject of names, what do you plan to do with those names when you get them? I mean, you can't just go out and kill them, can you? Even if it'd be doing the world a favor.'

'I don't know yet,' I admitted. 'I haven't decided. One thing at a time.' By now we were back in front of the Continental. The terrace café was still open. Maybe it stayed open all night. 'Come on,' I said. 'Let's have a coffee.'

'No, I'm tired.'

'There's something I want to show you.'

'Okay, I'll humor you, but just this once. Don't keep me up too late. I need my beauty sleep.'

The Vietnamese waiter seated us at a table next to one of the wide archways that overlooked the square. The ceiling of the terrace was high, supported by white pillars, the arches at least fifteen feet from tile floor to apex. Outside the arches, fanciful wrought iron braces supported an awning from which huge bamboo curtains were suspended. Now, at night, the curtains were rolled up. The lamps on the walls and the candles on the tables attracted bugs from outside, but this was the tropics, and in the tropics you live with bugs.

'So what did you want me to see?' she asked.

'Look around you.'

She complied. A number of the tables were occupied, mostly by Americans and Europeans, with a sprinkling of Asian businessmen. Many were half drunk, winding down from an evening in the bars and night clubs.

'Yeah, what am I supposed to be seeing?'

'Graham Greene was here in the early fifties. He set a scene of *The Quiet American* here on the terrace of the Continental.'

'I never read it. Never saw the movie, either.'

'It's about how the Americans blundered into Vietnam, walking into a situation where the French had screwed up horrendously and were fighting a war with the Viet Minh, the predecessors of the Viet Cong. An old European colonial power that had been here for nearly a century found its situation spinning out of control, and here were these Americans with their cold-war zeal and their book-learned theories on how to deal with Asia and their stupid, innocent arrogance, about to unleash unimaginable misery for all the right reasons.'

'Uh-huh. Your point being?'

'Look at this place. That was more than forty years ago, and nothing's changed. The Continental terrace was the favorite hangout for the foreign press corps during the French Indochina War. It still was when I was here in '68. Some of these drunks here tonight are probably journalists, even though Saigon's not a hot news-beat just now. The rest are mostly businessmen and government attachés, all of them with big plans for Southeast Asia. Nothing's changed, Connie. We could be looking at the origins of the next war right here. All that you and I went through in this place, all those guys whose names are on the wall in Washington, and the ones rotting away in VA hospitals or still having trouble sleeping at night after twenty-five years – none of it meant anything.'

'You know, I never really bought that domino theory stuff, but nobody asked my opinion at the time and I doubt they'd've listened anyway. What did you think, you were gonna find some sort of vindication here? My father charged up Omaha Beach and his brother was on Iwo Jima, and they're both still pissed that Germany and Japan are booming while America's in decline, like they should've stayed conquered and occupied countries forever. The world doesn't stop because something significant happened to us.'

'I don't expect it to. But do you know the one thing that's really unchanged, even though you'd think we all would have learned by now? In Greene's book, the quiet American of the title, a guy named Pyle, brings about all this tragedy with his high-minded good intentions, but he's such a wide-eyed innocent that the very people he's endangering are looking out for him. The narrator of the story's a burned-out, cynical, opium-smoking English reporter, and even he isn't immune. He says something that's stuck with me ever since I first read it, maybe thirty years ago.'

'What's that?'

I took a sip of the rich French coffee. 'He says: "Innocence always calls mutely for protection when we would be so much wiser to guard ourselves against it: innocence is like a dumb leper who has lost his bell, wandering the world, meaning no harm." Words to live by, Connie.'

'Have you lived by them all this time?'

'Nope. I fall for innocence every time.'

Still a little jet-lagged, I slept lightly, which turned out to be a good thing. The door was open to the balcony, the fan whirring slowly overhead, stirring the muggy air. I'm not sure what disturbed me – some faint alteration of the night-time noises. But there was absolutely no question about what jerked me wide-eyed, staring awake.

Like smells, there are some sounds you never forget, even if you haven't heard them in decades. The muffled pop, followed by the cobra-like hiss, then the heavy, metallic thunk as it landed on the thin carpet were so distinctive that I didn't waste a fraction of a second marveling at their improbability.

I rolled out of the bed as fast as I ever did out of my bunk during an attack. On all fours, I scrambled for it. The gunpowder stink of the burning fuse led me to the grenade as surely as its ugly sound, and I scooped it up.

In movies, people often dive on to grenades to save their buddies, but it's a stupid thing to do. In fact, it's about the only way a grenade is likely to kill you. Grenades are great wounders. You might be unlucky enough to catch a big frag in the brain or heart, but mostly they maim. What you do with a grenade is grab it and throw it as far from you as you can.

The problem was where to throw it. This wasn't exactly a demolition range. I knew it must have come in through the balcony door and it could go back out the same way, but there might be people in the square below; I couldn't spare the time to fool with the door to the hallway; the little bathroom was a possibility, but it abutted Connie's room and the wall might be thin enough to allow fragments to go through at dangerous velocity.

Needless to say, these thought occupied little time, a commodity in short supply when dealing with a live grenade. After a fraction of a second spent weighing the possibilities, I settled on the balcony itself. Most of the frags would be blown upward or be absorbed by the outer wall. Besides, the bastard who'd thrown it might still be out there and the idea of bagging him had genuine appeal.

I rolled the grenade out on to the balcony and dived for the bathroom, into a fetal crouch in the shower stall with my palms clamped over my ears. After the frantic haste, the ensuing second and a half seemed endless.

The explosion was amazingly loud, more like something you'd expect from artillery than a lousy little hand grenade. Glass and pieces of window sash and splinters of the door flew through the bedroom. The air was thick with choking dust, and then there was utter silence.

I unwound from my crouch and checked myself out. No injuries I could readily discern; not bad for an out-of-training old ex-cop long past his soldiering days. I hoped I hadn't killed anyone out there except maybe the assassin. There was a heavy pounding on a door.

'Gabe! Gabe! Are you all right? What the hell was that?'

I realized that it was the adjoining door to Connie's room that was taking the pounding and I flipped the latch. It opened and Connie was there looking disheveled and absurdly sexy in a T-shirt and panties. She threw her arms around me and I could feel her heart pounding beneath the ribs next to her spine. 'You're okay! Jesus Christ, Gabe, what the hell was that?'

'Grenade,' I wheezed. 'Someone tossed it into my room but I tossed it out on to the balcony.'

She coughed. 'I can't breathe in here. Come into my room, but watch where you step. There's glass everywhere.

We sidled into the other room and closed the door. With my arms wrapped around her warm solidity the reaction hit me all at once and I shook like a freezing dog.

'God damn!' I said, clenching my jaw to keep my teeth from chattering. 'More than twenty-five years and people in this town are still chucking grenades at me!'

Chapter Fifteen

The hotel management were embarrassed. The Saigon police were less embarrassed and a lot more curious. The government official in charge of foreign visitors was really, really embarrassed. This was not to say that any of them were exactly rattled. It takes a lot more than a little old explosion to unnerve the Saigonese. What I found most interesting was that none of them seemed to assume that I had been the intended target of the attack. They were just concerned that the story might damage the tourist trade. After all, this was Saigon, not Beirut or Sarajevo or even Londonderry.

Mr Pham was a gray little bureaucrat from whatever stamping factory turns out such men. With slight variations he might have been holding the same office in Tokyo or Moscow or Washington. He was there to soothe the ruffled feathers of visitors and minimize the government's involvement in the unfortunate incident.

'You must understand, Mr Treloar,' said Mr Pham, 'that this sort of thing is most rare in the People's Republic. It distresses us that a tourist such as yourself should be so inconvenienced, although there was thankfully no loss of life.'

There had been no body outside. The agile grenade chucker must have jumped down to the street and sprinted off as soon as he'd delivered his present: a foresighted course of action, as it turned out. I'd told no one that I had sent the grenade outside, and let them assume that it had been thrown on to the balcony from street level.

'Rare among the Saigonese, but more common among the criminals who come here to establish themselves.' This from Le Duong, police chief for central Saigon. 'With the easing of international tensions these social parasites have scented opportunity here in Saigon. A number of suspicious persons now reside in your hotel, Mr Treloar. It is likely that one of them was the intended victim.'

'Sure,' I said. 'It's easy to misjudge and get the wrong room from outside.' We were sitting in his office in the city hall, a huge Victorian-style building at the end of Boulevard Nguyen

203

Hue, a thoroughfare a block from Tu Do, laid out by the French when they were trying to make their colonial capital look like Paris; they came about as close to succeeding as could be expected in tropical Southeast Asia.

'We shall arrest the man responsible,' Le Duong assured me. Some things are universal. He sounded just like an LA police chief telling the press that an arrest was imminent. It's just one of those things they say. What they mean is that they're waiting for an accomplice to rat on the perpetrator. They don't have a prayer of locating him otherwise.

After I had told them everything I thought they should know for the twentieth time, I was once again assured that it was all just a fluke, that I should not allow it to spoil my visit to their beautiful country, that above all they would appreciate it if I did not complain to the consul or the foreign press. I told them, hell, what was travel to exotic places without a touch of adventure anyway? Amid smiles and handshakes I was sent back to my hotel in an official government Toyota.

'They gave us new rooms,' Connie said when I got back and we decided on a belated breakfast or early lunch on the terrace. 'They must be the best rooms in the place. I get the impression we could stay here free for a year if we just keep quiet about what happened. What *did* happen, by the way? I mean, I know somebody tossed a grenade into your room, but who and why?'

'Good question. The authorities think it's feuding gangs and somebody got the wrong room by mistake.'

'Yeah, sure.' We'd agreed to pretend even greater bewilderment than we actually felt. 'No sense endangering Nguyen Chi Thanh, assuming that he wasn't behind the grenade chucker. Think he might be?'

'It's conceivable. We don't know what's going on, who's on what side. Everybody's playing games here. At least that much hasn't changed.'

'I think it's time to clear out,' she said. 'The next time they might throw four or five grenades at once. You can't field them all. Or maybe they'll send a machine-gunner, like they did for your brother-in-law.'

'Agreed. I'll call the airline. Maybe we can get out of here tonight.' Suddenly I was as sick of Vietnam as I had been that last day at Tan Son Nhut.

'I've already done it. First flight we can catch leaves at six tomorrow morning. Saigon to LA with a stopover in Honolulu.'

'Let's be on it.'

She thought for a while, and so did I. 'While you were at the police station I went up to see our rooms. I pretended I was looking for something I'd left, but I was just curious. They were cleaning up and had most of the glass and plaster swept up already. There really wasn't much damage, just the glass and some wood. I went out on to the balcony and I saw where the grenade went off. I expected a big gaping hole, but there was just a little black smear about the size of my palm. There were a lot of tiny nicks in the outer wall, but you wouldn't even see them from street level. Somehow I expected more, with all that godawful noise and the glass and dust.'

'A grenade's got a bursting charge of about two ounces of TNT or one of the more modern explosives. It's not like a hundred-pound bomb or an artillery shell. It's mostly just concussion and a lot of tiny fragments flying around very fast. Those little frags are about the size of a paring off your smallest fingernail, but they can do a lot more damage to a body than you'd think. I still have a few of them in me. They'll scrub out that little black smear and plaster over the nicks in the wall. The glass and the door will be replaced. Go into those rooms this evening and you'd never guess that anything happened. They're good at that here. I guess they have to be.'

The new room was bigger than the last, and it had a small sitting room as well as a bedroom. It was on the third floor too, making it less accessible to bold grenadiers. Still no air conditioning, though. I took a shower and stretched out on the bed in a pair of thin cotton pajama bottoms to catch up on my sleep, but sleep wouldn't come to me. My mind kept flashing to the image of Connie in my arms the night before. It was certainly one of the more pleasant interludes of the last few days, despite the urgency of the circumstances. I'd felt that weird sexual rush that sometimes follows an intense jolt of adrenalin, and maybe she had as well – but we'd had to split apart and get dressed when the management came thumping on the door and the sirens drew closer.

She'd made no reference to it later, and that saddened me. There had been no flirtation between us thus far. I suppose she was too prickly and I was too long out of practice. I considered going over and knocking on the door to her adjoining room, but I hesitated. Then I wondered why. Fear of rejection? At my age? Who was I kidding?

I lay on my bed a long time, staring up at the fan, trying to make up my mind, work up my nerve. I could move plenty fast when I was dealing with a goddamned hand grenade. Why not this? Was it because I was in Rose's hometown? When we'd seen the cathedral up at the north end of Tu Do Street the day before, I hadn't told Connie that Rose and I were married there in one of the side chapels. My CO had stood as my best man and Duc gave away the bride. I'd been tempted to go see the place, but I was afraid the Communists might have turned it into a museum, like the Bolsheviks had done with St Basil's in Moscow.

Maybe that was a part of it – but Rose had died years ago. There had been women since, but only very few. Only very special ones. So why not Connie? Because we were working together and it would be unprofessional?

I decided that I could waste what remained of my life by endlessly asking myself questions. It was something I did too much lately. To hell with it. She could turn me down or she could laugh in my face. I could live with it. I had certainly lived with worse. One thing was certain: I didn't want to be alone.

I got up and walked to the adjoining door and made myself knock without hesitating.

'Come on in.' Her voice was a little thick, as if she'd been half asleep. I opened the door. It hadn't been latched on her side.

I could barely see her through the mosquito netting that draped the bed. The thick bamboo curtains were drawn, moving slightly in the breeze of the ceiling fan so that a few thin streaks of light from outside shifted on the floor. There was a haze of thin smoke in the air from a smoldering coil of the insect-repelling incense that is ubiquitous in the tropics.

I walked over to the bedside. She lay beneath the sheet, her bare shoulders gleaming above the white linen in the light of an errant streak of outside light. Her eyes were deep-shadowed, unreadable.

'Connie,' I started, my throat closing up on the next words.

'Yes?' She sounded the tiniest bit amused.

'Connie, last night ... I know you were scared and God knows I was. But ... I felt something, and I think you did too.' God, that was lame. I hadn't sounded that dumb as a teenager. I was glad she had the room darkened. It's a terrible thing for a grown man to blush.

I could see her teeth gleaming in the dimness. 'I felt something all right. Does danger always give men such a charge?'

'Not danger. It's the relief afterward, when you know you're still alive.' At least she hadn't laughed.

'Yeah. Being alive is nice, isn't it?' She flipped one side of the sheet back. 'Don't just stand there, Gabe. Get in.'

The mosquito netting parted before me like magic and I slid into the bed. She came into the circle of my arms without urgency, and the faint, flowerlike scent of her perfume came to me, driving away the pungency of the incense. Her flesh was faintly damp, as if she had just bathed.

'Just hold me for a while, okay?' she said. She rested her head on my chest and my hand trailed gently down her spine. No T-shirt and panties this time. 'Last night,' she said, her words almost slurred, her breath riffling the hairs on my chest, 'when I heard that awful noise, I knew what it was. I jerked wide awake and I was sure you were dead on the other side of that door. But I had to go and be sure.' Her hand crept up my chest and I covered it with my own. 'I couldn't believe it when you opened the door.'

We were quiet for a while, then she said, 'It's so easy to die. It can happen so fast. Something like that – it makes life look different, more precious, at least for a little while.'

'It does that,' I said, my arm bringing her even closer, her breasts pressing hard into my side. Her left hand laced with mine and for an instant our rings clicked together.

'This is the rough part, isn't it?' she whispered. 'It's like they never left us, your Rose and my Mick. They're not here, but we can't stop feeling their presence. I think they'd be happy for us, Gabe. Because we're still alive.'

'I know they would,' I said, lowering my lips to hers. She released my hand and her arms went around me and I slid my palms up and down her length. She gripped and stroked and our tongues danced together.

Her breath came faster through her nostrils, then her mouth broke away from mine so that she could gasp as I touched and caressed her. The body that had looked so hard in the gym and by the pool was soft and pliant and infinitely responsive. Her fingers kneaded my flesh, her nails tracing the old scars, and her teeth nipped together on my ear when I touched the nest of tight, red-brown curls at the juncture of her thighs.

Then she was pulling me over her and she guided me with one hand while the other pulled my head down to her breast. I drew out the moment of entry as long as I could, savoring the rich carnality of it while she dragged in a long, shuddering breath. Her strong legs wrapped around me and held me still for a while as she readjusted herself beneath me. I drew back slightly, my hands framing her face. Those generous lips drew back in a smile and a laugh formed deep in her throat as her pelvis began to rock like a cradle.

We were in no hurry and we both knew how to draw this ancient dance out, adjusting our rhythms like the sea and the tides, first flowing urgently, then ebbing, pausing, delaying. We stopped from time to time to explore one another more fully. Then there came a moment when we both knew that we had to finish it and we surged into each other, pushing one another up that long slope that ended in the blinding, exquisite moment of merging.

In the time of pulsing aftermath we lay panting with our upper bodies separated, our lower bodies still joined, fingers interlaced, and sweat slowly cooling us.

'Gabe?' she said when she could talk again.

'Yes?' It was an effort to get out that one, short word.

'Let's not make too much of this just yet, okay?'

'Why do you say that? I want to make a lot of it.'

'We're not our usual selves right now. It's this place, Gabe. It's not real. It's exciting and sensuous and dangerous all at the same time. It does things to our heads. We'll be home soon and I may not feel the same about you and you may feel different about me.'

'I'll feel the same way about you,' I told her.

'Maybe. But maybe not. I just don't want you thinking we've made some sort of commitment here.' Her hand stroked my thigh, but it was a gesture of affection, not excitement. We were both thoroughly wrung out.

I patted the smooth pliancy of her belly. 'Okay, if you want it that way. When we get back I won't go around telling people we're engaged or anything. But I'm not forgetting, either.'

'Fair enough.' Her voice was thick, half asleep. 'Now go on back to your room. I've been sleeping alone for a long time. I don't think I can go to sleep with someone else in the bed.'

I gently disentangled our legs and pulled away. Before I left I bent and kissed her on the cheek. She was already asleep. I closed the net and went back to my own room.

It was fully dark when I awoke. I checked my watch in the light coming from the square outside: 11.35. I got up, splashed water in my face, brushed my teeth and generally made myself feel more human. I was pleased to note that the ringing in my ears from the grenade blast had stopped.

Dressed in clean clothes, I knocked gently on Connie's door. No answer. Was she still asleep or had she gone out? I put my ear to the door and listened, but I heard nothing. Either she was solidly asleep or she'd gone downstairs for a late dinner. Hell, maybe she was out jogging. I was about to try the lobby and terrace when the phone rang. I went over to the stand by the bed and picked it up.

'Treloar?' It was a man's voice and it sounded familiar.

'Hacker?' It was the guy from the bar at the Apple Orchard.

'That's right. Look, I wasn't expecting us to be doing business together so soon, but something's come up. Are you doing anything right now?'

There was something awfully abrupt about this. After my recent shock I wasn't in the mood for anything abrupt.

'What's this about?'

'I'd really rather not discuss it on the phone. They're pretty backward here, you know, hotel operators, things like that.'

Now I really didn't like it. 'Where are you calling from?'

'Right here in the hotel. I'm in the lobby. Why don't you come on down and we can discuss this?'

My mind raced. It was all wrong. 'I need to talk to Connie first,' I said, stalling. 'We're here on business together and I can't transact anything without her.'

'Well, I'm afraid you can't do that, Treloar.' He sounded hesitant, almost embarrassed.

Icy little feet started dancing on my spine. 'What do you mean?'

'The guy I'm working for – she's with him now. But it's you he really wants to see. What do you say I come up to your room and we can talk?'

'You stay right where you are.' I hung up and tried to gather my thoughts. Was it a bluff? I went over to Connie's door and pounded. 'Connie!' Nothing. I went back to the phone, dialled the desk and asked for her room. I stood by the door and listened while her phone rang twenty times.

I sat on the end of the bed and thought. I sure as hell wasn't going to confront him in my room. The lobby would be as good a place as any. Was there anyone I should notify? Not in this country.

I took stock of my situation. I didn't have a gun, a knife, a blackjack, even so much as a nail file. Not that any weapon would preserve me from people who ran in gangs and used explosives. Hell, I'd once been here heavily armed and with a whole army around me, and I hadn't been safe even then.

Well, so much for advantages. I didn't have any. He was holding all the cards. I got up and left the room. The decision wasn't as wrenching for me as for most people. I'd gone through long years of alcoholism, of self-loathing and suicidal depression. Once you've been there, the prospect of a quick death isn't all that frightening.

That doesn't mean I wasn't cautious. I took the emergency stairs down to the ground floor. They opened on to a corner of the lobby and I cracked the door. Hacker was sitting in plain sight on a settee in the middle of the lobby. A quick scan didn't reveal any suspicious characters lurking about, but that didn't mean a damn thing. He undoubtedly had backup and it was probably outside or in one or more of the rooms opening off the lobby. Nothing I could do about it in any case.

I left the stairwell and walked up to the settee. He was facing three-quarters away from me and was a tiny bit startled when I showed up by his shoulder.

'Explain yourself fast, Hacker. I'm not a patient man.'

He jerked around and his grin had a slight, shamefaced edge to it. 'Hey, Treloar. Look, don't get excited. Connie's fine, it's just this guy's kind of paranoid and likes to feel that he has an ace in the hole.'

'What guy?'

'Keep your voice down, for Christ's sake. I heard about your little excitement here last night. People may be watching you.'

'Yeah, I'm a local celebrity. Is there a good reason why I shouldn't kill you now?'

'Well, for starters, I'm armed and I'm not alone, but look, Treloar, we're not comparing dicks here. I'm not trying to prove I'm more macho than you are, okay? That's kid stuff. This is a straightforward business arrangement and I'm just the go-between, the facilitator.'

'And your business involves kidnapping?'

He sighed. 'He had her before he even contacted me. Be realistic, man. This is Asia. They never heard of the Lindbergh case here and kidnapping's no big deal. There's a long tradition of exchanging hostages before commencing negotiations. They're never harmed as long as people deal in good faith.'

'I notice I don't get a hostage.'

'You're the interloper here. If you had a power base he'd send somebody for your goons to watch. It's customary.'

'Who is he?'

'Are you going to come talk with him or not?'

'Lead the way.'

He gestured toward the main entrance. 'After you.' He stayed behind me and to my right. So the gun, if he was carrying one, was probably tucked under his waistband over his right kidney, covered by the Filipino shirt. Not that it made any difference. I wasn't about to jump him. It was just nice to have these things sorted out and after all my years as a cop it was automatic.

The car was waiting for us on the street outside – a late-model Honda big enough to be a limousine by Vietnamese standards. There was a driver in front and another man beside him. I opened the back door on the passenger side and slid all the way across. Hacker got in beside me and closed the door.

The car pulled away from the curb and the guy beside the driver turned around and covered me with an automatic. He didn't snarl or act antagonistic: just a guy doing a job he'd done a lot of times before.

'I guess you know the drill,' Hacker said. I went through the necessary contortions while he frisked me, a task he performed competently. 'Okay, relax,' he said when he was finished. 'It's not a long drive.'

I took my hands from behind my head. We were heading south along the river. Gradually, the horizontal Vietnamese signs grew more infrequent, replaced by the vertical Chinese signs. Once they had been bright with red and gold paint, but most were now chipped and faded, looking shabby even in the dim light from the streetlamps.

Cholon had been pretty slummy even when I was there. Now it looked as if it had fallen on really hard times. There were sizable sections that looked as if they had been bombed or burned out and never rebuilt. It was early in the night for the streets to be so deserted. Was there a curfew for the Chinese, or had they all been run out? Cars and trucks passed by us occasionally, but I could see nothing through their windows.

We pulled into a wide garage entrance in the blank wall of a hulking riverside building. The tarry smell of the wharfs was strong in the air, and I could hear the horns of ships cruising up and down the channel. I had a vague idea of where we were: about a quarter of a mile from my old MP barracks.

The driver cut the engine and everyone got out. The garage doors rolled shut and it got even darker, then a light came on.

'Over this way,' Hacker said. I let him nudge me toward a small room that looked like some sort of dispatcher's office. Connie sat in a rickety wooden chair in the middle of the room. She wasn't bound or gagged but she was blindfolded. Beside her sat a thug with a pistol in his lap, smoking a cigarette. Behind us, the driver and the gunman had already lit up. As long as there's an Asia, the tobacco companies will never go broke.

'See?' Hacker said. 'I told you she was okay, and she'll stay that way as long as you behave yourself.'

'Gabe?' Connie said. 'Is that you? I told that white-haired bastard you'd never be stupid enough to come here with him.'

'She didn't say it with a lot of conviction,' Hacker informed me. 'I know this has put a strain on our friendship. I guess this means your movie company won't be hiring me?'

'Are you all right, Connie?'

'I'm not bleeding, but I'm not dancing, either. I stepped out of the hotel and Hacker's there in a car like, hey, fancy meeting you here. I step over to talk to him and this goon sticks a gun in my ribs and they hustle me into the car and put a blindfold on me.'

'Just keep cool. It looks like somebody wants to see me.' I didn't tell her I hadn't been blindfolded. She'd know that it probably meant they didn't care what I saw since they intended to kill me.

'Where are we?' she asked.

'Don't tell her,' Hacker said. 'If she knows the location, she'll have to stay here for the whole interview. Treloar, you're going to see somebody now. I'm going to take Connie back to central Saigon, to a place where there's a phone. As soon as I get the call that the interview is concluded, she'll be released, unharmed. I promise you that.'

'Yeah?' she said. 'And what about Gabe?'

'I guess that depends on how he decides to play it. But there's no reason why anyone should get hurt. You two have come over here and you've upset some people who are accustomed to taking drastic action to protect themselves. The man Gabe's going to see is about the most easygoing of the lot, but he's not someone you want to fuck with. Connie, you can go now.'

She got up and the thug took her arm, started to guide her out of the room, toward the car.

'See you back at the hotel, Connie.'

She stopped, turned to face me. She might have yelled that I was talking like an idiot since I didn't have the first goddamned idea what was going to happen to either of us, but she knew that any show of fear or weakness in a situation like this would be a bad move. It would have been nice to hug her, tell her that everything would be all right, but that too would be unwise. Any slightest display of affection would make each of us a more effective lever to use against the other. I think she understood that, too.

'Yeah,' she said. 'Don't be late. We have a plane to catch in the morning.'

I followed them out into the garage and Hacker pointed to a doorway in the far wall. 'Up those stairs there. Just be cool, hear what the man has to say, and you'll catch your plane in the morning with no sweat.' He got into the car with Connie and the door shut with the solid thunk of well-engineered machinery. The engine started smoothly, somebody slid the garage door open and the car backed into the dark Cholon street. With a quiet acceleration it disappeared in the direction of Saigon proper.

I turned around and the garage door slid shut again. The goon who'd been watching Connie stood by the office with his pistol dangling in his fist. Another man stood in a darkened corner where I could see only the red glow of his cigarette tip. There had to be at least one more, the one who had opened and shut the garage door. Too many men, too many guns. What the hell. I crossed the garage and stepped through the doorway.

There was no light in the stairwell, just what filtered through from the garage and down through a skylight, maybe some distant neon reflected from the clouds above. Just enough to see that there was a man standing at the top of the stair, wispy and insubstantial, visible only because he was dressed in a pale suit. I started up.

'Yesterday upon the stair,' I said, 'I met a man who wasn't there.'

'He wasn't there again today,' he said, finishing the old nursery rhyme, 'oh, how I wish he'd go away.'

I reached the landing. 'Hey, Martin. Long time no see.'

'It has been a while, hasn't it, Mr Treloar?' The hairline was higher, the fine-boned, almost girlish face a little harder, but Martin Starr had changed amazingly little. His hands were folded atop a slender cane and I could see that his suit was raw silk of unmistakable Hong Kong tailoring. He was as elegant and immaculate as Fred Astair.

'Make it Gabe,' I said. 'Old comrades-in-arms like the two of us should be on a first-name basis.'

'Gabriel,' he said, the tiny teeth I remembered showing in a thin crescent of a smile. 'The archangels have such majestic names: Raphael, Michael, Gabriel. I wish my parents had had such good taste. I had to settle for a second-rate saint.'

'He divided his cloak with a beggar,' I said. 'You ever done that, Martin?'

'I have, and probably more often than you, Gabriel.' He turned his head slightly, and I saw that his graying hair was tied back in a short ponytail. It lent an eighteenth-century dignity to his fine-etched profile. 'Let's take a walk, shall we?'

'Why not? I have nothing else to do for a while.' I followed him down the hall and detected no infirmity in his steps. The cane was an accessory. He opened a door and we were on a landing overlooking the wharfs and the river. For a minute we watched the moving lights of the river traffic, everything from tankers to sampans dotting the slowly roiling waters of the river that descended from the fastnesses of inner Asia.

'I've always preferred Cholon to Saigon proper,' Starr said as we descended the rickety wooden stairs. 'Once they were separate cities. In the French days, Cholon was actually larger than Saigon itself. But the cities merged and Cholon became a suburb.' We stepped out on to the long boardwalk from which the piers jutted out into the water like ribs on a clean-picked carcass.

'In those days,' he went on, 'you attended to politics in

Saigon and you came to Cholon for the nightlife. They maintained enormous brothels and inside the entrance of each one was a Foreign Legion MP post to maintain order.'

'Those were long gone by the time I got here.'

'Yes, American authorities were having no part of such civilized decadence. Abused streetwalkers and vicious pimps are our style. Wherever we go, we bring Puritanism and sin.'

'Why the grenade, Martin?'

'That is one reason why I wanted to meet with you.' He walked easily, unwarily. I couldn't see any of his men lurking in the shadows, but they were probably there. Or maybe not. Who can fathom a man like Martin Starr?

'Why didn't you just call?'

'Would you have believed that it was I on the other end? I thought not.'

'You could've met me on the terrace, in a bar somewhere. You didn't have to kidnap Connie. That doesn't improve my opinion of you one bit.'

'For many years I've moved in an unrelievedly hostile environment, Gabriel. Certain precautions have become nearly reflexive with me. She is an outsider of no real significance and she was in little danger. The grenade was not mine.'

For no remotely sane reason, I believed him. 'Whose, then? Was it Nguyen Chi Thanh?'

He produced a dry laugh. 'Nguyen Chi Thanh is the sad survivor of a toppled regime, dreaming of the day he and his cronies will wield power again. In the latter 1700s, the French court played host to old Scottish Jacobites who were always about to restore the Stuarts to the thrones of Scotland and England. French Bourbons played the same role after the Revolution. After 1917, there were Romanovs tending bar and running restaurants all over the globe, waiting for the world to come to its senses and put them back in power in Russia.

'These are futile people, not to be taken seriously, Gabriel. Nguyen Chi Thanh talks too much to too many people. He endangered you, although he acted in good faith within his limited capabilities.' As he walked his cane tapped on the old, soft wood.

'Is that a Malacca cane?' I asked him.

'As it happens, yes.'

'I've read about Malacca canes all my life. I don't think I've ever actually seen one.' He handed it to me and I examined it. It was surprisingly light, reflecting the distant lights from its rich, gleaming lacquer finish, as slender and elegant as its owner. Best of all, it didn't seem to conceal a sword or gun. I handed it back.

'Each day brings a new experience,' he said, 'if we keep ourselves open to it. On the contrary, Gabriel, I once saved you from a hand grenade. Surely you remember?' He gave me that almost shy, sidelong glance that I remembered, up from beneath the long lashes.

I paused, pinched the bridge of my nose, took a deep breath of the river air. Somehow it smelled wonderful. 'People keep reminding me of old debts these days. A few seconds after you pulled your magic trick with the grenade, I had you right in my sights and I didn't pull the trigger. We're even on that count, Martin. That spook major, Gridley or Gregory or whatever his name was – Gresham, that's it. He was so pissed off he wanted to have me court-martialled.'

Starr smiled with childlike delight. 'Did he? Well, he was very angry with me. But later, that night by the river not so far from here, you shot me. That was not kind, Gabriel. But then, you were more experienced at war by that time. It does harden a man, and I've forgiven you.'

'Actually,' I said, recalling the scene, 'it wasn't you I shot at. It was that tall guy who'd been yelling at you. He pointed a gun at me and I jerked off a round and my buckshot hit the table between you. I guess you caught some and he didn't. You were raising a gun too. If you hang around in bad company you've got to expect to get shot from time to time.'

He stopped and turned, facing me. 'A gun?' Then he smiled. 'Oh, I see, yes. There we were, in the middle of our dealing and carousing, and at the most improbable instant I saw you come out on that landing. I recognized you immediately, you know. I thought: How splendidly ironic are the fortunes of war! It was a Shakespearean moment, Gabriel.'

'I followed you and your buddies, shot one of them. I think I would've had you, but I turned back to get the one I'd shot. I didn't want to think of him burning. How the hell did you get through our cordon?'

'How like you to go to all the trouble of shooting a man only to turn back and save him from fire. Compassion is a grave error in some people, but altogether fitting and proper in

216

others. I read that in you that long, slow evening at Long Binh, when you and I and your friend the young sergeant formed our peculiar bond. He was a creature of little depth – all hard, glossy surface and a glib tongue, but in you I saw that capacity for love and suffering, for seeking and finding redemption in violence.' He paused. We stood in front of a ruined warehouse that was the nest of night birds and other nameless creatures. Inside it something, perhaps an owl, caught another benighted creature and a shrill squeal formed its self-bestowed elegy. A long, narrow pier stretched from the warehouse far into the river.

'To answer your question, we escaped by river. We surrounded ourselves with corpses and pretended to be among their number. The river patrol was fully occupied with those who were still alive, and we just drifted down with the current. We made our way ashore very near this place.' He tapped his cane a few times on the wood, meditatively. 'Being alive, being dead – once one has achieved a certain state of being, it becomes possible to slip back and forth from one to the other without great effort.'

'Who are you, Martin? Why were you in the LBJ? Why did they send a spook to pick you up? Why were we taking you to the embassy?'

He stepped out on to the old pier and I followed. The treacherous wooden decking creaked beneath our feet.

'It was all spook stuff, Gabriel. The whole war was a spook operation gone wretchedly wrong. I was one of them. I was extremely young, a mere lieutenant, but I had a flair for eastern languages and I was sent to do the work of more responsible but lazier and less competent men. We had an abundance of those. I will not say that I was idealistic, a quality alien to me then as now, but I was passionate and threw myself fully into whatever I undertook.

'My superiors sent me into Burma, Laos, Cambodia, wherever the dominoes had to be propped up. These were wild and savage places, Gabriel. I wish you could have been there, I believe you would have appreciated it: crossing gorges in the Burmese highlands on rope bridges that looked insufficient to support the weight of a butterfly; meeting with Kampuchean warlords in the moonlit ruins of Angkor – it was like something out of Haggard, a Victorian boy's adventure story come to life! Well, I *was* a boy.'

'I guess you're just a romantic at heart, Martin.'

'I set up a great many of those Air America bases where we funnelled money and arms and mercenaries in and moved them about from one country to another. Of course, there was a price to pay for the co-operation of all those bandits and warlords and complacent governments.'

'Drugs,' I said. 'You ran drugs for them.'

'What other wealth does south Asia have? It's now an old story, told by many indignant journalists and historians, scraping one finger across another and crying, "Fie! For shame!" And that wasn't the end of it. When you side with a bandit or a warlord, you have to participate in his wars and massacres. If a government accommodates you, you have to help it eliminate its enemies. But what are a few massacres? They were just gooks, weren't they? And what's a little dope when the goal is to slay the dragon of Communism? After all, it would never touch the children of the white establishment, and who cared about the rest?'

'But you got sick of it, huh?' We'd reached the end of the pier. Nothing left but the two of us and the deep, black water below.

'Not of the evil of it. I never balked at that. It was the sheer, blundering incompetence of it all. I could have put up with any amount of honest lying and hypocrisy, but not the puerile, sickly protestations of idealism, patriotism, even religious morality. It isn't difficult to deal with a genuine butcher, Gabriel. You can accomplish your bloody work and feel clean afterward. Nothing contaminates your soul like a pipe-smoking desk officer with a gray suit and a degree from Harvard who fancies himself Genghis Khan come again but who would never, never soil his own fingers.'

'So what did you do?'

'I set up in business on my own. I left the company, without notice but taking care to eliminate the two operatives most familiar with my latest movements, and I became a freelance consultant. For a while I specialized in organizing raids on opium trains and Air America dumps. I plotted mercenary operations, set up pipelines to Hong Kong, sold intelligence to whoever was paying. Who could be better at the work? I knew the personnel and schedules, I knew where everything was, I could find whoever I wanted to and avoid whoever I wanted to. I was young and voracious and I sought knowledge.'

'Knowledge?'

'In the end, that's all that there is: to know the nature of everything, to encompass it all, to experience it all. You contemplate the abyss, you descend into the abyss to face the monsters, you become the abyss.'

'If you were so good,' I asked him, 'how did you get caught?'

'In time, my information became less current, operations and sources were shut down. I was less effective, and I was in search of new experience anyway. I became involved in a classic farce; Asian theater of the absurd. I undertook a mission for a Laotian warlord, to negotiate for the services of a band of Chinese Nung mercenaries. They were operating in Montagnard country, working for the American Special Forces. The Nung were the remains of old Nationalist regiments driven out of China by the communists. Their commander indicated that they would look favorably upon a change of employers if a price could be agreed upon. My guides for the first leg of the journey were Pathet Lao and they were to turn me over to some Viet Cong operating in Montagnard country who needed a Laotian base and undertook this service in exchange. I assure you this was not a particularly complicated arrangement for that time and place. It did, however, allow wide latitude for disaster, which duly occurred.

'The Lao and the VC were brothers in the cause, but that didn't mean that they trusted one another. One thing they agreed on was that they hated the Chinese as much as they hated each other, and with good reason, as events were to prove. The site agreed upon for the meeting was perilously close to the Green Beret encampment, but we were assured that the Americans were off on a long-range mission.

'Of course it was an ambush. I should have expected it, but for once my instincts were dulled. I had been too successful for too long – and let that be a lesson to us all, Gabriel. The claymores shredded most of the VC, and the rest were shot. I was standing right between two of the claymores when they were detonated, in the space between their fragmentation patterns, but the concussion knocked me unconscious.

'The Nung were collecting heads for bounty, but I was a special prize and they took me to the Special Forces camp alive. There I was: an American consorting with the enemy. Naturally, the Green Berets assumed I was a deserter and a turncoat. They choppered me out to the LBJ, where I remained in a self-protective daze while the Army tried to figure out who I could be.'

'What did the other prisoners make of you? I recall the LBJ as a notably rough pen.'

'There is an order in such things, an order long established by nature and biology. In prisons as in dog packs you merely see it in its pure form: assertion and establishment of dominance. It's been going on since the first microbes. Several men mistook me for an effeminate and I disabused them. Others challenged my primacy and I dealt with them. In the LBJ men were carried out every morning, dead of mysterious and unexplained injuries. It happens in prisons every day.'

'So you were in your element?'

He shrugged. 'It was a way station, between one life and the next; a limbo, a purgatory. Actually, it was agreeable to be among men who did not pretend to be other than what they were. But I didn't like it that the world outside was going on without me, and I did not like to contemplate the company finding me there.'

'But they found you anyway, did they? And they sent Gresham to get you?'

'Not exactly.' He gazed downriver where the water and silt and all the past years washed down to the sea. 'Gresham was a rogue, as I was a rogue. But he was – how shall I put it? – a safe rogue. He operated on his own, outside the company, but he did it from snug within the company's arms. He lacked the spiritual fortitude to be a true rogue, a solitary. He lived in constant fear that he would be found out. This desire for order and safety has been the downfall of many otherwise superior men, Gabriel.

'During my independent operations we continued to have dealings together. His realm was the Saigon underworld, as mine was the outlaw milieu of the surrounding countries. It was an extremely profitable partnership. Getting word to him was not easy. The LBJ was so overcrowded that only the most serious cases were being sent there – men were not being released to their companies. But I managed to pass the information through a guard of less than sterling character.'

'So that's why he came down to Cholon to get his MPs instead of using the Seven-Sixteenth. I've been wondering about that ever since.'

'As always, he was being careful. Actually, there would have been little risk except that, under influence of concussion, I'd given those Special Force people my real name. Poor Gresham was very upset about that. We had a long talk in a solitary cell while the LBJ people tried to cope with my paperwork. They were terribly put out because there was no proper procedure for processing a non-person like me.'

'I remember that we waited around for a long time.'

'Anyway, Gresham tried to be reassuring, but I could smell the fear coming off him. He was going to get me out of the country without either the Army or the company knowing about it; the handcuffs were purely for the sake of appearance. Surely I understood, he'd come out with MPs and their suspicions should not be aroused. You can see where it was leading. He didn't need any MPs. He had authority to pick me up on his own and the means to cover it up afterward. But he was afraid of me.'

'So why the embassy?' I asked him.

'We wouldn't have gone there. He had a secure office on Tu Do Street. He'd have told you to drop us there, you'd have handcuffed me to a wall ring in one of the basement rooms, and he'd have dismissed you and you'd have gone on your way, perhaps pausing for a few beers at one of the local bars. Just one more inexplicable errand completed in a war where nothing was really expected to have a rational explanation. Had it not been for the remarkable occurrences of that night you would have forgotten it long, long ago.'

'Did you know the Tet offensive was coming?'

'No, I had been away from Vietnam for too long. I believe Gresham's own astonishment was the one thing he wasn't faking. It caught everyone by surprise and badly shook the company's sense of omniscience and omnipotence.'

The mist off the river was thickening, making distant things invisible, putting rainbow haloes around all the lights. 'So you knew where to go when you went underground. How did you survive that night, in handcuffs and prison fatigues?'

'It was one of the grand experiences of my life,' he said fondly. 'In those years I was hopelessly addicted to the adrenalin rush. There was a safe house by the Khanh Hoi docks – a place run by an old Chinese opium smuggler who had the Saigon police firmly in his pocket. It was a good place to stay, for deserters who could make enough big scores to meet his rates. I had to make my way from the shanty town to central Saigon through streets full of VC combat teams, MP jeeps spraying fire in all directions, whole blocks of buildings in flames. And I did it, Gabriel. I believed that night that I really had become a ghost, that I could make myself invisible to the eyes of mortals.

'Once, I paused for breath and refuge in a little Buddhist temple. An old priest sat before the image of Buddha, burning joss sticks and chanting prayers. He took no notice of the battle raging outside, never even glanced at me. Was I truly invisible? Even now I sometimes wonder.'

'But you didn't have any money,' I said. 'Why'd the old Chinese take you in?'

'He knew me. He knew that I would soon have plenty of money. He cut off my handcuffs, gave me new clothes and a room high beneath the eaves, some bottles of excellent French wine, a pipe and opium of the first grade. While the others crouched in the basement I went out on the lovely balcony with a glass of Cabernet and enjoyed the show. I cannot express or describe the sublimity of that dawn, when chaos achieved full human expression. I knew then that there was beauty even in futility.'

'I remember the morning,' I said. 'I spent it getting shrapnel carved out of my back.'

'Doubtless your experience was in its way as illuminating as mine. In any case, it was the beginning of my new life; the richest and fullest life I have ever known.'

'The life of a ghost?'

This time he paused for a while before speaking. 'How can I describe it to you, or to anyone who was not there and never shared my joy at taking life unadulterated, like uncut heroin through a needle straight into an artery? Can you even imagine an outlaw society of utterly deracinated men? Men who live their days submerged in a hostile sea, cut free from all strictures of behavior deemed acceptable by ordinary humans? There were men among them from the bayous and men from ivy-league colleges, black-power advocates and klansmen, men like fallen angels, and I became their master.

'I'll not romanticize. We were not some sort of buccaneer republic, like Tortuga or Madagascar. That is a fantasy for those who dream of a criminal life with the comfortable amenities of an ordered society. Many were merely unintelligent, or lazy, or had disordered minds. I was the only one among them who valued the life for its perfect reward: total, utter, complete freedom of thought. There can be nothing more liberating on earth. It was as if all my life I had been fettered with a short chain and unaware that I had wings. I tried to communicate this, but met only blank stares.'

He looked at me. 'And yet I was one of them, and I loved them, even the ones dope had turned into skeletal revenants and the ones who hated me because I was white. The ones who challenged me for supremacy I loved even as I killed them; loved them for their audacity and their willingness to die rather than be second.' For a moment he seemed unable to speak, then: 'I wish you had deserted, Gabriel. I wish you could have been one of us.'

I couldn't even begin to wonder what that meant. 'What happened to them? How did you stay alive? How did you get out?'

'Like all such societies, ours had only its fleeting moment. The attrition was high, you understand, from capture and from battle with the Vietnamese and Chinese gangs, and from internal squabbles and duels. When the Americans pulled out in '73 there was no more new blood coming in to replace that spilled here. When the North took over in '75, they proved to no one's surprise to be unsympathetic people. I made my way out, to Hong Kong at first. By then my contacts and wealth made this an easy task. I could have left years earlier, but this had become my world. In time, most of my friends ended up right here, in this river, and made their final journey to the sea.'

He gazed into the black waters for a long time, then murmured: 'Too late. Too late, my brothers.'

'What's that?'

'Just words from an old song.' He began to turn and I thought: Now it happens. Off this pier into the dark water, and then no more.

He stopped and turned back. 'Come along, Gabriel. You have a plane to catch.'

I let my breath out and followed his pale, narrow back.

'Connie isn't an outsider,' I said when we reached the boardwalk again.

'What do you mean?'

'Before, you said she was an outsider. But she was here, Martin. She was on the roof of the US Embassy during the big bug-out in '75.'

He turned, smiling with childish pleasure. 'Really? I'm sorry I didn't speak to her, then. I had assumed her to be too young for our war and its aftermath. Yes, America provided the world with a fitting curtain call for its débâcle in Vietnam. It was something totally unexampelled, Gabriel: an existential spectacle.'

'She said she heard your name mentioned in connection with the forged evacuation passes that were everywhere: all sorts of fat cats who didn't work for us had them.'

'To this one villainy I fear I must plead innocent,' he said. 'By that time I was blamed for all manner of things with which I had no involvement. Such a reputation as mine is a handy thing, for people who would keep their own fingers clean. You would do better to investigate my former colleagues, and learn who most of those fat cats were truly working for.'

We were almost back to the warehouse. 'What became of Gresham?' I asked him.

'He grew ever more cautious with age. His nature was always pre-vertebrate. When the environment no longer suited him, he metamorphosed, wove a chrysalis around himself and re-emerged as a different creature.'

His goons were right where he'd left them in the garage. The light now seemed bright, after the blackness outside. He crossed to a work bench that was empty except for an ink pad and some 3 × 5 cards.

'I know that you will soon have doubts, Gabriel. It's easy to suspend one's critical faculties on a foggy night in a Southeast Asian port. They are places of mystery and magic. The sense dissipates with sunrise. Soon, you'll have nagging suspicions that you've given ear to the deranged babblings of a drug-addled derelict enhancing his sordid past with self-aggrandizing romance.' He placed his hand beside the pad, fingers spread. 'You know how this is done.'

'You want me to print you?'

'Yes, and you have to do it personally. I want you to be satisfied that no sleight of hand was performed. Take my fingerprints, then pick up the card and put it in your pocket.'

I shrugged. 'Okay. But what's the point?' I picked up his hand, pressed the fragile-seeming forefinger into the ink, then rolled it on the card.

'You picked me up at an Army prison, a supposed deserter. Every soldier has his fingerprints taken and filed upon induction. This was done to you and to everyone else who served. When you return to the States, have my prints checked. You'll find no record of me under any name whatever.'

I finished with the last finger, picked up the card, examined it to make sure they were clear impressions, waved it for a few seconds to dry the ink, placed it in a breast pocket and buttoned it. Then, belatedly, I remembered something.

'Martin, did you send those threats to Mitch Queen and Selene Gibson? Are you planning to torpedo this film project?'

'I sent them,' he said, smiling. 'But I just wanted to attract the attention of certain parties, and I got it. Actually, I have little to do with Vietnam these days. They can come here and make their film and build a Vietnam War theme park without the slightest interference from me. Somebody probably will, anyway.'

The whole question of the movie seemed impossibly trivial after the last few days and I didn't feel like pressing him about it. I had my answer for Queen and he could believe it or not, as he chose.

The car was waiting. It was the same Honda and the same driver and goon were in it. I got in back and shut the door, then leaned out the window.

'Martin, you won't forget to make that call, will you?'

'Call?' he said. Then: 'Oh, Miss Connie, it slipped my mind. No, I told Pat to take her straight back to the hotel. They aren't holding her anyplace. She couldn't lead anyone back here, and in five minutes I'll be gone anyway, never to return.' He put a hand on the window frame and leaned close. 'She means something to you?'

'Yes, but I didn't know until last night.' The garage door slid open behind me and gray light flooded in. 'Hell, I guess it was the night before last. Maybe you wrote your threatening letters to manipulate someone, but the one to Selene brought Connie into my life. Thanks for that much, anyway.'

'Then my fund of good karma is increased. I am much in need of it, believe me.' He started to pull back, but I put a hand on his fine-boned wrist and he hesitated.

'Yes?'

'Martin, Saigon fell twenty years ago. What have you been doing all this time?'

He pulled away, disengaging. 'The war was what you and I

had in common, Gabriel. I've been alone since then. Have a safe flight.'

The car pulled out of the garage and he stood there with his hands atop his cane in the silvering fog, and then we drove away into the streets of Cholon.

I found Connie sitting in the lobby of the Continental, surrounded by our luggage. The look of relief on her face when she saw me was almost comical.

'My God, Gabe!' She jumped up, hugged me fiercely, then said: 'I didn't know whether to call the police or what! I was giving it another five minutes, then I was gonna go get the American Consul or whatever and—'

I shushed her. 'Come on, let's go catch our plane.' I grabbed up two of our bags and she grabbed the others and we went out and got into a taxi.

'Airport,' I told the driver.

'Well, what happened?' she demanded, fuming with impatience. 'Was it him?'

'It was him. We've got a long flight ahead of us. I'll tell you all about it when we're away from here.' I watched the sprawling city go by, so much the same, so changed.

'What's he like?'

I thought about that. How in God's name, in any human language, to describe the phenomenon of Martin Starr? 'I don't know. He's just a lonely guy, I guess.'

An hour later, our 747 was banking over Saigon, headed out toward the sun rising over the South China sea. I got a last glimpse of the city with the big, silt-brown river cutting through it. Down at the end of Tu Do Street I saw the cathedral and for some reason the name of it came back to me: The Basilica of Our Lady of Peace.

Chapter Sixteen

'You're jerking me off, right?' Lowry said. 'You want me to run these prints on a guy who deserted from the Army back in the sixties?'

'Just see if they're on file anywhere. If he was ever really in the Army, they've got to be on file, and I picked him up at a military stockade.' We were sitting in a café not far from the West Hollywood station. I'd landed less than two hours before and what I wanted to do more than anything else was sleep for about two days and get over my multiple Pacific crossings. The human body was never intended to cope with ten time zones all at once.

'This is a little distant from my investigation,' he said. 'The connection is – what's the word? – tenuous.'

'It's there,' I insisted.

'If so it's pretty damn vague. Because Duc was Vietnamese and this freak used to be a wheel in Saigon? Having a country in common doesn't make much of a case. If I had an Italian mob hit to investigate, I wouldn't assume that Luciano Pavarotti had to be involved.'

I'd told him some of the more credible parts of the story. Even those had raised his eyebrows all the way to his hairline. I handed him the card with the prints and he took it. 'It's not your customary sort of case, but you went into police work for the intellectual challenge, didn't you?'

He grinned. 'Come on, admit it: this is some piece of weird movie shit you and your producer friend cooked up, isn't it? All this stuff with spooks and ghosts and gangs and stars and death threats.'

'Maybe it was dreamed up by a scriptwriter,' I said, 'but people are dying for real.'

He got up, sticking the card in a pocket. 'It won't take too long. You remember how to get a good, clear set of prints, even if you had to use a stamp pad.'

'Like riding a bicycle,' I said. 'You never forget.'

I left him, went out and got into my car, still revelling in the paradisical Southern California climate, so different from the choking mugginess of the monsoon latitudes. The whole idea of the tropics as Eden is greatly oversold, if you ask me.

I'd tried to reach Queen as soon as we landed but he wasn't in his office. The woman who sounded like a starlet said he was away at a meeting, which seemed to be pretty much what Hollywood is all about: meetings. Connie had taken off to check with her boss, with Selene and her colleagues, and probably to work out. The long flight seemed to have energized her as much as it had exhausted me. She had slept much of the trip, after giving my story an incredulous hearing.

I thought I might be getting high on the blissfully cool air, decided I was just groggy from jet-lag and lack of sleep, and headed for Beverly Hills.

Julia told me that she hadn't seen Mr Queen since the morning of the previous day, but that was nothing unusual for him. Sometimes he disappeared for a week or more without informing her, the same way he sometimes showed up with unannounced guests and expected her to put on dinner for them. I guess the domestics of the big rich have their own litany of woes.

I made myself swim laps for more than an hour, to add muscle exhaustion to the mental kind, because I believe in disabling myself in a balanced and holistic fashion. I thought maybe by doing this I would wake up fully refreshed in body and mind. There is something about California that makes you prone to delusional health practices.

I managed to wait until it was almost dark before crashing. I set the alarm for 7.00 a.m. in hopes of re-establishing myself on a rational day-night basis. I crept between the sheets and was asleep before my eyes had a chance to close.

I woke up and glanced at the bedside clock. The red-glowing numbers said 4.12. I shut my eyes again and tried to summon back sleep. Fat chance. Back in Saigon it was time to be making dinner plans after an afternoon of sightseeing. I yawned, stretched a little, and the back of my hand hit something on the pillow next to my head.

I froze. It was one of those dreamlike moments when you know something is absolutely wrong but you can't quite figure out what. When I'd gone to bed, there had definitely been absolutely nothing on the pillow except a pillowcase. Whatever it was felt like it was made of paper, like a big paperback book or a stack of magazines or something. What with my recent experiences my mind went immediately to a jumbo-sized letter bomb. It made no sense, but why should anything start making sense at this late date?

Very slowly, with infinite caution, I rolled away from whatever it was, reached out to the bedside lamp and turned it on. Then, just as slowly, I turned my head to look back over my shoulder.

It lay there in seeming innocence: a bundle about ten by twelve inches, maybe four inches thick, lying on the pillow next to the indentation left by my head. It was wrapped in what looked like a silk scarf and tied with string. It wasn't ticking, but then real bombs don't. I told myself I was being a fool, that if somebody had come in while I was asleep, there were any number of more sensible ways to kill me than that.

I reached across and very gingerly tugged at the string. The knot slipped easily and the cloth slithered away. What was left was a stack of paper as thick as a typewriter ream, bound with heavy paper covers stamped in a leather pattern. I picked it up and set the heavy mass on my lap. In the upper center of the front cover was pasted a label and on it was typed, in caps: TU DO STREET. Below that: 'by Jared Rhine'. Then, in the lower right corner of the label: 'Copy 4'.

What the hell? I'd asked Mitch to see a copy of the script. Why had he delivered it like this? I decided that it was just the sort of halfassed behavior that appealed to him. Hell, maybe he'd tried to wake me and I'd been dead to the world. It was possible.

Out of curiosity I looked at the last page: page 205. In my recent conversations with Mitch he'd mentioned that each page of script translated roughly as one minute of screentime. This thing was going to be as long as *Ben Hur*.

It was a long time until daylight and I wasn't going to get back to sleep. I started to read.

I was immediately gratified to see that it didn't begin with a gigantic napalm explosion. Somehow, napalm has become a major star in Vietnam war movies. On the contrary, this one began with a wedding in a chapel on the campus of one of those ivy-draped New England colleges, circa 1962, the fondly remembered Camelot years.

I was unfamiliar with the formalized presentation of a script. Conventional books are easy, and plays are mainly just dialogue with a little stage direction here and there. Script format turned out to be wildly different, with lots of camera direction, shifting points-of-view indicated by different spacing, erratic punctuation, eccentric and seemingly whimsical use of capitals, massive use of parentheses and other singular arcana of language usage, all of it bewildering to the untutored eye.

It made for heavy going at first. I could tell that most of the non-dialogue verbiage helped to supply the visuals, some of it to make clear what the writer intended for the actors to convey in a particular scene, just in case their lines didn't make it obvious. Mitch had told me that the director usually paid no attention to all that stuff, that he'd most likely use just the dialogue and work it out with his cinematographers and actors to get exactly what he wanted up on screen. That didn't stop the writers from putting it in anyway. I could see how this often leads to hard feelings and recriminations, and why directors sometimes order the writer to be barred from the set.

The buildup to the Vietnam scenes was, to my eye, leisurely, with much backstage maneuvering, conferences on Capitol Hill and the Pentagon and CIA headquarters at Langley, with a young Kennedy protégé, whom I assumed to be the Lawrence McKay character, being gradually seduced, sucked in by the maneuvering spooks and power brokers, his youthful idealism tainted even before he goes to Southeast Asia, where over the years his corruption is to become nearly complete; only a tiny core of that old Camelot idealism holding out and yearning for redemption.

The Selene Gibson character was the bride in the first scene, a young college graduate marrying one of her professors, a much older man from a distinguished Boston family who was about to be named ambassador to South Vietnam, a nation most Americans had never heard of in that long-ago year. He was, naturally, one of those Asian scholars who think they know exactly how to handle the country and have nothing but contempt for the long-service diplomatic pros and the businessmen who have dealt with Vietnam since the French left or even before. They were the reason why, in the early years, the Vietnam conflict was called 'the professors' war'.

The sequence touched on some seldom-explored territory, but most of it seemed draggy and boring to me, not cinematic at all. But then, I wasn't experienced at this. It occurred to me that far more is conveyed by visuals than just action and spectacle. Much of this sequence took place in the halls of power, which many people find aphrodisiacal in itself. Also there was the touch of glamor conveyed by the nearness of America's true royal family. Most Americans are utterly enthralled by anything having to do with the Kennedys of Hyannisport, a family with whom I am utterly bored after three and a half decades of oversaturation. Maybe, I thought, that bit of reflected, necrophiliac glamor was sufficient to carry the opening sequence.

Some other major characters were introduced at this time: a CIA bureau chief based in Saigon, a young company cowboy to whom the passionate young diplomatic bride is powerfully attracted despite herself, a reptilian Army spook cum CIA liaison, of whose precise status nobody seems sure but who seems to wield frightening and arbitrary power.

Things pepped up when the action moved to Saigon early in the war. I was beginning to get the hang of reading the writer's directions, and I realized that a lengthy sequence in which the cowboy gives the ambassador's wife a tour of Saigon, which would look like a travelogue as well as help establish the romantic tension between the two, would also serve to give the viewers a sound mental picture of the geography of that confusing city.

I was mildly amused to see an early scene on the terrace of the Continental, where the two meet with a boozy, case-hardened reporter who had been exiled to the paper's dead-end Saigon desk. He had begun to scent that something really big and important was in the air, something that might salvage his alcohol-ruined career and bag him that ever-elusive Pulitzer.

A whole plethora of Vietnamese characters appeared in that sequence: venal military men and their grasping wives, political hacks and *their* predatory wives, and a whole minor cast of double agents, undercover VC officers and cell leaders, plus numerous hangers-on and hustlers of no discernible political slant. Here it was made plain that, in Vietnam, men attended to politics and war while their wives ran businesses, something few Americans ever really understood. Politicians on fact-finding missions and diplomatic personnel could blandly assure Congress and the press that the men we were supporting were clean – and it was true, after a fashion: it was their wives who were arranging the deals and taking the bribes and kickbacks.

The military build-up began. Even after all the books and movies and TV shows, it still hit me with a slight jolt that all this was happening fully five years before I got there, ten years before we pulled out. World War Two only took us four, and we won that one.

The action began to move outside Saigon as other towns became important, firebases were established, and VC activity intensified. I noticed something else happening, and it explained the title: after all the early activity in the presidential palace and the American Embassy, more and more of the scenes took place in rooms above the bars and businesses of Tu Do Street and the alleys leading from it: the offices of the confusing and grotesquely intertwined spook operations, foreign espionage cells, organized crime syndicates, and shady businesses, even shadier than the ones that operated right in the open, on the street.

In time, the ambassador's young wife, previously a wide-eyed booster for America's determination to rescue Southeast Asia from the Red Menace, grew disillusioned by the incompetence, bungling and unjustified arrogance of her countrymen, saw a few too many acts of brutality, refused to be cocooned within the embassy, and traveled out to see the real war. She started writing embarrassing letters to the newspapers back home, and got her husband recalled in disgrace.

At this point I stopped reading and set the heavy screenplay aside for a while and thought, rubbing my sore eyes. I glanced at the window and saw that a faint gray light was beginning to appear in the east. I'd been reading for two hours and was barely halfway through the damned thing. With its plethora of characters, their melodramatic, interconnected lives, their steamy love affairs (and there were many of those) and their wild swoops from glamor to squalor, it resembled nothing so much as a daytime soap on steroids. But it also had the soap's compelling, addictive quality of sucking you into the characters' lives and involving you with them. The writer definitely knew how to keep you interested.

I thought about him: Jared Rhine. Connie had found out that he began writing kung fu epics for the Asian market. Selene had said that he'd done all his Hollywood work with a little group of buddies from the USC film school, but she'd never said that *he* came out of the same school. Queen had told me that he'd made his name and become one of the hottest writers in the business with a string of action-adventure-sex-violence films of the currently fashionable type. That was as much as I knew about the guy except that he was something of a hermit in a business where schmoozing was the principal activity, and notably eccentric in a business where it's hard to raise an eyebrow.

Somehow, this didn't seem like the work of a man who wrote scripts for grunt-and-kick martial arts movies. Nor did it seem to have much in common with the sort of movie where the principal sound effects are gunshots and squealing tires, where people are constantly rappelling down the sides of high-rise office buildings and smashing through the tinted glass with sub-machine-guns blazing, pausing only for bouts of sweaty, athletic sex while the bad guys voyeuristically gaze on through hidden cameras.

This guy, on the contrary, had what might be called a stately sense of pacing. His concern with subtle nuance and detail of character bordered on the obsessive. Almost two hours into what purported to be a war film, there had been no real battles and the scenes of violence had been few, although they had been exceptionally shocking and graphic – appalling in the way real violence is. The modern cinema, with its bodies, limbs, blood and viscera flying through the air in slow motion, prides itself on being graphic when in fact it is only a near-comic burlesque of the real thing. Jared Rhine was going for the real thing.

Most of all, he seemed to have a scholarly and downright encyclopedic knowledge of the era, of its ambience and what I'd guess you'd call its zeitgeist, of the locales that formed the axis upon which spun a tortured decade: Washington and the ivy-league East, and Southeast Asia, centered on Saigon; arrogance and power on one end, corruption and incompetence on the other, misunderstanding along the whole length of the connection. Somehow, it didn't seem to compute with kung fu epics.

But then, what did I know? Maybe he'd known all along that this was his magnum opus, but that in cut-throat Hollywood he'd never get the budget the project called for without a track record of big, splashy hits. Maybe the Hong

Kong movie mills were a good place to learn the trade.

Then again, maybe this was just a classic case of the slapstick comedian who wanted to play Hamlet. For all I knew, he was just a competent hack who was trying to write way beyond his abilities. I only had the word of two people that this was a dynamite script: Mitch and Selene. How the story would translate into pictures on the screen I had no idea. I was a babe in the wood in this place. I admitted I just didn't know enough.

I picked up the script and resumed reading. It glossed over a couple of years with a montage of battle scenes, troop build-ups, newspaper headlines, TV anchors making solemn pronouncements, Congress debating the Gulf of Tonkin resolution, the worried, seamed face of LBJ, the sly, opportunistic face of Nixon, biding his time in the background, with the increasing presence of a new element: growing protest in the US.

The story picked up back in the States with the ambassador's wife, now divorced, leading nationwide protests. The prim little ivy-league ingenue had become a tousled, braless combination of Jane Fonda and Betty Friedan, not only leading rallies on the Mall in Washington but running for Congress while J. Edgar Hoover planted bugs in her bed.

I noted that Rhine was less than wholehearted in his admiration for the student protest movement. He showed a sort of patronizing fondness for their fuzzy-headed idealism, together with an all too plain contempt for their shallowness. He noted that most took no notice of the war until they lost their student deferments, having been perfectly happy as long as it was just poor white Southerners, blacks and Hispanics who were being drafted. He took a special delight in skewering their halfassed enthusiasm for pop versions of Eastern religions, mixing up yoga and the *I Ching* and Zen indiscriminately. Rhine himself seemed to know a great deal about the ancient religions, or wanted to give that impression.

Toward other leaders of the protest movement he was even less charitable. These were the political opportunists who adopted the cause as a shortcut to power and prominence, bypassing the tedious process of doing scut work in the traditional political parties. One such type became the Selene character's second husband: a cold-blooded political creep who usurped her congressional campaign to reinforce his own. She began to undergo a second disillusionment.

I wondered about Rhine's stance in all this. He seemed equally contemptuous of the meddling professors, the military, the spooks, the Washington establishment, the South Vietnamese government *and* the antiwar movement. What was he *for*?

The scene shifted back to the war, and now the focus of attention moved to the machinations of the spooks. The way they set up their operations gave whole new meaning to the term 'reckless disregard'. They spoke about their doings in a jargon so obscure that it was tortuous to follow. I hoped the hotshot director had some idea of how to keep the audience following all this. Rhine's camera directions kept drawing the lens to calendars on walls and desktops. He seemed very concerned with dates.

The cowboy and the Pentagon-Company spook ran maverick operations all over the nations of Southeast Asia, and the by-now-all-too-familiar story of the Air America escapades, of the sleazy compromises with all manner of Asian criminals, was told all over again. After so many books and even a few films about this period and its base truckling, I was a little surprised that Rhine devoted so much screen time to it – but once again his knowledge seemed to be pretty comprehensive, and maybe he wanted to show it off.

The South Vietnamese government was depicted throughout as venal and deeply corrupt, and Rhine showed no sympathy for the North nor for the Viet Cong. The Northerners were a virtually unseen presence: party fanatics with an endless store of propaganda broadcasts, seldom seen by the Americans except from the air. The VC were shown as cruel oppressors of the peasantry no better than the Saigon regime, but enormously capable fighters motivated by something other than greed for a change.

Then the ghosts showed up.

The cowboy, wounded and feverish after a dope-for-gold exchange was raided by a rival of the warlord his organization was cultivating, was pulled out of Laos by a team of men who seemed at first to be American soldiers but who were wild and savage-looking even by the standards of longtime boonie-busters. As a part of their mission, they also raided the successful bandit and recovered both the gold and the dope.

Just within the Laotian border, they were picked up by a

chopper with American markings and carried south, stopping at a couple of nameless bases in Cambodia, and finally dropped in a field outside Saigon where a truck picked up the Americans, the dope and the gold, and took them into the warren of the city. There the cowboy met with his colleague, the Pentagon-spook liaison, and learned that he was not merely a maverick but was running a full-fledged criminal operation in league with the Vietnamese and Chinese gangs of Saigon. He had tipped the Laotian bandit about the gold-for-dope exchange that he himself had set up.

The cowboy, understandably upset, found himself none the less attracted to the sheer audacity of the operation; its total freedom from any civilized standards of right and wrong. Having reached something of a philosophical epiphany in the world of covert operations, this seemed to him to be the logical next step in his odyssey of aberrance. He became the leader of the renegade spook's enforcers: Saigon's underground of American deserters.

I put down the script again. This was beginning to sound way too familiar. My scalp had begun prickling the instant those deserters appeared, and now I was tingling all the way to the base of my spine. We were no longer in territory long charted by the endless post-mortems on the war, written by a generation struggling to come to grips with the unthinkable.

Something occurred to me. I was more than three-quarters of the way through the thick screenplay and it was only 1967. Queen had said that it followed the lives of the characters right up to the present. I looked at the last page again. Before now I had only noted the page number; now my eye was attuned to script format, and I saw immediately that it ended in mid-scene, right in the middle of someone's line. Just how the hell long was this thing, and why had I been given only a part of it?

I quickly read through the rest. To my disappointment, the remaining part was mostly involved with the romances and political maneuverings of the other main characters, LBJ's fight to protect his war powers, embattled both by Congress and by the burgeoning campus antiwar movement, and the wonderfully rapacious shenanigans of the Thieu regime. On the final page the heroine, if that's the proper word, was preparing for a highly publicized trip to Hanoi, à la Jane Fonda.

The sun was up and I got up, went to the little kitchen and got the coffee machine going. I stepped outside and breathed in the southern California air, still early-morning fresh before the inevitable toxic fume build-up that would begin as the freeways filled with vehicles. But at this hour it was still possible to imagine what it was like before the white people arrived. Except that, back then, there weren't nearly so many pretty flowers or palm trees. It's hard now to believe that at one time there was practically no vegetation in the area except scrub oak and brush. The only reason anything grows there now is that Los Angeles brings in water from hundreds of miles away by gigantic pipelines. Shut off the water and it reverts to desert. I guess the Angelenos spend too much time worrying about riots, mudslides, earthquakes and brush fires to worry about the whole place drying up.

I crossed the fresh-mown lawn and went into the big house. I found Julia in the kitchen, leaning on a counter and reading a Spanish-language magazine.

'Is Mr Queen up yet?' I asked her.

'He never came in last night, Mr Treloar,' she said. 'Can I fix you something for breakfast?'

'Are you sure? He dropped some stuff at the guest house sometime last night.'

She frowned. 'I didn't see his car in the garage this morning. Jus' a minute.' She left the kitchen. Minutes later she came back. 'He ain' been in his bedroom. If he come in las' night, he went right back out again. What can I fix you?'

I turned down the offer of breakfast and went back to the guest house. My thoughts were full of suspicion, but it was just too damned early to do anything. I put on shorts and my running shoes, determined to run while the air was still clean enough to breathe safely. I left the script on the kitchen table with a note: *Connie, take a look at this.* I could hear stirring sounds from behind her door as I left the poolside cottage.

I wasn't the only runner on the sidewalks of Beverly Hills. Lots of people were putting in their miles before going out to work or hustle or whatever they did. Some ran with dogs, some ran in groups, many wore headsets that played music to shut out as much of the outside world as possible. They could run in safety, because this was Beverly Hills, just as they could run safely in Brentwood or Bel Air, because these areas are well patrolled. It was nice.

I wondered what sort of reaction I would have elicited if I'd dressed like this and gone running through the streets of Saigon. People would have assumed I was crazy, I guess. Not because it was unsafe, but because they couldn't fathom such a waste of energy. I tried to imagine myself explaining this to a Vietnamese peasant, or an old Buddhist monk: that we Americans did this because we felt so guilty about eating so much and using up so much of the world's resources; that, in the last century, we wore high, stiff collars to punish ourselves; that, in this century, we ran instead; that if we could induce enough fatigue and sweat and pain, we felt good about ourselves again. If they didn't think I was crazy when they saw me run, they sure would have known it when they heard me explain.

But that wasn't the thing weighing most heavily upon my mind as I thudded along the sidewalk, dodging other early runners and their dogs. I wondered about that script, and how it got on my pillow, not forgetting that someone had put a threatening letter on Selene Gibson's pillow, although she wasn't there at the time. I wondered why this script had infuriated person or persons unknown, if indeed it had. I wondered about Mitch Queen and Jared Rhine and what they were really up to with their hundred-million-dollar budget. I wondered, most of all, why Queen hadn't told me that the movie was going to involve the ghosts.

And I wondered what Martin Starr had been doing for the last twenty years, since the fall of Saigon.

Chapter Seventeen

When I got back to the guest house I took off my shirt, shoes and socks and jumped into the pool. I swam laps as hard and fast as I could, until my arms, back and abdominal muscles were burning with oxygen debt. Then I got out, towelled off, picked up my stuff and went inside.

Connie was sitting at the little table with a cup of something steaming in one hand. She had the script in front of her and her eyes were tracking fast from side to side as she flipped pages, apparently speed-reading.

'Go away,' she said. 'I'm not a nice person this early.'

I walked past her into my room, stripped off and showered, shaved, blew my hair dry and put on clean clothes. To my great amazement, I felt just fine, maybe better than I had in months. I felt refreshed, invigorated, rejuvenated and ready for anything. Either I was fully recovered from my jet-lag or else I really had gone crazy. In Southern California, sometimes it's hard to tell.

When I went back out she was finishing up the script. She looked up at me as I poured myself a cup of coffee, grown powerful after sitting so long in its steaming pot.

'So this is the terrific script? It's boring as hell,' she said, disappointed.

'It does seem a little draggy,' I said. 'But that's what I thought about *Hedda Gabler* when I read it for freshman lit. It wasn't until I saw it on stage that I understood why it's a classic.'

'I read it *and* saw it on TV with what's-her-name, Glenda Jackson. I thought it was boring as hell both times.'

'You're just hard to please,' I told her.

'No, I'm easy to please. Just give me Mel Gibson, Redford maybe. I like something where there's decent action, lots of heart pitty-pats, or funny lines. All three if I can get them. I just have standards, that's all.'

'Maybe it's too cerebral.'

'Are you saying I'm dumb?'

'No, I don't like cerebral movies either.'

'Gee, you and I have so much in common, we might as well get married.' She slugged down the last of her tea or whatever it was. 'Okay, enough of the witty banter. What's our next move?'

'I'm waiting to hear from Deputy Lowry about those fingerprints. And I have to talk to Queen.'

'Good luck on that last one. He's not an easy man to get hold of. I'm beginning to wonder why he hired you, since he doesn't seem all that interested in what you find out.'

'I'm wondering that myself. What did you tell your boss and Selene?'

'That it's looking like the threat was bogus but not to call off the security. There's just too damn many lunatics involved.'

'Lunatics do have a way of complicating a situation,' I admitted. 'Give me plain, no-frills career criminals any day.'

'Amen. What do you expect the fingerprints will prove?'

'Nothing much. But if Starr was ever in the military he'd have been printed, and he had no business being in the LBJ if he wasn't military.'

'Wouldn't he have been printed at the brig or the stockade or whatever you call it in the Army?'

'He probably was, but Gresham was carrying a big envelope when he joined us and it was stamped "Confidential" in red letters. That probably held all his LBJ paperwork. If his prints aren't on file that backs up his story of being a spook who ran off the reservation.'

She tapped the script. 'Getting to be a familiar story.'

'I noticed. Anyway, it'll be one more little bit of corroboration. You know how it's done.'

She'd been in the business long enough to know that the big revelations and the hysterical last-minute confessions are strictly for getting the story finished in time for the last commercial and the final credits. Mostly it's this sort of drudgery, going over the same old evidence again and again, waiting for the little anomalies to show themselves, catching the falsehoods and the half-truths, building what scientists call a model and testing the model to see if it works. It's slow and it's dull but it gets the job accomplished.

I rustled myself some breakfast from the refrigerator and pantry. I was whistling.

'You're chipper this morning,' Connie observed. 'I didn't read you as a morning person.'

I sat down and began to eat voraciously. 'I have these cheerful, energetic spells from time to time. It'll go away.'

She got up, fixed herself a plate of fruit and cottage cheese, and sat down again. 'How'd you come to be a cop?'

I thought about it. 'Part of the blame goes to early TV. Remember *Dragnet*? Not the later one, but the black-and-white series, when Ben Alexander was Jack Webb's partner? I thought that seemed like a great career, solving crimes. I never bought the street stuff and gunplay and all that. Friday and Smith did real detective work. They showed up *after* the crime and solved it.'

I downed a slug of coffee. 'I remember when we moved to LA and I started my last year of high school. I'll never forget my first sight of City Hall. It was the same building they showed all the time on *Dragnet*, the building on the shield. I was in heaven. And LA wasn't like small-town Ohio. I saw the black-and-whites cruising the streets and the freeways, saw the uniforms patrolling in the rough parts of town. It looked like serious, important work.'

Some of the darker parts came back to me. 'It was around that time that my parents started drinking heavily. I got that feeling most kids get when they realize that the grownups aren't in control any longer. Either you start hanging around the juvenile gangs for a surrogate family or you try to find something to give you a sense of order in your life. That's what the police meant to me: order. Not far-right law-and-order crap, but people maintaining the boundaries, protecting the citizens, putting criminals away.'

'Good guys against bad guys, huh?'

'That's the way I saw it back then. I was lucky in my timing. Just a couple of years later the police became fascist pigs. I guess if I hadn't gone into the Army, I might have ended up thinking that way too. By the late sixties college girls weren't dating guys who admired cops, and that's a pretty powerful inducement to boys that age. But the Army kept me insulated from the movement during its most influential years. By the time I was a civilian again, I didn't care what the coeds thought. I was married by then, and I still wanted that uniform and that shield. How about you?'

'Family business. My father was on the San Antonio PD back when it wasn't easy for a Mexican to get on the force. In Texas you're a Mexican if your surname's Spanish – doesn't matter if your family's lived in Texas since before the Republic.'

'I thought he was a minister.'

'He's been in the ministry full-time since he retired, but he spent thirty-five years in uniform. After he got back from the war, he and a lot of other Tex-Mexes joined the vets' organizations. They started doing that after World War Two, agitating for more Hispanics in government jobs. In Texas, when the vets' organizations talk, the politicians listen. He retired as a captain. I went into the Houston Police Academy right after I got out of the Navy. That was where I met Mick, my husband.'

In other places people tell one another their life stories after a long dinner, over drinks. In California they do it at breakfast. The really personal confidences they reserve for the coffee breaks.

We caught up on paperwork for a while, as the city roused itself all around us. I turned on the radio to the news station, keeping the sound low. My Angeleno habits were reasserting themselves. I found that I couldn't relax unless I had those periodic updates about freeway conditions. Other people were out there investigating last night's murders, sorting out the traffic accidents, taking down witnesses' statements, flying over the freeways, driving black-and-whites through sullen neighborhoods, while Connie and I sat in a poolside guest-house in Beverly Hills making out our expense accounts. It made for sort of a cozy feeling.

The phone rang and I got it. 'Gabe Treloar here.'

'This is Lowry. Your boy's clean, prints not on file anywhere.'

'Thanks, Lowry.'

'I expect to hear from you real soon, Treloar.'

'Don't worry, you'll be the first to know, as soon as I have anything.'

'Yeah, I believe that one. Keep in touch.'

'Bingo,' I said, hanging up. 'We've had one definite, incontrovertibly truthful statement out of all this, and it came from Martin Starr. He was never fingerprinted. At least, not by any agency that turns its prints over to the FBI.'

'But why would he give you a set of his prints? I mean, maybe it confirms something for you – but he's still leaving the sort of trail a man like him usually avoids.'

'He's not risking much,' I said. 'His prints still aren't on file.

He wasn't printed at any sort of official facility. I've got some prints on a three-by-five card. It means nothing. I could've got them anyplace, from anybody.'

'Maybe,' she said dubiously. 'But it just seems wrong. Do you think he might be retired?'

'What do you mean?'

'Maybe he's not worried because he's no longer involved in criminal enterprises. Maybe he's left all that behind him and this whole man-of-mystery-in-the-orient business is nothing but shuck and jive.'

'Come on. You know as well as I do that career crooks don't just change and go straight. That's for movies-of-the-week.'

'You said yourself that he's no ordinary scumbag. He's something so bizarre that shrinks don't even have a name for it.'

'Yeah, I . . .'

'What?'

'Look.' Coming up the little drive was a kid on a bicycle. A Vietnamese kid, I was sure of it, even with the bike helmet and the sunglasses and headphones. There was a basket mounted on his handlebars and it held some sort of package.

'It's just a kid.' She looked at me sharply. 'Gabe? What's wrong with you? Don't get all weird on me now.'

I couldn't help it. Absurd as it was in this setting, I was suddenly scared. It was the old image of the grenade-throwing Vietnamese kid on the bike. It was one of the big myths of the war, but it functioned in the way myths usually do. It served as the paradigm for all the mystifying dangers in an absurd war where you never knew who the enemy was. Men, especially those newly arrived in country, were more afraid of boys on bikes than they were of their far more dangerous and better-armed elders. It was sort of like the way people are terrified to fly but think nothing of driving out on the far more hazardous freeways.

Connie put a hand on my arm. 'It's okay, Gabe. I'm sure of it.' Even so, I saw her surreptitiously glance into her purse, making sure her pistol was handy. 'You wait here.'

I shook myself. 'No, I'm all right.' It was just pride. I didn't want her to go out and confront this possible terrorist, who had to be all of sixteen, while I cowered indoors. The machismo of the American male triumphed again.

We went outside just as the kid braked in front of the door.

He took off his headset and grinned. I could hear rock music resonating tinnily from the minuscule earphones.

'Are you Mr Treloar?'

'That's right.'

'Got something here for you.' He reached into the zippered canvas pouch in his basket and my stomach tensed. Then his hand emerged with a thin envelope.

I accepted it. 'Who is this from?'

He shrugged. 'Beats me.' He rezipped the bag and stuck a foot back into a stirruped pedal.

'Wait. Do I need to sign anything?'

He grinned again as he put his headset back on. 'You shittin' me? Bye bye, now.' He leaned his weight on to the pedals and sped off.

'See?' Connie said. 'He was just a messenger.'

I looked down at her hand, which was buried in her shoulder bag. 'Yeah. You were just reaching for a tip, huh?'

Her face colored. 'Being around you is turning me paranoid. Come on, what's in the letter?'

I opened it. It contained a single sheet of fax paper. I opened it and saw it contained only three lines. 'It's not signed, but it must be from Nguyen Chi Thanh. He sure didn't waste any time. I didn't know you could fax stuff between Saigon and LA.'

'What's it say?' she demanded impatiently, trying to look over my shoulder like a kid.

' "The men from Saigon who called on Nguyen Duc are Dang Thai Mai and Truong Chinh. Dang controls the Khan Hoi docks. Truong is head of the Chinese/Vietnamese drug cartel in Saigon. The man—" ' Suddenly my throat closed up.

'What is it?' she said, almost bouncing up and down on her toes. 'Come on, tell me!'

' "The man known as Big Ghost now uses the name Henry Armitage." '

'Armitage!' she said. 'Is that all?'

'That's enough.' I folded the fax and stuck it in a pocket. 'Come on,' I said, walking toward the parked cars.

'What? Where are we going?'

'We're going to Santa Barbara. I want to call on Jared Rhine.'

'Just a minute. Let me get some stuff.' She hurried back into the guesthouse. After a minute's thought, so did I.

'We may have to stay overnight,' I told her as I packed an overnight bag. 'Better go prepared. And take along some clothes and shoes you can hike in. According to Mitch, Rhine's place is in rugged terrain. Not that I'm putting much confidence in what Mitch says right now.'

'Oh, this is turning into an expedition, is it?' she said from her room. 'I'd better report to my—'

'No,' I said. 'Let's not use the phone or tip anybody. Like you said, I'm getting real paranoid. People have been leading us around since Chattanooga. I'd like to take a little independent action for a change.'

'Sounds good to me,' she said.

When we got into my car she was dressed in a variant of the safari outfit she'd worn in Vietnam, to which she'd added a pair of well-worn hiking boots and a cowhide shoulder-bag the size of a small rucksack. I backed on to the drive and headed out for highway 101.

'So it must've been Armitage I saw in front of Duc's house,' I said, feeling that silly euphoria you get when maddening, mystifying anomalies begin to click together and the picture starts to emerge, like those repetitive patterns of meaningless colors and shapes that, if you stare at them long enough, suddenly turn three-dimensional as an image begins to take shape, even if it's a vague and inchoate image. 'Archie Dupre was one of his cohorts from Saigon in the old days, now working for him as chauffeur and who knows what else.'

'Pretty damn ballsy of him to show up at Duc's wake,' she said.

'He's doing business in the Vietnamese community,' I pointed out, 'establishing himself as a wheel. It's a gesture of respect, and it serves to remind the rest what can happen if they won't cooperate with him and his buddies Dang Thai Mai and Truong Chinh. But he didn't want to be seen by me.'

'Because you'd recognize him.'

'Uh-huh. I'd assumed that Starr was the Big Ghost, but it's Armitage. And Armitage used to be Major Gresham, the CIA spook bastard who was running Starr in his outlaw operations and tried to kill him when he ended up at the LBJ. Starr's waited more than twenty-five years but now it's payback time.'

We drove up over the hills and into the San Fernando Valley, where signs of the most recent earthquake were almost completely gone, in the usual California fashion. Then it was up the range of hills on the other side of the valley and through the pass, and the LA basin was behind us. It was ten degrees cooler and the air was clean. The urban sprawl was gone and we were in something that resembled old-time California, rustic and agricultural, the California of Art Deco orange-crate labels, Steinbeckian fruit pickers, bee-buzzing groves of trees and paddocks where horses prance as if waiting for the Californio dons to throw silver-mounted saddles across their backs and ride out to inspect the herds and the vineyards.

It's still one of the prettiest drives in the southern part of the state, although I suppose one day LA will spill over the pass and creep northwest, and Ventura will expand southeast, and eventually the two will meet in the middle. Until that happens, the grass and cattle and the fragrant eucalyptus will continue to be a soul restorative only a few minutes from downtown.

Between the strangely named Oxnard, with its naval air station, and Ventura, the ocean came into view once more and the air became salty. The unsightly but enormously profitable offshore oil rigs appeared like the ships of a predatory invasion fleet in the channel. Intrepid surfers rode the waves as they have since the fad really got going in the fifties: Gidget's grandchildren.

Just after Carpinteria we passed the surreal little roadside tourist trap of Santa Claus, where it's Christmas all year round and which used to have a pretty good restaurant. Now, though, it was looking even more shabby and rundown than usual, a good sign that the developer's axe was about to fall.

The blue tile roofs of the Miramar Hotel just off the highway let us know that we were approaching Montecito, the little, gemlike rich man's community where people from Santa Barbara move when they've really made it.

Then we were coming into Santa Barbara. I hadn't been there in years and for a moment I was disoriented by the new bypass. Like the Malibuvians, the Santa Barbarans had fought for decades to keep the freeway from plowing through their community. When it reached Santa Barbara, highway 101 had taken a breather and became just another street, stopping every couple of blocks for red lights before reverting to freeway status on the other side of town.

No more. A series of overpasses arched above a couple of the old cross streets. The rest just stopped at the highway. The locals had improved the flow of highway traffic, at some cost to mobility, from one side of town to the other. The shoreline on this stretch of coast runs east-west and so does the highway. South of the highway lies the beautiful shorefront with its bird refuge and luxury hotels and restaurants. North of it is Santa Barbara proper, an expensive but immensely livable Spanish colonial town where they actually narrowed the main street, State, to make the sidewalks wider and more convenient for pedestrians.

It looked as if the bypass had been acquired at an even higher price. 'My god!' I gasped. 'Where's my tree?'

'What now?' Connie said sourly. It had taken almost two hours to drive to Santa Barbara from Beverly Hills and she'd been miffed that I was so reluctant to talk. I'm not much of a conversationalist when I'm thinking, and I'd been deep in thought the whole way. But now I was outraged.

'My tree! The giant fig tree! Even these greedy bastards wouldn't've cut it down!'

'What are you talking about, Treloar?'

But I wasn't listening. I pulled off at the first exit beyond State and began a frantic search, doubling back through the maze of little streets, most of them one-way, that paralleled the highway, wending among old houses and small businesses, a district that dated from the days when Santa Barbara was just a sleepy little resort town where people from LA came to get away for the weekend.

Then I found it and breathed a sigh of relief, but I almost wished they'd cut it down instead. It stood, abandoned and forlorn, in a little weed-grown lot next to the high wall of the new elevated highway. Its thick, rugged trunk was squat and enduring as ever, its branches so massive and widespread that some of them dipped to the ground, its high, exposed roots like the sharp spurs of an eroded mountain range.

'What a beautiful tree,' Connie said as I pulled up at the curb. 'But it's like they hid it away. You'd think they'd make this a showplace, a park maybe. There can't be many like this.'

'It's the giant Santa Barbara fig,' I told her, getting out of the car. '*Ficus* something-or-other. It's hundreds of years old. Before they put in this bypass it stood right next to the road. It was a famous landmark.' I walked over to it and stroked one of the radiating roots that arched as high as my waist. The roots and trunk were etched with initials carved by generations of kids, doing the old tree no harm. It was proof against pocketknives, anyway.

'In California it's illegal to hitchhike on the freeway. Here in Santa Barbara the freeway ended.' I pointed back the way we'd just come. 'From Anacapa Street at the east end of town down to Butts Buick at the west end, it was the only stretch on 101 where it was legal to hitch for a hundred miles or more. In the summers there'd be hitchers all along here and half of them would be lounging here under the fig, sitting on the roots, shooting the breeze. In the summers, when I was a kid, I'd be here at least a couple of times every month, going back and forth from one summer job to another or visiting friends. There was an old lady in a sunbonnet who always came along to hand out religious tracts. You'd meet all the local characters, and Santa Barbara sure had them, for a small town.'

Connie looked up at the broad-leaved branches. 'Sounds like fun.'

'It was. In the late sixties and early seventies it was a great hangout for hippies, a real psychedelic show. You could get high just walking by and inhaling. People were scandalized then. I don't know why. It all seems pretty innocent now.' I kicked at the leaf litter and turned up a flat wine bottle and a couple of hypodermic syringes. The place must be a night-time haunt for derelicts, I assumed, although it was deserted at this hour.

'Well, you found your tree and it's okay. Maybe someday when cars are obsolete they'll tear out this highway and people will be able to enjoy it again. It's survived a few centuries; it'll survive this. Now, how do you propose to find Rhine?'

'Come on,' I told her, getting back into the car. I took a last look at the sad old tree, all alone in its weedy lot with only drunks and junkies for company. I figured I'd never be back until the elevated bypass was gone, and that probably meant not in my lifetime. I pulled away from the curb and back to reality.

'What you're going to do,' I told her 'is check out the land registration records. He's supposed to be reclusive, but he can't really be hiding and still deal with Hollywood. It shouldn't take long.'

'You're in no position to be giving orders, but I'll humor you, just this once. What if he's renting the place?'

'Then it's the phone company, the newspapers, the local police – you've done this stuff before. You can always find someone as long as they're not in the witness protection program or something.'

'Yeah, but it's too pretty a day to be doing this sort of work.'

'It's too late for a career change now.'

'What'll you be doing in the meantime?'

'Getting some stuff that we'll be needing. May be needing, anyway. I don't know exactly how we're going to have to play this. I won't know until we're closer and have more information. But we may have to spend some time in the hills and I'm going to pick up some gear.'

'You had to spend your war year in Saigon,' she said. 'So now you want to pretend you're a grunt out in the bush.'

'I just like to commune with nature. Ah, here we are.' I'd pulled up to the county court house, a California dream building that was a vision of Spanish colonial architecture but that only dated back to the thirties. It was a Hollywood confectioner's fantasy, faithful to tradition in detail, but on a scale about four times larger than anything built by the Spanish in California.

'Damn!' Connie said, marveling. 'It looks like Zorro could come riding out any minute now.'

'Happy hunting,' I told her as she got out.

On one of the streets off State I found a map shop. It sold wall charts and atlases, navigator's charts, globes, geography books, diskettes and CDs. After a little discussion with the clerk, I found what I needed and walked out with some detailed topographical maps of the Santa Barbara hills.

Next stop was an Army-Navy surplus store on lower State. The district had been pretty seedy when I was a kid, full of bars, pawnshops and thrift shops. Now it was gentrifying, but a couple of blocks of it were still pretty raffish and the surplus store was still where I remembered it.

I picked up some Army blankets, a couple of canteens with cups and covers, a pair of anglehead flashlights and a big thermos bottle. My last purchase was a GI lensatic compass. There are newer types much more favored by outdoorsmen, but this one I knew how to use. An amazing amount of the stuff in the place was from East Germany and Russia, but I stuck with GI goods. Buy American is my motto.

When I drove back to the Spanish fantasy I found Connie sitting on the lawn next to some flowering bushes, drinking pineapple juice. When she saw me she got up, brushed a few stray grass clippings from the seat of her pants, and walked over to the curb.

'No problem,' she said, getting into the car. 'He bought the place in '82. It's in a little canyon in the hills near where Santa Barbara abuts Montecito. I got a Xerox of the plat and the property survey.'

'You find out who he bought it from?'

'County auction. It was seized for back taxes. Apparently, the rich folks' estates are on the lower slopes of the hills. Above that it's too hard to pump in much water, the fire hazards are high, not many people want to live there.'

'Good work.' I looked at my watch. 'We may have a long night ahead of us. Let's find someplace to eat, then we'll go look in on Mr Rhine.'

'Sounds good to me.' She looked in the back seat. 'We going to war, or what?'

'Just some comforts to make the long night easier.'

'You really want to pull an all-night surveillance? Why not just walk up and knock on the door?'

'First I want to have a better idea of what's on the other side of the door. My partner got killed knocking on a door because we assumed we knew who was inside and we were wrong.' I said it without thinking, and steered away from the subject. 'Anyway, it doesn't hurt to be prepared, like the boy scouts. What do you feel like eating?'

'Something substantial, if we're gonna be out in the hills with nothing but cheese and crackers to munch on.'

We found a good Mexican place near 101 and fueled up on tacos, enchiladas, guacamole and the inevitable fortifying rice and beans, eschewing all the upscale, yuppie items like fajitas. I found it all wonderful, but Connie complained that California Mexican food wasn't hot enough, that Tex-Mex had much more character. The problem didn't seem to affect her appetite. With plenty of Hispanic soul food under our belts, we headed for the hills.

Chapter Eighteen

The hierarchy of social status and wealth according to altitude of dwelling was interesting. What passed for proletarian Santa Barbara was on the flat land at or near sea level. Even in these areas, I learned, housing was hideously expensive. The toiling classes had to share tiny apartments at inflated rents just to be near the people they worked for. There were some fine houses on the flat lands near the old part of the town, but these were mainly owned by families of long residence, and they seldom had spacious grounds.

The mansions began with the foothills, and these were mostly set well back from the roads, screened by brick walls and tall plantings, and protected by fanciful wrought-iron gates. As the hills grew higher and steeper, the estates grew grander and the property values ever higher, for these were the houses with breathtaking vistas of the Pacific and the beautiful Channel Islands. The people who lived in these mansions had fought to keep the huge drilling rigs out of the channel. They spoiled the view. The oil companies had fought back. When wealth fights wealth, the greater wealth wins. In this century, there is no wealth greater than oil.

Narrow, twisting roads wind along the slopes and along the crests of these hills. Here and there you see unobtrusive little driveways with mail boxes, and these lead to the vast houses that are almost impossible to view except from the air. In these hills are country clubs that don't admit mere movie stars or similar riffraff. It was rumored that, when the Shah's sister had wanted to buy an estate in Montecito, the residents had banded together to keep her out, oil wealth or no oil wealth. Montecito would not countenance trashy Middle Eastern royalty in their midst. They'd let in Prince Charles, maybe, if he behaved himself.

For a while as we ascended, it seemed as if there was a correlation between altitude and wealth, with the unutterably wealthy owning whole hilltops from which to lord it over the peons. But this ended abruptly at a certain level, and the line of demarcation was as plain as that between the sea and the beach.

The terrain of the rich seemed to go on forever, a tame wilderness of bushes that put forth flowers in almost obscene profusion all year round. We continued to climb and then it was gone. Suddenly, without warning, we were in California before the invention of the lawn sprinkler. The land was sere and brown, studded with clumps of tough grass and brush, the deeply eroded gullies choked with snarled scrub oak. This was primeval California, the land as the dons found it. Above that level, there wasn't much except for broadcast stations and ranger towers.

'I think this is it,' Connie said as we drew up to a little canyon that cut back into the scrubby mountainside like an open wound. She had a map open in her lap and was concentrating on the maze of relief lines, complex as a thumbprint, that made maps like that so mystifying to the inexperienced.

The bare hills climbed steeply from one side of the road. On the other the land sloped dramatically away, the almost jungle-clad hillsides dotted here and there with mansions and their rectangular tennis courts, their putting greens and their gemlike blue swimming pools. All of it framed the town below in a semicircular theater, beyond which was the spectacular ocean, the islands and, beyond them, nothing but clouds. Whoever lived up here had a billionaire's view and a dust-bowl Okie's real estate.

I turned up the road, drove a couple hundred years and found the gate, just as described to me by Queen days before and far away in Chattanooga. 'This is the place,' I affirmed. Then I turned around. For a moment I considered getting out and looking for recent tire prints, but I was no Indian tracker. Besides, in this place, between the infrequent rains, signs would last like they do on the moon, with nothing to disturb them.

'Don't you want to try to get in?' Connie asked.

'Not from here. Check that map and find the nearest fire break. That'll probably make for the easiest approach.'

She looked it over and I paused as we got back to the road. There was almost no traffic this high up.

'We passed one about a quarter mile back,' she reported. 'The next one's a half-mile on.'

'Then let's take a look at the closer one.'

In southern California with its frequent droughts and their attendant brush fires and forest fires, fire breaks are a way of life. They are broad swathes cleared of vegetation, cutting straight up the slopes and sometimes along the crests of hills. The idea is that fires will burn up to the break and, with luck, won't leap across. Sometimes it works. In any case, they give fire-fighters access to the burning areas. They're unsightly and destroy the otherwise pristine aspect of the old hills, but they're necessary and they've been around so long that the Californians no longer even see them.

The one we were looking for started just off the road and it was blocked by a chain-link fence with signs posted warning people of the consequences should they try to take motorcycles or off-road vehicles on to the firebreak. It also said that hiking on the firebreak was forbidden and threatened dire punishments for starting fires should you choose to ignore the no-hiking warning. A lot of hikers had obviously ignored it, because there was a deep path around the fence worn by their plodding boots.

'What'll we do with the car?' Connie asked.

'We park it here. If it gets ticketed, we'll bill Mitch for it.' I started hauling stuff out of the back. After a pause, Connie began helping me.

'It could get towed,' she said.

'I doubt if this place gets checked more than once a week. If it happens, well, at least it's downhill all the way into town if we have to walk.' I locked up the car.

'Okay,' she said, a rolled blanket across her shoulders and a canteen belted around her waist. 'Lead on, Jeremiah Johnson.'

Similarly burdened, and carrying the thermos, I went around the fence and stepped out on to the firebreak. The area was shaded by big clumps of scrub oak that grew right up to the fence and to both sides of the break. It was surprisingly pleasant, with a steady buzzing and clicking of insects and a clean smell of sun-warmed vegetation. The only other sounds were very faint, distant traffic noises.

'Let's go,' I said, in what I hoped was a resolute, man-of-action tone. I began to stride uphill.

Before long, the stride turned into more of a trudge. The bare dirt of the firebreak had recently been plowed or disc-harrowed or whatever it is that they do to keep the vegetation suppressed in these herbicide-conscious days. The loose soil was constantly turning and settling beneath my feet and I had to compensate for the continually altering stresses. We hadn't been climbing for ten minutes before I was sweating profusely, even though the day wasn't especially hot. I began to feel deep pains in my ankles and knees.

'While you were playing quartermaster,' Connie said, 'you should've bought yourself a better pair of boots.'

'What's wrong with jogging shoes?' I said, knowing perfectly well.

'No ankle support, for one thing, soft soles for another. I don't figure on carrying you back down, Treloar.'

'Even I know it's a mistake to wear new shoes on a long hike. I just had to go with what I'd brought along. I'll be okay, don't sweat it.' That was one piece of advice she didn't need. She wasn't yet showing a drop of perspiration and I figured her heartbeat and respiration and blood pressure were probably about what they'd been when she was sitting on the courthouse lawn sipping pineapple juice.

'How high up do we go?' she asked.

'All the way to the top, I guess. We don't know how far over Rhine's place is, or how far up the canyon.'

'Can't be too high, not if he has water piped in. He sure as hell can't have a well dug up here. I wonder what fire insurance costs in a place like this? The fire hydrants must stop down in the rich folks' territory.'

'I guess you just live with the hazard,' I said. I almost jumped when something slithered from just in front of my toe. 'Damn! That was a rattlesnake!'

She laughed. 'Not unless they come in black around here.'

'This is southern Cal. Designer rattlers aren't out of the question.'

We climbed for another twenty minutes and the crest seemed almost attainable, but not just yet. 'Let's take a break,' I said, sitting down. 'There's no rush.'

'How come?' she asked. 'I mean, why stop now?'

'You're a fitness freak. I'm not. Civilized jogging I can handle but this frontiersman stuff is different.' She sat beside me and for a while we said nothing while I caught my breath and the sweat slowly dried on my body. Now we were so high that even the faint traffic noises were gone. For a moment we could hear the whopping of a helicopter that was too far away to see, then even that was gone and we heard only insect noises. The air was utterly still and the huge sweep of ocean far below us was like a painting, the miniature city like something seen in a dream.

'People crossed a thousand miles of desert and mountains like this to get here,' Connie said after a while. 'Why'd they do it?'

'The Spanish came for land,' I told her. 'The Anglos came for gold. Movies and real estate are fairly recent, I guess.'

'We should've brought some pans. Maybe we could look for gold on the way to Rhine's place.'

'I think you need water for that. The only water around here is what we're carrying.' I lurched to my sore feet. 'Come on, we can't sit around all day like this.'

As I'd expected, the firebreak continued along the top of the mountain. A short walk along it brought us to the cleft of the little canyon.

'This must be it,' I said. 'The bottom of the gully's overgrown, probably full of snakes and tarantulas and scorpions and assorted wildlife. Let's go down along the ridge. It'll be easier walking too.'

'It'll also make us easier to see,' she objected.

'But nobody's looking for us. Besides, these hills are always full of hikers, although I'll never understand why.'

'Let me go down first,' she said. 'That way I can catch you if you fall.'

Descending turned out to be little easier than climbing. It just stressed different muscles and was even harder on the ankles – my ankles, anyway. Connie, in her clunky boots, was acting like she was on a stroll along Rodeo Drive. Just putting on an act, I figured, showing me up for the decrepit old fart that I was.

'Hold it,' she said as we came up to a thick clump of something mean-looking, all thorns and dry, dusty leaves that made you sneeze. 'There's a house down there.'

I walked up to the brush and peered cautiously around it. About a hundred yards below us was a house made of stone and logs and what appeared to be windows scavenged from another house entirely. But it was no shack, the whole thing was put together masterfully and blended into the side of the canyon above the flash-flood line like a desert animal sunning itself on a rock. On the hillside just above the house was a dish arrangement like a satellite antenna, undoubtedly the uplink Queen had mentioned. A roofed porch ran around three sides of the place.

Behind the house a parking area had been cut into the hillside, paved with sandstone flags, one end of it covered with a shingled roof supported by peeled log posts. A dusty Land Rover was parked in its shade, a cable coiled neatly on the drum of a winch mounted on its front bumper. Unlike so many ORVs, this one looked well-used.

'Is this the place?' Connie asked, keeping her voice down. Sound really carried in these canyons.

'It must be. I don't think there's enough room for another house to be between here and the road and still out of sight. The dish is where Mitch said it was.'

'I don't see any phone wire going into the house. Just a power wire. He must use the dish for his phone, too.'

'First class all the way.' There was a fairly flat, sandy patch of ground just behind the evil-looking bush. I dropped my blanket and set the thermos atop it. 'Might as well settle,' I said. 'We're going to wait for a while.'

She didn't argue. 'How long?' she asked, spreading her blanket.

'Until dark, at least. I want to get closer, but I don't want to be seen doing it.' I squinted westward. We were too far into the canyon to see the ocean, but the sun was already touching the hilltops to the west. 'It'll be dark in a couple of hours. Let's rest and recuperate.'

At least she didn't make any smartass remarks about how much more severely in need of recuperation I was than she. Within a few minutes we were in shade and the temperature dropped. The sweat evaporating on my clothes made me chilly, but after the exertion of the climb and the descent it felt good.

'What are we—' She cut off as the sound of an approaching vehicle came from down the canyon, drawing closer. We sidled toward the bush and bellied-down to peer around its base. A few seconds later the vehicle came into view. It was a red Bronco, and from the laboring sound of the engine it had power going to all four wheels, although the condition of the road didn't seem to call for it. It looked brand new, with a dealer plate still mounted on the front bumper. It pulled up in front of the cabin and stopped.

'Damn!' I muttered. 'I forgot to bring binoculars.'

'Some commando,' she said, drawing a beautiful little pair of Zeiss glasses from her shoulder-bag. She handed them to me and I put them to my eyes, focusing with the central screw. By the time the image jumped clear, the driver was getting out of the four-wheeler. It was Mitch Queen, and he didn't look happy. I could see his mouth moving. In fact, I reflected, it wouldn't have looked like Mitch if his mouth *hadn't* been moving. Even across the distance I could hear his voice, although I couldn't make out the words. He paused and looked like he was listening while somebody spoke back, but that one wasn't speaking loud enough to be heard, or else the house blocked the sound of his voice.

I moved the binoculars down to get a look at the other man, but in the perspective-flattening field of vision all I could see was the roof and two sides of the house. When I looked back at Mitch he was climbing back behind the wheel. He shut the door, put the Bronco in gear and pulled around to the rear of the house.

Connie tapped impatiently on my shoulder and I handed her the glasses with some reluctance. While she peered through them I watched Queen get out and unload some stuff from the back of the vehicle. There were two grocery sacks and a cardboard box and he shuttled these into the back door of the house. Last of all he took in a couple of cases about three feet long, making four trips to get it all. Then he drove the Bronco under the carport and parked it. He went back inside and the screen door slammed behind him. The other man never showed himself. Connie took the glasses away from her eyes and we scooted back behind the bush. It was getting darker by the minute.

'So now we've got Queen located,' she said. 'And he's been shopping at Von's, if it matters. Probably laying in supplies. Looked like enough for a long siege or a short party. Did you get a look at the other guy?'

'Not a glimpse. Soon as it's dark I'm going to work my way closer and try to get a look inside.'

She gave me a dubious look. 'Maybe you'd better let me do that.'

'I can do this stuff,' I insisted. 'I'm just a little out of shape, that's all.'

'Okay, I'll buy that for now. But this guy seems to be a paranoid of the first order. He may be doing the whole crazed-

Nam-vet-hiding-in-the-park scenario – tripwires strung with tin cans all around his hideaway. He looks like he's into high-tech in these low-tech surroundings. There might be sensors out there.'

'In these hills? Listen.'Already, we could here yipping noises from up-canyon as darkness fell. 'Those are coyotes. In the foothill communities they come down and raid people's garbage cans. There's raccoons, possums, all sorts of nocturnal critters. If he put out warning devices, he'd never get any sleep.'

'Okay, it's your call.' She stretched out on the blanket. 'I'm going to try to get some sleep. It's gonna be a long night. Wake me if anything interesting happens.'

I unscrewed the top of the thermos and poured myself a cup of coffee. It was hot, which I like, and black, which I don't, but I needed it to stay alert, not for the sensual enjoyment of the act. Before I took my first sip, Connie was breathing deeply. People that healthy can be depressing, but I found that I didn't mind. After all, how many people would have gone along with this nutty trek through the hills for a night-time surveillance without giving me a lot of lip over it? Especially after two truly vicious scares back in Saigon. If she wanted to be Superwoman, that was all right with me.

The moon came up, silvery and three-quarters full. The coyotes yapped happily to see it. Now and then I heard things rustling and slithering in the weeds. Overhead, bats flittered between me and the moon, perfectly silent, hunting down night-flying bugs with the remorseless efficiency of millions of years of evolution. Well, hundreds of thousands anyway. I'm not terrifically knowledgeable when it comes to winged mammals.

Far from the light pollution of the city, the moonlight was amazingly bright, casting sharp, clear shadows and nearly intense enough to read small print by its light. I found something enormously satisfying about the experience. I'd been kidding about communing with nature. I'm really a city boy. But I decided maybe those Sierra Club characters had something, after all. It was incredibly soothing just to sit and meditate, with only natural sounds all around. I decided that I'd have to try this again sometime, when I wasn't working.

After a couple of hours Connie woke up. She sat upright and shook her curly head, then picked up her canteen. She took a slug of water, rinsed her mouth and spat, then got up. 'Be back in a minute,' she mumbled. A little while later she came back, adjusting her clothes. 'Okay, now what?' She seemed wide awake.

I held out the thermos. 'Coffee?'

'Uh-uh. I hate that stuff.'

'Then do you feel ready for a little creepy-crawling down to the house?'

'Sure,' she said brightly. 'Shouldn't we paint our faces black or something?'

'Did you bring along any black make-up?'

'No.'

'Neither did I. I guess we'll just have to do without. Come on. I'll be moving slow. We have plenty of time. If we make a noise, we just hope they think it's an animal. If anyone comes outside, pretend to be a rock.'

Cautiously, I began to make my way down the side of the canyon. The old lessons came back to me without conscious effort. They were in the files, waiting all these years to be called up. I lifted my feet high with each step, came down on the instep and rolled the foot inward. I wasn't perfectly silent, but I wasn't making any sounds that could be heard ten feet away. Connie, behind me, was as quiet as a shadow. Or maybe my hearing wasn't as good as it used to be.

We took around twenty-five minutes to negotiate the hundred yards of slope. We paused for a minute beside the dish. A cable as thick as my forefinger ran from the box at its base down to the house. The post in the center of the dish pointed at the heavens, as if someone were attempting to contact another planet. Maybe someone was.

There were lights on in the cabin, but it leaked around drawn curtains. We slowly worked our way close and began to circle the house. Every window was curtained and shut. From inside we could hear muffled voices and a stereo. When we got to the house I could hear the Byrds singing 'Turn, turn, turn'. It didn't make it any easier to make out the conversation from inside. Queen's voice was unmistakable. The other was just a mumble.

We were at what was, roughly speaking, the northern end of the house. Slowly, in a duck-waddling crouch, I began to circle it. I had to clamp my teeth shut against the pain this caused to my already battered knees. They popped in protest.

The back was no more revealing. From the southwest corner a power line stretched taut to a pole about fifty yards away, down the canyon. Rhine's connections to the outside world were pretty minimal. I saw a garden hose attached to an outdoor faucet. That meant a water line underground. There was no trace of plantings, so I figured he used it to wash the Land Rover.

There was no help at the southern end of the house. Another curtained window. From inside I could hear that the two were arguing although Queen's voice was still the only voice I could make out, except for Petula Clark's. She was singing 'Say a Little Prayer'.

The eastern side held a set of broad steps descending from the encircling verandah to the driveway, which was just a sort of cul-de-sac with enough room for a car to turn around without backing, and a spur leading from it around the rear of the house. There wasn't much floor to the little canyon, the ground ascending steeply just beyond the drive. If Rhine liked privacy, he sure had it here.

I signalled to Connie and we began to climb back to our vantage point. From the house I could hear the sound of Creedence Clearwater singing 'Bad Moon Rising'.

Getting back went swiftly and quietly. I was beginning to get the hang of this. I plopped down on the blankets, picked up the thermos and unscrewed the cap.

'That was fun,' Connie said, sitting beside me. She reached into her shoulder-bag and came up with another bottle of fruit juice. 'I can see how you guys get into this stuff – midnight recon, long-range patrolling, ranger operations. I'm beginning to understand how the male bonding business works. Now, except for an earful of golden oldies, what've we got?'

'For one thing,' I said, 'we can be pretty sure there's only two of them in there: Mitch and one very patient listener. They have water and electricity coming in. There's no dog. And they're expecting visitors.'

'How's that?' she asked.

'Those windows are all but blacked out. Rhine doesn't live up here because he hates nature, so he's not shutting that out. He sure as hell isn't worried about the neighbors or casual passersby looking in his windows. He's avoiding being a back-lit target at a window.'

She took a slug of her juice. 'Then why no warning devices?'

she said. 'If he's expecting an attack tonight, he would've put some out, to hell with the coyotes.'

'Good question. An ambush springs immediately to mind.'

'Then they're trying to suck us in?'

'Us or somebody else. I don't want it to be us. We wait here until somebody else shows up.'

'That could be a long wait.'

'Do you have anything better to do just now? We get paid the same, no matter how long it takes.'

'Looks that way. Gabe, you're enjoying this, aren't you?' She gave me one of her rare smiles.

I thought about it. 'Yeah, I guess I am. It seems like I spend most of my days just marking time. Doing PI work I'm almost always either at the typewriter or the telephone. I miss being out on the street doing real police work.' I knocked back some coffee. 'And people have been jerking me around on this case. I don't like being led around by the nose. It's time to take some personal action.' I turned and grinned at her. 'And, what the hell, every once in a while I get this urge to do something stupid and self-destructive and suicidal. If I come through the next few hours alive, I'll feel great for weeks. I'm getting where it takes a lot to get me high, at my age.'

She grinned back. 'You know, Treloar, when this started I figured you for kind of a square. I mean – you're sort of slow and laid-back and, to be honest, you seemed so easygoing you were downright passive. But since Saigon I've seen a new side of you. You're really weird, Gabe.'

'Shucks, I'm glad it's too dark for you to see me blush. I don't get compliments like that every day.'

'No, I mean it. That business with the grenade at the hotel impressed me, Gabe. And I don't care for melodramatics, but when Hacker and Starr snatched me I didn't really expect you to come for me on your own, but you did. It was stupid, but it was really chivalrous. I appreciate that. And now you're expecting a battle here, aren't you?'

'Somebody's been killing people. And those two down there, Mitch and Rhine, have been manipulating things to bring it to a head right here. I intend to be in on the kill, but on my terms, not theirs.'

'And you don't even have a gun.'

'You do. You'll protect me, won't you?'

'You jerk.' She grabbed my ears, yanked my head down and

kissed me. My hands gripped her waist, beneath her safari shirt.

I pulled back for a second. 'You mean you haven't forgotten that last night back in Saigon?'

'Let's just say I'm still considering our future. And don't start making any big plans just yet. Remember, you haven't met my kids yet.'

'Like you said, we have plenty of time.' This time my mouth came down on hers. Generous lips, big teeth and a lot of tongue – it was a hell of a combination. Then she pulled away.

'Okay, that's enough. I'll take this watch. Get some sleep.'

So much for dereliction of duty.

When Connie woke me the moon was almost down and there was a gray tinge in the sky. It was getting near dawn and she'd been on watch a couple of hours, nudging me with a foot any time I started to snore.

'Gabe!' she hissed. 'Wake up. There's someone out there!'

I rolled over on the blankets and low-crawled to her, using my elbows and knees, just like they'd taught us back in basic training.

'Where?' I whispered. She passed me the glasses and pointed toward the dish. I put them to my eyes and focused. Near it I spotted a moving shape, visible only because of the motion. It was a man dressed in dark clothing, commando-style. Either his face and hands were darkened or he was wearing a ski mask and gloves. Like the two of us earlier in the night, he was creeping forward, crouched with his knees deeply bent, placing his feet carefully. In one hand he carried an object that was about two feet long.

'Party's starting,' I said.

'What's he doing?'

'Can't tell yet.' I didn't see any light showing around the curtains below. They were asleep or waiting.

The man crept up to the dish and fumbled with the thing in his hand. It opened up into a V shape and he gripped the ends, then placed it against something on the ground. With an abrupt motion he brought his hands together. Apparently satisfied with his work, he backed away from the dish, then turned and made his way back the way he'd come, moving as cautiously as before.

'He cut the cable to the uplink,' I said, lowering the binoculars.

'The power line?'

I raised them again and looked. The line still stretched taut from the house to the pole. 'Not near the house. It could be cut farther down the canyon. I wish we knew. It could be important.'

'Why important?'

'They've taken out the communications. If they cut off the power and the water line, it could mean they want to wait it out, besiege the place, maybe negotiate for whatever it is everyone's so hot about. If they simply don't want anyone calling out, they'll just attack, kill everyone and get the hell out.'

'Yeah, I guess it would be nice to know what's going to happen,' she mused. Then she jerked around because I was getting up. 'Hey! What are you planning to do?'

'I've got to go down there. Warn them.' I was straightening, stretching the kinks out of my back and legs.

'What the hell for?' she said, exasperated. 'They set this up! Let them live with it!'

'I'm working for Mitch.'

'And he's played you for a fool – a fall guy. What do you owe him?'

'It's something that goes a long way back. I don't know how to describe it. It's blood and bread and salt.'

She stared at me speechlessly, then shook her head. 'I was wrong. I will never, *never* understand you people!' She reached into her shoulder-bag. 'Here, take this with you.' She held out her pistol.

I tucked it under my belt beneath my shirt. 'Keep watching the approaches. If it looks like trouble's going to start, skin out of here, go call for help. If you go back along the way we came, you won't be seen.'

'The hell with that. It'll take me half the day to go back up to the crest and then back down the firebreak. I'll go straight over that ridge.' She pointed to the high ground behind us. 'The firebreak's just a little way on the other side. It's rough ground, but I can cover it a lot faster that way.'

I squinted up the slope toward the ridge. In the still-faint morning light it was hazily visible. 'I don't know. The cover's pretty thin. You might be seen from down there.'

'Yeah, and I'll be moving damn fast.' She got up and put her arms around me. 'Get going, you idiot. It's getting light. If you

263

get killed I'll never forgive you.' She turned me around and gave me a shove between my shoulder blades to speed me on my way.

I stopped and turned around. 'I wish we could've met a long time ago.'

'Go!' she hissed. I thought I saw tears in her eyes but it was too dim to be sure.

Then I shut her out of my mind because I had to. When you're on a mission, the mission has to occupy your whole attention or you die and everyone else dies. My eyes swept the terrain, looking for movement. When it's dark your eyes react to movement first, shapes second. Color doesn't register at all. I listened for approaching vehicles but heard nothing. Even the birds weren't awake yet.

I crouched and sidled from cover to cover. If a sniper was out there with a starlight scope he might see me, but I was counting on their attention being focused on the cabin. When my brush cover ran out I dashed up to the northeast corner of the house. That bullseye was burning between my shoulder blades the way it had more than twenty-five years before in Saigon.

I ran to the back door and rapped on it. 'Don't shoot and open up! It's Treloar and you've got Charlie in the wire out here!'

The door swung open and I bulled my way inside and slammed it shut behind me.

'Gabe, m'man! Good of you to join us!' Queen was grinning and I balled the front of his shirt in both fists and rammed him against a wall, almost making him stand on tiptoes.

'You son of a bitch! What have you been pulling? Why have you been lying to me?'

'I can explain, Gabe. 'Ey, ah can 'splen!' For some reason, he'd gone into his Ricky Ricardo impression.

'Do it quick, you asshole, or I'll kill you before whoever's out there gets here.'

'Now, my friends,' said a voice from the doorway of what was apparently a small bedroom, 'let's have no unseemliness.' Martin Starr stood there, dressed in the kind of white cotton trousers favored by martial artists. He wore no shirt or shoes and his body was as lean and taut as a twenty-year-old gymnast's and laced with dozens of old scars.

I jammed a finger toward him. 'I want to hear your story

later! You're just a conniving crook. This prick betrayed me!'

'Let's not use any words we'll regret later, Gabe,' Mitch said, palms out in a plea for sweet reason. 'I did what I had to do, and I'm sure you'll agree that it was the only thing I could do under the circumstances.'

'May I offer you some tea, Gabriel?' Starr asked.

I turned around, still holding Queen against the wall. 'Coffee if you have it. One of them just came in and cut your satellite cable. You're cut off from the rest of the world, Martin.'

'As I have been for thirty years,' he said, firing up a compact little gas range. 'I have nothing to say to the outside world. I've ended all my contacts. Soon the last actors in this little drama shall be here and we will finish a play that has run on for far too long.'

'Gabe, are you gonna let me go so we can talk like civilized human beings?'

I turned Mitch loose and went to sit at a table. Like everything else in the little house, it was exquisitely made from some blond wood, lovingly polished. I ran my fingertips over the incredibly smooth surface. Starr wasn't looking my way but he seemed to know what I was doing.

'It was made by Shakers, as were the chairs. They worked wood as an act of faith and devotion. I wish they hadn't died out through enforced celibacy before I was born. They must have been something like Zen masters. A strange thing to find in America.'

'See, Gabe,' Mitch said, taking a chair opposite me, 'last year I got in a little trouble. Nothing big, just a sort of financial hole.'

'I thought your movies made millions.'

'They do. Unfortunately, some of my partners spend even more millions. Anyway, on my last film I was working with a director who thought most of the budget was for his bimbos and nose candy, I had a financier committed to a big chunk of the budget who went bankrupt before he came up with his end, and I had an accountant – his name was Arminius von Ribbentrop, if you can believe it – he had the books looking good in spite of it all, but that was only because it was just ink while the actual money was going into his numbered Swiss account. Remember how I told you that you don't see many big ripoffs in my business? Well, it's true, but it's also true that a lot of little ripoffs can really add up.'

I was listening, but I was also looking around. The interior was spare but beautiful, the pine floor and walls as harmonious as the exterior was helter-skelter. There were no rugs. The only wall decorations were some Chinese scrolls and a pair of Japanese swords, one long and one short.

'It's not like any of this was my fault, but in Hollywood word gets around. I pride myself on running a tight ship and it made it look like I was losing my grip on things. People weren't returning my calls, Gabe!'

'You really think I'm going to pity you for your unreturned calls?' I asked him.

'The clash of value systems is always touchy, even within our own culture,' Starr said. 'You see why there was so little basis for understanding between ourselves and the Vietnamese?'

'So when none other than Jared Rhine himself contacted me, I jumped at the opportunity. I mean, all is forgiven if you have a hot script.'

'And you went on with it when you saw it was *him*?' Once again I pointed at Starr. He was carrying steaming cups to the table.

'Actually, Gabe, I didn't recognize him at first. I mean, Tet was a long time ago, our acquaintance was brief and we had a lot of distractions that night. Admit it, Gabe. Would you have known him if you hadn't just been thinking a lot about him?'

'He hasn't changed much,' I said.

'He's not the kid he was and neither are we. I knew something seemed familiar about him, but what I was really interested in was the script. I thought he was just another freaked-out writer. The industry's full of them.'

'I didn't find the script all that compelling,' I said.

'Yeah, but you only saw half of it,' Queen said. 'And you don't know how to read cinematically.'

'Half? You mean this thing is supposed to be almost eight hours long?'

'A little over seven hours and twenty minutes,' Queen said. 'Depending on how we handle the visuals. You should've seen Towne's original script for *Greystoke*. The sucker would've been even longer! Okay, okay, I admit it: *Tu Do Street* calls for a little editing.'

'I would not have allowed any cuts,' Starr said. 'You don't

improve the *Mahabarata* by shortening it.'

'You talk like you still intend to make this thing,' I said, marveling.

'Well why not?' said Queen. 'We get this little business here out of the way, there's no reason why we can't pick up other financing. Plenty of people in the business will still want in on this project.

'So, I was telling you – Jared, that's to say Martin, puts me on to these kids with their magic rejuvenation process and I know I just have to have this thing, but he wants to be in charge of picking the financing, too. Now this is unprecedented but the guy's got my nuts in a vise, y'understand? So I go along. Now Schuster and the Paramount boys we agreed on, but he wanted me to contact this dickhead Morris, who's rolling in cash, and he wanted me to get Morris to bring in this money-laundryman—'

'Armitage,' I said, interrupting the flow of words.

'Yeah, that's right.'

'And you didn't ask him why he wanted Armitage?'

'What for?' He seemed honestly puzzled.

'Never mind. When did you figure out who Jared Rhine was?'

'About two days after I came up here to look at the script. You know how you file away little things in your memory and they sort of shift around back there in your subconscious and then – pow! – everything clicks together?'

'I'm familiar with how it works,' I told him.

'Well, that night I sat up in bed thinking, *that's* where I saw that guy before. Now, Gabe, you have to understand my reasoning here. I mean, with this guy's record, he's sure as hell not going to use his real name, is he? And whatever his past indiscretions, he sure as hell has a good reputation as a screenwriter these last few years. Should I hold his past against him? It's un-American!'

I looked at Starr. 'Some hotshot. He used to write kung fu scripts for the Hong Kong movie mills. He probably killed Bruce Lee!'

'I found myself at loose ends in Asia and the cinema had always intrigued me, red-blooded American boy that I was. I found that the martial arts films closely mirrored the way I had lived my life.'

'Hey, everybody's got to start somewhere, Gabe.'

'So why the stupid threats?' I asked Starr.

'That was so Mitchell would have an excuse to hire you. I was sure you would want to participate.'

'Why?' I asked, so thoroughly boggled by this time that I'd stopped expecting any form of earthly logic. I just needed answers, even if they made no sense.

'I knew that Gresham and his Asian cohorts were about to move against Nguyen Duc, and that your honor would demand that you avenge him.'

'Wait a minute,' I said. 'You knew Duc was my brother-in-law?'

'I keep up with my old friends, Gabriel. I've followed your career from a distance.'

'And you couldn't warn Duc?'

He sipped at his tea. 'I had no right to interfere with his karma. Really, it is a tragedy for a man to live beyond his war, as we all have. All of our lives took a new course on that momentous night in 1968. Perhaps it would have been better if we had died then. We've all done much to be ashamed of in the years since.'

'Hey, speak for yourself, Martin,' Mitch said.

Starr ignored him. 'I have a strong sense of symmetry, Gabriel. It may be because of my years in Asia, the principle of yin and yang, the cyclical wheel of time, that sort of thing. It's an important quality to a screenwriter. For years I've felt that, to bring these events to a fitting conclusion, the four of us should all be together again.'

'Saigon,' I said. 'The grenade attack. Was that Gresham's friends?' I wasn't interested in Starr's lunatic world-view. I wanted facts.

'I doubt you would have survived had it been,' Starr said. 'No, poor Nguyen Chi Thanh is a frightened man, yet another revenant of the war. He spoke to his companions and one of them must have decided that you could stir up too much trouble, just as things were turning better for them. Frightened men do foolish, ill-considered things.'

I got up, carried my coffee to one of the windows beside the front door, and pushed the curtain aside a bit to see outside. It was bright enough to wash the last stars from the sky and bring out a little color from the land.

'They'll be here pretty soon,' I said.

'Well, we're ready,' Mitch said. 'Come here, Gabe.' He was

crouching beside the long boxes he'd brought in from his Bronco and he opened them as I stepped up to him. 'Aren't these pretty?' They held two massive, dark gray automatic rifles of a type recently outlawed in the state of California, not the cheap Chinese AKs but precision-made European weapons, what are technically known as battle rifles as opposed to the lower-powered assault rifles.

'Let me guess,' I said. 'Your buddy Ahhnuld had a garage sale and these are props from his last movie, right?'

He picked one up. 'They're Swiss. Cost thirty-five hundred bucks apiece. Guy who supplies weapons for the industry found them for me. Accurate to six hundred meters, built-in scope, twenty-round magazines, 7.62 millimeter and selective fire. Wouldn't we have loved these back in Saigon?' He handed one up to me and I took it. It was shockingly heavy and substantial.

'Hell, our old M-16s only weighed about five pounds and we complained about carrying that much weight. This has to weigh more than twice that. We'd've chucked these in the river and looked for something lighter.'

'Mitchell's flair for the cinematic never leaves him,' Starr said. He seemed to take no interest in the exotic weaponry.

I heard the sound of approaching engines. 'They're coming,' I said. 'At least two vehicles. Mitch, if you knew it was going to come to this, why did you do it? Your movie won't get made. Even if we live through this you'll be ruined.'

'In my business there's no such thing as bad publicity, Gabe. There's only publicity.'

I gave up. I was trapped among lunatics. Oddly enough, I felt all right about it. I went back a long way with these guys and we had some old, old scores to settle. I felt that I was in exactly the right place and I didn't want to be anywhere else that morning.

'Did Armitage order the hit on Duc?' I asked.

'The decision would have been reached by consensus, Asian-style,' Starr said. 'But the consensus could not have been reached had he not wished it so. I suspect that the trigger was pulled by Archie Dupre. He was an artist with the sub-machine gun in the old days. He had a little Swedish K, the sort the spooks favored.'

'Then they're mine,' I said.

'Individual duels may be impracticable,' Starr said. He

came up to the window and we saw the two vehicles coming up the canyon, moving slow. 'Don't you hate them, Gabriel? Don't you hate them all: the planners and the dabblers, the ones who send the warriors out to die and never let blood stain their own fingers? The schemers and the manipulators and the profiteers? Such people have destroyed the ancient purity of war, made it an ugly little game for cowards.'

Queen came up to join us, the big Swiss rifle suspended horizontally at waist level by a long sling over his shoulder, just like those pictures out of the world's trouble spots.

'You were born in the wrong era, Martin,' he said. 'The Crusades would've been more your style, the Hundred Years War, maybe. Liege lords and warriors, all fighting together, that's what you'd go for.'

Starr nodded. 'Yes, I would have been an exemplary knight or samurai. During my rogue years I enjoyed myself immensely, fancied myself a true swashbuckler. But now I look back on what I did and it seems cheap and unnecessary, paving the way for the likes of *them*.' He made one of his very few gestures, pointing at the vehicles that were pulling up at the bottom of the driveway, about a hundred feet away.

A little team got out of the lead vehicle and began setting something up on its hood. It was a machine-gun. Not a piddly little burp gun, but a full-sized, belt-fed machine-gun mounted on a tripod.

'Jesus, they brought some real firepower,' I said.

'They know whom they are up against,' Starr said.

The driver of the second vehicle got out. Thin and black, he held a sub-machine gun as he limped around to open a back door. The man who got out wasn't wearing a pinstriped suit this time. He was dressed in khakis, like an engineer on a field job. His white hair formed a fringe around his temples, the top shiny bald, and his white mustache was full and neatly trimmed. Had I seen him casually, I probably wouldn't have recognized him. But I'd been thinking about him a lot lately.

'Well, well,' I said. 'Major Gresham. It's been a long time since we were all together.' The sun cleared the hilltops and struck fire from his wrist and I saw that he was still wearing the brass native bracelets he'd worn the night of Tet, and it brought back another, later night, when someone had turned and pointed a weapon at me. I turned to Starr. 'It was him! That night down by the river, he was the one yelling at you across the table! I thought he was pointing a gun at me but it was those brass bangles on his wrist.'

Starr smiled. 'And that distracted you from shooting me properly. How these little misunderstandings do complicate our lives.'

'And Dupre was the guy I shot in the leg that night. I thought he was one of your men but he was one of Gresham's.'

'We were all working together. Archie was one who never really accepted my leadership. He let Gresham seduce him, poor boy.'

'Good thing for me and Connie it was the Vietnamese who opened up on us in that playground. Old Archie would've made a better job of it. Speaking of which,' I glared at Queen, 'how did they know where to find us? We couldn't find a tap on our phone and the kid wasn't calling us from Duc's office.'

'Oh, that was my fault and I really apologize, Gabe.' Queen was shamefaced, repentant: Eddie Haskell talking to Mrs Cleaver. 'The tap was on my phone and I knew about it. Taps are okay as long as you know they're there. I just forgot that they could listen in on the pool house from my phone line.' He caught my look. 'Hey, man, I can't think of *everything*!'

My mouth had gone almost dry. 'Martin, the ball's about to start. I have to know. Why are you doing this?'

He paused for a moment, studying the men outside with infinitely sad eyes. 'I want to end it. I gave my life to a war and it didn't end when it should have. Ghosts we were and ghosts we remain unto this hour. I'm tired, Gabriel, and I want it finished.'

There were five men who got out of the lead vehicle, all Asians, two older men and three younger ones, two of the latter manning the machine-gun. The rest were armed with smaller weapons. Three had been riding in the other vehicle. Besides Gresham/Armitage and Dupre, there was a hulking thug of a Caucasian.

'Are two of those guys Dang Thai Mai and Truong Chinh?' I asked Starr.

'Yes, the two older ones.' He smiled faintly. 'It's unusual for them and Armitage to take a personal hand, but they want to keep this operation small and they don't trust one another. Very convenient for us, though.'

'And that guy next to Dupre would've been the wheel man on the hit.' I nodded. 'Okay, Martin. Let's finish it.' I worked the operating handle on the Swiss rifle, chambering a round. I set the selector switch to semi-automatic.

Starr nodded too, and he smiled and whispered, almost too low for me to hear, 'O, my beloved brothers.'

Gresham, or whatever his real name was, raised a bullhorn to his mouth. 'Martin, I know you and Mitch Queen are inside. I want you to come out. I want every copy of that screenplay, and any software that contains any part of it. I will give you one minute to comply with my instructions.'

'Hey, Major Gresham!' I yelled. 'You're the same pompous ass you were almost thirty years go. Just thought I'd tell you that, now that you don't outrank me.'

'Who is that?' he said. 'Treloar? Now aren't you sorry you didn't kill that madman when you had the chance?'

'Hell, no,' I said. 'Martin and I are old buddies. I wouldn't've missed this party for the world. You shouldn't've killed Duc, Gresham.' I turned to Starr. 'What's in that script that's got him so desperate?'

'Operations, code names, dates, officials. I wove it all into a marvelous story, Gabriel, but I used all their real names. Much of what was done wasn't just criminal. It was treasonous.'

'So why's he upset? He's as big a crook as he ever was. It's not like he has a reputation to protect.'

'But he was not alone then, nor is he now. Many, many of those people are still in government, Gabriel, safe and respectable and sure their ancient misdeed will never come back to haunt them, as long as he keeps silent. It is what he's held over their heads all these years. Why do you think he has been able to operate so freely, never even coming under investigation?'

Queen chuckled. 'That man's got more dirt on more important people than J. Edgar Hoover. Hey, Martin, what do you say we make that our next movie?'

'You are obsolete, Treloar,' Gresham said. 'Martin is obsolete. You are relics of a world that no longer exists. You didn't move with the times and there's no sense keeping you around any longer.' He lowered the bullhorn and turned to the machine-gun team.

Just then one of the Asians yelled something and pointed up toward the slope behind us. Another raised a sub-machine gun and loosed a long, ripping burst. I raised the heavy rifle, took a quick sight and laid him out with one shot. Then they were all ducking behind the vehicles and the muzzle of the machine-gun swung around.

'Hit the floor!' I yelled, but they were flattened out there ahead of me.

'What was that guy shooting at?' Queen said.

'That was Connie. She's running to get help.' My mind boiled. Was she hit? It was extreme range for one of those little burp guns, and the Asian probably wasn't an expert like Archie. But even a fool can score a lucky hit.

'She should not have risked her life,' Starr said. 'All will be over here long before she can come back with aid.' Then the machine-gun opened up.

The powerful bullets ripped through the windows and the wooden parts of the outer walls. The air filled with flying splinters that stung my face and hands. If it hadn't been for the soft wood of the walls absorbing most of the bullets we probably would have been minced by ricochets. As it was, there was more noise and confusion than real danger from the machine-gun bullets. It was what the military calls suppressive fire. They use the firepower of the machine-gun to make you keep your head down and keep you from shooting back while the rest of the soldiers move in for the kill.

I looked around and saw Queen still hugging the floor. I saw Starr tucking something into the cloth belt at his waist. I glanced at the wall. The Japanese short sword was missing. We had battle rifles, they had heavy ordnance, and he was going to fight with the sword, and a short one at that. It figured.

'The fools will come to the end of that ammo belt soon,' Martin said, speaking quietly but still somehow making himself heard over the ungodly racket. 'When they do, give me some cover fire. I am going to make a call.'

The instant the machine-gun paused, Mitch and I each got up on a knee and fired out through the windows flanking the door. The gunners were fussing with the breech of their weapon. They'd not only fired up the belt, they'd let the weapon overheat. An air-cooled gun is supposed to be used in fairly short bursts, no more than nine or ten rounds each, letting it cool for a few seconds between bursts. They'd just held the trigger down until the belt was gone and now they were burning their hands trying to get a fresh belt loaded.

Mitch hosed the front of the vehicle on full-auto, making them duck behind it. I squeezed off individual rounds, shooting at the gun. With its breech open like that, I had a good chance of disabling it. Vicious little sub-machine gun bullets spanged off the stone of the lower wall, striking sparks, but I kept firing and watching the gun jerk around on its pintle. Then the return fire was too intense and I ducked back down again.

'Good shootin', m'man!' Queen was laughing like a hyena, jamming a fresh magazine into his rifle. He tossed me one and I stuffed it in a side pocket. 'Hell, Gabe, those peckerheads don't have a chance. I'm bulletproof, Martin can make himself invisible and you shoot like Annie Oakley.'

More of the little bullets were coming in and the machine-gun was still quiet. Maybe I'd done it. The problem was, fire was coming in the side windows now. They were moving into position to encircle us. I saw movement at the north side window and twisted around, trying to bring my big rifle to bear, but Gresham's wheelman already had his gun levelled at Queen. I tried to shout but before I could get a sound out somebody was standing behind the gunner and it was like Starr was tapping him on the shoulder, breaking in for a dance. The hulking thug disappeared and so did Starr and neither of them had made a sound.

Mitch laughed uproariously again. 'Did you see that? Ain't Martin a wild son of a bitch?' He rolled over on his belly and propped himself up on his elbows. 'Come on, Gabe. I figure he'll go for Gresham next. Let's give him a little help.'

We jumped up and I saw the two younger Asians still trying to get their gun into action. We laid fire into the vehicle and Queen must have punctured its gas tank earlier because the sparks we raised set it off with a flat whump. The two didn't run from the flames so I knew we'd nailed them too.

'Bingo!' Queen yelled, ducking again. 'That's – what? Four down and four to go?' A hail of bullets came in through one of the front windows from two guns firing at once. 'Well, hell, let's see if the old Gunslinger hasn't lost his touch.' Mitch lurched to his feet among the slivers of glass and the wood splinters and expended cartridge cases.

'Mitch, no!' I shouted but he was lost in a cowboy fantasy, the celluloid reeling in his head the way it had since the day I met him. He kicked the door open and stepped out on to the porch and opened fire. I saw him jerk and stagger back in as I jumped to my window. Out there, crouched behind a rock, were the two older Asians, Dang Thai Mai and Truong Chinh. I didn't know which was which, but what did it matter? Their war was long ago like ours and they'd forgotten how to fire from cover efficiently. They were standing a little too high and I cut them both down with one shot each.

I heard a thud behind me and whirled. 'Mitch!'

He was sitting propped against a wall, his feet straight out, his big rifle across his lap, four or five holes leaking blood in steady streams down his chest. Idly, he fingered the holes, a puzzled look on his face.

'Well, shit. I was sure I was bulletproof.' He looked up at me and for the first time I saw something resembling fear on his face.

I low-crawled over to him. 'Mitch, you dumb son of a bitch, why'd you do that? We could've picked them off.'

'No style in that.' He looked at the bullet holes like they had personally offended him. 'It's not fair, Gabe,' he cried indignantly. 'That script was a winner!' He held out his hands, his fingers clawed as if he were holding something between them. 'I could feel that Oscar right here in my hands!' He looked at me and I saw that madman glint come back into them, that familiar smile working the corners of his mouth. I knew what was coming. 'Gabe . . .'

'Don't say it, Mitch. I swear to God, if you say it I'll finish you off right here and now!'

'Gabe . . . I coulda been a *contender*!' He started to chuckle, but instead of a laugh, foamy blood poured out of his nostrils. He coughed and more blood came out of his mouth. I grabbed him around the shoulders, my rifle forgotten, but there was no way I could help him. He wasn't hit in the heart or the spine but it looked like he was lungshot. A hospital might save him, but he would have to be evacuated fast.

Then something hit me in the side and I spun around, half-sitting on the floor, and I heard nothing except the ringing in my ears. Then that went away and I saw Archie Dupre standing in the back door, holding his little sub-machine gun almost idly at his waist. I clutched my side beneath my shirt and felt a big, bloody tear in the flesh, right where I'd been shot beneath the racetrack on mini-Tet. It felt like it had obliterated the old scar. I was afraid to probe too hard for fear my fingers would go right inside and I'd feel my own viscera. That would be a little too much to take.

'Hey, Archie,' I said, surprised that my voice was working. 'You get around pretty spry for a middle-aged gimp. Looks like we're even.'

'Not by a long shot. Where's Starr?'

'Find him yourself. He's not an easy man to pin down.' I knew he could have put those bullets through my head instead. Maybe he wanted to talk over old times. 'It was a war and people were shooting each other, Arch. I could've let you burn in that warehouse by the river. I went back for you and I dragged you out.'

'You think I take that for a favor?' His dark face twisted. 'You shoulda let me burn, man. I done three years in the LBJ. You got any idea what that was like? Then I done nine more at Leavenworth, an' if that shit-for-brains cracker Carter hadn' wanted to stick it to Reagan I'd still be there!' He should have killed me right away but he'd been waiting too long for this. He had to gloat.

'So go ahead. What're you waiting for?'

He lowered the muzzle a little bit more. 'Beg, man. Beg.' His face untwisted and relaxed into a grin.

'Sure,' I said, my hand coming out from under my shirt with Connie's pistol in it. '*Chieu hoi*, motherfucker.' I pulled the trigger as fast as I could, starting at his belt buckle so the recoil would make the shots track up his body. He jerked up the burp gun and got off two shots before he fell back through the door. I felt something tear into the muscle where the neck and shoulder join, and I was on my back staring at the ceiling.

Gradually, I regained my orientation. I rolled on to my unwounded side and slowly, painfully pushed myself up until I had my feet under me. I felt my neck and there was lots of blood, but it wasn't pulsing out in a bright-red stream, so maybe I'd make it. I saw Mitch, pale and still. The blood was no longer running from his wounds, but I thought I could see a tiny bit of movement in his chest. Maybe the dumb son of a bitch would get his movie made yet. I was sure there was someone left unaccounted for.

My rifle was lying in front of the door and I stooped to pick it up, almost passing out in the process, but I managed to straighten with its weight in my hand and I stumbled out the front door. The light outside seemed to brighten and dim in irregular pulses, but all was quiet. I did see motion, though. It was by Gresham's vehicle. I began to walk that way, and through the spots that swarmed in my vision I saw that two figures were locked together in something that looked like an exotic dance.

Martin Starr and Gresham were locked in a close embrace like lovers, and Martin was bleeding from a number of wounds, but his right arm was working between them. I was pretty sure that I didn't want to see this, but I kept going forward. I couldn't feel the desert beneath my feet and I wasn't sure whether it was really quiet or I had just gone deaf. Then Gresham was sliding down between Starr and the jeep and Martin turned to me, smiling like a happy child.

The dark spots sort of coalesced and I was blind. Then I was floating along, seeing the ground pass beneath me. But there were two bloody legs below me and I knew they weren't mine. Someone was carrying me. It went black again.

When I came to, I was sitting against a wall. It took a minute for me to place my surroundings. I saw someone lying on the floor and I recognized Mitch Queen and it all came back. There was someone in the room with me and I looked to one side and saw Martin Starr sitting crosslegged with the Japanese short sword in his lap.

'Are you awake, Gabriel?' He smiled gently. 'I was waiting so that I could bid you farewell.'

'Oh, God, don't do this, Martin.' But it seemed like nobody was listening to me these days.

'Some of us are cursed to live too long, Gabriel. But others choose not to. I have never submitted to fate in my life and I will not do so now. I hope you will live a long and happy life, Gabriel, but I doubt that it shall happen that way. You accept fate, and yours is a melancholy one.'

He was silent for a while, then. 'You recall that we stood by the river in Cholon and we spoke of Saint Martin and the beggar?'

'I remember.'

'To divide his cloak, Saint Martin had to draw his sword. I urge you to remember that.'

He placed the point of the sword just beneath his sternum and gripped the handle with both hands. Then, without any trace of hesitation, as neatly and elegantly as he did all things, Martin Starr drove the blade inward and upward, hilt deep, into his heart. He gave the handle a half-twist, then his hands fell away, into his lap. Slowly, his head lowered, until his chin rested on his chest.

I was unconscious for a while, and when I came to it was like old times again. I heard the thunderous whop-whop-whopping of a big helicopter coming in for a landing and the sound of screaming sirens as if all the most dramatic moments of my life were being played out all at once, here in this unlikely place. Dust flew in through the open door and the shattered windows and the multitude of bullet holes.

Amid the sirens I heard those loud, squawking police radios and shouting voices and someone bawling incoherently through a bullhorn. I guessed that Santa Barbara cops didn't often come across a scene like this.

Heavy boots thudded on the porch and two figures came through the door, comically huge in their flak jackets and helmets, arms extended stiffly, holding their pistols in both hands. A couple more came in, everyone with the appalled look of men who find themselves unexpectedly on the wrong planet.

Then Connie came in, her face pale and drawn with dread. She looked at the bodies numbly, then she saw me and her face was hard to read. She walked over to me and crouched by my side. Her hand reached out and gently stroked my cheek, wiping away blood or tears, I'm not sure which.

'Hey, Gabe,' she said softly. 'It looks like you finally got to win the war.'

I looked at her, the words struggling to form in my throat. 'Yeah,' I said at last. 'I guess I did.'

Too late. Too late, my brothers.

Epilogue

For the first time she saw the sun setting over the ocean in the West.

'It seems wrong,' Rose told me. 'Always before, the sun rose over the ocean. It set in the mountains.'

'You have a lot to get used to,' I said. I had thirty days' accumulated leave before reporting for duty at Fort Ord. Rose and I were going to take a long, leisurely drive all the way down to the tip of Baja California. We'd begun that morning, as soon as I finished in-processing. An old school friend had brought my car up from LA. This was our first stop. I'd seen the sun almost touching the water and had pulled over at one of those incomparably dramatic spots that are all along that stretch of coast, all baroque rock formations and thunderous surf. We'd picked a rock and sat with our feet dangling over a breathtaking cliff. Now half the sun was above the water, half below, and between stretched a fog bank dyed an incredible orange.

'It is so quiet here, so peaceful,' she said. She leaned back into my arms, a tiny woman with black hair so long that she was sitting on it. Behind us the radio was on in my old '56 Chevy. A folk singer I'd never heard of was singing in a heart-achingly pure soprano something called 'Both Sides Now'.

I smiled, feeling warmed and light as a breath after the brutal year overseas. 'That's something else you'll have to get used to, Rose. Peace.'

She snuggled more deeply in my arms. 'I know it is true, but I can hardly believe it. It is over, isn't it? For us, for our children and grandchildren, it is over. The war will never touch us again, will it, Gabe?' She looked up at me and there was the slightest doubt marking her features, as if what had started out as a statement had turned midway into a serious question.

I held her more tightly. 'I promise,' I said, my lips brushing her exquisitely fragile ear, 'I'll never let it touch us again.'

The sun went down beneath the fog, and then beneath the sea, and in a few minutes the stars came out, one by one.